AFTER GLOW

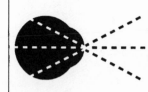

This Large Print Book carries the
Seal of Approval of N.A.V.H.

AFTER GLOW

Jayne Ann Krentz

writing as

Jayne Castle

WHEELER PUBLISHING

Published in 2004 by arrangement with The Berkley Publishing
Group, a member of Penguin Group (USA) Inc.

Wheeler Large Print Hardcover.

The text of this Large Print edition is unabridged.
Other aspects of the book may vary from the original edition.

Set in 16 pt. Plantin by Christina S. Huff.

Printed in the United States on permanent paper.

Library of Congress Cataloging-in-Publication Data

Castle, Jayne.
   After glow / Jayne Ann Krentz writing as Jayne Castle.
      p.   cm.
   ISBN 1-58724-729-1 (lg. print : hc : alk. paper)
   1. Women museum curators — Fiction.   2. Women
archaeologists — Fiction.   3. Large type books.   I. Title.
PS3561.R44A74 2004
   813'.54—dc22   2004045834

For Fuzz lovers everywhere.
The dynamic dust-bunny returns . . .

As the Founder/CEO of NAVH, the only national health agency solely devoted to those who, although not totally blind, have an eye disease which could lead to serious visual impairment, I am pleased to recognize Thorndike Press* as one of the leading publishers in the large print field.

Founded in 1954 in San Francisco to prepare large print textbooks for partially seeing children, NAVH became the pioneer and standard setting agency in the preparation of large type.

Today, those publishers who meet our standards carry the prestigious "Seal of Approval" indicating high quality large print. We are delighted that Thorndike Press is one of the publishers whose titles meet these standards. We are also pleased to recognize the significant contribution Thorndike Press is making in this important and growing field.

Lorraine H. Marchi, L.H.D.
Founder/CEO
NAVH

* Thorndike Press encompasses the following imprints: Thorndike, Wheeler, Walker and Large Pr int Press.

1

The tiny burner and the little bowl next to the body told the sad story. Professor Lawrence Maltby had finally managed to kill himself. Judging by the dark residue and the lingering scent of exotic spices, he had done himself in with a common street drug known as Chartreuse.

Lydia Smith left the doorway of the shabby bedroom that Maltby had converted into a study and crouched beside the professor's scrawny, crumpled form. She did not expect to find a pulse, and when she put her fingertips to the throat beneath the scraggly white beard, she proved herself right.

She shivered, rose quickly, stepped back, and reached into her shoulder bag for her personal phone. Her fingers trembled when she punched out the emergency number.

"Yes, that's right," she said to the overstressed operator. "Number Thirteen, Hidden Lane. First floor, apartment A. It's in the Old Quarter near the Wall."

"I'm sorry, ma'am, but that street isn't coming up on my city grid," the operator said brusquely. "Are you sure about the address?"

"Yes, I'm sure. Hidden Lane isn't on most city maps." Lydia took another step from the body. "Probably why they named it Hidden Lane. Look, just tell the medics to take Dead City Way to South Wall Street and turn left at the tavern on the corner. Once they're in the neighborhood, anyone can give them directions."

"All right." There was a short silence before the woman came back on the line. "They're on the way. I'm also sending a police car since you say there's a body."

The operator sounded as if she wasn't at all certain that Lydia could tell the difference between a dead body and the other sort.

"There is definitely a dead man in this apartment. Trust me, I've seen one before."

"Do not under any circumstances leave the scene, ma'am. Since you're the one who found the body, there will be a few formalities."

Formalities. Lydia felt the hair on the nape of her neck stir much the same way it had a few minutes ago when she had walked into Maltby's gloom-filled apartment and realized that something was horribly wrong.

In her experience *formalities* was not a good word.

Just a few formalities was the phrase the pompous members of the Academic Council had used to describe the farce of a formal inquiry they had staged before they had fired her from her position at the university seven months ago.

8

We need to go through some formalities, was how the police detective in charge of the investigation into Chester Brady's murder last month had termed the grilling that Lydia had been obliged to endure.

It wasn't her fault that she had been the first person to stumble across Chester's body in that ancient alien sarcophagus, she thought. And there was no reason to hold her responsible for the fact that she had been the first one to find Maltby's body today.

It was just her bad luck that she had walked in on this mess, she told herself. It could have been anyone. The door of Maltby's apartment had been unlocked when she had arrived a few minutes ago, so naturally she had put her head inside to call his name. After all, he was the one who had asked her to stop by his place this morning.

Actually the message that he had left on her answering machine while she had been occupied with a museum tour group had been a demand, not a request.

". . . This is Dr. Lawrence Maltby. I must see you immediately, Miss Smith. Please come to my apartment as soon as possible. I have extremely urgent news concerning the incident in the catacombs a few months ago that led to your dismissal from the university. . . ."

Although he had been let go from his own position at Old Frequency College more than a decade earlier, Maltby had evidently not lost his air of professorial authority. The tone of his

9

voice on her answering machine had been that of a department head summoning a junior staff member to his office.

In spite of the rudeness, Lydia had wasted no time. The magic words *urgent news concerning the incident in the catacombs a few months ago* had gotten her full attention.

But the expensive cab ride to Hidden Lane had been for naught. She was too late.

She saw no reason to mention the reasons she happened to be standing over Maltby's dead body to the emergency operator, however.

"Look, this isn't a crime scene or anything," she said quickly. "Professor Maltby wasn't murdered. It looks like he OD'd on Chartreuse. There's no point in having me stick around to answer a lot of questions. I don't have any answers."

The operator was unmoved. "I'm sorry, ma'am, but rules are rules. Stay right where you are until the police and the medics arrive."

"Yeah, sure." Lydia ended the call abruptly. She glanced once more at the body and then quickly looked away.

She had not known Maltby personally, but she had heard the gossip along Ruin Row for years. His tragic end had been forecast for some time by all of the gallery owners who had dealt with him. In his heyday he had been a respected, tenured professor of para-archaeology. But his career had foundered after he had sunk into the dark netherworld of drug addiction.

After his dismissal from the staff at Old Frequency College, he had moved here to Cadence City where he had attempted to make a living as a private consultant to collectors and gallery owners along Ruin Row. But the drugs had made it impossible for him to function reliably. Eventually his deteriorating reputation had caused his consulting work to dry up.

In the end, Maltby had descended to the lowest rung in the antiquities trade. He had become a ruin rat, eking out a meager living by sneaking illegally in and out of the catacombs in hopes of turning up the occasional valuable relic.

Several of Lydia's acquaintances in the Old Quarter had told her that, during the brief spells when he was able to kick his habit long enough to go underground, Maltby sometimes showed up with some spectacular finds. No one knew where he did his secret excavating work down in the catacombs and, honoring the unspoken rules that governed the less legitimate side of the antiquities trade, no one asked.

She listened intently for a few seconds and heard no sirens. She had a few minutes before the medics and the police arrived. Surely there was no harm in looking around.

Trying not to look at the body, she moved to the desk and surveyed the cluttered surface. There were several aging copies of the *Journal of Para-archaeology* stacked randomly on one corner. Pens, papers, and a notebook were scattered about in a careless fashion.

She unfastened her shoulder bag, removed a tissue, and used it to open the notebook. The scribbling inside appeared to be a series of angry rebuttals to various papers that had appeared in recent editions of the *Journal of Para-archaeology*; letters to the editor that would never have been published.

She closed the notebook and surveyed the desk. Something about the arrangement of the items on it seemed off. All of the things that one might expect to see on an academic's desk were present, including a small pad of paper, heaps of reference books, a lamp, and a blotter. There was no computer but that was not a surprise. Maltby had probably sold it long ago to buy Chartreuse. Either that or it had been stolen. This was a rough neighborhood.

She took a closer look, trying to figure out what was bothering her. And then it struck her that the blotter was not positioned squarely in the center where it could be properly used. It had been dragged or pulled too far to the right so that one corner hung off the edge. The lamp was in the wrong place, too. The shade was cocked at an odd angle that would send the beam of light straight down, quite uselessly, to the floor.

It was easy to see what had happened. No doubt belatedly aware that he was in serious trouble from the overdose, Maltby had evidently tried to get to his feet, perhaps to call for help. He would have been dazed and unsteady and had probably flailed wildly about, grabbing at the nearest objects in a vain attempt to steady himself. He had knocked the lamp and blotter askew in the process.

She leaned down to open the top desk drawer. What could it hurt to just glance inside to see if Maltby had left any clue to what it was he had wanted to tell her?

She paused in the act of reaching for the drawer knob when she noticed the little sheet of paper lying on the worn carpet. It was just the right size to have been torn off the small note-pad that sat next to the phone.

Curious, she crouched down and angled herself under the desk to pick up the paper. When she turned it over she saw that someone had started to scrawl a couple of words in a very shaky hand.

Amber Hil

A knock sounded loudly on the front door of the apartment, shattering the unnatural stillness of the death room. Startled, she started to straighten. Her head collided smartly with the underside of the desk.

"Damn." She scrambled out from under the desk and dropped the paper into her purse.

There was a second knock. A shiver went through her. Whoever was out there in the hall managed to make a simple rap on the door sound like a summons to doom.

She hesitated, uncertain whether or not to respond. She still didn't hear any sirens, which ruled out the possibility that Maltby's visitor was a medic or a cop. Given the character of the neighborhood, that left a lot of unpleasant possibilities.

She pondered the wisdom of simply ignoring the knock. Then she recalled that the door was unlocked. Whoever was out there in the hall might decide to try his luck with the knob at any moment.

It would probably be a really good idea to go into the front room and lock the door.

She hurried out of the study, went down the short hall, and traversed the dingy sitting room on tiptoe. There was a peephole in the heavily reinforced door. Trying not to give away her presence, she put her eye to the little circle of glass. At the same time she reached out to throw the bolt.

She stopped when she saw the man standing in the shadowy hall. A day's growth of dark beard, scarred boots, rugged khaki pants and shirt, and a battered leather jacket added up to one conclusion. This was the kind of guy who looked like he'd make an interesting date if you were in a mood to take a walk on the wild side, but you would definitely not want to run into him in a dark alley on a moonless night.

His eyes were a disturbing combination of gold and green. He had the hard, implacable features of a man who was accustomed to being in command.

14

The face of his watch was a circle of amber. She knew this because she knew the man.

There was nothing special about the amber watch, of course. Almost everyone wore amber in one form or another. Two hundred years ago the colonists from Earth had quickly learned that here on Harmony the unique gemstone had a very special property: Amber made it possible for humans to focus their latent psychic energy, paranormal powers that the environment of the new world had somehow released.

Given the fact that, by the second generation, all of the colonists' offspring exhibited some degree of psi talent and could control it with the use of amber, the stuff had quickly become the energy source of choice. Even little children could resonate with amber with sufficient skill to operate a door key or switch on the rez-screen to watch cartoons.

Lydia knew only too well that Emmett London was not into amber accessories because they were fashionable. He was a very powerful dissonance-energy para-resonator — a ghost-hunter. He had the psychic talent and the training required to neutralize the dangerous, flaring balls of chaotic dissonance energy, the so-called *ghosts,* that drifted at random through the endless underground corridors of the alien ruins.

Ghost-hunters were a necessary part of any excavation team. They were, in essence, professional bodyguards who were hired from their

15

Guilds to protect archaeologists, researchers, and others who explored and excavated the ancient catacombs beneath the Dead City.

Until she had met Emmett last month, she had held an extremely low opinion of hunters in general. She considered most dissonance-energy para-rezes to be little better than high-end mobsters. There was a hunters' Guild in every major city on Harmony and as far as she was concerned they were merely legalized criminal organizations run by ruthless bosses.

Emmett was the mysterious ex-boss of the Resonance City Guild. Shortly after his arrival here in Cadence last month, rumors had begun to circulate in the tabloids to the effect that he was the handpicked successor of the current boss of the Cadence City Guild, Mercer Wyatt.

Emmett denied any interest in assuming the leadership of the local Guild, but Lydia was not so sure he could avoid the job — not if Wyatt put pressure on him. There were a lot of old sayings about the hunters and the Guilds, one of which was, *once a Guild man, always a Guild man*. Granted, the conventional wisdom overlooked the fact that there were some female hunters but that was beside the point.

In the past few weeks she had tried very hard not to think about the fact that she was sleeping with the man Mercer Wyatt had chosen to take over as the boss of the Cadence Guild.

She yanked open the door and threw herself into Emmett's arms.

"You don't know how glad I am to see you," she said into his shirt. "How did you find me?"

"I called your office. Melanie told me you were here." He put an arm around her shoulders and glanced back to check the grimy hallway. Satisfied, he moved both of them into the apartment and closed the door. "What the hell are you doing in this part of town?"

"Maltby, the man who lives here, said he wanted to see me. When I arrived I found him lying on the floor of his study." She took a deep breath. "He's sort of dead."

Emmett looked pained. "Not another one."

She frowned. "This isn't like the last time. It looks like Maltby took an overdose of Chartreuse. I called for an ambulance." She sighed. "Not that it will do any good."

"Where is he?"

The stoic resignation in his voice annoyed her. "You don't have to act as if I make a habit of finding dead bodies." She waved a hand toward the study. "He's in the room down that hall."

Emmett walked to the doorway of the study. She trailed after him, clutching her purse.

"This is not good," Emmett said.

"Yes, well, it's a lot worse for Maltby."

"That's not what I meant. Some complications have come up. The last thing we need right now is a dead body."

He disappeared into the study.

Alarmed, she hurried to the doorway. Emmett

17

was standing over Maltby's remains, surveying the small space with a considering expression.

"What complications?" she asked. "Don't get me wrong, I'm glad to see you, but what are you doing here? When did you get home from the camping trip with Zane and his buddies?"

It was not at all surprising that Emmett looked a little rough around the edges today, she thought. Her young neighbor, Zane Hoyt, and his pals were all budding dissonance-energy para-resonators from a part of town where good male role models were decidedly scarce. The boys in the neighborhood were growing up fast with more psi power than any of them knew how to handle. It was a recipe for disaster. They desperately needed guidance and a firm hand.

The Guild-sponsored Hunter-Scout troops were a useful community resource for boys in Cadence but there had been none in the section of the city where Lydia and Zane lived. Emmett had taken care of the problem a couple of weeks ago when he had quietly prodded the Guild into establishing a troop in the neighborhood. He had even gone so far as to take an active interest in the newly formed group.

All of the boys, Zane included, idolized Emmett. He was, after all, one of the most powerful para-rezes in the city. Young males, Lydia had discovered, were very impressed with raw power.

"Got in around three o'clock this morning,"

Emmett said. "Dropped the boys off at their homes and went to my place to crash. Didn't want to wake you up. The phone rang just as I was walking in the door." Absently he rubbed his jaw. "I haven't been to bed yet."

Sirens wailed in the distance. About time, Lydia thought.

"Who called you?" she asked. "Why didn't you get to bed?"

"It's a long story. I'll explain later." He eyed her closely. "Meanwhile, please tell me this dead guy doesn't have anything to do with your new consulting job?"

"Oh, no, things are going great with the Hepscott project," she said, relieved to be able to give a positive, upbeat answer for once. She cast an uneasy glance at Maltby. "This was a, uh, private matter."

"Yeah, I was afraid of that." Emmett's expression hardened a little more. "This is connected to those questions you've been asking along Ruin Row for the past couple of weeks, isn't it? The ones about your so-called Lost Weekend?"

She should have known that he was aware of the discreet inquiries she had begun making here in the Old Quarter. Emmett was an ex-Guild boss. He had connections.

"Maltby called me," she said briskly. "I didn't call him."

"You just can't let it go, can you? You're determined to prove that you were the victim of some kind of ghost-hunter conspiracy. You won't accept that what happened to you was a really bad accident."

She narrowed her eyes. "This is precisely why I didn't tell you I was doing some investigating on my own. I knew I'd get a lot of rez-static."

"And this is *why* you would have gotten the static from me." He pointed at the body. "Things like this happen in this part of town. At the very least, you should have called me before you came to ask your questions."

"I knew that you would be getting back very late last night. I assumed you'd be sleeping late this morning."

"Would you have called to invite me along if you had figured I'd be up?"

She was starting to feel cornered. "I know my way around the Old Quarter, Emmett. I've lived here all my life. I don't need an escort."

"Maybe not in the district where you live, but that's over on the other side of the Quarter. In this neighborhood, you need an escort."

She tightened her grip on the strap of the purse. "You know, this really isn't the time for a lecture on personal safety."

"On my way to this flophouse I passed three drug dealers who offered to score me some high-grade Chartreuse, a couple of hookers, a guy who tried to sell me a hot rez-screen, and one of those smiling idiots in green bathrobes who promised to reveal the secrets of true bliss if I would buy a book. And that was just in the half block between here and where I parked the Slider. I'll be lucky if the car's still there when I get back to it."

"I'm sure you'll find the Slider right where you left it. No one would dare touch it. Everyone knows who you are, now, Emmett, thanks to that stupid article in the *Cadence Tattler* last week."

Much to Emmett's disgust, the popular supermarket tabloid had featured a photo of him on the front page. The picture had been accompanied by some breathless prose questioning the real reason for his presence in Cadence. The headline, *Next Guild Boss?* had said it all.

Emmett fit his hands to his hips. "You scare the living daylights out of me, Lydia."

"Nah. You're a ghost-hunter. Nothing scares you."

She spoke lightly but deep down she was relieved that he was backing off the argument. They were only a few short weeks into this very complicated relationship and things were unsettled enough as it was. They did not need a major confrontation.

They listened to the sirens halt abruptly outside in the lane.

Emmett raised his brows. "Mind if I ask what you plan to tell the cops?"

She winced. "I'm hoping they won't ask too many questions."

"This is the second time in a month that you've reported a dead body. Got a hunch there are going to be a few questions."

Someone pounded on the door of the apartment.

"I'll go let them in," Lydia said. She turned and went down the hall.

When she opened the front door of the apartment she found two medics, a uniformed police officer, and an all-too-familiar face crowded together in the dark hall.

"Hello, Miss Smith," Detective Alice Martinez said. "You do turn up in some interesting places." She switched her tough cop's gaze to a point beyond Lydia's left shoulder. "So do you, London. What is it? The two of you can't think of anything more romantic to do on a date than find dead bodies?"

One of the medics looked at Emmett. "Where's the dead guy?"

"Down that hallway," Emmett said.

The two medics and the officer headed for the study.

Lydia did not like the dark cloud she sensed gathering over her head. "What are you doing here, Detective?" she asked warily. "This isn't a homicide."

Alice did not take her attention off Emmett. "Actually, I was looking for you, Mr. London. I called Miss Smith's office to see if she knew where you were and was told that both of you were probably at this address. Imagine my surprise when I discovered that Miss Smith had just phoned in a report about a dead man."

"Detective." Emmett inclined his head politely.

Lydia got the impression he was not surprised to see Alice Martinez. The cloud overhead got darker and more ominous. There would be rain any minute.

"Why do you want to talk to Emmett?" she asked sharply.

"I need to ask him a few questions," Alice said. "Just a formality."

"*What?*" Lydia was outraged. "You can't be serious. Surely you don't think that Emmett had anything to do with Professor Maltby's death? I'm the one who found the body. Emmett is not involved in this. He just happened to be here when you arrived."

Alice and Emmett both looked at her. Lydia got a nasty feeling that she had overreacted. Not the smart thing to do around a cop, she told herself.

"I hadn't planned to talk to Mr. London about Maltby's death," Alice said calmly. "Although, I may have to revisit that decision. But we'll let that go for now. The reason I tracked him down this morning was to ask him some questions concerning another problem that I'm handling at the moment."

"Problem?" Lydia glanced from Alice's face to Emmett's and then back again. A fresh wave of dread ruffled her nerve endings. "What problem? What is going on here?"

"Someone tried to kill Mercer Wyatt early this morning," Emmett said quietly.

"Whoever it was nearly succeeded," Alice added. "Wyatt is in intensive care at Cadence Memorial Hospital under an armed guard. The doctors finished operating a couple of hours ago. His condition is listed as critical."

Lydia relaxed slightly. "I see. Well, that's unfortunate but I can't say that I'm terribly surprised. Wyatt is a Guild boss, after all. No one rises to that position without making enemies. Guild politics are notoriously messy. At least they are here in Cadence."

"True," Alice agreed in a very neutral tone of voice.

Lydia frowned. "So, why do you want to question Emmett?"

"Because the word on the street is that he's the new acting head of the Cadence Guild." Alice's smile was ice cold. "The way I heard it, he will take over permanently if Wyatt doesn't make it out of intensive care."

2

He had known this would not be easy.

Three hours later Emmett watched Lydia de-rez the lock on the front door of her apartment. She had not said a word during the drive home following the *formalities* at Detective Martinez's office. The continuing silence was a bad sign. Lydia was normally never loathe to let him know exactly what she was thinking.

It was as though she was suffering some form of shock but he was not certain how to deal with it. For starters, he was not sure what had upset her the most, finding Maltby's body or the news that the man whose bed she was sharing on a fairly frequent basis was the temporary chief of the Cadence Guild.

He had the unpleasant feeling that it was the second piece of news that had made her go tense and silent.

Lydia was convinced that she had good reason not to trust ghost-hunters and she made no secret of her negative opinion of the Guild. That she was involved in an affair with him did not mean she had changed her mind on either point, he reminded himself.

And the fact that she had been quietly pursuing her own private investigation of the mystery of her Lost Weekend without asking for his help really pissed him off.

They were sleeping together, damn it. That meant they were supposed to discuss stuff before she ran around doing potentially dicey things like trying to find proof of criminal actions on the part of a couple of Guild men.

The fact that he would have put his foot down very heavily on such a project did not constitute grounds for keeping her plans to herself, he thought. In spite of her low opinion of the Guild, she probably didn't have a clue of the kind of risks she was running.

He had grown up in the Guild and he had controlled the Resonance City organization for six years. He knew the risks all too well.

The first thing to do was to get her talking again, he decided. This was a relationship. According to all the advice gurus, communication was important in a relationship.

He followed her into the cramped foyer of her small apartment, trying to think of a way to get the conversation going.

"All things considered," he said, shrugging out of his leather jacket, "I thought that went well."

She dropped her purse on a small table. "Neither of us is sitting in jail, if that's what you mean."

Okay, it was a start. At least she was speaking to him again.

A large wad of lint scampered across the floor on six unseen little legs. Two bright blue eyes sparkled innocently from the depths of a tangle of ratty-looking gray fur.

"Hello, Fuzz." Lydia scooped the dust-bunny up, kissed the top of his head, and settled him on her shoulder. "You don't know how glad I am to see you. I have had a very difficult day."

The dust-bunny blinked his cute azure eyes at Emmett, who was not fooled for a minute. He had seen Fuzz's second set of eyes, the ones he used for hunting at night. The little fluff ball looked as harmless as something that had been swept out from under the bed but at heart he was a highly efficient little predator. There was a saying about dust-bunnies. *By the time you see the teeth, it's too late.*

Fortunately he and Fuzz had discovered that they had a couple of things in common. One of them was Lydia.

"Lookin' good, Fuzz." Emmett ruffled the dust-bunny's fur and was rewarded with a humming sound. Fuzz, at least, was happy to see him.

"I'm going to get out of this business suit," Lydia announced. She turned down the hall toward the bedroom. "And then I'm going to have a glass of wine. Probably two glasses."

"I'll open a bottle," Emmett said, trying to sound helpful.

He spoke to thin air. She had already disappeared into the bedroom.

"Ghost-shit." This was not going well at all.

He went into the small kitchen, opened the refrigerator door, and brooded for a while on the selection of items inside. Among the limited offerings was a carton of milk and some leftover macaroni-and-cheese casserole. On the top shelf was a bottle of the truly dreadful white wine that Lydia kept on hand. The stuff was, in his opinion, only a couple of steps above Green Ruin and Acid Aura, the beverages of choice among the derelicts and down-and-outers who drifted through the Old Quarter.

But there wasn't much choice so he hauled out the jug and set it down on the counter.

Lately he had managed to avoid having to drink Lydia's lousy wine because the two of them had been spending a lot of time at his new place a few blocks away. He not only had a better view of the Dead City from the terrace of his town house, he kept more palatable vintages on hand.

A few weeks ago when he had set out to find living space here in Cadence, he'd had his choice of properties. The real estate agent had tried to sell him one of the big gated estates up on Ruin View Hill. After all, money was not exactly an issue. He had made plenty of it while running the Resonance Guild and he had good instincts when it came to investments.

But he'd had a couple of major priorities when it came to housing. One of them was not wanting Mercer Wyatt and his wife, Tamara, for next-door neighbors. The other and far more important objective had been to be as close to Lydia as possible.

He figured that one month into this rocky relationship was probably way too soon to ask her to move in with him, let alone consider marriage, so he'd opted for proximity. That meant a house in the Old Quarter. Besides, he liked the vibes in the neighborhood.

The real estate agent had eventually given up trying to make him see the advantages of a mansion on the hill and had found him an attractive, post–Era of Discord town house that had been recently remodeled and redecorated.

Emmett had taken Lydia to the house one afternoon while he was considering the purchase just to see how she responded. The glow of delight in her lagoon blue eyes as she walked through the spacious rooms and out onto the terrace to see the glorious view of the Dead City had sealed the deal as far as he was concerned. She looked terrific in his house. Right at home.

He had been hoping that, in a month or two, the time would be right to point out how much money she could save if she gave up her cramped apartment and moved in with him. After that he had planned to ease her gently into the idea of getting married.

He would have preferred to go straight into a full-blown Covenant Marriage with all the legal and social bonds attached to such an alliance. Covenant Marriages were almost impossible to dissolve. Obtaining a divorce required teams of lawyers, a lot of money, and years of patience. And then there was the social stigma to live down.

Most people went first for the standard, easily renewable, one-year Marriage of Convenience to test the waters with a partner, although if someone accidentally got pregnant in an MC it was understood that the couple would immediately obtain a Covenant Marriage license.

The First Generation of colonists from Earth hadn't established the rigid strictures of Covenant Marriage because they had been a prudish lot; rather they had been a desperate lot. Two hundred years ago when the mysterious energy field in space known as the Curtain had opened, providing a gate between Earth and several other inhabitable worlds, the settlers had chosen to make their new homes on Harmony.

But shortly after they had established their colonial towns and villages, the energy field had vanished without any warning, stranding them. The Curtain had never reopened.

Cut off from all contact with Earth, with families separated from their home-planet relatives forever, the high-tech engineering and farming equipment falling apart because of a lack of replacement parts, the colonial leaders had buckled down and concentrated on drawing up plans that would ensure the survival of their communities.

In the effort to create a social structure that

could withstand the unknown rigors and stresses that lay ahead, they had fashioned the Republic of City-States that bound all of the colonial cities on the planet into a single federation. They had then proceeded to craft the stern laws that governed Covenant Marriage.

A Marriage of Convenience was the great loophole in the law. It was designed for folks who wanted to rez a little wild, untuned amber before getting serious and for prudent couples who wished to try out a relationship before making an unbreakable commitment. But eventually mature, responsible adults were supposed to settle into a Covenant Marriage. After all these years it was still considered the cornerstone of a stable society.

As far as he was concerned, there was no need to do any trial runs with this relationship, Emmett thought. He couldn't envision a future without Lydia. He would have been happy to go straight into a Covenant Marriage. But he had known that he would be lucky to get her to agree to start with an MC.

Lydia had a lot of issues when it came to ghost-hunters. He had tried to distance himself from Guild politics as far as possible, but he knew that she still fretted about his connections to the organization.

Now, thanks to the near-fatal assault on Mercer Wyatt a few hours ago, there was no point in even raising the issue of marriage in the immediate future.

He poured two glasses of the evil white wine and put the bottle back in the refrigerator. There was no sound from the bedroom. Lydia had had plenty of time to change into a pair of jeans and a sweater. What was keeping her?

Fuzz tumbled silently into the kitchen and looked up at him from the floor. The dust-bunny bobbed anxiously.

"What is it, pal? Want a pretzel?" Emmett removed the lid of the jar. Dust-bunnies were omnivorous. Lydia usually fed Fuzz whatever she had fixed for herself. But when it came to snacks, he had a pronounced taste for pretzels.

But Fuzz ignored the pretzel. Instead he made an odd noise, a sound that was very close to a tiny growl.

"Okay, no pretzel." Emmett replaced the lid of the jar. "Something wrong, buddy?"

A tremor passed over Fuzz's fur. He looked as if he was trying to bristle, not an easy thing for a ball of lint to do. Then he bounced a couple of times, turned and scampered a few feet back toward the bedroom, halted and tumbled back into the kitchen. He bristled some more.

"Right." Emmett picked up the two glasses of wine. "You want to play the Find Lydia game, is that it?"

Fuzz drifted swiftly back down the hall toward the bedroom.

Emmett followed warily. They had played this game many times in recent weeks both indoors and outside on the street or in a nearby park.

Fuzz loved it. The rules were simple. Emmett would look at Fuzz and say, *find Lydia,* and Fuzz would rush off gleefully to lead him to wherever she happened to be at that moment.

But this time there was a sense of urgency in Fuzz's demeanor that was new.

At the doorway to the bedroom Emmett paused, trying to get a handle on the situation before he made a move.

Lydia stood at the window, her back turned toward him. She was still in her severely tailored, skirted business suit. She hadn't even removed the jacket. Her face was in her hands and her shoulders were shaking.

His insides turned to ice. He had seen Lydia in a lot of moods, including angry, passionate, happy, and scared. He had seen her confront energy ghosts, a murderer, and Mercer Wyatt's ambitious wife, Tamara, all without flinching. But in the short time he had known her, he had never seen Lydia in tears.

Fuzz hopped up on the windowsill near Lydia and huddled there, peering at Emmett with an air of agitated expectation. Dust-bunny body language for *do something,* probably.

Sorry, pal, Emmett thought. I haven't got a clue how to deal with this.

But he sure as hell could not continue to just stand here watching Lydia sob quietly into her fingers. She was tearing the heart out of him.

"Lydia? Honey?" He put the wineglasses down on the dresser and went to stand behind her.

She sniffed a couple of times. The tears continued to flow. Aware that he was way out of his depth, he seized a couple of tissues from the box on the nightstand and pushed them into her hands.

Lydia took the tissues from him without comment and blew her nose. Unable to think of anything else to do, Emmett gave her more tissues.

She dabbed at her eyes and took a deep breath. He put his hands on her shoulders from behind and massaged gently.

The flood of tears eventually subsided but she did not turn around. Instead she gazed fixedly out the window at the old building across the street. She sniffed a couple more times.

"Sorry," she muttered. "I hate when this happens."

"It's okay." He continued to knead her tense shoulders. "You've got a right. It's been a rough day."

"You think so? Gosh, I only came across one dead body, went through a police interrogation, and found out that you are now the chief of the Cadence Guild. Just an ordinary day." She wiped her eyes with the back of her hand. "No good reason that I can see to break down in tears."

He winced. "It's the last item on the list that made you cry, isn't it? The fact that I've agreed to take over the Guild on a temporary basis."

"Why did you do it, Emmett?" she asked starkly.

"It's . . . complicated," he said.

"Tell me one thing. Does it involve Tamara Wyatt?"

The question surprised him. "Hell, no. Tamara has nothing to do with this."

"She's your ex-fiancée. She ended the engagement and married Mercer Wyatt when she found out that you were going to step down as boss of the Resonance Guild. And now you've just taken over the Cadence Guild, her husband's job. You two have a lot of history."

"Whatever Tamara and I had together ended when she made it clear that she wanted to be the wife of a Guild chief more than she wanted to be my wife. I told you that the night you met her."

"If this isn't about Tamara, what is it about? Is the old saying true? Once a Guild man, always a Guild man?"

"The Cadence Guild is in a very delicate situation right now," he said, choosing his words carefully. "Wyatt says he's preparing to step down in another year or two. He claims he is committed to modernizing the organization along the same lines as the Resonance Guild before he leaves office."

"You really think he intends to turn the Cadence Guild into a respectable business enterprise with a board of directors and an elected CEO at the top? After running the organization with an iron fist for over three decades? Give me a break."

"Wyatt is nothing if not a cold-eyed pragmatist." Emmett wondered, even as he spoke the words, why he was bothering to try to defend the boss of the Cadence Guild. Probably because he had just agreed to take over the job himself, he thought. Deep down he had been praying that when Lydia found out what had happened she wouldn't consign him to the same category as Wyatt, that she wouldn't conclude that he really was a low-life mobster.

"I agree he's probably one heck of a realist," Lydia muttered.

"He is genuinely concerned with the future of the Guild. He took a good hard look at the current position of the organization and realized that the Cadence Guild must change if it wants to stay relevant."

"Hah."

"Wyatt admits that he's having trouble attracting and keeping good, well-qualified hunters. There was a time when a talented dissonance-energy para-rez signed up with the Guild for life. Now a lot of them join for a few years, make some quick money ghost-hunting, and then get out in order to enter a more respectable profession." He hesitated. "That's especially true for hunters who want to marry outside the Guild."

"Uh-huh."

She didn't say anything else, but there was no need for further comment, he thought. They were both well aware of the facts. Ever since they had been established during the Era of Discord, the hunters' Guilds had operated as closed, insular societies with their own traditions and their own rules. Historically, if you were raised in a Guild family, the odds were very high that you would choose a spouse from another Guild family.

"Wyatt wants to change the image of the Cadence Guild," he said. "His goal is to turn it into a professional business organization."

"The way you did with the Resonance Guild?"

He wasn't sure where she was going to go with that. Her tone was a little too neutral for his peace of mind.

"That's the general idea," he said.

"No offense, but Wyatt seems to be off to a rather poor start, what with nearly getting himself murdered this morning." She blew her nose into a tissue. "That sort of thing isn't good for the professional image, you know. Tends to make people think in terms of gangland feuds and mob boss rivalries."

He said nothing. He had no more arguments to give her.

She sniffled again, blotted up the last of her tears, and wadded up the tissue. "You're supposed to be a business consultant now, Emmett."

"I *am* a business consultant. As far as I'm concerned this job with the Guild is just that, a short-term consulting position."

"If you go back into the Guild, you may not get out a second time."

Very deliberately he took his hands off her shoulders. "And if I return to the Guild, you'll end our relationship? Is that what you're trying to tell me?"

"*No.*" She whirled around, eyes glittering with sudden fury and outrage. "I'm trying to tell you that the idea of you running the Cadence Guild, even for a few weeks, scares me more than all the illusion traps and energy ghosts in the Dead City, *that's* what I'm trying to tell you."

He felt his own temper start to slip. "Does the thought of sleeping with a Guild boss offend your delicate sensibilities so much? I figured that you and I had something more going on than just a casual fling."

"Don't act dense."

"Sorry, but it's not an act. I feel dense at the moment. I'm also real tired of playing guessing games. Why don't you tell me exactly why you're crying? Keep it simple. Short sentences and no more than two syllables, okay? After all, I'm a hunter, remember? I don't do big words."

"Fine." She threw up her hands. "You want to know why I'm crying? I'm crying because I'm terrified that if you take Mercer Wyatt's position, whoever tried to murder him last night will try to get rid of you, too. I'm scared to death that if you take over the Cadence Guild, you'll be putting yourself in grave danger." Tears welled up in her eyes once more. "And I can't bear to think about what I would do if you got hurt or worse."

He stared, dumbfounded, at the fresh tears running down her face. "That's why you're so upset? You think whoever went after Wyatt will come after me?"

She swiped her eyes with her sleeve and nodded mutely.

"Ah, honey."

He stopped, not sure how to proceed. He had been braced to hear her tell him that she would break off their relationship if he took over the Guild. He had been so intently focused on arguments designed to convince her to tolerate the situation for a short period of time that he could not wrap his brain around this other thing. She had dissolved into a puddle because she feared for his safety?

He could not recall the last time anyone had been overly concerned about his health and well-being. Back in Resonance it was understood that he could take care of himself.

Admittedly, over the years he had managed to reduce a couple of previous lovers to tears but the aggrieved parties had always made it clear that the reason was the usual masculine sin of failing to understand and respond properly to a woman's needs. None of those old lovers had ever cried because she was concerned that he might get hurt or killed.

Relief and a strange sense of satisfaction surged through him. Lydia was worried about him.

"It's okay," he said. "There's no reason to be

concerned about me. What happened to Wyatt looks like something personal, not Guild politics."

"Is that right?" She turned away to grab another handful of tissues. "How do you know that?"

"I'll explain later. Right now I've got something more important to do."

She dabbed a few more tears and glowered at him over her shoulder. "Such as?"

He smiled slowly and reached out to pull her back into his arms.

"Such as this," he said.

He caught her face in both hands and raised her mouth to his. She stiffened. And then, with a soft, muffled cry, she practically leaped on him, wrapping her arms very tightly around his neck, holding on as if she was afraid that he would slip away from her.

"Emmett."

Everything in him went from zero to full-rez in a rush. Desire swept through him, heating his blood and making him heavy and restless with need.

He had intended a gentle, soothing embrace, a few cuddles and kisses designed to calm her and reassure her. But her sudden, impassioned response sent any gentlemanly plans he might have had up in smoke.

"Okay, this works, too," he whispered against her throat.

He pulled her with him down onto the bed.

Out of the corner of his eye he saw Fuzz tumble off the windowsill and scamper across the carpet. The little ball of dryer lint drifted out of the bedroom and disappeared discreetly down the hall. Probably embarrassed him, Emmett thought.

He turned his attention back to Lydia, who had landed on top of him and was straddling his thighs. The position had forced her skirt high above her knees.

"Promise me you'll be careful." She unbuckled his belt.

"I'll be careful."

She unfastened his shirt. "Promise me you won't take any chances."

Acid green ghost light danced at the edge of his vision. It winked out quickly only to be followed by another shower of sparkling energy. *Flickers,* he thought; the little flashes of unstable dissonance energy often appeared when he and Lydia made love.

Psi energy leaked and whispered out of small cracks, hidden openings, and invisible vents in the ancient green quartz walls that surrounded the ruins in this part of town. Often, when he found himself highly aroused with Lydia the wavelengths of his sexual energy resonated with the stuff. The result was the small bursts of harmless ghost light that winked out as quickly as they appeared.

"Right," he muttered, crumpling her skirt up around her waist. He touched the crotch of her panties. She was already damp. Satisfaction roared through him. "No chances." *Except with you,* he added silently. Loving Lydia was far and away the biggest risk he had ever taken.

She released him from the prison of his zipper. Her fingers slid along the underside of that part of him that was now rock hard. When she cupped him he stopped breathing for a few seconds.

She flattened herself on top of him, threading her fingers through the hair on his chest and kissing him with her mouth open.

Energy stirred and shimmered in the air around them. Not ghost light, just a frisson of sensation. Lydia was the source this time, he realized, although he didn't think she was aware of the invisible currents shifting across the bed.

She was an ephemeral-energy para-resonator, otherwise known as an illusion trap tangler. Her para-talents took a different form than his own. She could not summon ghost light, but she could de-rez the dangerous snares of illusion shadow that the long-vanished aliens had left behind to guard their secrets in the ruins. She was the best tangler he had ever worked with, he thought. When it came to wielding raw psi power she was, in her own way, as strong as he was.

She slithered down his body, touching him with the tip of her tongue at various points along the way. He realized where she was headed and knew that if he didn't gain control of the situation he would lose it before he got to his own favorite destination.

He rolled her onto her back. With a few efficient moves he got himself out of his pants and shoes. When he came down on top of her, anticipation had seared away all coherent thought.

He unfastened her jacket and then her blouse and took one sweet, ripe nipple between his teeth.

Her eyes were bottomless pools of intense blue by the time he had finished undressing her. He bent his head and kissed her until she was shifting and twisting beneath him, until she moaned. The soft sound of her need was the sweetest music he had ever heard.

He settled between her warm thighs. The scent of her passion sharpened his need until he could think of nothing else but losing himself inside her.

Ghost light sparked again when he found his way into her tight, wet heat. She raised her hips to take him deeper. He felt her fingers rake his back beneath his unbuttoned shirt.

He stroked into her and her body clenched. He thrust again, very slowly this time, withdrawing almost completely. She gave a little scream. He sank himself to the hilt. She convulsed around him.

Her climax rippled through her, drawing him inexorably toward his own release.

He held on until the last instant and then he let the power of her orgasm sweep him away.

Although some instinct compelled him to try to master the flow of sexually charged energy that pulsed between them, in the end, he was never sure if he had accomplished his goal. When he was with Lydia the white hot boundary between surrender and control was impossible to define.

3

Lydia reluctantly swam up out of the delightfully vague state that had followed in the wake of the over-the-top climax. She was getting used to great sex, she thought. Maybe that was not such a good thing. Life would probably be a whole lot simpler had she never discovered what she had found in Emmett's arms.

Granted, her previous sexual experience had not been what anyone would call extensive. In fact, her friend Melanie, who was something of an expert on the subject, had warned her on several occasions about the dangers of her excessively dull sex life.

But the truth was that passion had never been a particularly high priority for her, Lydia thought. For as long as she could remember, her single great, shining goal had been to become a para-archaeologist. After the loss of her parents when she was in her late teens, she had found herself alone in the world. The dream of exploring the underground catacombs of the Dead City and cataloging the secrets of the ancient Harmonics had helped to fill up many of the empty places in her life.

The vision of herself as a brilliant, highly respected member of the faculty of para-archaeology at the university had consumed her. She had planned to achieve a sterling academic reputation, write brilliant papers and books, and announce stunning new discoveries in the *Journal of Para-archaeology*.

Her ambition, drive, and strong psi talent had carried her far for the first few years. She had been on track to fulfill all of her goals. But approximately seven months ago, everything had come to a screeching halt. The disaster in the catacombs that she bitterly referred to as her Lost Weekend had nearly gotten her killed. Worse yet, it had shattered her promising career.

The experience had also left her with a case of amnesia regarding the events of those two days. She had no clear memories of the forty-eight hours that she had spent wandering in the endless glowing tunnels and passages beneath the Dead City.

The details of the incident had been pieced together at the inquiry. According to her companions on the research team, she had disappeared down an unexplored and unmarked corridor and never returned. As soon as someone had noticed that she was missing, the team leader, Ryan Kelso, had sent the ghost-hunters to search for her, of course. But it was too late. She had vanished.

Forty-eight hours later she had awakened to find herself alone in a small, uncharted chamber. That was not the worst of it. The really bad news was that she had somehow lost her rez-amber. She had known then that she was doomed. Tuned amber functioned like a compass in the maze of the catacombs. Without it she had no means of making her way to any of the exits.

But Fuzz had found her.

To this day she did not know how he had done it, let alone how he had sensed that she was lost in the first place. But she would never forget the glorious sight of him crouched beside her, anxiously licking her face when she had at long last opened her eyes.

He had led her unerringly to the nearest exit. She knew only too well what her fate would have been had he not appeared when he did. The only question was whether she would have died of thirst before she went mad wandering aimlessly through the endless green night of the alien catacombs. The odds of being found by a search party were almost zero.

No one had been more surprised to see her reappear than her colleagues on the excavation team who had given up hope. There had been great joy and celebration all around — for about three days.

And then the reality of her new situation had sunk in: Everyone assumed that her experience underground had shattered her para-rez pitch. The shrinks who had checked her out afterward quickly filled her medical file with such ominous phrases as *sustained para-psych trauma* and *para-amnesia*. Typical aftereffects of an encounter with an illusion trap or a large energy ghost.

The most amazing aspect of the case, as far as the para-psychologists were concerned, was that she was able to function with any degree of normalcy after the experience. She was certainly not the first ephemeral-energy para-resonator to lose control of one of the nightmarish traps or blunder into a powerful energy ghost. She was, however, one of the few who had gone through such an experience and not ended up in an institution.

She was labeled *extremely fragile*, psychically speaking, and therefore unreliable on a professional excavation team. No one wanted to work with a tangler who had been badly fried.

At the formal inquiry the two ghost-hunters who had been charged with responsibility for protecting the team had blamed Lydia for taking off on her own without due regard for the very strict safety rules. She, in turn, had accused them of failing to do their job properly.

The findings of the investigation had been pretty much a foregone conclusion. Officially, the disaster was deemed to be a result of Lydia's failure to follow established procedures. She had been dismissed from her position at the university.

For her part, she had vowed never to trust a ghost-hunter again.

Life had certainly changed a lot in the past few months, she reflected. Instead of working on an academic research team, she was now employed at a third-rate museum, Shrimpton's House of Ancient Horrors, and she was dating a ghost-hunter.

On the positive-rez side, her sex life had definitely improved.

On the negative-rez side, she knew that she had fallen in love.

She was aware of Emmett sprawled heavily on the bed beside her, one arm flung around her waist in a casually possessive grip.

She stared up at the ceiling. "I can't believe that I'm sleeping with a Guild boss."

"Temporary Guild boss," he mumbled into the pillow. "Acting Guild boss. No, wait, let's make that *consulting* Guild boss."

"I'm sleeping with a Guild boss."

"*Former* Guild boss?" he tried.

"Guild boss."

He rolled over onto his back and folded his arms behind his head. "You can be a little too literal-minded at times, you know that?"

She levered herself up on one elbow. "Probably a result of my academic training."

"Probably."

For a few seconds she allowed herself to savor the sight of him in her bed. He still wore his shirt but that was all. The shadow of his untrimmed beard enhanced the stark, uncompromising planes and angles of his hunter's face.

"You didn't even get a chance to shave this morning, did you?" she said. "You must be exhausted."

"Like I said, the phone was ringing when I walked in the door around three A.M." He took one hand out from behind his head and rubbed his jaw, grimacing. "The doctors didn't know if Wyatt was going to make it so I just dropped the camping stuff and got back in the car."

"There's something I don't understand here. Why did the hospital call you? You're not even a member of the Cadence Guild."

He exhaled heavily. "Like I said, it's complicated."

"I'm listening."

"Wyatt was barely conscious when he dragged himself in to the emergency room. But he's a Guild boss to his bones. He stayed awake long enough to call a couple of members of the Guild Council and issue some orders. Then he made the hospital call me. He was being wheeled into the operating room when I arrived." Emmett shook his head. "And still giving orders."

"Wait a second." Lydia sat up, pulling the sheet around her. "Wyatt got himself to the hospital? But I thought you said he was nearly killed with a mag-rez gun."

"He should have been dead. Someone put two rounds into him. Both shots were probably intended to hit him in the upper chest. But he evidently sensed something was wrong when he got out of his car and tried to dive for cover. The result was that both shots went low and to the side. Still there was a lot of damage, not to mention shock and blood loss."

"It's a wonder he didn't bleed to death."

"He was in the Old Quarter near the South Wall when it happened. He managed to summon a couple of small energy ghosts. Used them to partially cauterize the wounds and slow the bleeding. Then he got behind the wheel of that big Oscillator 600 of his and drove himself to the ER."

"He used ghost energy on bleeding wounds?"

"No one ever said that Mercer Wyatt wasn't as tough as they come."

She caught her breath, astonished. Most of the green radiation given off by unstable dissonance energy manifestations everyone called ghosts was psi in nature, and the effects produced were most pronounced on the paranormal plane. But some of the eerie glow took the form of thermal energy. Ghosts were frequently hot enough to scorch paper or wood or a bedroom wall, as she had discovered the hard way last month.

Nevertheless, the thought of using one on an open wound was mind-boggling.

"I've never heard of such a thing," she said. "Theoretically, I suppose, it could be done. But the hunter would have to be able to exert an amazing amount of control in order to manipulate a ghost with the kind of precision it would require to staunch bleeding and not get badly burned at the same time."

"Hunters have some built-in immunity to the effects of ghost fire," he reminded her. "Comes with the psi talent required to handle them, I guess."

She shuddered. "Even so, I can only imagine how much pain it would cause on both the physical and the psychic planes."

He shrugged. "It hurts but not as much as you might think, not if you use some of the ghost's psi energy to distance your mind from the pain."

She frowned. "You've heard about this technique?"

"Sure. You get instruction and a little practice in basic training. It was an emergency medical procedure that was developed by Guild field medics during the Era of Discord."

Every child was taught the history of the Guilds in elementary school. They had been established a hundred years earlier as combat units to protect the cities against the threat of the charismatic fanatic, Vincent Lee Vance, and his followers.

Vance was a powerful dissonance-energy para-resonator — a ghost-hunter — who had spent his early years prospecting for amber. He had always been considered psychically unstable by those who knew him best but his eccentricities had not been much of a problem because for the most part he had shunned society to follow the solitary career path associated with the prospecting business.

At one point in his life Vance disappeared underground into the catacombs beneath Old Frequency City. When he had failed to reappear after several months, he had been presumed dead.

Eventually he had emerged, no longer a scruffy, half-daft amber man, but a visionary megalomaniac whose goal was nothing less than the conquest of all of the city-states. He claimed that he had discovered a great treasure house of ancient Harmonic secrets that would enable him to institute an ideal society. He promised that those who fought on his side would be rewarded with enormous power and wealth.

Life had been hard in the colonial cities a hundred years ago. The appeal of a utopian world was strong.

Vance had gathered an army of disaffected followers before anyone even started to take him seriously. He also acquired a lover named Helen Chandler, an extremely talented ephemeral-energy para-resonator who, it was said, could untangle any illusion trap that had ever been discovered.

From his secret headquarters somewhere in the complex of tunnels beneath Old Frequency City, Vance had drawn up detailed plans of conquest. His strategy had worked well at first because the colonial cities had never established standing armies. There had been no need for a military on Harmony. All of the city-states had been closely connected and had cooperated from the start in the effort to survive.

There were also no large arsenals on Harmony. The high-tech hunting rifles and handguns that had been brought from Earth by some of the colonists had ceased to function after the first few years because there had been no way to maintain them or reproduce the ammunition. In Vance's era there were only a couple of small, privately owned munitions manufacturing firms turning out revolvers and some rifles for the use of the cities' police departments and for farmers and hunters. The weapons were notoriously unreliable because the technique of making an amber-resonating trigger had not yet been perfected. In any event, none of those firms had possessed the capability of supplying arms in large numbers to Vance's recruits, even if they could have been made to do so.

But Harmony had provided its own weaponry: the dangerous and powerful energy ghosts in the catacombs.

Vance had fought a guerilla war in the maze of tunnels beneath the city-states. His hunters had summoned and manipulated great numbers of powerful energy ghosts. His tanglers had cleared the traps out of miles of uncharted underground corridors, enabling Vance's forces to strike swiftly and then disappear into the catacombs.

In a series of fast strikes, Vance's army produced early, devastating results. Old Frequency had fallen within days. Old Crystal had followed less than a month later. But the hunters in the two cities had put up more of a fight than Vance had expected and in doing so they had bought valuable time for Old Resonance and Old Cadence.

Under the leadership of a powerful hunter named Jerrett Knox, whose arcane, scholarly hobby happened to be the study of the history of ancient warfare on Earth, Resonance and Cadence had quickly brought their hunters together. The Guilds had been established to organize the fighting forces.

Knox had proved to be a gifted leader and a shrewd tactician. He also knew the catacombs extraordinarily well because he had spent years mapping them.

It had taken nearly a year to defeat Vance and his followers but in the end his minions had been crushed. After the final battle of Old Cadence, Vincent Lee Vance and his tangler-lover, Helen Chandler, had fled into an uncharted sector underground. They had vanished somewhere in the miles of unmapped catacombs, never to be heard from again.

"I've seen some accidents while working underground but I've never known a hunter to try to use a ghost to stop bleeding," Lydia said.

"It's an old-fashioned, low-tech procedure that is almost never needed these days," Emmett explained patiently. "Underground emergency teams carry modern medical kits that contain safer, more efficient equipment."

"But the Guilds still teach the old methods?"

"They teach them," Emmett said deliberately. "But not every hunter can make them work. Manipulating small ghosts that precisely is tricky."

"I'll bet," she muttered. "But Mercer Wyatt can no doubt do tricky."

"When called upon, yes," Emmett said dryly.

"Probably a Guild boss thing." She wrinkled her nose. "All right, finish your story."

"That's about it. Like I said, Wyatt made it to the ER, gave a few orders, and was rushed into surgery. Last time I checked, he was still unconscious."

"How critical is his condition? Do they really think he might die?"

"I don't know. The doctors are being very guarded at the moment."

"But in the meantime, you're the new Guild boss."

"Uh-huh."

She sighed. "Well, I suppose I can understand why you felt you had to take over for Wyatt when he asked you to help out. After all, you've been connected to the Guilds your whole life. You probably have a very ingrained sense of loyalty toward them."

"Let's get something straight here," Emmett said quietly. "It wasn't some kind of knee-jerk sense of Guild loyalty that made me agree to take over until Wyatt recovers."

She scowled. "Then why in the world did you do it?"

He exhaled deeply. "Another type of knee-jerk loyalty, I guess. I did it because Mercer Wyatt is my father."

4

She just sat there in the middle of the rumpled bed, speechless.

Wry amusement flickered in Emmett's eyes. "When I was growing up it was fairly common gossip back in Guild circles in Resonance."

She swallowed. "I see."

"Guess the stories didn't circulate here in Cadence, huh?"

"They certainly didn't circulate in *my* circles," she said briskly. "But, then, I've never socialized much with the Guild crowd."

"And you couldn't have cared less about gossip concerning any of its members, right?"

She raised one shoulder in a small shrug. "I had other interests."

"Yeah, like getting into a prestigious graduate school so that you could become a highly respected professor of para-archaeology and get to publish impossible-to-read treatises on tiny, insignificant artifacts that no one else gave a damn about and then do your socializing at boring faculty sherry hours where you got to trade witty repartee with a bunch of pompous academics."

"Hey, it was my life and I was real happy

with it until a couple of idiot hunters failed to do their job, nearly got me killed, and succeeded in getting me fired. Don't start with me, London."

His jaw jerked slightly. But all he said was, "Sorry. It's been a long day."

There was a short, tense silence.

"So tell me about your father," she said eventually.

"Not much to tell. The way I got the story from my mother was that before I was born she and her husband, John London, were on the point of ending a simple Marriage of Convenience. He'd had a fling with someone else." He paused a beat. "She'd had one, too."

"Her affair was with Mercer Wyatt, I take it?"

"Yes. But Wyatt was in a Covenant Marriage at the time and moving up fast through the Guild ranks here in Cadence. His wife was pregnant. There was no question of a divorce."

"No, of course not."

"John London was killed in an excavation accident underground. Mom had me a few months later and put London's name on the birth certificate. It was the only thing she could do under the circumstances."

"Wyatt knows the truth, I assume?" she said.

"I assume so. I never asked."

She widened her eyes. "You assume so?"

"We don't talk about it, okay?" Emmett sat up and swung his legs over the side of the bed.

"Mom has always made it clear that as far as she and the law and the benefits office of the Resonance Guild are concerned, I'm John London's son. Fine by me."

"I see. A real communicative family."

He stood and disappeared into the bathroom. "When I was growing up Wyatt came to Resonance City several times a year. Whenever he was in town to talk business with the leaders of the Guild, he would visit with me and Mom. He acted like he was some sort of honorary uncle. He always showed up with an armful of the latest toys and games. He gave me my first amber. Showed me how to summon a ghost. Kept track of how I was doing in school. Took my mother out to dinner."

"How long did that go on?"

Water ran in the bathroom for a moment.

"The dinners with Mom stopped when she married a member of the Resonance Guild Council a few years later," Emmett said after a while. "She was the one who ended the relationship. I got the impression there was a major battle of wills when she told him. Wyatt was not happy about it but in the end, he had no choice. When my mother makes a decision, she makes it stick."

"What about your own relationship with Wyatt? Did he continue to visit you?"

"We stayed in touch. When I started to move up in the hierarchy of the Resonance Guild he gave me some pointers, taught me the ropes of

Guild politics. But we had a major parting of the ways when he realized that I had my own ideas about the future of the Resonance Guild."

"What happened?"

"Wyatt was furious when he found out what I planned to do with the organization. He was still locked into Guild traditions in those days. He figured that if I managed to restructure the Resonance Guild as a modern business enterprise, the rest of the Guilds would eventually follow. We had several extremely colorful discussions on the subject. He finally gave up trying to change my mind."

"Then you proposed to Tamara and dear old dad showed up at your engagement ball and stole your fiancée?"

"To be fair, Wyatt's wife had died the year before. As for Tamara, she had already decided to end our engagement because I had told her that I planned to step down from my position with the Guild. She just didn't tell me until the morning after the reception."

"Heck of a morning-after surprise."

"My own fault. I should have seen it coming."

The shower went on in the bathroom, effectively cutting off all communication to and from the bedroom.

Annoyed, Lydia scrambled out of bed, pulled on a robe, and stalked into the steamy bath. She pushed the curtain aside.

Emmett was sluicing himself off beneath a blast of hot water. She tried to ignore the fact that he looked awfully good naked and wet. Water gleamed on his broad shoulders.

"It strikes me that Tamara's position is in jeopardy again," she said, raising her voice to be heard above the rushing water. "Her husband is in intensive care. If Wyatt doesn't make it, she will no longer be Mrs. Guild Boss. On top of that, you are the new Guild chief. She is not going to be a happy woman. Makes it look like she chose the wrong man, after all."

"Tamara will have to worry about her own problems." He reached for the razor. "I'm going to be a little busy for a while."

"You never got around to telling me why you don't think that you're in the same danger as Mercer Wyatt."

"He was fading fast because of the stuff they were pumping into him to control the shock and prep him for surgery. But the last thing he said to me before they wheeled him away was, *Don't let the Guild tear itself apart because of this. It wasn't politics, it was personal.*"

"You mean he knows who shot him?"

"I think so, but he didn't tell me. He said he'd take care of it when he got out of the hospital."

A shiver went through her. "Great. Just great. We're in the middle of a Guild family soap opera."

Emmett turned off the shower and grabbed the towel she held out to him.

"When it comes to dysfunctional families," he said, "I'll put mine up against anyone's, anytime."

5

She dreamed one of the Lost Weekend dreams.

She fled down an endless corridor that glowed green on every side. There was no sound behind her, but she knew that her pursuers were back there in the miles of catacombs searching for her.

She clutched something in one hand but she did not know what it was. She only knew that she dared not drop it.

Then, without warning, she was no longer in a corridor but a vast chamber with a ceiling far higher than any she had ever seen underground.

She was breathless. Her heart was pounding. Something very frightening had just happened but she could not remember what it was.

She stumbled and fell headlong on the green quartz floor. Terrified that she had just brushed against some object that might contain an illusion trap, she scrambled to her feet and turned to see what it was that had tripped her.

A human skull stared back. The eye sockets regarded her without pity or remorse.

The jaw moved. The death's head spoke. . . .

She came awake in a cold sweat, sitting straight up in bed. "The words."

Emmett stirred beside her. "What's wrong?"

At the foot of the bed, Fuzz raised his head. She could see all four of his eyes, the green set as well as the blue glowing in the shadows.

"The words on the scrap of paper I picked up off the floor of Professor Maltby's apartment," she whispered.

Emmett levered himself up off the pillows. "What paper?"

"I dropped it into my purse just before you and Detective Martinez arrived." She pushed aside the covers and stood beside the bed. "I got distracted after that and forgot about it."

She grabbed her robe and hurried down the short hall to the small table where she had left her purse. Emmett pulled on his khakis and followed at a more leisurely pace, yawning. Fuzz perched on his shoulder, no doubt hoping that this midnight expedition would include a raid on the pretzel jar.

Lydia got the purse open and groped inside. "It's in here somewhere."

"Take it easy, honey." Emmett switched on the hall light. "What made you pick up that paper?"

"Because it looked like the last thing Maltby wrote." Irritated when she could not locate the scrap of paper, she turned the purse upside down and dumped the contents onto the table. "It was unfinished."

Emmett began to look interested. "You think he was trying to write a message just before he died?"

"Maybe."

"You didn't say anything about this to Martinez."

"There wasn't much to say. The message might have been the start of a grocery list, as far as I know. Besides, Martinez was only interested in you and Mercer Wyatt. I doubt that the death of one more down-and-out Chartreuse addict is a high priority for the Cadence cops."

Emmett watched her sort through the array of items that had tumbled out of the purse. The mix included her wallet, a small jewelry case containing one of the several spare amber bracelets she had purchased after her Lost Weekend, a comb, her business calendar, and a packet of tissues. He studied the round, green quartz object on the bottom.

"What the heck are you doing with a tomb mirror in your purse?"

"Zane found it the other day. He gave it to me."

Tomb mirrors were among the most common of alien antiquities. No one knew how the aliens had used them but since one side was usually glass smooth and produced a clear, green-tinged reflection, the experts concluded they might have actually been mirrors. One school of thought held that the mirrors had had religious significance.

Tomb mirrors came in a variety of odd shapes and sizes but like most of the other antiquities that had been discovered on Harmony they were made of the same ubiquitous green quartz that the ancient alien colonists had used to construct almost everything. The stuff was virtually indestructible. As far as the experts could tell it was almost completely impervious to the elements and the biological processes that nature used to recycle everything else.

Emmett picked up the little tomb mirror and studied the ornate carvings that surrounded the reflective surface.

"Nice one," he commented, turning it over in his hand to examine the elegantly worked design on the back.

"Yes, it is." She finally spotted the scrap of paper trapped in the fold of her wallet. "Thank goodness. For a minute there I thought I had lost it."

Emmett put the mirror down on the table and studied the torn bit of note paper she held up to the light.

"Amber Hil?" He frowned. "Doesn't mean anything to me."

"It didn't register with me, either, when I found it today. But tonight I had another one of those stupid Lost Weekend dreams. This time I was in some sort of massive chamber. There was a skeleton on the floor." She broke off, struggling to bring back some of the swiftly evaporating details. "Maybe two skeletons, I'm not sure."

66

"Sounds like a major anxiety dream."

"I knew I had to get out of the chamber and keep moving. They were chasing me." The little piece of paper in her hand trembled.

"Easy, honey." Emmett put his arm around her shoulder and pulled her close against his hard, warm body. "Just a dream."

Fuzz hopped from Emmett's shoulder to Lydia's and rumbled soothingly in her ear. She raised her hand and patted him.

"I know," she said, shaking off the aftereffects of the nightmare. "I'm okay. The dream tonight was just my unconscious reminding me about this little note."

There was no point in telling Emmett that the Lost Weekend dreams were getting more frequent and more bizarre. He would only worry. He had problems enough at the moment.

The truth was, she was hopeful that the nightmares were a sign that her amnesia was starting to clear. In recent months she'd had an increasing number of fleeting glimpses into the dark place where her memories of the Lost Weekend were hidden. To date she had seen nothing solid or identifiable, though. It was like catching sight of a wraith at the corner of her eye. When she turned to look, it disappeared.

But she was convinced now that one day soon she would remember exactly what had happened to her down in the catacombs. When that day arrived, she planned to file the mother of all lawsuits. To that end, she was already drawing up a list of inexpensive lawyers. The problem would be finding one who was gutsy enough to take on the Cadence Guild.

She turned briskly away from the table and went toward the kitchen. "There's something familiar about what Maltby wrote down. I know I've seen these words somewhere else."

"Any idea where?" Emmett asked behind her.

"Yes." She yanked open the refrigerator and peered into the glowing interior. "On a milk carton."

Emmett moved close behind her and studied the carton of milk sitting on the top shelf. "Amber Hills Dairy."

"*Yes.*" She waved the piece of paper. "Frankly, I just can't see a man who was preparing a fix of Chartreuse worrying about picking up a carton of milk at the grocery store, can you?"

"He could have written the words earlier and gotten distracted."

"Emmett, when you make out a grocery list, you write milk, not the name of the dairy."

"Huh."

"I take it you don't make out a lot of grocery lists."

He shrugged. "I just go into the store and buy what I want."

She shook her head and closed the refrigerator door. "Another thing, Maltby's handwriting was very good and very precise. I saw some examples of it on his desk. But look at the penmanship on this piece of paper. *Amber Hil* was written with a hand that was shaking badly."

"Maybe," Emmett said, clearly unconvinced.

"Know what I think? I think Maltby was trying to write Amber Hills Dairy because he knew he was dying. He was leaving me a clue."

"Slow down, honey. Why would he use those last few moments of his life to write the name of a commercial dairy?"

"Good question." She swung around and started toward the bedroom. "I'm going back to his place to see if I missed something else."

"Now?" Emmett asked warily.

"I can't think of a better time, can you?"

"Damn," Emmett said. "I was afraid of that."

6

The fog had rolled in off the river earlier in the evening. It had flooded Hidden Lane, thickening the already deep shadows that nestled in the narrow passage. It was one-thirty in the morning. Only a handful of the windows in the aging apartment buildings that rose on either side of the lane were lit at this hour.

Emmett was well aware that the lack of illumination did not mean that there was not a lot of lively business activity going on in the vicinity. Most of the entrepreneurs who plied their trades and sold their goods in this part of town preferred to work at night and in the shadows. The sole exception might be the Greenie huddled at a small table beneath the lane's single streetlamp, books stacked in front of him. He did not look all that happy to be on the job at that hour. Emmett didn't blame him.

The Slider fit, just barely, into a tiny space near the entrance to the flophouse where Maltby had lived. Emmett de-rezzed the engine and looked at Lydia with what he hoped was an expression of stern authority.

"Stick close to me," he ordered. "I go in first.

70

If anything happens, you let me handle it, understood?"

"Relax." She unbuckled her belt and opened the door. "What can go wrong? I told you, I just want to have a quick look around Maltby's place. We'll be in and out in five minutes."

"Why doesn't that reassure me?" he said, cracking the door.

Fuzz, crouched on Lydia's shoulder, blinked his blue eyes and then, when he realized that Lydia was about to exit the Slider, opened his second set. His small body quivered with what looked like anticipation. He loved the night.

Emmett met Lydia and Fuzz at the front of the vehicle. He summoned a few stray wisps of ghost energy and fixed them to the license plate.

"Well, that should certainly ensure that the car is still here when we get back," Lydia said with wry appreciation. "No one in his right mind is going to steal a Slider from a ghost-hunter who is strong enough to attach a small ghost to it on a city street."

He shrugged. "Don't know about the fear factor but I do know that the ghost energy clinging to the car makes it a hell of a lot easier to find if it does get swiped."

He opened his para-rez senses as far as possible and knew that Lydia was probably doing the same.

Traces of psi energy trickled, seeped, and flowed all around them. There was nothing unusual about that, not in this part of town. But they felt stronger now than they had earlier in the day. Emmett was not surprised. Although the researchers had never been able to prove it, most people with even an ounce of para-rez sensibility — and that included virtually everyone since the second generation of colonists — were convinced that the ghostly currents whispered a little more loudly after dark.

One popular theory held that it wasn't the psi energy that was more powerful at night, rather it was that humans were simply more sensitive to it when the sun went down. It made sense, Emmett thought, that without the distraction of the solar radiation that came with daylight, the human mind might be better able to focus on other kinds of energy.

Whatever the reason, there was no denying that here, in the shadows of the walls of the Dead City, things got a lot more interesting between sundown and dawn.

It was difficult to see much of the Greenie at the table. The flowing robes and heavy cowl concealed gender, age, and features very effectively. It was only when the figure spoke to them that Emmett knew for certain it was a man.

"Have you found true bliss?" the Greenie murmured, thrusting a book toward Lydia.

"Not yet," Lydia said. "But I'm working on it."

"Read this and learn the thirteen steps that anyone can follow to the secrets of perpetual happiness. The keys to bliss were given to Master Herbert by the spirit of the ancient Harmonic philosopher, Amatheon. They are yours for the taking." The Greenie pushed the book into her fingers.

"Okay, thanks." Lydia dropped the book into her purse with an impatient movement.

The Greenie smiled from the depths of his cowl and held out a bowl. "A small contribution is expected. Little enough to ask when you consider that I have just shown you the path to bliss."

"Forget it." Lydia yanked the book out of her purse and dropped it on the table. "I'm not paying for perfect bliss. The best things in life are supposed to be free."

"If you cannot afford to make a contribution now, perhaps you will be able to make it later," the Greenie muttered.

"Sure," Lydia said, moving right along.

The Greenie glanced speculatively at Emmett.

"Save your breath," Emmett advised. "I'm a Guild man. I don't read much."

The Greenie sighed and huddled down into his robe.

Emmett took Lydia's arm and steered her away from the table and up the steps of the apartment house. The door that opened onto the small, dank foyer was unlocked, just as it had been that morning when he had arrived in search of Lydia. The smell in the front hall seemed to have gotten worse in the past few hours.

The entryway was lit by a dim, sputtering, fluo-rez bulb. If there had ever been a light in the narrow corridor beyond, it had burned out long ago.

"Apartment A," Lydia said. She started forward eagerly.

Emmett wrapped his hand around her arm and hauled her back. "I'll go first. I'm the hunter here, remember? The overpaid bodyguard?"

"Really, Emmett, we're not on an expedition underground. I really don't think —"

"Yeah, I've noticed that tendency. You ought to watch it."

He moved into the hall, every sense rezzed.

Nothing shifted in the shadows but he noticed that there was a thin line of light beneath the bottom edge of the door of the apartment directly across from Maltby's. That was interesting, he thought. There had been no sign of a neighbor when he had arrived earlier today.

He halted in front of Maltby's door and tried the knob. To his surprise, it turned easily in his hand. The cops and medics hadn't even bothered to lock up after they removed the body.

He eased the door open. Rusty hinges squeaked.

A faint scraping sound came from somewhere inside the apartment. It was followed immediately by the heavy weight of an unnatural silence; the tense, quivering stillness of someone who has been startled.

He reacted instinctively, pushing Lydia, who was right behind him, back down the hall.

"Stay there." He gave the order the way he had in the old days down in the catacombs when he had been responsible for the safety of an archaeological team: in a flat, hard voice that let everyone know that he expected full and immediate compliance. He had discovered the hard way that it was the only surefire means of securing the attention of the P-As who tended to get completely distracted by their work and often became oblivious to what was going on around them underground.

Lydia did as she was told, hovering in the corridor. Fuzz quivered in excitement.

Inside the apartment he heard a frantic scrambling sound. Not the rush of movement that indicated someone coming toward him, Emmett realized. More like the noise a person made trying to squeeze through an open window. The intruder had chosen flight rather than a confrontation.

Emmett entered the apartment swiftly, staying low and moving at an angle so that he would not be silhouetted against the weak light from the hall. Adrenaline kicked in, wild and potent. His prey was escaping.

He reached the doorway of the study in a matter of seconds but he knew at once that he was too late. Night air poured through the open window but the room was empty.

He started across the floor, unable to see anything except the pale square of gray light that marked the window. His booted foot struck a heavy bundle of what felt like thickly wadded up fabric.

Hell, not another body. He glanced down as he caught his balance. There was just enough light from the alley outside to reveal the bunched-up carpet that had snagged his boot. The intruder must have removed it to get at the floorboards, he thought. The guy had been searching for something.

The delay cost him a crucial few seconds.

By the time he reached the window and flattened himself against the wall, he knew he was too late.

From where he stood he could see a section of the fog-bound passage that ran the length of the building. The combination of river mist and darkness made it impossible to spot his quarry but he heard footsteps pounding toward the entrance of the alley.

A *lot* of footsteps, he thought. Two people, not one.

He considered summoning a ghost to stop the fleeing intruders out in the street. The problem was that he had no way of knowing who else might be in the vicinity. It would not look good in the morning papers if the headlines implied that the new Guild boss made a habit of singing innocent bystanders with wild ghost energy. The damn image thing.

"Emmett?" Lydia's voice came from the

front room. She sounded anxious and alarmed. "Emmett, are you okay? Answer me."

"I'm okay."

So much for following orders. Out of nowhere he suddenly recalled the records of the inquiry into Lydia's Lost Weekend. They had been marked confidential, of course, but he had not had any trouble getting a copy through his Guild connections.

The two hunters who had been assigned to Lydia's team had testified that she had gotten into trouble because she had not obeyed their orders.

Sometimes it was all too easy to comprehend just how that might have happened, he thought. She was, by nature as well as by training, strong willed. In the pursuit of an objective, she could be very, very determined.

He turned away from the window and saw four eyes glowing in the darkness a short distance away.

"Thanks for the backup, Fuzz." He reached down and scooped up the dust-bunny, who was sleeked into full hunting mode. "But we missed 'em."

Carrying Fuzz, he walked out of the study and went into the living room. Lydia was a silhouette in the doorway.

"They're gone," he said.

"What happened?" she asked, closing the door.

"Some other folks got here first. They made it

out through the window before I could grab them."

"You're all right?" she asked sharply.

"Fuzz and I are both fine. Probably a couple of burglars. Not a big surprise in this neighborhood. They must have got the word that Maltby was dead and thought they'd drop in to see if he left any drugs around."

"Hmm."

He did not like the sound of that *hmm*, but he chose to ignore it. Instead, he removed the flashlight from his pocket, rezzed it with a small pulse of psi energy, and played the beam across the room. "They really tore this place apart looking for his stash."

Together they surveyed the chaos that had overtaken the tiny living room. The carpet had been rolled up and shoved to one side. Foam spilled out of ripped cushions on the sofa. Books had been swept off the shelves and dumped unceremoniously onto the floor.

"They were certainly looking for something," Lydia said ominously.

"Leftover Chartreuse, like I said."

"Maybe." She directed her own light at a dismembered sofa. "But there's another possibility."

He glanced at her. "You think they wanted to see if he left some clue about whatever it was he wanted to tell you? Don't go there, Lydia. We don't need any conspiracy theories to explain this search. Maltby did drugs, remember? Odds are this was done by a couple of opportunists looking for some free dope."

"You've got to admit that Maltby's accidental overdose today, the very day he chose to leave a message saying he had something important to tell me, is what you might call a very interesting coincidence."

"It's a coincidence. Period." Resigned, he led the way back to the study.

"I really hate when you get that tone in your voice," she said, hurrying after him.

"What tone?"

"The tone that says you know I'm right but you don't want to admit it."

"I'm a bigger person than that," he said. "I can admit when you're right."

"Really? Try it sometime when I've got a rez-corder handy."

She peered over his shoulder while he aimed the light into the room. "Jeez, they really made a mess in here, didn't they? Look, they even pulled up a couple of floorboards."

There was no denying that the study was in far worse shape than the other room. The drawers had been removed from the desk, the contents dumped on the floor. The reading chair had been overturned, the underside ripped open.

"Let's make this fast," he said, moving to the desk. "Someone else may decide to stop by tonight."

"We're looking for anything that has to do

with Amber Hills Dairy." Lydia studied the floor. "I wonder if he had a hidden safe."

"If whoever was here ahead of us didn't find it, I doubt that we'll get lucky," he warned. "The intruders obviously spent a lot of time taking this place apart."

"You know what your problem is, Emmett? You're a worst-case scenario type of guy." She pushed aside some tumbled books to take a closer look at a seam in the floorboards. "You've got to learn to think positive."

"The beauty of planning for the worst-case scenario is that I'm rarely disappointed." He picked up a heavy textbook and flipped through it. There were hand-scribbled notes on every page. "Looks like Maltby never lost his interest in his old profession, in spite of the drugs."

"I told you, once upon a time, he was considered an expert in his field."

Ten minutes later Lydia gave up on the bookcase and stood looking around, her hands on her hips. "I hate to say it, but you may be right. Whoever got here ahead of us had a chance to search this room very thoroughly."

He resisted the temptation to say *I told you so.* "I agree."

"But they were still here when we arrived," she added thoughtfully. "Starting in on the living room, from the looks of it. Which implies that they did not find whatever it was they were looking for."

"Maybe there were no drugs left to find."

"Okay, let's say that the intruders were looking for Chartreuse." She folded her arms. "If that was the case, they wouldn't have had any interest in whatever it was that Maltby wanted to tell me. Which means his secrets are still here."

"Honey, there is nothing here that has anything to do with a dairy," he said as gently as possible.

"A milk carton," she whispered.

"What?"

"The poor man was dying. Maybe he wasn't trying to write a cryptic note in code. Maybe he was simply attempting to get an obvious message across to me." She unfolded her arms and rushed back out into the short hall.

"Now what?" he said to Fuzz.

They followed her into the small kitchen. She opened the door of the refrigerator. The interior light illuminated her face. He saw her eyes widen with excitement.

Moving closer he looked over her shoulder. There was half of a sandwich covered in mold and some unidentifiable sliced meat that had turned fuzzy and gray.

A carton of Amber Hills Dairy milk stood on the top shelf.

Lydia picked it up with great care. "Empty, I think." She hesitated and smiled slowly. "No, not quite."

He picked up a tiny tingle of psi energy.

"Trapped?" he asked.

She nodded. "Yes." Gingerly she opened the top of the carton and peered inside. "No milk, just a very nasty little illusion trap. Well, well, well. Wonder what it's hiding?"

"Don't try to de-rez it now. Let's get out of here."

"Fine by me." She closed the top of the carton with satisfaction. "I've got what I came here for."

He switched off his flashlight, went to the front door, and checked the corridor through the cloudy peephole. No one stood in the hall.

He eased the door open and moved out of the apartment with Fuzz on his shoulder. Lydia followed silently, cradling the milk carton.

Without warning the door directly across the corridor opened a bare three inches. The chain rattled. A slice of a face appeared.

"You're the new Guild boss, ain't ya?" the man rasped. "Saw your picture in the papers tonight."

One of the many downsides of his new position was the very high profile that came with it, Emmett thought. On the other hand occasionally it could be useful.

"I'm Emmett London," he said. He did not introduce Lydia who was standing very quietly in the hallway.

"Thought so. Name's Cornish." He squinted at Emmett. "This thing with Maltby. Guild matter, huh?"

"Yes, it is."

Emmett sensed rather than saw Lydia's surprise and disapproval, but he paid no attention. He hadn't lied to the old man. As far as he was concerned, as long as Lydia was involved in this mess, it *was* a Guild matter. After all, she was sleeping with him and he was running the Cadence Guild. It was a simple enough equation.

"Maltby was murdered, wasn't he?" Cornish grunted, as if something he had been thinking all along had just been independently confirmed. "Knew he didn't accidentally OD. He didn't always resonate on what you'd call well-tuned amber but he was no fool when it came to his Chartreuse. He knew how to handle the stuff. Been using for years, y'know."

Lydia moved forward. "We're trying to find out what, exactly, happened here today. Can you help us?"

"Me? Nah." Cornish shook his head very fast. "I didn't see nothin'. Just heard a lotta noise out in the hall late this morning. Next thing I know there's you and the new Guild chief and a bunch of cops and medics cluttering up the place. Then I seen 'em carry out poor old Maltby."

"There were two people inside Maltby's apartment when we arrived tonight." Emmett reached for his wallet and deliberately took out a couple of bills. "Did you happen to see them enter?"

Cornish examined the cash with great longing. "Well, now —"

"Like I said, this is a Guild matter," Emmett

said evenly. "I'm only in the market for the right answers."

Cornish hesitated, obviously pondering the risks of lying to the new boss of the Cadence Guild. Then he sighed heavily and shook his head with deep regret.

"Didn't see anyone go in the front door," he said. "Must've used the alley window. Heard 'em tearing the place up but never got a look at 'em."

"Thanks." Emmett handed the cash through the crack in the door. "The Guild appreciates your honesty, Mr. Cornish."

Cornish brightened at the realization that he was going to be paid, even though he hadn't been able to supply any useful information.

"Thank you, Mr. London, sir. Much obliged. Sorry I couldn't help you out a bit more. Glad you're takin' an interest in what happened to poor old Maltby. Me and him was neighbors for a lotta years. Gonna miss him, even if he was half barmy."

Cornish made to close his door.

"Wait, please," Lydia said urgently. "I have one more question. Did Professor Maltby have any visitors recently? Say, in the past two or three days?"

"Not that I seen." Cornish paused, pondering. "Didn't hear anyone knock on his door yesterday or the day before for that matter. But —"

"Yes?" Lydia prompted.

"Maltby went out the night before he took a little too much Chartreuse or whatever it was that really happened." Cornish shifted slightly, one shoulder bunching in a shrug. "There was nothing unusual about that, though. Long as I knew him he went out two, sometimes three times a week, always at night."

"To buy his drugs?" Lydia asked.

"Nah. Gone too long for that. Besides, he got his Chartreuse from the same guy who sells me —" Cornish stopped in midsentence, belatedly aware that he was about to implicate himself. "Uh, what I mean is, everyone around here knows that a Chartreuse buy don't take more than about sixty seconds. Dealers don't like to stand around chatting with the customers."

"How long did Maltby stay out at night?" Lydia asked.

"Hours," Cornish said. "Sometimes he didn't get back until damn near dawn."

Emmett removed some more cash from his wallet. "Any idea where Maltby went at night?"

"Sure. He had himself a secret hole-in-the-wall. Went down into the catacombs all by himself to hunt for relics. Didn't even take a hunter to watch out for ghosts. He was a tangler, a real good one. Worked on plenty of legal excavation teams back when he was a professor at some college. He knew how to find the good pieces and he knew the galleries on Ruin Row that would buy 'em without askin' too many questions."

"Maltby dealt in illegal antiquities?" Emmett asked.

Cornish shrugged again. "That was how he paid for his Chartreuse."

7

Lydia walked into her small living room and set the milk carton down very carefully on the low table.

"Poor Maltby." She kicked off her shoes. "He was no doubt hoping to make a spectacular antiquities find down in the catacombs and use it to try to regain his professional reputation. I know just how he must have felt."

Fuzz bounced onto the table and leaned forward to sniff cautiously at the milk carton. He backed away immediately, growling.

Emmett slung his leather jacket over the back of an armchair. "It would have been incredibly dangerous for Maltby to work alone underground all those years."

"The risks have never stopped the ruin rats from going into the catacombs, you know that. Besides, Maltby was an excellent trap tangler and a fine P-A in his day."

"Traps aren't the only hazards down below." Emmett stood behind the sofa, strong hands lightly braced on the back. He studied the innocent-looking milk carton. "Wonder how he avoided getting fried by a stray ghost all these years."

"Everyone knows you can outrun a ghost if necessary," she reminded him.

"Only if you see it coming in time and only if it doesn't corner you." He showed her a few teeth in a dangerous smile. "Come on, admit it, you fancy, elite academic types need us low-class hunters when you go underground and you know it."

She made a face. Tanglers, in general, preferred to play down the dangers of the highly unpredictable energy ghosts primarily because of the long-standing rivalry with ghost-hunters. The relationship between the two types of para-resonators often reverted to a brains-versus-brawn thing.

Tanglers considered themselves the scholarly, intellectual side of the research teams. They were usually well-educated, multi-degreed, professional para-archaeologists who took pride in their academic status. Hunters, on the other hand, traditionally had no more than Guild training in the techniques of handling ghosts and other safety issues in the catacombs. In short, they were merely bodyguards as far as tanglers were concerned.

But the truth was that the ghosts, technically known as unstable dissonance energy manifestations or UDEMs, were a serious problem because they appeared at random and with very little warning. It only took the slightest of brushes against the green energy fields to knock you unconscious and land you in an emergency room. A more extensive encounter could kill. Only a person with a natural talent for resonating with the chaotic psi energy that formed ghosts could summon or destroy a UDEM.

"Okay, okay." She sank back into the sofa cushions and flung her arms out to the sides along the top. "I'll agree that ghost-hunters have their uses underground."

He leaned slightly over the back of the sofa. She felt his fingers on the nape of her neck. A shiver of awareness went through her.

"I got the impression somewhere along the line that you find me useful occasionally aboveground as well," he said softly.

She hid a smile. "I've been testing the old saying about hunters being very good in bed. You make an excellent research subject."

"Yeah?" He traced a design on her nape. "Come to any conclusions?"

"I'm still doing the research." The hair was stirring pleasantly on the back of her neck now. "I expect it will take me a while. I plan to do a lot of extensive tests."

He removed his fingers from her skin, walked deliberately around the sofa, and stopped on the opposite side of the low table. He regarded her with a disturbing intensity.

"So long as I'm your only test subject, I don't mind a lot of extensive research," he said. "But if that's not going to be the case, I need to know now."

Something hard and grim had slipped into his

voice. She knew him well enough to know that he rarely used that tone, at least not with her. She swallowed uneasily.

"Emmett?"

"Sorry," he said, not sounding sorry at all, just cool and determined. "This probably isn't the right time for this conversation but given the circumstances, we're going to have to have it soon so we might as well get it over with tonight."

She stilled. "Are you talking about a trip to the dentist or our relationship?"

His smile was brief and humorless but at least his hard mouth curved slightly. "Our relationship."

"I see."

It was a subject they had both managed to avoid discussing openly. After all, they were only a few weeks into this affair, she reminded herself. They were still exploring new ground here. There had been no need to rush into decisions or commitments. There were issues. No one had said anything about love. They needed time.

Blah, blah, blah.

But there had also been a couple of underlying assumptions in their current arrangement, at least as far as she was concerned. One of them was that as long as they were seeing each other, neither of them would sleep with anyone else.

Maybe they should have talked about that assumption earlier, she thought.

"The problem is," Emmett continued in that same too-even tone, "because of this situation with Wyatt and the Guild, I'm going to be busy for a while. I won't have time to play the game the way you've got every right to expect me to play it."

Her mouth went dry. "I don't consider our relationship a *game,* for heaven's sake."

"Bad choice of words. Look, I don't consider it a game, either. But that doesn't mean that there aren't some expectations and conventions that apply to our present arrangement."

She felt the first flicker of temper. "Expectations?"

He moved one hand in a negligent, open-handed gesture. "Flowers, dinners out, theater tickets, long walks by the river. You know, all the stuff that goes with being involved in an affair."

"Sure. Right. Expectations." It only went to show how little she knew about having affairs, she mused. She hadn't even thought about their relationship in terms of expectations. Maybe she had been afraid to look at it in such specific terms because some part of her had been afraid that it wasn't going to last very long.

"What I'm trying to get at here," Emmett said, "is that I won't be able to spend a lot of time with you until Wyatt takes back his old job. I'm going to be tied up in meetings during the day and I'll be working late most evenings."

She sat up on the edge of the sofa, knees pressed tightly together. "For goodness sake,

Emmett, I don't expect you to entertain me constantly."

"I know that." He shoved a hand through his hair. "I'm not talking about entertainment, damn it. I'm talking about making sure that you and I have the same understanding of our current arrangement."

"Arrangement," she repeated neutrally. Something told her that she was going to learn to hate that word.

He gave her a brooding look. "I'm not handling this very well, am I?"

"You do seem to be floundering. Why don't you try being a little more direct? You're usually pretty good with direct."

"All right, I want to be sure we both agree that what we've got going between us is an exclusive —"

"Arrangement?" she finished icily.

"Yes."

"Hey, no problem, London." She gave him her brightest, most polished smile. "As it happens, I'm pretty busy myself these days. I've got my new private client and I'm still working full time for Shrimpton. And then there's this business of trying to figure out why Professor Maltby sent for me the day he died. Yep, I think it's safe to say that I won't have a lot of spare time available to hop into bed with other men."

He rounded the table in two long strides, clamped his hands over her shoulders, and hauled her to her feet.

"If you give a single, solitary damn about me," he muttered, "you won't joke about sleeping with other men."

Stunned by his fierce reaction she splayed her fingers across his broad chest and searched his face. A sense of wonder unfurled within her.

"Are you telling me that you would be jealous if you found out that I was seeing someone else?" she asked cautiously.

"I won't share you with another man," he said in a low, rough voice. "I can't. I'm pretty sure it would make me crazy."

She touched his face with her fingertips. "Oh, Emmett."

"While we're involved in this arrangement," he said evenly, "it has to be all or nothing."

She stood on tiptoe and kissed him lightly on the mouth. "Same goes for me, London. All or nothing."

The battle-ready tension eased out of his shoulders. He smiled slowly and raised his hands to cup her face. "No problem. You're the only woman I want in my bed. Sounds like we've got a mutual understanding here."

He pulled her close and kissed her before she could get too depressed about semantics. When his mouth closed over hers she felt the hot, urgent need that flowed through him, a need that was harnessed by the self-mastery and control that was so much a part of his nature.

A low rumble made Emmett raise his head. They both turned to look at Fuzz, who was still on the table, circling the milk carton, tatty fur alternately bristling and going flat.

Emmett released her reluctantly. "You'd better do your thing with that trap before your dust-bunny accidentally triggers it." He glanced at his amber watch. "If you hurry, we can still get a couple more hours of sleep tonight."

So much for that passionate interlude. She was jolted by the swift, efficient manner in which Emmett had just changed the subject. Apparently having achieved his objective — assuring himself that she would be true to him while he worked long hours at his new job — he was ready to move on to the next item on the agenda.

It occurred to her that the ability to switch his focus so quickly was probably one of the character traits that had helped him rise to the top echelons of Guild leadership. The skill no doubt made him a terrific CEO but she had a feeling it would prove disconcerting in a relationship.

Make that an *arrangement*.

But he did have a point, she thought. Time to find out what Maltby had concealed in the milk carton.

"I doubt if Fuzz could spring the trap," she said, turning toward the table. "Back in the early days of underground exploration there were some attempts made to use animals to identify and trigger the illusion snares, but they failed. The psychic vibes of the traps seem to resonate only with humans. Some experts think that's because the aliens set them to resonate with minds that had evolved to the point that they were vulnerable to the downside of creativity and imagination."

"In other words, minds that could be overwhelmed by nightmares, but you don't need him tipping over the carton while you're working on the trap." Emmett picked up Fuzz. "I'll keep him out of your way."

"Thanks." She opened the milk carton again and studied the dark shadows inside. "You know, we're very lucky those intruders we surprised didn't think to check Maltby's refrigerator."

"My guess is they did check it but never thought twice about the milk carton."

"Mmm." She peered into the carton, studying the shadows within. The amber she wore on her wrist warmed slightly as she used it to tune into the psychic frequencies of the little trap.

It was small, but the resonating patterns were extremely complex.

"Maltby was a real pro," she murmured. "This is not a simple trap. He probably found it somewhere down in the catacombs and managed to de-rez it without destroying it. Then he reset it inside this carton. Couldn't have been easy."

"Can you see what he used to anchor it?"

"Not yet."

An illusion trap had to be anchored to some material of alien construction, usually an object fashioned of green quartz or the far more rare dreamstone.

She probed with the sure, firm touch required. A tentative approach was often disastrous because the effort resulted in a disturbance of the trap's pattern that could trigger it.

Picking up the rhythm of the underlying currents she sent out a few psychic pulses designed to dampen the waves of psi energy.

This was the most dangerous part of the operation. One misstep at this juncture and the energy pulses would rebound, overwhelming her and locking her into an alien nightmare that would last until she went unconscious. It might take her brain only a few seconds to shut down but it would feel like an eternity.

The uncoiling energy waves would also catch anyone else who happened to be standing too close when the illusion snare snapped. The fact that Emmett had not bothered to retreat several discreet steps said a great deal about his respect for her skills as a tangler.

She felt the energy of the trap gradually subside and then cease altogether. She held the frequency for a moment longer until she was certain that the trap had been destroyed permanently and could not be reset.

"Got it," she said, struggling to suppress the little flash of euphoria that always followed a successful untangling. It was considered uncool, not to mention extremely unprofessional, to let anyone see you getting off on the small rush.

"You're good," Emmett said softly.

"Thanks." The praise made her smile. Hunters were notoriously churlish when it came to giving credit to tanglers. "Coming from a Guild boss, that is praise, indeed."

"Credit where it's due, I always say." He leaned closer, trying to get a view of the interior of the carton. "What's inside?"

She looked down and saw a tiny green quartz tomb mirror and what appeared to be a piece of paper that had been folded into a square. "I'm not sure."

Picking up the carton, she upended it. The mirror clunked when it hit the table. The folded paper landed on top of it.

"He used a mirror for the anchor," Emmett said.

"Uh-huh." She picked up the paper and unfolded it with care.

"It's a copy of an old newspaper article," she said.

She spread it out on the table. Together she and Emmett studied the piece.

Local Student Disappears Underground; Feared Dead

Troy Burgis, a student at Old Frequency College, vanished into an unexplored underground passageway sometime late yesterday. A search team was sent down but reported no trace of Burgis. He is presumed lost.

College authorities said that Burgis and two companions had gone into the catacombs beneath Old Frequency without official permission. Evidently the unauthorized venture was instigated by Burgis.

Jason Clark and Norman Fairbanks, the two students who accompanied Burgis on the illegal expedition, said that they became separated when Burgis insisted on trying to untangle a large illusion trap that blocked access to one of the corridors.

Burgis failed and in the process accidentally triggered the trap. Clark and Fairbanks said that they were standing as far away as possible but when the illusion energy rebounded on Burgis, they felt some of the effects. They were unconscious for almost an hour. When they awakened, Burgis was gone.

College officials reported that Burgis's parents died when he was very young. He had no siblings. The authorities are still searching for next of kin.

"The date of the article is nearly fifteen years old," Lydia said. "Why on earth would Maltby have gone to all the trouble of copying it and protecting it with an illusion trap?"

"Beats me." Emmett picked up the small tomb mirror and studied it closely. "Maybe this was what he wanted to hide. Looks pretty ordinary, though."

She glanced at the quartz mirror, assessed the

simple carving that surrounded the reflective surface, and shook her head. "There's nothing special about it. I'm sure he only used it to secure the trap." She tapped the paper. "It was this article he wanted to conceal. But I can't imagine why."

"Lydia, I think you should keep in mind one very important fact about Professor Lawrence Maltby."

She raised her head, frowning. "What's that?"

"He was a Chartreuse addict," Emmett said. "That means that his brain probably got badly de-rezzed a long time ago. If I were you, I wouldn't try to make too much out of this newspaper article or the fact that he left you a message in the first place. He no doubt heard you were asking questions around the Old Quarter and it sparked a couple of delusions."

"I'm not the only one who took him seriously. What about those two guys we surprised in his apartment?"

"I told you, they were most likely looking for his stash, not an old newspaper story about a student who went missing underground."

She tapped the copy of the newspaper clipping lightly against her palm. "Hmm."

"I really hate when you do that," Emmett said.

8

The offices of Hepscott Enterprises, Inc., radiated class and financial success. The furnishings and décor were in various shades of gray punctuated with occasional hits of black and crimson. The reception lobby alone was twice as large as her apartment, Lydia thought.

On the way to the front desk she passed a number of glass cases that contained models of several Hepscott projects. Among them was a gated community of expensive homes and a new banking and financial tower that were going up downtown.

A neatly folded copy of the *Cadence Star* was on the low table in front of a long black leather sofa. She glanced at it and saw the large headlines, *Wyatt Critically Wounded. Guild Officials Appoint Acting Head.*

She had read the story that morning at breakfast, sitting across from Emmett. There was nothing in it that he had not already told her. The reporter had stuck to the facts and not descended into gossip. There was no mention of Emmett having once been engaged to Tamara Wyatt. The *Star* left that sort of thing to the tabloids.

Lydia was very glad that she had splurged on the new suit and a pair of heels that matched the conservative rusty brown color of the outfit. The ensemble had cost her a month's income but it was worth it. She looked almost as serious and businesslike as the receptionist.

"May I help you?" the woman behind the desk asked politely.

"I'm here to see Mr. Hepscott."

The receptionist looked doubtful. "Your name?"

"Lydia Smith." Lydia gave her the special smile she had developed for handling the secretaries who guarded the offices of senior faculty members at the university. "I have an appointment."

The woman's brow cleared instantly. "Yes, of course, Miss Smith." She leaned toward the intercom and pressed a button. "Miss Smith is here, sir."

"Send her in please, Elizabeth." Gannon Hepscott's voice was well modulated and infused with self-confidence. It went well with the décor of his reception lobby.

"Yes, sir." Elizabeth got to her feet. "This way, Miss Smith."

Lydia followed her to a tall door paneled in red amber-oak.

The interior of Hepscott's private office was even larger than the lobby. It was done in the same colors. The view out the wall of windows was nothing short of spectacular. It encompassed a long, meandering swath of the river and most of the Dead City of Old Cadence.

In spite of her determination to project oodles of cool, professional competence, Lydia caught her breath at the glorious scene outside the windows. Last night's fog had burned off early this morning and the green quartz towers of the alien city sparkled and shimmered in the sunlight.

She had always wondered if the ancient Harmonic architects had been trained in art and poetry in addition to structural mechanics and design. The buildings they had left behind aboveground had an airy, ethereal quality that never failed to fascinate her. The soaring spires, arched roofs, colonnaded balconies, and sweeping walkways dazzled the eye and summoned forth a deep sense of wonder.

"I know just how you feel," Gannon Hepscott said from somewhere behind her. He sounded amused. "Every morning when I walk into this office I go straight to the windows and spend a few minutes looking at the ruins. And every day I ask myself the same question."

She smiled in understanding. "Why did they leave?"

"We'll probably never know the answer."

"No, but I doubt that we'll ever stop asking the question." She turned around and smiled at the man standing next to the large, semicircular desk. "Keeps things interesting, doesn't it?"

Gannon Hepscott chuckled. "Yes, it does."

This was the first time she had met him in person. Until now she had dealt only with members of his staff.

Hepscott appeared to be in his mid-thirties. He was tall, with long-fingered hands and a slender, graceful build that did wonders for the beautifully tailored suit he wore. His features were sharp, almost ascetic.

She had been warned, albeit respectfully, that Hepscott affected a rather eccentric style. Now she comprehended why he had acquired that reputation. He was a study in pales.

His eyes were a very light shade of gray. He had striking platinum hair that she knew could not possibly be natural. Even more arresting was the fact that he wore it shoulder-length and tied back at his nape. It was a look favored by a lot of macho, khaki-and-leather-wearing ghost-hunters but not by CEOs and presidents of corporations. Yet Hepscott managed to pull it off brilliantly. On him the style was at once very masculine and very elegant.

His suit and shirt were white on white. His accessories were silver.

"Please, have a seat, Miss Smith. Thank you for making the time available this morning."

"My pleasure." She took one of the pair of black leather chairs he indicated and set her portfolio case on the plush gray carpet. "I'm looking forward to hearing more about your plans."

"As my architect and designers no doubt told

you, I intend to call the project the Underground Experience." He picked up a sheaf of papers and lowered himself onto the black sofa directly across from her. "My goal is to create the most exciting casino resort to be found in any of the city-states. I plan to locate it near the South Wall." He paused, mouth tilting slightly at one corner. "For the atmosphere."

"I see."

"It's taken me five years to acquire the adjoining properties required for the resort but I've finally put together a parcel large enough to suit my purposes."

"Your staff said that you wanted to create a theme based on the underground ruins."

"Yes." He spread some drawings out on the table. "What I want is a dazzling, fantasy version of a trip through the catacombs. From the moment a guest walks into the lobby of my resort, I want him to be surrounded by genuine relics and artifacts, not reproductions."

"That's where I come in, I take it?"

Gannon smiled and sat back against the sofa. "Yes, Miss Smith, that is precisely where you come in. I want the settings to be as authentic as possible. You'll have a generous budget. I want you to use it to acquire only museum-quality antiquities. Attend the auctions. Contact your connections on Ruin Row. Get the word out to the private collectors. Do whatever it takes. I want only the best pieces. My design team will incorporate them into the décor."

"It sounds like a very exciting project," she said.

"I'm not one to micromanage." Gannon rose to his feet. "I hire qualified people and I let them do their job. However, this project is very important to me and I will expect to be kept informed. I'd like weekly status reports in person. Will that work with your schedule?"

She realized that he was terminating the meeting already. "No problem, Mr. Hepscott."

"Please. Call me Gannon." He studied her with a warm, considering expression. "Something tells me that you and I are going to make a great team, Lydia."

Forty minutes later she leaped out of the cab in front of Shrimpton's House of Ancient Horrors, paid the driver, and rushed through the entrance. The meeting with Gannon Hepscott had gone smoothly and swiftly enough, but the cab had encountered a rush-hour traffic jam on the way back downtown and as a result she was twenty minutes late for work. She hoped that her boss was not yet aware of that fact.

The elderly man behind the ticket booth waved to her. "Morning, Lydia."

"Morning, Bob. Is Shrimp here yet?"

"Nope, you're in the clear."

"Great. Thanks." Relieved, she slowed down to catch her breath.

Thirty years ago, Shrimpton's had started out as a third-rate museum featuring low-end alien relics. The establishment had gone rapidly downhill from that point. By the time Lydia had put in an application for a position on the staff seven months ago, it was considered more of a carnival fun house than a legitimate museum. No respectable antiquities expert took it seriously. Certainly no one with her credentials would have even considered working in the place under normal circumstances.

But she had not had a lot of career options after the university had let her go. Her professional reputation had been in shreds.

Shrimpton had given her a job when she had needed one desperately and she would be forever indebted to him. Although she was trying to build a new career as a private antiquities consultant she had vowed to give her employer his money's worth. She would work through lunch to make up the twenty minutes, she promised herself.

She walked quickly along a long exhibit hall that was dramatically shadowed and lit with glowing green fluo-rez lamps designed to provide the eerie, creepy atmosphere that was the hallmark of Shrimpton's.

In spite of its low reputation, the museum had acquired, under her direction, some rather nice relics including several wonderful carved urns and a matching pair of green quartz columns.

Her greatest acquisition, however, one that had forced the more upscale antiquities community to sit up and take notice, was a little vessel of pure, worked dreamstone. It occupied a place of honor at the end of the main gallery and was protected by a state-of-the art security system that had been donated by Mercer and Tamara Wyatt. The placard next to the beautiful little object read, *Unguent Jar. Dreamstone. A gift of Mr. Chester Brady.*

Unfortunately, the gift had been posthumous because Chester, a shady ruin rat who had made a career working the illegal side of the antiquities trade, had run afoul of an illicit excavation operation. He had been murdered, his body dumped into a sarcophagus here at Shrimpton's.

Lydia had been escorting Emmett on a tour of the Tomb Wing when they had discovered the body. She knew that she would never again be able to walk past the display of not-quite-human shaped coffins without thinking of Chester.

She opened a door and walked into the small suite of museum offices. There was no light showing through the opaque glass panel of Shrimpton's door. Bob had been right, the boss had not yet arrived. Shrimpton had probably stopped for a box of doughnuts.

The door to the office of Shrimpton's secretary and all-around general assistant, Melanie Toft, stood wide. Lydia put her head around the corner.

"Morning, Mel."

Melanie looked up from the tabloid she was perusing. She was an attractive, dark-haired woman with lively eyes and what could only be called a very fashion-forward sense of style. Lydia sometimes wondered if she shopped for all her clothes in the lingerie departments of the stores. Melanie had an extensive collection of sheer blouses, very short skirts, and daring little dresses that resembled nightgowns and slips.

"About time you got here," Melanie said. "How was the meeting with Hepscott?"

"Fine. He gave me a budget that is several times what I get to spend here in a year. I can't wait to start buying."

She went into her office and set her portfolio case against the shelves holding her extensive collection of the *Journal of Para-archaeology*.

She was stuffing her purse into the bottom drawer of her desk when Melanie appeared in the doorway, rattling the copy of the tabloid.

"Have you seen the papers?"

"Hard to miss the headlines. The news that someone tried to murder Mercer Wyatt is above the fold of every newspaper in town. I also caught the report about it on *Good Morning, Cadence* on the rez-screen before I left my apartment."

"How can you sound so calm and casual?" Melanie sashayed into the office and propped one well-rounded hip on the corner of the desk. "For goodness sake, woman, you're dating the new boss of the Cadence Guild."

"*Acting* boss."

Melanie winked. "The job could become permanent if Wyatt doesn't make it."

"Got a hunch Wyatt will survive. He's a tough old specter-cat."

Melanie held up the tabloid. "You never told me all the juicy details about Emmett London's connections to the Wyatts. How could you keep that kind of gossip from your very best friend? I'm crushed, *crushed* I tell you."

Lydia glanced at the cover of the *Cadence Tattler* and froze. A large, grainy photo of Tamara Wyatt and Emmett going into the main entrance of Cadence Memorial Hospital together filled most of the available space.

The headlines screamed *New Guild Boss Involved in Lovers' Triangle?* The type had to be at least an inch high.

"Let me see that." Lydia snatched the tabloid out of Melanie's hand.

"Be my guest," Melanie replied.

Lydia raced through the article, her stomach growing colder by the second.

Emmett London, newly appointed chief of the Cadence Guild, was formerly engaged to wed Tamara Mcintyre (now Mrs. Mercer Wyatt) in a Covenant Marriage in Resonance City. According to sources who spoke on condition of anonymity, the wedding was called off abruptly after the bride-to-be was introduced to the boss of the Cadence Guild, Mercer Wyatt, at the engagement ball.

In a magazine interview last month, Mrs. Wyatt maintained that she had been "swept off her feet" by the dynamic Wyatt and that the two intended to convert their current Marriage of Convenience into a full Covenant Marriage in the near future.

A spokesperson for the Resonance Guild assured this reporter that the engagement between London and Tamara Wyatt had ended amicably. But other sources, speaking off the record, hinted that London was furious about the breakup and vowed revenge.

"Revenge?" Lydia reread the last line of the story, appalled. "This idiot reporter is implying that Emmett wanted revenge because Mercer Wyatt stole his fiancée."

"Yes, indeed."

"Oh, jeez." Lydia sat down hard on her desk chair. "This is terrible."

"You'll notice that the article stops short of actually suggesting that London may have been the one who shot Wyatt," Melanie said dryly. "But the implication is a little hard to miss."

"It's impossible to miss." The chill in Lydia's stomach turned into an even more unpleasant sensation of hollowness. "This could turn into a disaster."

"Forget that. Let's get to the interesting stuff. Any of it true? Was the lovely Mrs. Tamara Wyatt London's fiancée at one time?"

Lydia cleared her throat. "Well, yes."

Melanie's eyes rounded. "Oh, my."

"But the engagement didn't end because Tamara got swept off her feet by Mercer Wyatt." Lydia thumped the cover of the tabloid in disgust. "Good grief, he's forty years older than she is."

"Still in great shape though, I hear," Melanie said cheerfully. "At least he was until yesterday. Why did the engagement end?"

"Emmett informed her just before the engagement party that he had accomplished his objectives for the reorganization of the Resonance Guild and planned to step down. He wanted to go into private consulting. That did not suit Tamara. She had other goals."

"Wanted to be Mrs. Guild Boss, huh?"

"She sure did. As it happened good old Mercer Wyatt had recently been widowed and was apparently in the market for a new bride." Lydia turned one hand, palm up. "Tamara ended the engagement."

Melanie drew up one bare knee and clasped her hands around it. The motion hiked her lacy skirt dangerously high on her thighs. "How did Emmett feel about being dumped?"

"He had a very narrow escape and he knows it."

"It says in the paper that they were planning a Covenant Marriage. It would have been a legal and financial nightmare to get out of it once the vows had been spoken." Melanie shook her head. "Wonder why they didn't go for a standard Marriage of Convenience, first?"

Lydia cranked back in the squeaky desk chair and swiveled slightly from side to side. "Emmett is a long-term planner, one of those types who sets goals and then does whatever it takes to accomplish them. He probably applied that management approach when he set out to marry Tamara."

"Well, you've got to admit, she does seem to be the perfect Guild boss wife. She's not only beautiful, she's stylish and smart. Heck, she's an executive in her own right. Look how active she's been on the boards of all those charities and social clubs this past year. She's done more to promote a more modern, mainstream image for the Cadence Guild in the past year than anyone else has done since Jerrett Knox defeated Vincent Lee Vance."

"I know." Lydia drummed her fingers on the top of her desk. She did not need to be reminded of the long list of Tamara Wyatt's personal assets and accomplishments. "I've met her. She's impressive but she would have been the wrong woman for Emmett. I'm pretty sure he knows that now."

"Of course he does," Melanie said loyally. "It's obvious that you are the right woman for him."

They both thought about that for a while.

Melanie cleared her throat. "So, where was Emmett London in the early morning hours when Mercer Wyatt was getting shot in the back?"

"The leader of Zane Hoyt's Hunter-Scout troop asked him to help supervise the boys on a camping trip. They got back around two in the morning. By the time Emmett dropped the kids off at their various homes and got to his place it was three. Wyatt had just arrived in the emergency room."

"The paper says that Wyatt was shot sometime between two and three," Melanie pointed out.

"Uh-huh."

"Sounds like Emmett might have a little trouble accounting for the time between dropping off the last Hunter-Scout and answering the phone call from the hospital."

Lydia leveled a finger at her. "Don't even think of going there, Mel. At the most, we're talking twenty minutes."

Melanie pursed her lips but refrained from pointing out that twenty minutes was long enough to murder someone.

Lydia sighed. "Luckily, Detective Martinez seemed satisfied that Emmett was not a suspect. After all, it was Wyatt himself who appointed Emmett to take over on an interim basis. He wouldn't have done that if he thought that Emmett had tried to murder him."

Melanie rocked back and forth on the desk a couple of times. "But Wyatt was shot in the back, according to the papers, and never saw the person who tried to kill him. Plus, I'll bet that Martinez didn't know about this lovers' triangle thing when she questioned you and Emmett. Her view of the situation may change when she finds out those three had a tangled past."

Lydia slumped deeper into her chair.

"On the other hand," Melanie continued on a brighter note, "this is a Guild matter and everyone knows that the Guild polices its own." She hopped off the desk. "Well, gotta run. Things to do. By the way I meant to tell you that Shrimp is feeling very pleased with himself."

"Why is that?"

"He got an offer from a private collector for the Mudd Sarcophagus. The guy apparently saw it in the Tomb Wing last week and wants it badly because it fills out his collection. He's willing to pay a lot more than it's worth. Shrimp is thrilled, as you can imagine. He says you can use the profits to get a more interesting coffin." She rolled her eyes. "What a concept, huh? An *interesting* coffin."

"Thanks for the heads-up."

"The client is making arrangements to pick it up Friday at five. Shrimp wants you to supervise the crating and packing and see that it gets safely out the door with all the paperwork in order."

"I'll make a note." Lydia pulled her desk calendar toward her and flipped the pages to Friday's date.

"Also, just so you'll know, I'm going to slip

out of here a little early today. Got a date with Jack tonight."

Jack Brodie, Lydia knew, was another in a long line of ghost-hunter dates for Melanie.

"Don't tell me, let me guess," Lydia said. "The two of you are going to spend the evening somewhere in the Old Quarter."

Melanie wiggled her brows. "Jack promised me that he'll summon a little ghost or two to burn before we go back to my place."

"Have fun," Lydia mumbled.

"Oh, I'm sure I will. You know what they say, there's nothing like a hunter in bed after he's burned a ghost. We're talking hot, hot, hot." Melanie grinned from the doorway. "But you already know that, don't you? After all, you're dating the top hunter, himself."

"Emmett is stuck in an office for the foreseeable future." Lydia knew she sounded unbearably prim. She couldn't help it. Melanie's easy way with sexual innuendos and her casual lust for hunters was always a bit disconcerting. She could feel herself turning a vivid shade of pink. "He hasn't got time to zap ghosts for fun and games."

"Too bad." Melanie disappeared around the corner.

Lydia sat for a long time, staring morosely at the front page photo of the *Tattler*. The gossip about a scandalous lovers' triangle at the top of the Cadence Guild was only going to get worse. The story was simply too juicy to fade away.

If anyone could take care of himself, it was Emmett, she thought. But he had his hands full at the moment.

Something told her that the next few days and weeks were going to be very difficult for all of them.

9

Emmett opened the file that Perkins, Wyatt's administrative assistant, had just handed him. "This is the list of people who phoned Wyatt the day before he was shot?"

"This is the list I gave to Detective Martinez, when she interviewed me," Perkins said with clipped precision. "It includes all of the business calls, both incoming and outgoing, that were made from this office on that date."

Emmett looked up. Perkins probably had a first name but no one in Wyatt's headquarters had used it in so long that it had been forgotten. Perkins evidently preferred it that way.

He was a small, dapper man who looked more like a butler than a professional secretary. A circle of close-cropped gray hair surrounded his gleaming bald pate. He peered at Emmett through gold-framed spectacles.

"Can I assume from the way you responded to my question that there were some calls of a personal nature that were not included on this list?" Emmett asked evenly.

Perkins cleared his throat. "There was one that I saw no reason to add."

Emmett raised his brows. "You made that decision on your own?"

Perkins drew himself up to his full height. "I have worked for Mr. Wyatt for twenty-three years. I think I know him well enough to say that he would not have wanted me to give the caller's name to the police."

"Because?"

"Because the call was from an old friend of his who was, I'm sure, in no way connected to the dreadful events."

Emmett rubbed the bridge of his nose. "I'll need the name, Perkins."

"Yes, sir, I understand, sir. The caller's name was Sandra Thornton."

Emmett frowned. "She gave you her name when she phoned?"

"No, sir, but I recognized her voice immediately."

"She calls frequently?"

"She hasn't called at all in the past two years, but before that Miss Thornton and Mr. Wyatt had a close, extremely personal relationship for a period of several months. During that time, she called Mr. Wyatt's private number on several occasions."

One of Wyatt's former mistresses, Emmett thought. Great. Talk about complications. He closed the file and stacked his hands on top of it. "Let me get this straight, Perkins. One of Mercer Wyatt's old lovers who hasn't been in touch in two years just happens to call the day before Wyatt gets shot and you didn't think that was worth mentioning to the cops?"

Perkins looked down his nose at Emmett. "I beg your pardon, sir, but this is Guild business of the most personal nature."

Emmett tried not to grind his back teeth. He reminded himself that this was the Cadence Guild, not the new, reformed Resonance Guild. In spite of Wyatt's avowed intentions to modernize the organization, they still did a lot of things the old-fashioned way in this town. And by long-standing tradition, Guild affairs were guided by one unshakable precept: *Guild business stays within the Guild.*

"What's the story on Sandra Thornton?" Emmett asked, reigning in irritation. "Think she's still got feelings for Wyatt? Was she angry when he broke off the relationship?"

Perkins blinked a couple of times in obvious surprise. "My understanding is that Miss Thornton was the one who ended the affair, sir, not Mr. Wyatt."

"Did she call it off because Wyatt was seeing other women besides her?"

"I have no idea why she ended the arrangement, sir." Perkins cleared his throat. "Mr. Wyatt did not confide that information."

He wished Perkins hadn't used the word *arrangement.*

"Did Wyatt say anything after Thornton called? How did he react? Was he annoyed?"

"Perhaps a bit preoccupied, sir, but that was all." Perkins hesitated. "He did ask me not to mention the call to Mrs. Wyatt, however."

"Why not?"

"Mr. Wyatt cares deeply for Mrs. Wyatt. I believe he was afraid that she would be hurt or upset if she knew that an old flame had contacted him."

Tamara would not have been pleased, that was certain. Emmett considered his options. He would turn the information over to Detective Martinez, but given the extensive resources and manpower available to him through the Guild, he could probably find Sandra Thornton a lot sooner than the cops.

Wyatt's last coherent words before he went unconscious rang in his ears: *It wasn't politics, it was personal.*

"Get hold of Verwood," Emmett said. "Tell him I want to see him immediately."

Lloyd Verwood was in charge of Guild security here in Cadence. The only thing Emmett knew about him was that Wyatt had appointed him to the position. That was enough. Verwood wouldn't have gotten the job if he wasn't good.

"Yes, sir," Perkins said. "Shall I —"

He stopped when the door opened without warning. Tamara Wyatt walked into the office. One look at her tense, drawn expression and Emmett knew that she was very tightly rezzed. The stress she was under was taking its toll.

"Perkins." She nodded at the little man. "Wondered where you were."

"Mrs. Wyatt." Perkins bobbed his head deferentially and then looked at Emmett for directions.

"That's all for now, Perkins," Emmett said. "Let me know when Verwood gets here."

"Yes, sir." Perkins left, closing the door discreetly behind him.

Tamara went straight to the window and stood looking out at the view of the Dead City and the mountains beyond. In spite of the strain she had been under since the call that had summoned her to the hospital, she was as sleek and polished as ever. Her dark hair was neatly coiled in an elegant chignon that focused attention on the excellent bones of her striking face. She wore her amber in her earrings.

Tamara was a ghost-hunter, a strong one, although she had never worked much underground. Her interests lay elsewhere. Tamara preferred the halls of Guild politics to the alien catacombs.

She was a beautiful woman, endowed with that subtle aura that people called glamour. The old meaning of the word implied sorcery and magic and looking back he figured he must have been under some kind of spell when he had proposed to her. Or maybe he just hadn't been paying much attention, he thought. Either way it was hard to explain why he hadn't noticed the single-minded, all-consuming thirst for power that guided Tamara's every move.

The tabloids had got it wrong this morning. His engagement to her hadn't ended because she had been swept off her feet by Mercer Wyatt. Tamara would never have allowed herself to be distracted from her objectives by anything so mundane and inconsequential as passion.

The truth was that Mercer and Tamara were in many ways a perfect match, he thought. In spite of the fact that Wyatt was nearly four decades older than her, they had a lot in common. They both had a talent for manipulating Guild politics and they were both obsessively loyal to the organization.

But last month Mercer had informed Emmett that he intended to retire so that he would have more time to enjoy life and his lovely new bride. Emmett was pretty sure that news must have come as a shock to Tamara.

"I assume you've seen the headlines in the tabloids this morning," Tamara said curtly.

"Hard to miss 'em."

"They couldn't get much worse. What if the media picks up those old rumors about you being Mercer's illegitimate son?"

"My birth certificate states that I am the son of John London. As far as I'm concerned that's the way it's going to stand."

"What a hideous mess." Tamara turned away from the window and began to pace the room. "Any news from the police?"

"No. I assume they are following their own leads." He leaned back in his chair. "I'm going to start a private investigation using Guild resources."

She nodded in a distracted manner. "I just came from the hospital. Mercer's two daughters are there now. They arrived a couple of hours ago." Her jaw tightened. "They are not particularly fond of me, you know. They tolerate me because they have no choice, but as far as they're concerned I married their father for mercenary reasons."

"Well, look at the bright side. They'll probably want to stay in a hotel while they're in town. You won't have to put them up at your house."

"That is not very funny, Emmett." She halted on the far side of the room. "There are a couple of problems that have to be dealt with immediately. First, you do realize that your temporary appointment has to be ratified by a majority of the Guild Council as soon as possible?"

"I've scheduled a meeting of the Council on Thursday. Can't do it any sooner than that because three of the members are out of town."

She frowned. "Confirming you as the acting head of the organization may not be a sure thing, even though everyone knows that Mercer handpicked you to take over in his absence."

"I think that, under the circumstances, there won't be any problem getting a majority."

"Maybe not, but there's always the possibility of a challenge from one of the members of the Council," she warned.

"I don't think that's very likely, do you?"

"I'd like to say that it won't be an issue. After

all, you've only been appointed on a *temporary* basis." Her eyes narrowed. "It's not like you're taking charge of the Guild permanently, is it?"

"No," he agreed mildly. "Wyatt can have this desk back as soon as he wants it. What's the problem, here, Tamara?"

"Foster Dorning may be the problem."

Emmett raised his brows. "What makes you think that?"

"He was elected to the Council a few months ago. He came up through the ranks very quickly. Mercer thinks Dorning greased the way with a lot of bribes and favors."

"Sounds like Guild politics as usual."

She looked at him from across the room. "I think he has his eye on this office. He may try to take advantage of the current situation."

"By issuing a formal challenge?"

"If Dorning won the challenge and claimed the position before Mercer gets out of the hospital it might be impossible to unseat him. You know how murky Guild law and tradition are when it comes to this kind of thing."

"Let me worry about Dorning."

"Emmett, I know you're a very strong pararez. I've seen you work. But the word is that Dorning is extremely powerful, too. What's more, I don't trust him. If it comes down to a formal challenge —"

"I said, I'll deal with Dorning. What was the other problem?"

Frustrated and angry, she opened her mouth

to argue. But whatever she saw in his eyes must have convinced her that it would be useless to pursue the issue. In the end she went with the forced change of topic.

"The Restoration Ball is the other problem," she said stiffly. "It will be held on Thursday night. Mercer and I had planned to attend."

"Don't worry," he said. "I think under the circumstances everyone will understand if you send your regrets."

"It's not that simple, damn it." She resumed her restless pacing. "You know how important the annual ball is in Resonance City. It's no different here. It's the social event of the year. Everyone who is anyone will be there. The Cadence Guild *must* be represented."

"You can't be serious about showing up at the ball, not with Wyatt in intensive care. If you think the scandal sheets were bad this morning, just imagine what the headlines would look like if you danced the night away while your beloved husband fights for his life."

"Of course I can't go." She gave him a repressive glare. "You will have to go, instead."

"Forget it." He sat forward and reached for a pen. "I've got more important things to do than put on a tux Thursday night."

She came to stand directly in front of the desk. "Listen to me, Emmett, you not only have to go, you've got to take a date."

The absolute conviction in her voice and face gave him pause. Tamara might be single-minded, even ruthless, but she did not do things without good reason.

"You're worried about the image of the Guild, I assume?" he asked quietly.

"Yes. Mercer and I have worked very hard in the past year to make the Guild part of the mainstream here in Cadence. You know how difficult it is to change the way the public views the organization. It took you six years to do it in Resonance."

"You don't have to remind me."

"I know the politics in this city, Emmett. Trust me on this. It is critical that the Guild is represented at the ball this year."

"I'll send someone from the Council."

"No." She flattened her hands on the desk. "That's not good enough, not now with all this ridiculous gossip about a lovers' triangle at the top of the Guild. We have to put a stop to that nonsense or at least try to contain it. The best way to do it is for you and your friend, Miss Smith, to show up at the ball looking like a besotted couple."

He meditated on that for a long moment. She had a point, he thought.

"All right," he said eventually.

Tamara subsided wearily. "Thank you." She took her hands off the desk and turned toward the door.

"Lydia and I will be there," Emmett said, "but I can't guarantee that Lydia will do the besotted thing."

"As long as everyone gets the idea that you're sleeping together, it should work. I'm going back to the hospital. The press is keeping a twenty-four-hour watch and it's vital that the reporters see that I'm sticking close to Mercer's bedside."

"Sure, good for the image," he said neutrally.

"Exactly."

She went out the door and closed it firmly behind her.

He bounced the end of the pen against the surface of the desk a couple of times. Then he reached for the phone and punched out Lydia's office number.

She answered on the first ring, sounding tense.

"Shrimpton's House of Ancient Horrors, curator's office."

"I need a date for the Restoration Ball," he said without preamble. "Tamara says we need to be there. A Guild image thing."

There was a short silence from Lydia's end of the line.

"Gosh whiz," she said finally. "I haven't got a thing to wear."

"Go shopping tomorrow. Get whatever you need and tell the shops to bill me. If they give you any trouble, have them call this office."

"Maybe I could rent a dress. I know there are shops that rent gowns for special occasions."

For some reason that irritated him. "You are not wearing a rented gown to the Restoration Ball."

"Why not?" she said persuasively. "It's the logical thing to do. It's going to cost a bundle to buy a designer dress and all the accessories. It's not like I would ever be able to wear the gown again in this lifetime."

"Forget it. Buy the damn dress and whatever you need to go with it."

"You sound upset. Are you upset?"

"I'm not upset," he said through his teeth. "But I am way too busy to waste time on this argument."

"Okay, okay, I take your point." Her tone was soothing now. "I guess it would be kind of tacky to show up in a rental gown."

"Yes, it would. Very tacky."

"I mean, everyone knows that the clothes are a big part of the whole Restoration Ball scene. It's always televised. Everyone will be watching at home. The media will film all of the guests as they walk into the Hall on that long red carpet and there will be pictures in the papers the next day. I can see where it might look bad if it leaked out that the new Guild boss's companion for the evening wore a cheap rental."

"I'm glad we're clear on that issue," he muttered.

"Maybe I can find something nice on sale."

He made a fist around the pen. "If it's on sale, it's because no one thought it was good enough to buy at full price, right?"

"That's one way to look at it. But I'm sure I can find something that will do."

"Damn it, Lydia —"

"I just don't want you to get stuck for the cost of a very expensive gown, that's all," she said quickly.

"I can afford it."

"I know, but it's the principle of the thing."

"The principle of the thing? What the hell is that supposed to mean? We're talking about a dress. I'd like to know just what kind of principle is involved here."

"It's not like you and I are married," she said very coolly. "As you pointed out, we're involved in an *arrangement*. I don't feel right about letting you buy me a lot of expensive things. Don't you understand? There's a name for women who accept costly gifts from men."

He went very still, aware that something inside him had just gone stone cold. An arrangement. Well, it wasn't like he was in any position to deny it. An arrangement was exactly what they had.

"If it makes you feel any better," he said, working hard to keep his voice even, "I'll put the dress down as a business expense and let the Guild reimburse me."

"Don't be ridiculous. You can't pass off a fancy ball gown as a legitimate business expense."

"Sure I can," he said grimly. "I'm the boss here, remember?"

There was a lengthy pause.

"You're angry," she said.

"Lydia, I'm out of time and out of patience. Get the damn dress. Look at it this way, you'll be doing me a favor." He rubbed his temples. "By the way, I'm going to have to call off our dinner date this evening. I'm sorry but I've got a hunch I'll here until at least eight or nine. I'll just go on back to my place."

"What will you do about dinner? Eat at your desk?"

He hadn't given the problem any thought. "Yeah, probably."

"I've got a better idea," she said firmly. "Come to my apartment when you're ready to pack it in for the day. Fuzz and I will hold dinner for you."

"You don't have to do that."

"We don't mind."

"Thanks," he said. The part of him that had gone cold thawed a bit.

When he hung up the phone a short time later he felt as if he'd had a couple of cups of strong rez-tea. The prospect of going home to Lydia tonight would fortify him for the long afternoon ahead.

10

At ten minutes after nine that evening, she heard him open the door with the key she had given him a couple of weeks earlier. Every time he walked into her apartment this way she got a fizzy sensation in her chest followed by a little tingle of panic. She had never given any other man the key to her apartment.

"There he is, Fuzz." She put down her notebook. "Go tell him hello. I'll pour the wine. He's going to need a drink."

Fuzz tumbled off her lap and drifted eagerly toward the door. Lydia hurried into the kitchen, yanked the jug of white out of the refrigerator, and poured a sizable amount of the contents into a tumbler.

Carrying the large glass in one hand, she followed Fuzz into the hall. Emmett had dumped his briefcase on the floor and hung his jacket in the closet. When he saw her, he paused in the act of unfastening the top buttons of his black shirt and gave her a wry smile.

"I warned you I might be late," he said.

"No problem." She handed him the wine and stood on tiptoe to kiss him. "The salad is ready and the ravioli will only take five minutes."

"Sounds good." He kissed her back and then he took a long swallow of the wine. When he lowered the glass, he looked amused. "I must be in pretty bad shape tonight. Even this stuff tastes good right now."

"Maybe you're finally developing a cultivated palate." She turned and started toward the kitchen. "How did it go today? Aside from finding out that you have to put in an appearance at the Restoration Ball, that is. Any news on Wyatt's condition?"

"Still in intensive care but holding his own, according to Tamara. She says that they've got him so loaded up with meds and painkillers that he sleeps most of the time. When he is awake, he's very groggy and incoherent. The hospital is restricting visitors to family only."

Which would not include him, Lydia thought. Officially he was no relation to Mercer Wyatt. She wondered if it bothered Emmett that he could not claim the right to see his father in a time of crisis.

He followed her into the kitchen and lounged against the door frame. Fuzz scampered up onto the counter beside him and looked hopefully at the pretzel jar.

"I assume you saw the headlines in the tabloids this morning," he said.

"Sure did." She tried to keep her voice light as she rezzed the burner beneath the pot of water. "All that stuff about a lovers' triangle at the highest circles of the Cadence Guild certainly made for some exciting reading."

"It's pure ghost-shit. You know that."

She concentrated on opening the bag of ravioli. "I know it, but a lot of folks are going to be thrilled to believe the worst. The tabloids are hinting that you had a motive for trying to kill Wyatt. They're suggesting that you came here to get revenge against him because he stole Tamara away from you."

"It'll all blow over eventually."

"Uh-huh." She dumped the frozen ravioli into the boiling water.

"You're really worried, aren't you?" He took a step forward, caught her chin with his thumb and forefinger, and brushed his mouth across hers. His eyes softened. "Don't worry about the tabloids, honey. They can't do us any real harm."

"I'm afraid they'll try you in the court of public opinion," she said, anxious for him to understand the danger. "If they make you look guilty, the police might begin to wonder if there's something to the gossip. The last thing you need is for the cops to start investigating you as a suspect."

"I appreciate your concern, sweetheart." He kissed her forehead. "But this isn't the first time I've had to worry about stuff like this. Don't forget, I was a Guild boss for six years in Resonance. I know how to handle the press."

"Famous last words."

Emmett spent an hour on paperwork after dinner and then fell into her bed with only a mumbled "good night." He was sound asleep when she came out of the bathroom.

She climbed in beside him very carefully so as not to awaken him. It wasn't easy because he took up a large portion of the bed.

Fuzz blinked his baby blues from the foot of the bed, yawned, curled into a ball of lint, and went to sleep.

She lay awake for a long time, studying the shadows on the ceiling. She thought about the anonymous phone call she had made that afternoon, the one to a reporter who worked for the *Cadence Tattler*, and she wondered what the headlines in the newspapers would look like in the morning.

It was a long time before she got to sleep.

11

Two newspaper vending boxes flanked the entrance to Shrimpton's House of Ancient Horrors. The one on the right belonged to the *Cadence Star*. Lydia picked up a copy of that paper first. The headline was commendably restrained, as befitted a family newspaper. *New Guild Chief Takes Command.*

Lydia breathed a sigh of relief and moved on warily to the box on the left and peeked inside. There were only a couple of copies left of that day's issue of the *Tattler*. She was forced to conclude that the headlines plastered across the cover in type that was at least two inches high probably explained the brisk sales.

NEW GUILD BOSS HAS MYSTERY MISTRESS.

The smaller headline underneath read, *Will London Bring Her to the Restoration Ball or Keep Her Hidden Away in Secret Love Nest?* The accompanying photo showed a picture of Emmett getting out of his Slider in front of the Guild office tower.

Lydia reluctantly shoved some coins into the

slot and took out one of the remaining copies. A flashy amber-colored Coaster pulled up to the curb with a flourish just as she started to walk toward the front door of the museum. The hood and tail fins of the vehicle were decorated with flames the color of green ghost light.

The door of the Coaster slid open and Melanie popped out. She leaned down to blow a farewell kiss to the man at the wheel. The pose caused her short, stretchy red skirt to ride up so high in back that the lacy edge of a pair of black panties was revealed.

"Thanks for a great evening, Jack." She spotted Lydia and waved. "Well, good morning, Mystery Mistress."

"Hey, is that her?" The door on the other side of the Coaster opened. Jack climbed out and grinned across the low roof of the Coaster. Sunlight glinted on a tiny, faceted crystal set in his left incisor. "Introduce me, Mel."

"Sure." Melanie swept a hand out with the air of a magician. "Lydia Smith, meet Jack Brodie. Jack, this is the Mystery Mistress herself, and I am happy to tell you that she *will* be at the Restoration Ball. I know this for a fact because she asked me to help her pick out her gown. We're going shopping this very afternoon."

Jack ducked his head. "An honor to meet you, ma'am. When we saw the papers this morning Mel told me that she not only knew who you were, she actually worked in the same office with you. I didn't know whether she was just putting me on or what."

Jack seemed pleasant enough, Lydia thought, and he was certainly very good-looking. He was turned out in typical, swaggering, ghost-hunter style — lots of rugged khaki and leather. He wore a chunk of amber in his belt that was big enough to serve as a hood ornament for the Coaster. A lot of male ghost-hunters seemed to think that people equated the size of their amber with the size of another portion of their anatomy.

"Thank you," Lydia replied. "A pleasure, I'm sure."

"Wait'll I tell the guys down at the Guild Hall that I met the boss's, uh, lady friend, in person. They're all real curious about him, you know. Heard about what he did while he was in charge of the Resonance Guild. Lotta guys are a little worried, to tell you the truth."

Lydia clutched the *Tattler*. "Why in the world would they be worried about Emmett?"

"Well, they say he's not what you might call a big supporter of some of the old Guild traditions." Jack glanced both ways along the sidewalk, leaned over the roof of the Coaster, and lowered his voice. "They heard that he turned the Resonance Guild into some kind of damned business corporation."

"Jeez," Lydia murmured. "What a concept."

"Yeah, weird, huh? Course, London's here now, not in Resonance, and things work a little different in Cadence. We still got Guild law and Guild tradition in this town."

Lydia gave him a thin smile. "Good to know the old ways haven't been forgotten by the Cadence Guild."

"No, ma'am, that's for sure." Jack rechecked the sidewalk to make certain no one else was within earshot and lowered his voice a little more. "Speaking of tradition, I heard a rumor that Mr. London might have to handle a real Council challenge at the confirmation meeting on Thursday afternoon."

She had no idea what a Council challenge was, Lydia thought, but she did not like the sound of it.

"A Council challenge?" she repeated carefully.

"Yeah." Jack's eyes glinted with anticipation. "Never seen one, myself. Haven't had one of those since Mercer Wyatt took over thirty years ago. Should be interesting."

Alarm bells clanged loudly.

"What is a Council challenge, Jack?" Lydia asked.

"It's an old tradition that dates all the way back to the founding of the Guilds. Any member of a Guild Council can issue a challenge to a boss. If the challenger wins, the Council has to choose another leader. The guy who beat the boss usually gets the job."

Lydia frowned. "I take it this challenge thing is not a multiple-choice quiz?"

"No, ma'am." Jack chuckled and then did another quick survey of the vicinity. His voice went down to a raspy whisper. "It's a full-on hunter duel."

Lydia went ice cold. "Duels between hunters are illegal."

"Sure. But small duels go on all the time. You know how it is. A couple of guys drink a little too much Green Ruin and decide to go into some dark alley and see who can pull up the biggest ghost. Nobody pays much attention unless someone gets fried real bad and turns up in an emergency room. Then there's an investigation and a few hands get slapped, but that's about it."

"So typical of the way the Guild handles things," Lydia stated.

Jack either did not hear her or else he failed to pick up on the sarcasm.

"Now a Council challenge duel is different," he said. "It's not like an ordinary hunter match."

"In what way?"

"Well, for one thing, it's held at a secret location somewhere deep underground. Hell, been so long since they used the old dueling grounds, I doubt if anyone but the Council members even know where they're located."

"I see."

"The other thing that makes a Council challenge duel a little different from your average Saturday-night back alley burn-fest is that you're talking about a match between two of the most powerful hunters in the whole damn Guild. Nobody gets that high in the organization unless he can melt amber."

Lydia exchanged a quick glance with Melanie who was starting to look intrigued.

Melting amber was an expression. Very few hunters had the power to do it. The stuff didn't actually melt when a lot of psi energy was forced through it, but a very strong ghost-hunter could pull so much para-energy that the tuned amber he used to control it lost its focus. When that happened, it was said that he had melted amber.

Ruining a chunk of amber that had been exquisitely and expensively tuned by a specially trained focus-energy para-resonator was not a problem for other types of para-resonators. Most people, even very strong ephemeral-energy para-rezes such as herself, used psi energy in subtle, nuanced ways. But ghost-hunters were all about raw power.

She happened to know for a fact that Emmett was one of the small percentage of hunters who could melt amber. Presumably all of the other members of the Cadence Guild Council were capable of the same feat. A duel held underground where each duelist could summon very large, extremely dangerous ghosts might well prove lethal to the loser. At best, he would be lucky to survive and if he did make it he would no doubt be so badly psi-fried that he would be a candidate for a nice, quiet para-psych asylum for the rest of his life.

Lydia was suddenly aware that her mouth had gone dry. She stared, wide-eyed, at Jack.

"You said that there hasn't been a Council challenge since Wyatt took over the Guild. Do you mean that in the entire time he's been running things no one ever tried to take him? I find that a little hard to believe."

Melanie raised her brows. "She's right. Is Mercer Wyatt so strong that no one ever dared to challenge him?"

"Wyatt's strong, all right," Jack said easily. "But a couple of the other Council members like that new guy, Foster Dorning, are probably just as strong or stronger."

"So why hasn't anyone ever issued a challenge to Wyatt?" Lydia demanded.

" 'Cause he's smart, that's why." Jack winked. "Way too smart to leave himself open to a challenge."

Lydia glared. "I'm waiting for the amber to resonate here, Jack. Go ahead, tell us how Wyatt has managed to avoid a challenge for three decades."

The bit of crystal set in Jack's tooth sparkled when he gave her a knowing grin. "Because, except for about a year after his first wife died when he was covered because he was officially in mourning, Wyatt has always been real careful to make sure he's married."

Lydia stared at him, openmouthed. She noticed that Melanie had a similar blank expression on her face.

Lydia recovered first. "What's marriage got to do with it?"

Jack shrugged. "There's a damn good reason why the Guild chiefs of all the cities are usually in either a Marriage of Convenience or a Covenant Marriage."

Melanie tipped her head inquiringly. "And that reason would be?"

"A little thing called Guild wife rights." Jack's handsome features screwed up in what might have been close thought. "I guess technically it would be Guild spouse rights. But the fact is, there's always been so many more male ghost-hunters than female hunters that I don't expect it's been much of an issue. And for sure there's never been a woman Guild boss in any of the cities."

"I've never heard of these so-called Guild wife rights," Lydia said tersely. "Explain."

"Old tradition," Jack said. "Goes back to the early days when the Guild Councils worried about the organizations being torn apart by in-fighting and rivalries. They wanted to make sure that there were as few challenges as possible, especially in the upper echelons, because they needed trained, experienced hunters badly during the Era of Discord. Couldn't afford to waste good para-rezes in duels."

Lydia exchanged a quick glance with Melanie and turned back to Jack. "How do these Guild wife rights work?"

"Heck, I'm no expert in Guild law." Jack

waved one hand across the roof of the Coaster. "Way I understand it, the Councils each instituted a rule that allows a Guild wife to go before the Council and halt any challenge that has been made that involves her husband."

Melanie whistled softly. "And that actually works?"

Jack spread his hands. "Sure seems to have worked for Mercer Wyatt all these years. Works for the other Guild bosses, too. Rumor has it there's only been one boss who was challenged in recent years and that was because he wasn't married."

"Which one?" Melanie asked.

"London." Jack's teeth flashed in another grin of anticipation. "He didn't have a wife when he took over the Resonance Guild six years ago and there's talk that he had to deal with a Council challenge."

Melanie looked quickly at Lydia and was clearly alarmed by whatever she saw there.

"Hey, obviously he won," she said very brightly.

"Yeah." Jack nodded cheerfully. "They say London is strong, all right. Should be one hell of a match if they go for it."

Lydia could not move. She felt as if she had been carved from quartz.

"Gotta run," Jack said. He ducked his head at Lydia. "Like I said, nice to meet you, ma'am." He winked at Melanie. "See you Thursday night, babe, right?"

"My place," Melanie agreed. She twinkled at Lydia. "I'm having a few friends over for drinks and pizza. We're going to watch the Restoration Ball festivities on the rez-screen. Can't wait to see you walking up that red carpet."

"For sure," Jack said. "Never knew anyone personally who got to go to that fancy shindig. Wait'll I tell the guys at the Hall."

He slid back into the Coaster and rezzed the engine. Flash-rock melted and the vehicle shot away from the curb with a low, throbbing whine.

Melanie frowned at Lydia. "Hey, are you okay? You look a little sick."

"No, I am not okay, I'm horrified. I *knew* this job was risky."

"Yours or Emmett's?"

"Not funny, Mel. I'm talking about Emmett's new position, of course. Damn, damn, *damn*."

"Take it easy. You're overreacting."

"At the start of this mess, I was afraid that whoever tried to kill Wyatt might go after Emmett. He assured me that wasn't likely to happen because he's convinced that the attacker was only interested in Wyatt. But nobody said anything about this stupid Council challenge tradition."

"I'm sure Jack was just spreading hunter gossip." Melanie patted Lydia's shoulder. "Don't worry about it. After all, everyone knows this is just a temporary job for Emmett. Why would anyone bother to challenge him to a duel?"

"Who knows? Guild Law and traditions are so

murky that no one outside the organizations can say how they work."

"Look, London knows how to handle a Guild Council. He did it for six years in Resonance, remember?"

"I know, but this is Cadence. Things might work differently here, for all we know."

Melanie urged her gently through the entrance of the museum. "Don't worry about London. He can take care of himself."

"That's what he keeps telling me. I just wish I could believe it."

Melanie smiled very slowly. "Well, well, well."

"What's that supposed to mean?"

"You've got it bad, don't you?" Melanie was genuinely sympathetic. "You're in love with Emmett. That's why you're letting your imagination make you crazy."

"I'm dating him," Lydia said tersely. "Obviously I'm fond of him."

"Sounds like something a lot more intense than fond, if you ask me."

"We have an arrangement," Lydia mumbled.

"Oh, sure, an arrangement." Melanie chuckled. "Lydia Smith, Mystery Mistress, has an *arrangement* with the boss of the Cadence Guild. Nope, sorry, I'm not buying that one, pal. Sadly, as I've so often pointed out, you just wouldn't know how to have a casual, no-strings-attached affair with a man."

12

The secretary of the Old Frequency City College Alumni Association called just before lunch. Lydia put aside the schedule of group tours that she was slated to escort through the museum that week and reached for the phone.

"This is Jan Ross," a perky voice said on the other end of the line. "I understand you've been trying to get in touch with me?"

"Yes, thank you so much for returning my call." Lydia quickly opened her top desk drawer and took out the copy of the newspaper story she had found inside Lawrence Maltby's milk carton. "I'm trying to get some information about a former student. His name is Troy Burgis. According to a newspaper account that I came across, he disappeared in the course of an unauthorized trip into the catacombs about fifteen years ago."

"I see. I don't recall the name but unfortunately there have been a few such incidents over the years. The college does its best to protect the students but you know how it is. Sometimes the fraternities get carried away with their initiation rites or a group of young people get drunk and decide to go underground through a hole-in-the-wall. Accidents happen."

"I understand. Is there any way I can get more information on this particular student?"

"I can look him up in the yearbook, if you like," Jan Ross offered.

"I would really appreciate that."

"Hang on."

Alumni associations, Lydia thought, best investigators in the world. You could hide from your family, friends, tax collectors, and creditors but you could not escape the long reach of your alumni association.

She tapped her pen anxiously against the edge of her desk. She did not know what she hoped to discover about Troy Burgis. She knew only that she had to try to find out why Maltby had gone to the trouble of concealing the article in a trapped milk carton.

She heard movement, the squeak of a desk chair, and then the sound of pages being turned.

"Yes, here he is," Jan Ross said a moment later. "There's not much information, though, just his name and major and favorite extracurricular activity."

"Is there a photo?"

"No, just a blank square and a note that says photo not available."

Damn. Then again, what good would a photo have done her? Lydia thought. It would have been fifteen years old and besides, Burgis was dead.

"What subject was he majoring in?" she asked.

"Para-archaeology."

"I guess that figures, given his interest in the catacombs. What about extracurricular activities?"

"One. Music. It says here that he formed his own band that played at an off-campus club. The members included Jason Clark, Norman Fairbanks, and Andrea Preston."

Lydia paused in the act of taking down notes. "Clark and Fairbanks were with Burgis when he disappeared. Any chance you could put me in touch with either of them? I'd really like to talk to Andrea Preston, too, if possible."

"I'll see what I can do, but it will take me some time to pull the contact information and then I'll have to get in touch with each of them first to see if they wish to speak with you. I'm sure you understand."

"Of course. Please tell them that I'm only interested in Burgis." She cast around for another question that the alumni secretary could answer. "Does the yearbook give the names of the academics who were in the Department of Para-archaeology there at the time?"

"No, but I've got that information on file. Just a sec."

Jan Ross came back on the line a short time later.

"Looks like it was a small department in those days," she said. "There were only two full professors, a couple of assistant profs, and four instructors."

Lydia tightened her grip on the pen. "Can you read me the names?"

Ever helpful, Jan Ross read the short list of the members of the department. When she was finished, Lydia thanked her and hung up the phone.

She sat there for a long time, contemplating the one name that she had underlined very heavily: Dr. Lawrence W. Maltby.

It was Melanie who spotted The Dress.

Melanie had, in fact, taken charge of the entire shopping expedition when she had deduced that Lydia was incapable of focusing on the problem.

Lydia knew that finding the right gown was important but she could not seem to concentrate on the business of finding it. She kept getting distracted by memories of Jack's comments concerning the dangers of Council challenges and the risks involved in being an unmarried Guild boss.

"If I don't keep an eye on you you'll end up with another dull business suit and a pair of low-heeled pumps," Melanie declared when they got into a cab outside of Shrimpton's that afternoon.

Lydia did not argue the point. She settled in beside Melanie and closed the door. "It was very nice of Shrimp to let both of us leave the office early so that I could shop."

"Nice, my sweet patoot. He practically begged me to take you shopping after I pointed out the advantages."

Lydia frowned. "What advantages?"

"Are you kidding?" Melanie chuckled. "This is going to be one of the best things that's ever happened to Shrimp and he knows it. Just wait until the newspapers find out that the new Guild boss's Mystery Mistress works for none other than Shrimpton's House of Ancient Horrors. Folks will be lined up around the block outside our tacky little museum to get a look at you."

"Oh, jeez, Mel." Lydia was appalled. "This is a nightmare. I've become a museum attraction."

"You're going to be an even bigger draw for us than the dreamstone jar," Melanie said with great satisfaction.

"Oh, *jeez*, Mel."

Melanie's brows jumped together in sudden concern. "You don't look too good. You're not going to faint or anything, are you?"

"I am not going to faint." Lydia paused, considering the matter. "But I might be sick."

"Mother of pearl." Melanie's eyes got huge. "You're not pregnant, are you?"

"No," Lydia said flatly. "That is absolutely impossible." *I think.* "We've been very careful." Most of the time.

"Too bad. A pregnant Mystery Mistress would have been an incredible attraction for Shrimpton's."

"Since when did you become so concerned with the financial future of Shrimpton's House of Ancient Horrors?"

"A woman has to think about her career."

"Got news for you, Mel, a position at Shrimpton's is a job, not a career." Lydia broke off as the cab turned the corner into an exclusive shopping district. "Where are we going?"

"Designs by Finella," Melanie announced with relish. "I've read about it for years in the fashion and style magazines. The wealthiest, most important women in town shop there."

"Good grief, I know I need a nice dress but there's no reason for us to go to the most expensive shop in town."

"Will you please calm down? You're not going to pay for it, remember? You said that Emmett told you that the Guild is picking up the tab for the gown."

Lydia fell back on the argument she had attempted to use when she'd had this conversation with Emmett. "It's the principle of the thing."

"Listen to me, friend." Melanie turned partway around in the seat, rested her arm along the back, and gave Lydia a ferociously intense stare. "Here's the only principle you need to keep in mind: This is your big chance to really stick it to the Cadence Guild. You know you've been wanting to get revenge against ghost-hunters ever since that disaster in the catacombs seven months ago. What better way to do that than to send them a huge bill for a fabulous ball gown and all the accessories?"

"Hmm." Jolted out of her dark musings, Lydia contemplated that logic. "You know, you've got a point. I hadn't looked at it quite like that."

Melanie relaxed against the seat. "Revenge is sweet, ain't it?"

At Designs by Finella, Melanie had to do some fast talking to get the attention of one of the elegant saleswomen.

"My friend will be attending the Restoration Ball," she said with a grand air. "We want a very special gown suitable for the occasion. Mr. Emmett London will be her escort for the evening. You do know who Mr. London is, don't you?"

The woman's eyes widened in shock and then lit with interest.

"The new head of the Cadence Guild? Yes, of course. I read all about him in the newspapers." The saleswoman flicked a quick, speculative glance at Lydia. "I heard that he had a companion, but I was under the impression that the relationship was a very private matter. I didn't realize that he took her out in public."

Lydia's temper flared. She bared her teeth in a steely smile. "Figured he was keeping me stashed away in a secret love nest? Don't believe everything you read in the tabloids, lady."

The saleswoman turned red. "I assure you I never meant to imply —"

Melanie waded in smoothly. "Shall we get busy looking at some gowns? By the way, Mr. London wishes the bill to be sent directly to him at Guild headquarters. You can call his office for confirmation."

The saleswoman pulled herself together immediately. "Let me introduce myself. I'm Mrs. Davies." She snapped her fingers for an assistant. "The private viewing salon, Jennifer."

"Private viewing salon?" Lydia grimaced. "Sounds like a funeral parlor."

She and Melanie were ushered into a mirrored room, seated on pink velvet chairs, and served delicately scented rez-tea in dainty cups.

One spectacular gown after another was brought out for inspection. Each dress was nothing short of a work of art and each seemed more beautiful and more expensive than the last.

Her temper cooled and Lydia returned to her brooding thoughts. It really wasn't fair, she reflected. Under any other circumstances, she could have enjoyed herself enormously. After all, what were the odds that she would ever again get an opportunity to shop for the ultimate ball gown and accessories?

But the potential pleasures of the experience were buried beneath the weight of a sense of impending doom. Her intuition was kicking in and she knew better than to ignore it.

Melanie had no such nagging doubts to distract her, however. She took on the responsibility of selecting the right dress with great zest, turning thumbs down on one gown after another.

Too boring. Too beige. Too ordinary. Too much lace. Too much skirt.

At one point the assistant produced a shimmering, sparkling silver lamé number. The sight of it glittering there in front of her brought Lydia out of her dour reverie.

"That's rather nice," she said.

"Are you out of your mind?" Melanie made a face. "I could carry it off but you would look like a high-class hooker in that thing."

"Oh."

The next offering was pink.

Melanie lost her patience. She scowled at Mrs. Davies and the assistant. "I thought I had made it clear that Miss Smith will be attending the Restoration Ball with one of the most powerful men in the city. She needs to look exotic and mysterious and elegant. Do you see where I'm going here?"

"Hmm." The saleswoman hesitated and then motioned to the assistant. "Bring in *Midnight*, Jennifer."

"Yes, ma'am."

Jennifer disappeared for a moment. When she returned she carried what appeared to be a shapeless length of fluid fabric in a shade of blue that was so dark it was almost black.

"This gown is not one of Finella's own designs," Mrs. Davies said hesitantly. "That is why

I haven't shown it to you until now. The majority of our most important clients insist on wearing only creations designed by Finella herself. She is, of course, a goddess in the world of couture."

Melanie frowned at the limp material. "Who designed this one?"

"Finella's new apprentice, Charles, a gifted young man whom she feels has great potential. It will require a certain degree of daring to wear this gown to the Restoration Ball, however, precisely because it is *not* a Finella original. Most of the other women will be in dresses created by her or one of the handful of other exclusive designers in Cadence."

Melanie narrowed her eyes and tapped one toe. "I see what you mean. Going to the ball in a dress by an unknown designer is risky but it could turn out to be a brilliant move if the gown works." She motioned to Lydia. "Try it on. What have we got to lose?"

Lydia eyed the unprepossessing material draped over the assistant's arm. "Are you sure?"

"Let's get you into it and see what we've got."

Lydia peeled off her business suit, stepped out of her pumps, and allowed the assistant to pour the midnight blue gown over her head.

When it was properly fastened, the assistant stepped back.

"Yes." Melanie got to her feet and walked in a circle around Lydia. "Oh, my, yes, indeed. This is the one."

Lydia turned to study her reflection. For the space of a couple of heartbeats she did not recognize the woman in the mirror. Then it hit her that she was looking at herself and for the first time that day, her attention was riveted on the project at hand.

"Good heavens," she whispered. "I feel like Amberella in this gown. All I need is a couple of wicked stepsisters and a fairy godmother and I'll be all set."

"Don't know about the wicked stepsisters," Melanie said, "but you've got me for a fairy godmother."

Lydia grinned at her in the mirror. "It doesn't get any better than that in my neighborhood."

Midnight was stunningly simple in design, a narrow column of fine, liquid material that discreetly hugged her slender frame. It was cut demurely high in front and plunged deeply at the back. Long, slim sleeves fell to her wrists. The hemline hit at her ankles. A cleverly designed opening trimmed with a dashing ruffle made movement possible. The overall effect was sophisticated, exotic, and mysterious.

She caught sight of the saleswoman's face in the mirror. Act as though you buy clothes like this all the time, she told herself.

"It'll do," she said crisply to Mrs. Davies. "Thank you. You've been very helpful."

"My pleasure." Mrs. Davies was clearly as surprised as everyone else in the room by the effect of the gown, although she struggled to conceal her reaction. "It is absolutely perfect for you and for the occasion, Miss Smith." She flapped a hand at the assistant. "Jennifer, go get Charles. I want him to see this."

A moment later a slender young man with delicate features and dark, curly hair appeared. He hovered shyly in the entrance.

"You sent for me, Mrs. Davies?"

"Miss Smith will be attending the Restoration Ball with Mr. Emmett London, the new head of the Cadence Guild. She will wear your *Midnight*." Mrs. Davies gestured toward Lydia. "I thought you would like to personally oversee whatever minor alterations are needed."

Astonishment and then joyous wonder transformed Charles's finely boned face. "My *Midnight* will be going to the Restoration Ball with Mr. London?"

Lydia smiled at his expression. "Well, it won't be going alone. I'll be inside your beautiful gown, Charles, but I'll try not to detract from it too much."

Charles blushed furiously. His smile lit up the room. "I don't know what to say. Thank you, Miss Smith."

"I'm the one who should be thanking you," Lydia said sincerely. "Left to my own devices I might have ended up looking like a high-class hooker."

Charles glanced at the row of rejected gowns and raised one brow. "The silver lamé?"

"I'm afraid so."

"Don't worry," Melanie said. "I would never have let her buy that one. Anyone can see it would have been all wrong for her. Now, then, let's talk about accessories. I'm thinking gold. What do you think, Charles?"

"Yes." He nodded approvingly. "Nothing else but gold and not a great deal of it."

"And my amber, of course." Lydia glanced at her bracelet.

"No," Charles said with absolute conviction. "No amber. Just gold."

"He's right," Mrs. Davies said. "You must limit the accessories to gold. Anything else will interfere with the statement that the gown makes."

"Carry your amber in your purse," Melanie advised quickly when she saw Lydia open her mouth to argue. "You don't want to ruin Charles's creation, do you?"

"Well, no, but —"

"Relax, you're going to be stunning," Melanie said.

"Don't get too excited," Lydia warned. "I clean up okay but I don't do stunning."

"You will do stunning in my *Midnight*," Charles said very quietly.

An hour later, laden with shopping bags, Lydia and Melanie exited the boutique.

They ran smack into a throng of reporters. Cameras popped and flashed. Microphones were thrust forward. The questions came fast and furious.

"*Which one of you is London's Mystery Mistress?*"

"*Is it true London is going to take you to the Restoration Ball tomorrow night?*"

"*Where did you two meet?*"

"*How long have you been seeing each other?*"

Lydia froze.

Melanie, however, was unfazed. "Don't look at me," she said to the hungry crowd. "I'm not your mystery woman." She waved gracefully in Lydia's direction. "Allow me to present Lydia Smith, Mr. London's date for the Restoration Ball."

The gaggle of reporters and cameras swerved toward Lydia and the questions rained down upon her head with the force of hailstones.

". . . How would you describe your relationship with London?" a female reporter with short blond hair demanded.

"Tell us what it's like to date the boss of the Guild," gushed another woman.

"According to my sources you aren't from a Guild family," someone else called out. "Does that mean that marriage is out of the question?"

The word *marriage* pierced the spell of immobility that had gripped Lydia. Pull yourself together, she thought. Think of this group of reporters as one giant illusion trap that has to be untangled before it explodes into a full-blown alien nightmare.

Melanie grabbed her arm and started to drag

her toward a cab. "Miss Smith doesn't have any comment for you."

"Oh, yes, she does." Lydia dug in her heels, forcing Melanie to come to a halt. She drew herself up to her full height and gave the cluster of journalists her most sparkling smile. "As a matter of fact, Miss Smith has a very important comment for the media."

13

The desk intercom burbled, interrupting Emmett's conversation with Verwood, the head of Guild Security. Irritated, he punched the button.

"I thought I told you that I did not want to be disturbed, Perkins."

"I assumed that you would make an exception in case of an emergency, sir."

Emmett gripped the phone a little tighter. He did not need any more problems.

"What is the nature of this emergency?" he asked evenly.

"I'm not sure, sir, but according to Miss Smith, there definitely is one in progress. She insists on speaking with you immediately."

Lydia's name in the same sentence with the word *emergency* made him go cold.

"Put her through, Perkins."

"Yes, sir."

Emmett picked up the phone. "Lydia? What's wrong?"

"I'm really sorry about this, Emmett. I don't have a good excuse. But I don't think it will do too much harm. Honestly, the time will go by before you know it, what with you being so busy and all these days. You'll hardly even notice."

"Are you all right?"

"Yes, of course, I'm fine, why?"

"Perkins said there was some sort of emergency."

"Yes, that's what I'm trying to explain."

He called on what was left of his store of patience. "What the hell is wrong?"

"It's a long story. You see what happened was, Melanie and I came out of the dress shop and there were all these reporters waiting in front."

He allowed himself to relax a little. "Honey, they were bound to find you, sooner or later. It's not like we've tried to keep our relationship a secret."

"I know." She cleared her throat. "The thing is, they wanted a comment about us, Emmett."

"You should have told them to call my office."

"I'm sure you'll be hearing from the media at any moment," she said dolefully. "Because I gave them a comment. That's why I'm calling you now. To warn you."

Confusion was starting to take the place of concern. "Warn me about what?"

He heard her take a deep breath on the other end of the line. "I hope you won't be too upset about this. I guess I was just feeling cornered. They were going on and on about the Mystery Mistress thing and I just couldn't take it anymore. It's embarrassing."

"What did you say to the press?" he asked, spacing each word very carefully to get her attention.

162

"I told them that I was not your mistress."

For an instant it seemed as if the whole world went away. *She had denied their relationship.*

He stared blankly at the view of the Dead City outside the window. He was aware that Verwood was looking at him with concern.

"I see," he said softly.

"I'm really sorry about this, but I don't think it will do too much damage."

The only damage being done was to him, he thought wearily. Well, what had he expected? He had known from the start that his connection to the Guild would be a huge issue for her. The media circus surrounding the Mystery Mistress had probably pushed her too far.

"Emmett? Are you still there?"

"I'm here."

"I've made an appointment at the registrar's office for three o'clock this afternoon." She sounded crisp and assured now. A woman with an objective. "I know you're awfully busy, but it won't take long. Can you make it?"

He was definitely not tracking here. "The registrar's office?"

"The clerk said they would make an appointment so that we wouldn't have to stand in line."

"Why do we have an appointment?" he asked.

"Something was said about being only too happy to do a favor for the Guild, as I recall."

"I meant, why do we need an appointment at the registrar's office?"

There was another brief pause. "I thought

you understood. I just got through telling the media that I was your fiancée, not your mistress, and that we were going to file for an MC this afternoon."

The world snapped back into focus. "You told the press that we're getting married? Today?"

"I'm afraid so."

"I see," he said again.

"How mad are you?" she asked, sounding resigned.

"I'm not mad. Just a little surprised, that's all." More like stunned, but there was no reason to tell her that.

"I realize that I probably should have talked to you first," Lydia said apologetically. "But like I said, the reporters caught me by surprise and I just couldn't stand all those stupid questions about the Mystery Mistress."

"It's okay. I understand. Don't worry about it."

"I know a year sounds like a long time but it will go by before you know it and it's not as if you and I weren't spending a lot of time together, anyway."

"I said, don't worry about it." He glanced at his watch. "I'll meet you at the registrar's office at three."

"You're okay with this?"

"I'm okay with it."

He hung up the phone and looked at Verwood. "Congratulate me. I'm getting married this afternoon."

Verwood, a big, square man with very little

neck, did not alter his politely impassive expression. "Congratulations, sir. A sudden decision?"

"No, I've been thinking about it for a while." Emmett picked up the file on Sandra Thornton that Verwood had given him earlier. "I was just waiting to be asked."

14

Lydia stood on the second-story terrace of Emmett's newly acquired townhouse, looking out at the view of the green quartz wall and the spires and towers of the Dead City. The night air was cool and damp from the fog that was coalescing off the river. In another hour or two the mist would blanket the Old Quarter.

The house was much closer to the ruins than her own apartment. The only thing between her and the great wall was the large city park down below. Proximity made a difference. Here she was even more aware of the psi energy that leaked from the Dead City than she was in her own place. When she went out on the balcony of her apartment she picked up only occasional stirrings of the stuff. But in this neighborhood it permeated the atmosphere.

She could tune out the little currents of energy or ignore them if she wished but she rarely bothered to do so. It was, after all, a pleasant sensation. The part of her that was sensitive to psi power resonated with the whispers coming from the ruins.

She leaned on the terrace railing and contemplated the events of the day.

Things had definitely not been dull.

The good news was that Emmett appeared to be completely unperturbed by the hasty Marriage of Convenience she had orchestrated. The bad news was that for some reason she could not explain, she was a nervous wreck tonight.

Emmett had arrived at the registrar's office on time, accompanied by a very large, square individual named Verwood whom he introduced as his chief of security. To her astonishment, Emmett also brought along a ring. She experienced a very odd sensation when he slipped it onto her finger. It was as if the simple gold band somehow made the promises they spoke far more binding than the associated paperwork indicated.

It was just a Marriage of Convenience, she reminded herself, not a Covenant Marriage. It would automatically expire in one year, leaving them both free to go their separate ways if they so chose.

The MC didn't really affect their relationship in any material way, she thought. She and Emmett had already been involved in a monogamous arrangement. The formalities were just that — formalities.

Tonight was no different than any other night she had spent with Emmett during the past few weeks.

Except that she had a ring on her finger.

She heard a quiet footstep behind her and

turned to watch Emmett walk out onto the terrace through the open glass doors. He carried a bottle of champagne in one hand. In the other hand he held two flutes by their long stems. Fuzz was perched on his shoulder, gnawing on a pretzel.

She glanced at the champagne. "We're celebrating?"

He set the bottle and the glasses on the terrace table. "Don't know about you, but this is my first marriage. Figured it warranted something by way of celebration."

Guilt trickled through her, not for the first time today. "I'm sorry about this."

"Stop apologizing." He poured champagne into the two flutes and handed one to her. "It's just an MC. No big deal."

No big deal. How depressing.

Fuzz finished his pretzel, skittered down Emmett's arm, hopped onto the railing, and sat gazing at the ruins. He opened his second set of eyes, the ones he used for hunting at night.

"I wonder what he sees out there in the park that we can't see," Lydia said.

Emmett smiled. "Maybe a female dust-bunny."

"Huh. Hadn't thought about that." She took a large mouthful of champagne and swallowed it in one gulp.

Something went wrong about halfway down. Probably the fizzy bubbles, she thought. She wasn't accustomed to good champagne.

She gasped, sputtered, turned red, and coughed. Her eyes watered.

"You're welcome to as much champagne as you want," Emmett said, slapping her lightly between the shoulders. "But you might want to take it a little slower. You can enjoy it more that way. Not that it matters, but that particular bottle cost a hundred and fifty bucks. Sort of a shame to gulp it."

"Good heavens." She recovered her breath and stared, horrified, at the flute she had just emptied. "You opened a hundred-and-fifty-dollar bottle of champagne just to celebrate our MC?"

He shrugged. "I told you, this is my first marriage."

"Well, it's my first one, too, but still, a hundred and fifty bucks?" She frowned. "Wait a second, are you going to bill the Guild for the champagne as well as my new gown?"

"Why not?" He picked up the bottle and refilled her glass. "Just another business expense."

She brightened a little. "Well, in that case, who cares how much the stuff cost?"

He was amused. "I take it you like the idea of sticking the Guild with the tab for your expenses?"

"I know it's small and petty of me, but, yeah, I like the idea a lot. I figure it's the least the Guild can do for me after the way those two hunters refused to take responsibility for what happened during my Lost Weekend."

He nodded.

A long silence descended. Fuzz seemed entranced with the view of the fogbound park. So did Emmett.

She grew increasingly uneasy. Why was it suddenly so hard to make conversation? she wondered. The fact that Emmett was officially her husband for the next year didn't change anything about their relationship, did it? Tonight was no different than last night.

Except for the ring on her finger.

She cast about for something to say.

"So," she said, going for casual and blasé. "This really is your very first MC?"

He lounged against the railing and looked out at the night-shrouded ruins. "Yes."

She took a more cautious sip of the champagne and decided that it tasted quite good. The alcohol and the cloak of darkness emboldened her. "You must have had plenty of affairs over the years. Why didn't you ever go for a Marriage of Convenience?"

He was quiet for a long moment.

"I guess it just never felt right," he said eventually. "Or maybe it never seemed necessary. I could never see the point of an MC. Always figured that when the time came, I'd go all the way with a Covenant Marriage."

She looked down at the dark shapes of the trees in the park, aware of another wave of guilt rolling over her. Emmett was a romantic at heart, a man who had planned to wait until he found the right woman. Who would have believed that a Guild boss would have had such a sentimental side to his nature?

"What about you?" he said. "How come you never got into an MC until now?"

She pulled herself out of the sea of guilt and tried to formulate an answer to his question. "I've been very busy for the past few years, what with getting my degrees and starting my career."

"No time for marriage?"

"Not exactly." She hesitated. "I suppose what it comes down to is that I never dated anyone I wanted to actually share a home with, if you know what I mean."

"Ryan Kelso," he said dryly.

She blushed and was grateful for the cover of darkness. She preferred to forget Professor Ryan Kelso, the man she had been dating at the time of her disaster. Ryan had dumped her even before the university had fired her.

"Ryan was obviously a mistake," she conceded. "Sort of like you and Tamara."

"Uh-huh."

"But at least I was only thinking of an MC with Ryan." She grimaced. "Not a Covenant Marriage like you and Tamara were planning."

"I would take it as a great favor if you would not remind me of that period in my life."

The cloud of depression got heavier.

"Well, we both had extremely narrow escapes and we should be grateful fate intervened," she declared, trying to sound positive.

"This is true." Emmett put one foot on the lowest bar of the terrace railing. "But the bottom line here is that due to fate, some narrow escapes, and your announcement to the Cadence media this afternoon, we find ourselves confronted with a wedding night that neither of us had planned."

"I guess you could say that."

"Correct me if I'm mistaken, but I seem to recall that it is traditional to consummate the marriage on the wedding night."

She couldn't have moved if a ghost had materialized right in front of her. What was the matter with her?

After a minute that felt like half an eternity, Emmett moved. He straightened, reached out, and took the flute from her nerveless fingers.

When he turned to set the glasses on the table the low light spilling through the glass doors glinted on his strong cheekbones. She could not even breathe now.

It's only an MC, she chanted silently. It's only an MC.

Ah, but he's mine for a year and I do love him so.

Emmett pulled her into his arms and smiled very slowly. "Hello, Mrs. London."

"Emmett." She flung her arms around him.

He wrapped her close, tilted her chin up, and kissed her very deliberately, as though he sought to stamp an impression on her mouth.

She stopped trying to tell herself that this

night was the same as the others that she had spent with Emmett. There was something new between them. The vows that they had spoken today, even though they were only meant to bind them together for a year, made a difference and so did the ring on her finger.

This was her husband. At least for a while. Desire and a curious sense of possessiveness soared through her.

Emmett picked her up in his arms and started toward the glass doors.

He halted abruptly on the threshold, setting her on her feet with such shocking suddenness that her head spun. She had to grab the door frame to steady herself. Somewhere in the shadows, Fuzz rumbled a warning.

She finally caught the pulse of invisible psi energy in the air around her. Not the soft whispers that seeped from the Dead City, she realized, but the unmistakable chaos of unstable dissonance energy.

Acid green light flared at the edge of the terrace. The ghost took shape with terrifying speed. In seconds it was a swirling, pulsing ball of crackling energy moving straight toward them.

Fuzz leaped off the railing and streaked across the terrace to Lydia. She picked him up quickly, holding him close.

"Take him inside and stay out of the way." Emmett gave the order in a flat, cold voice.

She did not hesitate. When it came to dealing with a ghost, there was nothing like a really good hunter and Emmett was one of the best.

With Fuzz cradled under one arm, she hurried through the glass doors, giving Emmett all the space he needed on the terrace to do what he did so well.

When she turned around she was shocked to see how large the finished UDEM was. The core was a very hot green, indicating that the pattern in which the psi energy resonated was extremely complicated. Not your average ghost, by any means.

She had seen such UDEMs inside the catacombs, but never here outside the walls of the Dead City. Whoever was manipulating this one had to be an extremely powerful hunter. She also knew that he had to be somewhere nearby. It wasn't possible to energize and control a ghost from a distance any greater than half a city block at most. A hunter had to be fairly close to be effective. The one who had sent this one up onto the terrace was probably down below in the park, hiding in the trees.

Emmett was taking his time, analyzing his opponent. In her experience, hunters generally liked to move in fast and kick up a lot of flashy energy. Emmett was certainly capable of summoning a ghost as quickly as any other hunter when the necessity arose. But given an option, he preferred to work more deliberately.

It took a ghost to stop a ghost. Nothing else

could do the job. You couldn't de-rez one with a bullet, fire, water, amber-generated electricity, or any other force that had yet been discovered. Since ghosts were a fact of life in and around the Dead Cities, ghost-hunters had a lot of job security.

The pulsating mass of dissonance energy was so close now that Lydia could feel psi currents rolling across the terrace and into the room where she stood with Fuzz. Acid green light illuminated the scene.

Fuzz's fur was slicked back so tightly that she could see his ears. The hair on the nape of her neck lifted. There were goosebumps on her arms.

The dangerous ghost wasn't the only source of psi power in the vicinity. Emmett was brewing up a storm of his own.

Outside on the terrace another ball of roiling energy took shape. Emmett was constructing a smaller but far denser ghost to counter the threatening UDEM. Lydia could see that the energy he had summoned and manipulated into a resonating pattern burned more hotly at its core than that which powered the attacking ghost.

She knew theoretically what he was doing. Technically, de-rezzing a ghost wasn't much different than untangling an illusion trap. The trick was to tune in to the resonating patterns of psi energy and counter them with an opposing pattern that gradually dampened and neutralized the core. Like so many things in life it fell in to the category of easier said than done.

There was so much wild green energy whipping around on the terrace now that psi power lit up the night. Somewhere down below in the park Lydia heard a dog bark. A window was flung open.

"It's a ghost, Harry, a really big one," a woman yelled. "And it's right next door. Get the dog back inside. Hurry."

The mutt barked louder. Lydia heard more windows open.

"What the hell?" a man shouted from the terrace of the house on the other side of Emmett's. "There's two of 'em. The guy who lives in Number Seventeen has one going. Woo-hoo. Hey, Martha, didn't I tell you it was a good idea to have the new Guild boss living right next door?"

"I'm not so sure about that," Martha shot back. "We never had any ghosts in this neighborhood before London moved in."

"I don't get it," someone else said. "Ghosts aren't supposed to be able to get that big outside the catacombs."

"I told you, I didn't think it would be safe living this close to the Wall, didn't I, Joe?" a woman snapped. "But, you wouldn't listen to me, would you? The neighborhood has so much *character*, you said. It will be a terrific *investment*, you said. Well, you know what I think? I think we're going to be damn lucky if those two ghosts don't set fire to our fabulous real estate investment. And you know our insurance policy doesn't cover ghost damage."

At that moment Emmett's ghost drifted into the very heart of the advancing UDEM. Green energy spiked high into the night sky and then both ghosts winked out of existence.

An unnatural silence gripped the street. Lydia allowed herself to exhale. Fuzz wriggled out of her arms, tumbled back out onto the terrace, and leaped to the top of the railing. He crouched there, staring out into the night with all four eyes.

"He's down there, isn't he, buddy? Let's see if we can catch him." Emmett snatched up Fuzz and plunged back into the house.

"Emmett, be careful," Lydia called as he swept past her.

He was already on the stairs. She heard the front door open before she was halfway down. When she reached the entrance she confronted a wall of fog that glowed with the reflected glare of the old-fashioned streetlamps. Visibility was limited to a few feet. She could not even see the town houses across the street.

Somewhere in the misty distance she heard the sound of Emmett's swift footsteps. When they grew more muffled and faint she knew that he had gone down one of the narrow walks that led into the park.

She was almost positive that he would not

find his quarry. The fog and the night would provide cover for the rogue hunter who had conjured the attacking ghost.

Emmett released Fuzz as soon as they hit the park. It was worth a try, he thought, although he was not feeling very optimistic. By now the other hunter would be long gone.

"Find him, Fuzz."

The dust-bunny's night vision and sense of smell were a lot more acute than his own, Emmett thought, and the little creature seemed to understand what was expected of him. Fuzz was, after all, a natural-born hunter of another kind.

Fuzz vanished into the night-and-fog-drenched park. Emmett followed, listening for sounds that might indicate stealthy movement. He had melted amber de-rezzing the ghost and his senses were still humming at high-rez. The potent bio-cocktail unleashed into his system as a result of the heavy expenditure of psi power would take a while to wear off.

He knew the pattern all too well. He was going to be very wide awake and very aroused for about an hour and then he would crash for several hours. That was how it went after a major burn. There wasn't a damn thing he could do about it.

Hell of a way to spend a wedding night, he thought.

A few minutes later Fuzz tumbled out of the

shadows and into the light of one of the park lamps. He scampered up Emmett's pant leg with a piece of paper clutched in one front paw.

"What have you got there, pal?" Emmett took the scrap of paper from Fuzz. He rezzed the flashlight he had grabbed from one of the drawers in the hall cabinet on the way out the door. "A parking garage receipt."

He glanced at the logo stamped at the top of the receipt. *City Center Garage.* Yesterday's date, he noticed.

He knew that garage well. It was the one that was located most conveniently to the office tower that housed the headquarters of the Cadence Guild. Everyone who worked in the building used it.

In theory that deduction gave him several hundred suspects not including all those people who might have parked there yesterday simply because they had some business in the building. But he knew that he could rule out most of them immediately.

There were not many hunters who could conjure a ghost the size of the one on the terrace tonight outside the catacombs. Most of those who were capable of such a feat sat on the Guild Council. That left him with ten suspects.

He was pretty sure he could narrow that number even more — all the way down to one.

15

Lydia was waiting for them when they walked back into the front hall of Number Seventeen. Her face was etched with anxiety.

"Are you okay?" she demanded, closing the door behind them.

"We're both fine."

That wasn't strictly true. The afterburn was hitting him very hard now. With no threat in sight to distract him, he was plunged into the grip of raw lust. But he had never allowed himself to give in to the sexual craving inspired by a meltdown and he had no intention of doing so tonight. He was in control; he was *always* in control.

Lydia stood directly in front of him, frowning in concern. He looked at her standing there in the hall with the light from the lamp overhead gleaming on her red-gold hair. Her eyes were so deep and blue that he wanted to dive straight in and swim to the bottom. The urge to pull her down onto the floor, spread her legs, and thrust himself into her was almost overwhelming. He wanted to take her again and again until he was spent and empty.

Not exactly the romantic wedding night scenario of every woman's dreams, he thought.

He pulled himself together with an effort, set Fuzz down on the bottom step, and showed Lydia the garage receipt. "I'm guessing our guy dropped it. Fuzz seemed to think it was important enough to bring back to me."

Her brows drew together. "It doesn't tell us much, just that whoever lost it probably works in the Guild building. That's no big surprise, but there must be hundreds of Guild employees there."

"Yeah." He was having trouble concentrating. He was too busy looking down the front of her dress. The urge to touch her breasts was so strong it made his palms tingle.

He forced himself to turn away and walk deliberately to the ornately carved wooden cabinet of curiosities that he had installed in the front hall. The relic was an antique from Old Earth that one of his ancestors had managed to smuggle onboard a ship carrying colonists through the Curtain to Harmony.

"Who would do this, Emmett?"

"Don't worry about it." He rubbed the back of his neck and tried not to think about how good she smelled when she was damp and aroused. "I'll handle the problem."

"Obviously someone doesn't like the idea of you taking over the local Guild even on a temporary basis."

"I said, I'll deal with it." He slammed the little drawer shut and raised his eyes to meet her reflection in the mirror that hung above the cabinet. Big mistake.

She blinked and then frowned in concern. "Are you sure you're all right?"

He glanced at his watch and set his jaw. "In about forty minutes I'm going to crash. Until then I should probably go stand under a cold shower."

"Ah, so that's it." She visibly relaxed. "You melted amber, didn't you?"

"Didn't have much choice." He scrubbed his face with his hand. "That was the strongest ghost I've ever seen outside the catacombs."

"And now you're in the postmeltdown stage? The one where you get all lusty for a while and then collapse and sleep for hours?"

"That pretty much sums it up, yeah." He made a face. "Sorry about this. Not exactly how I'd intended to end the evening."

"It's okay," she said gently.

Her response was no doubt meant to soothe him but it had the opposite effect. She didn't understand, he reminded himself. She couldn't know that he'd spent most of his adult life trying not to become the stereotypical ghost-hunter of folklore and legend, trying to maintain control.

"No, it is not okay." Frustration sizzled through him, sharpening all the edges. "Damn it, this is our wedding night. I had plans for this evening. Champagne and soft music and . . ." He broke off, moving one hand in a gesture of sheer disgust. "All the rest."

Her eyes filled with wonder. "Emmett, that is so sweet, so romantic."

Sweet? Romantic? He gave serious consideration to turning her over his knee.

Bad idea. Now he was obsessing on her lovely ass. *Think about something else.* Like all that paperwork sitting on his desk down at Guild headquarters.

"You'd better go to bed now, Lydia." He made to step around her. "You can have the guest room tonight."

"Don't be ridiculous." She blocked his path. "You don't have to worry about freaking me out. This isn't the first time I've seen you in this condition."

"Nothing happened last time and nothing's going to happen this time," he vowed. "In a little while I'll crash and sleep it off."

"But meanwhile you want to have hot, steamy sex, right?"

He wished she hadn't used the words *hot* and *steamy* in the same sentence. "I'll survive without it."

"It's all right." She put her arms around his neck and smiled. "I like having sex with you, remember?"

He stood very still. With an act of sheer will power he managed to keep his hands at his sides.

"That's not the point," he replied.

"Oh, yeah?" Her smile grew more tantalizing, more inviting. Her eyes were filled with sensual mysteries. "What is the point here? I just told you I'm not nervous in the least. Maybe you're the one who's running scared? What's the matter, London? Afraid you'll lose control?"

"What the hell is that supposed to mean?"

"Being in control is a very big thing with you, isn't it?" she whispered. "It took me a while to realize just how important it is. But you know what? Sometimes it's okay to just let go. This is one of those times."

She tightened her arms around his neck, pressing her breasts and hips against his tight, heavily aroused body, and kissed him with a bold, teasing deliberation. At the touch of her warm, damp mouth, his resolution was shattered.

Hell with it. Why was he fighting this so damn hard? Tonight was his wedding night and his wife wanted to make love.

His wife.

It was as if a prison door had suddenly opened, allowing him to walk free. A sense of spiraling anticipation rushed through him.

"So you're not scared of me tonight?" He cupped her face in his hands. "Think you can handle your hunter husband when he's in full afterburn?"

Her eyes widened a little but she did not try to back away. "You may be one heck of a hunter, Emmett London, but I'm one heck of a tangler. I can handle you."

184

Heat swept through him. "Oh, man, I can't wait to see just how you do that."

He moved, catching her wrists and pinning her against the wall beside the cabinet of curiosities before she even realized what had happened. Bending his head, he kissed her, not holding anything back, letting her know just how hot he burned tonight.

Her mouth opened for him. She kicked off her shoes and drew one bare foot up along his leg.

"You really want to play with fire tonight, don't you?" he said against her throat.

"Can't wait," she breathed.

He let her feel the edge of his teeth. "Neither can I."

He released her wrists. Her arms promptly wound back around his neck. He felt her fingers plow through his hair.

Leaning into her so that he could feel the swell of her soft breasts, he reached down, grabbed the hem of her skirt, and shoved it up to her waist.

She gasped when he put his hand between her legs. His temperature went up another few degrees when he discovered that her panties were already damp.

"Talk about melting amber," he murmured. "You're the real thing, you know that? Hot, liquid amber. Right here in the palm of my hand."

"You do have very good hands." She twisted against his fingers.

He liked how she sucked in her breath when he touched her. He liked it a lot. Impatience roared through him. He tugged the silky panties down out of the way. They fell to her ankles and she stepped out of them.

He was shaking a little now with the force of his need. He had to concentrate hard in order to unfasten his belt and unzip his trousers. When he finally freed himself, her eyes widened at the sight of his erection. Then she smiled slowly and reached down to stroke him.

He caught one of her smooth, sweetly rounded thighs, elevated her leg and folded it around his waist. She was open and ready. When he teased her tight little bud she gasped. He seized her other leg and tucked it around himself.

He braced her against the wall and thrust into her hot, snug body.

"Emmett." She clutched at his shoulders to steady herself.

Again and again he drove himself into her. She clung to him as though he were a life raft in a storm, hanging on as if she would never let go.

When he was on the brink of his own release he pulled out of her spicy heat.

"No, wait," she yelped. "I'm almost there."

"Don't worry, we're both going to get where we're going."

He turned her around and bent her over at the waist in front of the cabinet of curiosities. Automatically she reached out with both hands to grasp the edge of the cabinet to steady herself.

"What in the — ? Oh, my." She looked at him in the mirror. Her eyes glowed with a mix of astonishment and sensual delight. "This is . . . interesting."

He fitted his palms to her buttocks, savoring the firm, full curves. "It's even better from my point of view."

He positioned himself and entered her slick, tight vagina again, hard and fast.

She made a soft, exquisitely excited little sound and moved her lovely rear back a little, enabling him to go even deeper.

He took one hand off her waist and reached around and under her sleek belly to find the magic button.

When he made contact with her sensitive clitoris this time she gave a near soundless shriek and convulsed around him.

He went over the edge with her, pumping himself into her for what seemed like forever, until he was spent and dry.

She came back to her senses an eon or two later and discovered that she was lying on her back on the hall carpet. Emmett was sprawled heavily on top of her, his head pillowed on her breast. Somewhere along the line he must have turned off the overhead ceiling fixture because the space was drenched in shadows. A truly thoughtful gesture, she decided. Otherwise, in her current position, she would have been staring straight up into a very bright light.

"Emmett?"

"Mmmph?" He did not open his eyes.

She threaded her fingers through his hair. "Just wondered if you were asleep yet."

"Almost." He sounded as if he'd been drugged.

Once the afterburn buzz dissipated, exhaustion overtook a hunter very swiftly.

"We need to get you upstairs."

"Nah. I'll sleep here tonight."

"On the floor? I don't think that's such a good idea." She tried to wriggle out from underneath him. "You'll wake up all stiff and sore."

"Don't mind," he mumbled. But he shifted slightly, freeing her.

"Come on, you can make it up the stairs." She crouched beside him, grabbed him under one arm, and tried to haul him upright.

"Forget it." He opened one eye. "Isn't going to work."

"Yes, it is. Just stay awake for another three minutes and we'll manage."

He groaned but he got his feet under him and stood, swaying slightly. "You're sort of bossy, you know that?"

"We all have our talents."

She steadied him while he dragged himself up the stairs. When they reached the top she shoved him into the bedroom. He dropped like a large, heavy boulder onto the bed.

"Satisfied?" he mumbled into the pillow.

She smiled to herself, thinking of the events that had just taken place downstairs in the front hall. "Very."

"Hell of a wedding night, huh?"

"I'll certainly never forget it."

"Not the way I planned it," he said, barely whispering now.

"I know," she said gently. "But it doesn't matter." She unfolded the blanket at the foot of the bed and spread it over him. "Emmett?"

"Mmm?"

"There's something I want to ask you. Something very personal."

"This probably isn't a good time." His words were so slurred she could barely make them out. "Can't think straight anymore."

Which was exactly why she had decided to ask the question, she thought. But there was no need to explain.

"Earlier tonight you were afraid to make love to me while you were rezzed from the amber meltdown. Did you really believe I'd think that you were some kind of sex-crazed beast who couldn't control himself?"

There was such a long silence that she thought he'd fallen asleep.

"Didn't want you to think I was just another hunter," he muttered. "Your opinion of hunters is kinda low, y'know?"

"You're not like any other hunter." She tucked the blanket in around him. "You're different."

"Yeah?" he growled. "How?"

"You're my husband."

She walked out of the room and shut the door very quietly behind her.

16

The doorbell chimed imperiously the following morning just as Lydia started to pour a second cup of rez-tea for Emmett.

"I'm up, I'll get it." She put down the pot and walked out of the kitchen.

Fuzz, who had been eating his breakfast out of a dish on the floor, abandoned his eggs and toast to scamper after her.

"If it's one of the neighbors complaining about that little scene with the ghost last night," Emmett called after her, "let me handle it."

"Other than a few scorch marks on our terrace, there was no damage done," she said over her shoulder. "The neighbors have no grounds for complaint."

"They may feel a little differently about the matter," he warned.

When she reached the hall she took a quick look around to make sure that there was no evidence of the Grand Consummation. Everything appeared to be in order, she decided, but she knew that she would never walk into this house again without thinking of her wedding night.

She opened the door and found thirteen-year-old Zane Hoyt, her neighbor at the Dead City

View Apartments, on the front step. He was dressed in his favorite ghost-hunter-wannabe outfit complete with a big chunk of amber around his neck. Fuzz hopped into his arms.

"Hi, Lydia." Zane beamed at her as he scratched Fuzz. "Aunt Olinda says you and Mr. London got married yesterday. It's in all the papers, she says. I came by to see if it was really true."

"It's true."

Zane had lost his parents at an early age. He was being raised by his aunt. His greatest ambition in life was to become a ghost-hunter. He certainly had the psi-talent for it, but Lydia had been hoping to steer him toward a more respectable career path.

Now that Emmett had entered Zane's life, however, she had a hunch that she was fighting a losing battle. Zane had immediately glommed onto Emmett as a father figure. Hero worship was powerful stuff.

Zane leaned forward to examine her left hand. "Wow, you've got a ring and everything. That is so high-rez." His face lit with excitement. "You're married to the hottest ghost-hunter of them all. Mr. London's the boss of the whole Guild now, you know?"

"Trust me, I'm aware of that."

"Aunt Olinda says to give you her congratulations. She says we're gonna watch you and Mr. London walk into the fancy party at Restoration Hall on the rez-screen tonight."

"I'll be sure to wave." She glanced at her watch. "Shouldn't you be in school?"

"I'm on my way. Just wanted to see what was going on for myself so I could tell everyone in class."

Emmett sauntered into the front hall and opened the closet door. "Morning, Zane. How's it going today?"

"I'm doing fine, Mr. London, except for that stupid test I've got to take this morning. I just stopped by to see Lydia and you and tell you that I think it's really great that you two got married."

"Thanks. Appreciate that." Emmett hooked his jacket over his shoulder and picked up his briefcase. He gave Lydia a brief but thorough good-bye kiss. Then he looked at Zane. "I'm on my way into the office. I'll give you a ride to school."

"All *right*." Zane almost levitated with excitement. "Wait'll the guys see me getting out of the Guild boss's own personal Slider."

He handed Fuzz to Lydia and whipped around to race toward the vehicle.

"You've certainly made his day," Lydia said to Emmett.

A sexy gleam lit his eyes. "You certainly made my night, Mrs. London. Sorry I zoned out just as things were getting interesting."

She felt the heat rise in her cheeks. "If things had gotten any more *interesting*, I wouldn't be able to move this morning."

His amusement vanished. A watchful expression replaced the sensual laughter in his gaze.

"Are you . . . okay?" he asked very quietly.

She folded her arms and leaned one shoulder against the edge of the door frame. "I hope this won't dent your hunter pride too much but I gotta tell you that I'm just fine this morning."

The tightness at the corners of his mouth eased. "Just fine?"

She wrinkled her nose. "You didn't scare me one little bit last night, London, if that's what's worrying you."

His mouth quirked. "You're sure?"

"Positive."

"I didn't make you even a little bit nervous?"

"Nope."

"Huh." He took his foot down off the step. "Well, I'll have to see what I can do to improve my technique tonight. Maybe if I put my mind to it I can summon a really, really big ghost and induce an even hotter afterburn."

"Don't bother with the ghost. You don't need one." She grinned. "Got news for you, London. Last night was interesting, but it wasn't all that much different from your usual style."

"Damn. You didn't think the part where you were bent over the cabinet watching us in the mirror was just a little bit different?"

"It was merely a clever variation on one of your many excellent themes." She came away from the door frame, adjusted the collar of his shirt, and gave him a wifely peck on his cheek. "Now go to work like a good Guild boss. I'll see you tonight. What time do we have to leave for our big scene at the ball?"

"Hell, I've got so much going on I nearly forgot about the Restoration Ball." Emmett frowned. "Tamara said it starts at eight. She suggested that we plan to put in an appearance around nine."

Lydia stifled a sigh. Things had been going along quite pleasantly this morning until Tamara's name came up.

"She wants us to make an entrance, is that it?" she asked politely.

"The whole point of this exercise is to make sure that everyone, especially the media, takes note of the fact that the Guild boss and his wife are part of mainstream society here in Cadence."

Forget playing Amberella tonight, Lydia told herself. This isn't a romantic fairy tale. It's all about grabbing some good PR for the Guild.

"The image thing." She nodded. "Got it."

"There will be a lot of traffic downtown tonight. We'd better leave here around eight-thirty."

"I'll be ready," she promised.

He turned to head toward the Slider and then paused one last time. "You're sure there wasn't anything a little out of the ordinary about last night?"

"Seemed like a normal evening at home."

"Huh." He shook his head and continued on toward the car. "Sure seemed pretty unusual to me."

"Just goes to show how dull and boring your life was before you met me, London."

He looked back at her, his teeth flashing in a wicked grin. "Trust me, my eyes have been opened."

Melanie glanced up from the morning edition of the *Tattler* when Lydia paused in the doorway of the office. "Well, well, well, if it isn't the blushing bride. Shrimp's looking for you. He's busily scheduling about a hundred special tours to be escorted personally by the wife of the new Guild boss, her very own self."

Lydia grimaced. "Thanks for the warning."

"How was the wedding night?"

"That's an extremely personal question. But since you ask, one of the more interesting highlights occurred when a huge ghost materialized on the terrace at what can only be described as an inconvenient moment."

Melanie stopped grinning. "Uh-oh. Not good. Are we talking about a seriously large ghost?"

"It was nasty, Mel. Biggest UDEM I've ever seen outside the walls. It probably would have set fire to the house if Emmett hadn't been able to de-rez it."

"Sheesh. You think it had something to do with the attack on Mercer Wyatt?"

"That's my guess but Emmett is still trying to figure out the connection."

Melanie shuddered. "Looks like maybe there is some downside to being married to a Guild boss, after all. Who would have guessed?"

"I gotta tell you, life was a lot simpler when Emmett was just a business consultant." Lydia studied the copy of the *Tattler*. "What do the headlines look like today? The box out front was empty."

"I know. I got the very last copy. This issue is probably sold out all over town." Melanie propped the tabloid up in front of herself so that Lydia could read the giant headlines.

GUILD BOSS WEDS
MYSTERY MISTRESS IN MC
Couple Will Appear at Formal Ball Tonight

Lydia anxiously examined the photo of herself standing in front of the entrance to Designs by Finella. She breathed a sigh of relief.

"Could have been worse," she said.

"It is worse, in my opinion." Melanie shook the paper in amused disgust. "A lot worse. You will notice that they cropped me right out of the photo. I was standing next to you when you gave your big quote to the media, if you will recall. But there's no sign of me in this picture."

"I would have been delighted to have been the one who got cropped." Lydia made to move off down the hall.

"Wait a sec." Melanie put down the newspaper. "Jack is taking me to lunch today. Want to come with us? My treat?"

"Thanks, I'd love to, but I'm pretty busy at the moment."

Melanie cleared her throat. "Uh, as a favor to me."

That stopped Lydia in her tracks. "A favor to you? We have lunch together all the time. How would I be doing you any special favors if I let you treat me today?"

"It's for Jack, actually." Melanie's cheeks turned a surprising shade of pink. "I like him a lot. We're even starting to talk about an MC."

"You are? I hadn't realized it was that serious."

"He's a great guy and it would thrill him to pieces to be able to tell his pals at the Guild Hall that he went to lunch with the boss's wife," Melanie finished in a little rush of words.

"Ah, so that's it." Lydia smiled ruefully. "Sure. Let's all go to lunch together. Why not? I've got to eat to keep up my strength for my grand entrance at the ball tonight, anyway."

"Thanks, I appreciate this. Jack is going to get such a kick out of it."

"No problem. But under the circumstances, I insist you let me pay for the meal."

"No, really, that's okay."

"Forget it." She winked. "I'll put it on the Guild's tab."

Melanie blinked and then relaxed back into a

cheerful smile. "Well, in that case, I think I'll make reservations at the Riverside Grill. It's one of the most expensive places in town. I've always wanted to eat there."

"Go for it," Lydia said.

"You know, what with shopping at Designs by Finella and eating at high-end restaurants, my social life has certainly become a lot more classy since you got this Guild boss–wife gig."

The phone on Lydia's desk rang a few minutes before noon. She reached for the instrument without taking her attention off a catalog of newly acquired antiquities being offered for sale by one of the more reliable galleries on Ruin Row.

The object that had caught her attention was an example of what the experts called a funerary column. No one knew for certain that the elaborately worked objects had actually been used in alien burial ceremonies but since they were often found in the vicinity of sarcophagi, they were presumed to be associated with death rituals. Shrimpton's House of Ancient Horrors specialized in the spooky and the morbid. The funerary urn would fit in nicely with the rest of the collection in the Tomb Wing.

"Shrimpton's House of Ancient Horrors, curator's office," she said, mentally calculating how low she could go on the offer for the funerary column.

"I'm calling for Lydia Smith." The woman on the other end sounded hesitant.

"This is Lydia."

"Are you the person who phoned the Old Frequency College alumni office trying to locate people who knew Troy Burgis?"

"Yes." Lydia closed the catalog quickly. "I am. Who is this?"

"Karen Price. I was a year behind Troy Burgis at Old Frequency College."

"Did you know him well?"

Karen made an irritated sound. "I don't think anyone knew Troy Burgis well. He was a very bizarre person."

"What was your connection to him?"

"My roommate was a member of his band."

"That would be Andrea Preston?"

"Yes. In addition to playing the harmonic flute in his band, she dated him. They were a very intense couple for a while. I met him a few times when he came to pick her up or bring her back to the dorm after a date."

"What was Burgis like?"

"To me he was sort of freakish, scary, even. But Andrea seemed to be fascinated by him."

"What made you think that Burgis was weird?"

There was a short pause on the other end before Karen said hesitantly, "First, will you tell me why you're interested in him?"

"Yes, of course. A former professor of his died from a drug overdose recently. I found a copy of a newspaper story about Burgis's disappearance in the professor's apartment. He had called me shortly before he died and left a message saying that he wanted to speak to me about an urgent matter. But I got there too late. I'm trying to put it all together, if you see what I mean."

"You think that maybe this urgent matter the professor wanted to discuss was related to the old clipping about Burgis?"

"I think it's a distinct possibility, yes."

"What was the name of this professor who OD'd?" Karen asked.

"Dr. Lawrence Maltby."

"Maltby. I remember him. He was with the Department of Para-archaeology at Old Freq. I took a couple of classes from him. Troy Burgis was in one of them. So was Andrea. That's how she and Burgis met, in fact. They started studying together. The next thing I knew, she was in his band and staying out all night with him. Evidently Burgis's idea of a hot date was to go down into the catacombs to have sex."

"Was Burgis a hunter? Did he like to de-rez a ghost or two before making love with his girlfriend?"

"No." Karen sounded surprised. "Burgis wasn't a ghost-hunter. He was a tangler. A very, very good one, according to Andrea, although he hadn't had any technical training. But, then, Andrea idolized him. She would have believed anything he said."

"What was Andrea like?"

Karen sighed. "Well, for starters she was incredibly beautiful. Sort of ethereal in a way. When she walked into a room, everyone turned to look at her. I remember feeling sorry for her, though, because she had been badly abused as a child and was completely estranged from her family. She was all alone in the world."

"Do you think she really loved Burgis?"

"Absolutely devoted to him. But I am equally positive that he did not love her. Burgis was obsessed with only two things. One of them was pulse-rock music. He went so far as to rent a studio so that his band could record a half dozen tapes, but they never caught the attention of any of the big music companies."

"What was his other obsession?"

"Vincent Lee Vance."

"*Vance?*" Lydia was so startled that she dropped the pen she had been using to make notes. It rolled off the desk and bounced on the floor. "The rebel leader?"

"I told you, Burgis was weird. When she first started dating him, Andrea spoke about him fairly freely. She said that Burgis was fascinated with Vance and the Era of Discord. He dreamed of finding Vance's first secret headquarters. If you recall your history lessons, it was supposedly located in the catacombs under Old Frequency."

"Right." Lydia leaned down and picked up the pen. "They think that he established two secret underground bunkers during the Era of Discord. The second site is thought to be lost somewhere in the tunnels around here."

According to the old legends, Vance and his lover-tangler, Helen Chandler, had fled to the second headquarters to commit suicide after the defeat at the Last Battle of Old Cadence. A lot of people had searched for the sites of both of Vance's headquarters in the past hundred years but neither had ever been found.

"Andrea told me that Burgis was determined to discover the first site," Karen said. "He spent a lot of time underground, untrapping tunnels in the unmapped sectors around Old Frequency."

"Going down into the catacombs alone night after night without proper equipment or a trained team would have been foolhardy. Even if Burgis was good enough to handle the traps, what did he do about the ghosts? He would have encountered any number of them in the unmapped sectors."

"Burgis usually took a couple of his friends with him, two guys who were also in the band. They were both strong dissonance-energy para-rezes although I don't think either of them joined the Guild to get formal training."

Lydia sat up very straight on the edge of her chair. "Jason Clark and Norman Fairbanks, by any chance?"

"How did you know their names?"

"According to the newspaper article, they were with him the day he disappeared."

"That's right, they were," Karen said slowly.

"What about your roommate, Andrea? Any chance you can put me in touch with her?"

There was a short, brittle silence.

"She's dead, Miss Smith."

"What?"

"She died in a boating accident a couple of months after Burgis vanished. At the time some of us believed that she had killed herself because of what happened to Burgis. As I said, she was devoted to him."

Lydia exhaled and sank back in her chair. "How sad."

"Yes," Karen's voice sharpened. "But, as it turned out, not a unique occurrence."

"I beg your pardon?"

"Andrea wasn't the only one who had a fatal accident after Burgis disappeared. In the next six months Norman Fairbanks and Jason Clark died, too. One suffered a terrible fall in the course of a hiking trip in the mountains and the other was killed in a fire."

Lydia swallowed. "Every member of Burgis's old band is dead? Are you serious?"

"Very serious. What's more, none of the bodies was ever found." Karen paused a beat. "Not that anyone looked very hard."

"What about the families? Didn't they demand an investigation?"

"There were no families to be concerned. You see, Burgis, Andrea, Jason Clark, and Norman Fairbanks all had one thing in common. None of them had any close relatives. Each was alone in the world."

"This is getting stranger by the minute."

"Yes." Karen's voice was flat and grim. "And that, Miss Smith, is the reason I called when the alumni secretary contacted me and said that you were asking questions about Troy Burgis. I thought you should know that people who got close to Burgis fifteen years ago tended to disappear."

"What do you think happened to Burgis and the members of his band, Karen?"

"I don't know and I don't want to find out. But if there is a mystery connected with those disappearances I can tell you one thing for certain. It had something to do with whatever it was Burgis found down there in the catacombs."

Lydia frowned. "Hang on here. Are you saying you think Burgis and his friends have been living underground for the past fifteen years? That's impossible. They would have to eat. They would need sunlight. No one could tolerate living in the catacombs full time for years on end."

"Maybe it would drive most normal people crazy, Miss Smith. But what I'm trying to tell you is that Troy Burgis was not normal. What's more, he had the ability to attract other lost-soul types, people who were searching for something or someone to believe in, people like Andrea and Jason Clark and Norman Fairbanks. Those three would have followed him anywhere."

Lydia studied her notes. "Looks like he didn't

bother to make friends with *every* lost soul he came across, just a few who were useful to him. He obviously handpicked them: A beautiful woman to keep him company and two loyal hunters to act as bodyguards down in the catacombs."

"Exactly. Troy Burgis was one scary guy back in college. If he's still alive, he will be even more dangerous now."

17

The Riverside Grill was located, astonishingly, on the banks of the river. It was a known hangout for the city's powerbrokers, politicians, celebrities, and those who wanted to be seen dining in the company of such folk.

Jack Brodie was waiting for them. He lounged against a wall in the entryway trying to look cool. But his khaki-and-leather attire and the big chunk of amber in his belt buckle didn't blend into the elegant ambience of the Riverside Grill. Lydia could see that he was nervous.

He brightened with unabashed relief when he caught sight of Lydia and Melanie coming through the door. Detaching himself from the wall, he hurried toward them.

"I think there's some kinda mistake," he said in a low voice. He cast a quick glance back toward the maitre d's station where an imperious-looking individual directed the seating. "That guy says we don't have a reservation."

"That's not true." Melanie stiffened with indignation. "I called first thing this morning and was told that there was no problem getting a table for three."

"What name did you use?" Lydia asked.

"Yours, of course. Well, Emmett's, I guess, if you want to get technical. You think I could get us in here? I told them that Mrs. Emmett London and two friends would be arriving at twelve-fifteen sharp."

"I'll go talk to the maitre d'," Lydia said.

She went to the podium and tried a friendly smile. The maitre d' did not return the smile.

"I'm Mrs. London. I believe you have a reservation for me and my guests?"

The maitre d' frowned. "You must be mistaken, madam. The reservation I have is for Mrs. Emmett London, the wife of the new head of the Cadence Guild."

"That would be me."

The maitre d' looked down his long nose. "Are you claiming to be *the* Mrs. London?"

"Yes." Lydia put a little steel into her smile.

The maitre d' raised his brows and smirked at Melanie and Jack standing behind her. "And these are your luncheon guests?"

"Yes."

He shook his head, evidently amused. "I've had some brassy people try to talk their way into this restaurant but you, madam, take the grand prize for nerve. The real Mrs. London is the wife of one of the most powerful men in the city. I doubt very much that she would be dressed in a cheap little suit that was obviously bought on sale in the basement of a discount department store. Furthermore, I think it is safe to say that the real Mrs. London would not be lunching with a woman who dresses like a hooker and a hunter who is obviously from the very lowest ranks of the Guild."

"That does it." Lydia reached across the podium and grabbed the maitre d' by his discreetly striped tie. "Say whatever you want about my clothes, but you will apologize to my two guests right now or else I will pick up the phone and call my husband and have *him* tell you to apologize. Understood?"

Stunned outrage and then the first hints of uncertainty flashed across the maitre d's face. "Uh —"

"Do you really want to annoy the new Guild boss?" Lydia asked in a very low voice. "If so, I'll be happy to dial his number so that you can explain just why you won't seat me and my guests."

A woman in a severe blue suit rushed toward them from a narrow hallway.

"What is going on here, Barclay?" The woman stopped short, appalled at the sight of Lydia holding the maitre d' hostage by his tie. *"Mrs. London."*

Barclay's eyes widened. "This isn't the real Mrs. London." But he was no longer sure of himself. "It can't be."

"Of course this is the real Mrs. London, Barclay," the woman snapped. She gave Lydia an apologetic smile. "I recognize her. She was on the front cover of the *Tattler* yesterday."

"I'm glad somebody around here has the

sense to read the tabloids." Lydia released Barclay's tie. "Who are you?" she said to the woman in the blue suit.

"I'm the assistant manager, Julia Sanders. I'm so sorry if there's been a misunderstanding."

"Barclay, here, is the only one who doesn't seem to understand the situation," Lydia said. "My friends and I have a reservation for lunch. We'd like a table for three, please."

"Certainly." Julia shot a quelling glance at Barclay. "I'll handle this."

"Yes, Miss Sanders," Barclay said weakly. He readjusted his tie with trembling fingers.

"With a view of the river," Lydia added.

"Naturally."

"And I also want an apology from Barclay."

"Of course."

"The steak's not bad," Jack announced midway through lunch. "Not much to it, though. My mom usually cooks up about three times as much when I go home for dinner. And look at these itty-bitty veggies. Never seen anything like 'em. Wonder how they get them to grow that small?"

"The more expensive the restaurant, the smaller the portions," Melanie said with a wise air. "How do you think all these rich folks stay so slim? It's not like any of them actually work for a living."

"Huh." Jack put the last of the steak into his

mouth and chewed reflectively. "Hadn't thought about that."

"I can't wait to see the dessert tray," Melanie confided. She looked at Lydia. "Hey, you're not eating your fish. What's the matter? Is it bad? If it is, you're supposed to send it back in a fancy place like this."

"No, it's fine." Lydia jerked herself out of her reverie and forced a smile. "I'm just not very hungry today, that's all."

Melanie chuckled. "Too much excitement lately, what with getting married yesterday and the big Restoration Ball coming up tonight."

"Speaking of excitement," Jack said around a mouthful of miniature vegetables, "word down at the Guild Hall is that there might be a little at headquarters this afternoon."

"Excitement?" Lydia stopped pushing her expensive entrée around her plate and frowned at him. "What are you talking about?"

"You must have heard about that big ghost that someone sent after Mr. London last night?"

"I was there. I'm married to Mr. London, remember?"

"Oh, yeah, right. Well, some of the guys down at the hall say that was probably someone testing the boss in order to get a feel for just how good he is, y'know?"

Lydia got a sinking sensation in the pit of her stomach and knew she couldn't blame it on the fish. "What do you mean?"

"Remember I told you that there was talk

about a formal challenge? Well, word is that Foster Dorning may be planning to issue one this afternoon."

"A Council challenge?" Aware that her voice was rising, Lydia glanced hurriedly around and then leaned across the table. "You told me that no one could challenge a married Guild chief. Something about Guild wife rights."

Jack looked perplexed by her reaction. "Yeah, well, the way it works, see, is that the boss's wife has to demand her rights in front of the full Council. Didn't I explain that part?"

"No, you did not." Lydia tossed her napkin aside and leaped to her feet. "I think that meeting is scheduled for two o'clock. I've got to hurry."

"Hey, what's the rush?" Jack asked. "Melanie wants to see the dessert tray."

But startled comprehension had appeared in Melanie's face. She, too, was on her feet. "I'm going to skip dessert. Come on, Lydia, I'll drive you in my car. It's raining, you'll never get a cab."

Jack looked completely bewildered now. "Where are you two going?"

"To demand my Guild wife rights," Lydia snapped, struggling to keep her voice to a whisper.

"I get it, you're worried about Mr. London." Jack gave her a reassuring grin. "Don't sweat it, ma'am. Got a feeling he can take care of himself."

Lydia did not stop to argue. "Let's go, Mel."

Heads turned when they dashed across the restaurant toward the front door. Lydia ignored the attention. When she passed Barclay's station she paused briefly. Barclay cringed back.

"Be sure my other guest gets dessert," she snapped. "Send the bill to Guild Headquarters. Twenty percent for the waiters. Don't bother adding anything extra for yourself, Barclay. I'll check."

Outside she jumped into the passenger seat of Melanie's small Float. Melanie scrambled behind the wheel, rezzed the engine, and shot out of the restaurant parking lot.

She glanced in the rearview mirror. "I think it's probably safe to say that the management of the Riverside Grill will definitely recognize you the next time."

"I can't believe it," Lydia stated.

"The impression we made back there?"

"No, the way I screwed up with this Guild wife rights thing. Why didn't Jack *tell* me that just getting married wasn't enough? If only he'd explained sooner how it works."

Melanie whipped the little vehicle around a corner and then shot Lydia a strange glance. "That's why you told the media that you and Emmett were going to get married, isn't it? You did it to protect him from a Council challenge."

"He's got enough problems. He only took the job because Wyatt asked him to do it. It's supposed to be a temporary arrangement."

"Calm down. Emmett's one heck of a para-rez. You've seen him work. Jack's right, he can probably handle anything anyone on the Council can throw at him."

"After my Lost Weekend experience, I don't trust hunters. Two of them once set me up and then lied through their teeth about it."

"Admittedly you had a very negative experience with some members of the local Guild. I can understand why it left you with a poor impression. But we're talking about the Guild Council, here, not just a couple of low-ranking hunters. These guys are at the very top of the organization."

"The thing is, Mel, what if there's something big going on at the top of the Guild? What if a couple of the Council members are working together to stage a takeover? Maybe they're trying to destabilize the power structure. That would explain the attempt on Wyatt and the ghost attack last night."

"You're talking about some sort of conspiracy here?"

"It wouldn't surprise me. Emmett won't listen to me, but I can't get past the idea that this is old-fashioned Guild politics in action and that means there's a very good chance that someone on the Council is involved."

"You don't think maybe you're getting downright paranoid?"

"When it comes to the Cadence Guild, a little paranoia is a healthy thing."

Melanie whipped the Float around another corner and came to a sliding halt at the sight of the barricades that blocked the street. A marching band filled the intersection. Flags waved and music blared. People clogged the sidewalks, cheering.

"Damn," Lydia said. "I forgot that the Restoration Day parade always takes a route that goes straight past the Guild headquarters. I'll get out here. I can make better time on foot."

She opened the passenger side door of the Float and extricated herself from it. "Thanks, Mel. See you back at Shrimp's."

"Be careful," Melanie yelled after her. "And don't forget you've got an appointment at the salon later this afternoon."

Lydia waved reassuringly, gripped the strap of her shoulder bag, and plunged into the crowd. When she reached the entrance of the high-rise office tower that housed the offices of the Guild she had to wriggle through a knot of office workers who had come outside to watch the parade. No one tried to stop her from entering the building.

She raced into the lobby only to find her path blocked by a guard dressed in khaki and leather.

She assumed what she hoped was an air of authority and prepared to use Emmett's name once again as a talisman. "I'm Mrs. London. I'm here to see my husband."

The guard grinned. "Yes, ma'am. I recognize

you from the pictures in the papers. Private elevator on the left, ma'am. I'll rez the key code for you."

"Thank you."

She stepped into the hushed confines of the paneled elevator and was whisked to the top of the tower so quickly her ears popped.

When she stepped out a moment later she found herself in a plush, carpeted lobby.

"Good afternoon, Mrs. London." A small, tidy little man rose from behind a vast desk. "The guard informed me that you were on the way up here."

"Hello," she said. "Who are you?"

"I'm Perkins." He bobbed his head. "How may I assist you?"

"I'm here to see my husband."

"I'm so sorry." Perkins appeared genuinely distraught. "Mr. London is in a very important meeting of the entire Council at the moment. I couldn't possibly interrupt."

Oh, damn. She might already be too late. "When did it start?"

"Just a few minutes ago. It won't last long. There's only one item on the agenda."

"Where is this meeting held?"

"In the Council chambers, of course." Perkins angled his head in the direction of a closed door. "If you don't mind waiting —"

"No problem."

"If you'll follow me, there's a nice sitting area in here." Perkins turned to lead the way. "You'll have a wonderful view of the parade. Can I get you some rez-tea?"

"That would be great, Perkins. Thanks."

When he turned his back to her, she spun around and sprinted in the opposite direction, intent on reaching the closed door of the Council chambers before Perkins realized he'd been duped.

She actually had her hand on the gleaming doorknob before he comprehended that she had not followed him.

"*Mrs. London*," he squawked, appalled. "Wait. You can't go in there. You mustn't —"

She turned the knob, yanked open the door, and walked smartly into the chamber.

18

Emmett and ten other men, most of them much older than him, were seated at a great semicircular table. They were all dressed in modern business suits that looked oddly out of place. She realized that the popular images of the ghost-hunters' Council came from the historical films and photos that dated from the Era of Discord. In the old movies and pictures the members of the Council were always shown wearing the traditional robes of office that dated from that time.

But aside from the modern attire, she had a hunch that very little had changed. You could feel the power in the room, she thought. Not just the low-level buzz of psi power that was palpable when so many strong para-rezes were gathered together in a small space, but another kind, the sort that clung to a group that had operated under its own secret rules and codes for decades.

The Guild had functioned outside the mainstream legal system from inception. It accorded superficial deference and polite respect to the civil authorities and the courts but everyone knew in reality it was immune to them. The old-fashioned hierarchical system had worked reasonably well down through the years because there was a fair amount of truth in the old saying *the Guild polices its own.*

You had to hand it to the ghost-hunters, she thought. They had been able to maintain their traditional ways and clean up financially at the same time because they'd always had a knack for selecting strong, savvy leadership.

For the first time it struck her quite forcibly just how strong and savvy Emmett had to be if he had, in fact, managed to mainstream the Resonance Guild, as the media claimed. It meant that he had had to control and steer a bunch of tough, powerful men like these into a future that none of them would have welcomed.

She recognized the ten members of the Cadence Guild Council from photos that she had seen in the news over the years. All but one, Foster Dorning, were longtime members. In front of each man sat a chunk of solid amber carved in an octagonal design.

Tamara Wyatt was also present, looking elegant and very tense. She was not seated at the great council table but rather in a chair that Lydia suspected was designed for an honored guest.

Everyone turned to look at Lydia when she moved into the room. A shocked silence fell. With the exception of Emmett, everyone wore expressions of blank-faced astonishment. Clearly the members of the Cadence Guild Council were not accustomed to having their meetings inter-rupted.

Emmett's hard face and eyes gave no indica-tion of his reaction to her presence but she did not need to be a mind reader to figure out that he was not thrilled.

"Gentlemen," he said, rising deliberately from his position of authority at the head of the table, "allow me to introduce my wife, Lydia."

The men all stood politely, nodded brusquely, and murmured an acknowledgment of the in-troduction.

"Mrs. Wyatt, you've already met my wife," Emmett added, still speaking in that cold, formal tone.

"Yes, of course. A pleasure to see you again, Lydia."

Yeah, right, Lydia thought. She and Tamara had met on only one previous occasion, a small dinner party at Mercer Wyatt's mansion. She was pretty sure that both of them had known from the get-go that they were not fated to be great buddies.

She was a little taken aback by the signs of strain that marked Tamara's patrician profile. But the woman had been under a lot of stress lately, she reminded herself.

She inclined her head, once. "Mrs. Wyatt."

Perkins hovered anxiously in the doorway. "Mr. London?"

"It's all right, Perkins," Emmett said. "I'll handle this."

"Yes, sir." Clearly relieved, Perkins backed out of the room and closed the heavy door.

Emmett fixed Lydia with a look that would have frozen a ghost. "I'm a little busy at the moment, my dear. Perhaps you would be more comfortable waiting in my office."

She swallowed heavily and collected her nerve. "I'll be quite comfortable right here, thank you." She walked quickly across the chamber and sat down next to Tamara. "Mrs. Wyatt and I have so much in common." She gave all of the men at the table a cool smile. "What with both of us being *Guild wives* and all."

To Lydia's amazement it was Tamara who backed her up.

"As the wife of the acting head of the Cadence Guild, Mrs. London has as much right to be here at this meeting as I do," Tamara said with icy authority.

Lydia was not sure why Tamara was leaping to her defense but she decided she had better not waste the opportunity.

"Just another Guild wife right," Lydia said, crossing her legs very deliberately. She gave the Council members a blazingly bright smile. "You know what they say about rights, use 'em or lose 'em. I'm here to make sure mine get used. All of them."

At the table, ten jaws dropped. Emmett's went rigid. Veiled respect and something that might have been gratitude lit Tamara's eyes.

Understanding had dawned in the Council chamber. Lydia saw relief on the faces of most of the men. Only one of the council members looked angry.

"I'm delighted to see that, as a new Guild wife, you are aware of our traditions," Tamara said smoothly.

"You bet." Lydia regarded the table full of men. "Don't mind me, gentlemen. I'll just sit here very quietly and not bother anyone. Unless, of course, I feel I need to speak up in order to defend my Guild wife rights."

Emmett's eyes were ice cold but he turned his attention back to the meeting.

"We will return to the business at hand, gentlemen." He nodded at an older man at the far end of the table. "Mr. Chao, please call for a vote."

Chao rose quickly. "All those in favor of accepting the appointment of Emmett London as acting Guild Chief until Mercer Wyatt is able to resume his duties, please so signify with amber."

One by one each of the ten Council members moved his chunk of amber out toward the center of the table. The last to vote was the youngest member of the council. Lydia estimated that he was in his mid-thirties.

Foster Dorning, she thought.

Dorning hesitated before casting his vote. He stared straight at Lydia. She was shaken by the rage that flashed across his face. But he recovered quickly and pushed his amber octagon toward the center of the table.

She could have sworn that, with the notable exceptions of Dorning and Emmett, everyone else breathed a collective sigh of relief.

"There being no objections to the appointment, it is hereby confirmed," Chao announced. He sat down, pulled a handkerchief from his pocket, and mopped his brow. "This Council looks forward to advising you, Mr. London."

"Thank you, gentlemen." Emmett got to his feet. "The confirmation vote being the only item on the agenda today, this meeting is hereby adjourned."

One by one the members of the Council filed out of the chamber.

When the last of the men had departed Lydia took one look at Emmett and sucked in a deep breath.

She had never seen him look so angry.

She glanced at the door and considered a run for the elevator. That would be the coward's way out, she chided herself. She wasn't afraid of Emmett's wrath. Then again there was that Old Earth saying about discretion being the better part of valor.

"Thank you, Lydia." Tamara rose from her chair. "I must say, your timing was excellent. I warned Emmett that Dorning was planning to issue a formal challenge. That was the very last thing we needed right now." She frowned curiously. "How did you find out about it?"

"I heard a rumor," Lydia said. "At lunch."

"If you don't mind, Tamara." Emmett's voice was much too soft. "I'd like to talk to my wife in private."

Annoyance glittered in Tamara's eyes but she nodded calmly. "If you'll excuse me, Lydia, I'll be on my way back to the hospital."

Lydia told herself that some sort of polite inquiry was probably in order. "How is Mr. Wyatt doing?"

"He's in stable condition but he's still heavily sedated." Tamara sounded abruptly weary. "The doctors say that the most serious concern now is the psi burn he got from the ghost he used to stop the bleeding. It took a lot out of him." She hesitated. "He's not a young man anymore."

She walked out the door and closed it behind her.

A heavy silence descended on the chamber. Lydia braced herself.

Emmett circled the long table, halted in front of it, leaned back, and folded his arms.

"When did you first hear about the tradition of Guild wife rights?" he asked as if he was merely curious.

She cleared her throat. "Quite recently, as a matter of fact."

"I see. Who told you?"

"A friend of Melanie's mentioned it in passing."

"A hunter friend, I assume?"

"Uh-huh. Look, Emmett, I can see you're angry about this but I was only trying to help. When Jack told me that there were rumors of a possible Council challenge brewing and that there was a simple way to stop it, I figured, what the heck, why not just pull the plug on it before it got off the ground."

"I see."

"I knew you would never ask me to help you because you wouldn't want me to think that you were just using me. But we're pretty good friends now and I don't mind, honest."

"Good friends," he repeated neutrally.

"Okay, more than friends," she said cautiously.

"Yeah, I'd say that, seeing as how we're married and all."

She gripped the arms of the chair. "Please don't twist my words. I told you, I was only trying to help."

"That's the real reason for our MC, isn't it? You were just trying to help."

This was not going well. "Jack made it clear that the only way I could protect you from a challenge was if I was legally married to you."

"So your little slip of the tongue to the media yesterday didn't happen because you felt cornered or because you didn't want everyone referring to you as my mystery mistress. It was a calculated move designed to push me into marriage."

She sighed. "You're really pissed, aren't you?"

"Can I assume that the headlines in the *Tattler*

about my Mystery Mistress were not an accident, either?"

She drew a deep breath. "I did sort of pick up the phone and give the paper an anonymous tip."

"Knowing it would lead to us getting married?"

"No." She spread her hands. "Back at the start of this thing I just wanted the media to stop hinting that you had shot Mercer Wyatt because you and he and Tamara were all part of a lovers' triangle. I was afraid that the police might take the gossip seriously. I mean, let's face it, you don't have a very good alibi for the period of time when Wyatt was shot."

"So you figured that if it got out that I had a secret mistress the media would stop implying that I had a motive to shoot Wyatt?"

"Yeah, that's pretty much it." She sagged against the back of the chair. "And then Jack told me about the possible Council challenge and Guild wife rights and this big meeting today. One thing led to another. I just kept getting in deeper and deeper."

"And now we're married."

"Only for a year." She heaved another sigh. "Like I said, I was only trying to help."

He straightened away from the table and went to stand at the window overlooking the parade route far below.

"I don't suppose it occurred to you that I might have wanted Dorning to make a formal challenge?" he said neutrally.

She stared at his broad shoulders, dumb-founded. "For heaven's sake, why?"

"To get the opposition out into the open. In my experience, it's always a lot easier to deal with it that way."

"You mean you *intended* to give Dorning an opening to make a formal challenge?"

"Yes."

"Oh, lord." A terrible sense of doom descended on her. "I screwed things up for you, didn't I?"

"Yes."

She wished the floor would open up beneath her so that she could sink into a catacomb. "I'm sorry."

"Uh-huh."

"How was I supposed to know what was going on?" she demanded. "You never bothered to tell me your plans."

"Don't you get it?" He turned his head to look at her. "I've been doing my best to keep you at arm's length from Guild politics."

"You can't keep me out of this." She shot to her feet, thoroughly incensed now. "I'm your wife. I've got a right to help protect you."

He swung fully around to face her. "I ran the Cadence Guild for six years without the benefit of having a wife to shield me from a formal challenge. I can deal with the likes of Dorning. I don't need your protection, Lydia. Stay out of this."

She pulled herself together. "Of course.

You're absolutely right. What was I thinking? The Guild is your world, not mine. I should never have tried to interfere."

"Lydia —"

She looped the strap of her shoulder bag over her arm and went to the door. "There's one other thing you should know."

"What is that?" he asked.

"I took Jack and Melanie to lunch at the Riverside Grill today. There was a little scene with the maitre d' and I sort of tossed your name around somewhat freely in order to get a table."

"I see."

She drew a deep breath. "And I charged our meals to the Guild."

"The bill will be taken care of," he said quietly.

"Like the dress?"

"Like the dress," he agreed.

She nodded, more depressed than ever. "Just another Guild business expense."

"Yes."

Probably how he thought of their marriage, she decided. Just another business expense.

She let herself out into the reception area and closed the door of the Council chamber very quietly behind her.

He watched the closed door for a long time thinking about how much had gone wrong in the past couple of days. The derailing of his plans to force Dorning's hand was the least of the lengthy string of disasters, he thought. He was a lot more worried about his marriage, which appeared to be on the rocks after less than twenty-four hours.

After a while he opened the door and went out into the hushed lobby. Perkins watched him uneasily.

"I apologize for not handling that well, sir. I regret to say that I did not know what to do with Mrs. London when she arrived. I was completely unprepared —"

"Never mind, Perkins. Few people are ever prepared to deal with Mrs. London."

Perkins relaxed slightly. "She is rather unusual, isn't she? I recall Mr. Wyatt saying something similar when he instructed me to open the file on her."

"File? What the hell are you talking about?"

Perkins trembled in alarm when Emmett advanced toward his desk. "The file on Lydia Smith, sir."

"Wyatt had you open a file on her?"

"Yes, sir."

Emmett planted both hands on the polished surface and leaned toward Perkins. "When?"

"There was a formal inquiry following an unfortunate incident in the catacombs a few months ago. Miss Smith maintained that two Guild members had failed to carry out their assignments properly and as a result she very nearly died underground. The charges were quite serious so naturally Mr. Wyatt was apprised of the situation."

"Where is that file?"

"I'll get it for you, sir." Perkins leaped nimbly to his feet and went to unlock the heavily secured door of the file room.

Emmett watched him open a long, metal drawer and pluck out a yellow folder.

"The results of the inquiry were satisfactory." Perkins handed the folder to Emmett. "The two Guild men were completely exonerated of all charges. But Mr. Wyatt had some lingering concerns about that pair of hunters. He spoke with their commanders and instructed them to watch both men for a while. But in the end, the problem, if there was one, went away."

Emmett opened the file. "What do you mean, it went away?"

"The two hunters resigned from the Guild a couple of months after the inquiry. They said they wanted to pursue other careers." Perkins's shoulders moved in an elegant shrug. "As you are well aware, sir, it is not at all uncommon for hunters who have worked for several years and who have been financially successful to retire from excavation work."

"Yes, I know."

Active ghost-hunting tended to be a young man's, or occasionally a young woman's, game. The need to be constantly alert while underground, the risks of getting singed or badly psi burned, and the constant irritation that came from dealing with arrogant academics who generally viewed hunters as so much dumb muscle, took their toll. A hunter could make good money working the catacombs and many of them chose to take the profits and retire early.

Emmett studied the extremely limited data on the pair of hunters who had been involved in Lydia's Lost Weekend incident. "Where are these two now?"

"I have no idea, sir, but the people down in the retirement benefits department will no doubt have addresses."

Emmett closed the folder with a snap. "Find them, Perkins. I want to talk to them."

"Yes, sir."

19

Lydia was sitting in her tiny living room at six-thirty that evening, drinking a cup of rez-tea and watching the fog roll in over the Dead City, when the phone rang. Fuzz, curled on the sofa beside her, twitched a little in response.

"Don't bother," Lydia said to him, rising to her feet. "I'll get it."

She scooped up the phone. "Hello?"

"Where the hell are you?" Emmett asked. Each word sounded as if it had been cut from a block of ice with a chain saw.

The potent blend of anger and pain and dread that had been brewing in her ever since she had left his office that afternoon pulsed through her. She would not lose her temper, she vowed. She could be just as stone cold as any Guild boss.

"I'm home, of course," she said with exaggerated patience. "As you obviously know since you just dialed this number. Where are you? Still at the office?"

"I'm at my townhouse, which is where you're supposed to be. You live here now."

"No, I don't live at your townhouse. I spent a few nights there, including last night, but I

232

never actually moved my stuff into your place. I'm still paying rent here."

"Damn it, this is about what happened today in my office, isn't it? You're still upset."

"What was I supposed to do after you made it clear you didn't need or want a wife?"

"I never said that. I said I didn't want you involved in Guild business."

"Well, since you're all about Guild business," she retorted, "it's going to be a little tricky staying out of your affairs, isn't it? I'm doing my best, though. That's why I'm keeping this place."

"We're married, Lydia."

"It's just a Marriage of Convenience, remember? I figure *convenience* is the operative word."

"It's the key word, all right, and I don't find it very *convenient* to have my wife living six blocks away. I've got a piece of paper that says you're committed to me for a full year. As far as I'm concerned this MC of ours is the equivalent of a business contract."

She was starting to feel a lot more cheerful, she thought. Emmett wasn't nearly as cold-blooded as he sometimes appeared.

"Nothing in that contract says we have to live together," she pointed out politely.

"Marriage implies a shared residence and you know it."

"Careful, Emmett, you're starting to sound like a lawyer. What are you going to do if I don't move in with you? Sue me?"

"I think I can come up with something a little more creative than a lawsuit," Emmett said, sounding dangerous. "I'm a Guild boss, after all."

"Is that a threat?"

"It sure is. And now that we've got that settled, let's talk about tonight. I'll pick you up at eight-thirty. As soon as we've put in an appearance at that damned ball, we'll go straight back to your place, collect some of your stuff and Fuzz, and come back here. Tomorrow I'll arrange to have a moving van pack up the rest of your belongings and transfer them here."

She lounged against the kitchen counter. "Don't be ridiculous. You don't have time to go through the yellow pages and select a moving company. You're running the Guild."

"Who said anything about going through the phone book? I'll have Perkins handle it."

"Gee, it must be nice to have an administrative assistant."

"Comes in handy. See you at eight-thirty."

He de-rezzed the connection before she could respond.

Slowly she replaced the phone and smiled at Fuzz.

"I do believe that I got his attention, Fuzz. Pack your bags. We're moving into his place tonight."

She heard the key in the front door precisely at eight-thirty. Fuzz skittered eagerly toward the tiny foyer.

She went back to the mirror to check her reflection for what had to be the millionth time. She still couldn't quite believe that the sophisticated-looking creature in the glass was really her.

Midnight looked even more sleek and glamorous tonight than it had when she had tried it on in the boutique. The stylist at the salon that afternoon had sculpted her hair into a graceful, elegant chignon that called attention to the nape of her neck and emphasized her eyes.

Following the advice she had been given, she had kept the jewelry to a minimum and made sure that all of it was gold.

"Lydia?" Emmett's voice echoed grimly in the front room.

"I'll be right there," she called back.

She turned away from the mirror and went down the hall. One look at Emmett and she forgot all about her own image.

Dressed in formal black, amber eyes gleaming with power, he looked like an elegantly lethal specter-cat on the hunt. She felt a familiar tingling through all her senses and had to fight the urge to throw herself at him and drag him to the floor.

He watched her come toward him and gave her a slow, sensual smile. Energy hummed in the air. She felt the hair stir on the nape of her bare neck. Heat pooled in her lower body.

"Whatever that dress cost, it was worth it," Emmett said. The words were heavy with sexual promise. "Sure glad you're coming home with me tonight, Mrs. London."

The grand entrance of Restoration Hall was choked with reporters and cameras. In addition, a large crowd had gathered to watch the guests walk the gauntlet of red carpet.

Emmett eased the Slider to a halt directly in front. "Ready?"

Lydia forgot about being cool. A trickle of panic shot through her.

"Oh, jeez," she whispered. "It looks just like it does on the rez-screen every year. I'll bet Melanie and Jack and Zane and Olinda are all watching us right now."

"Whatever you do, just keep smiling," Emmett growled.

Uniformed valets leaped for the doors on both sides of the Slider before Lydia could respond. A hand reached down to assist her.

"It's the new Guild boss and his wife," someone shouted.

A murmur of excitement rippled across the crowd.

Flashbulbs went off like fireworks, dazzling Lydia as she stepped out of the Slider. She blinked rapidly, trying to clear her vision. So much for being cool, she thought. She was afraid to move for fear she would trip on the curb or the edge of the carpet, neither of which she could see because of the black dots dancing in front of her eyes.

And then Emmett was there, taking her arm to steady her. He walked her along the red carpet toward the elaborately gilded doors.

More flashbulbs burst. This time she was ready for them. She kept her smile plastered in place until she and Emmett were safely through the doorway.

She started to say *whew, glad that's over* but then she caught sight of the long reception line composed of dignitaries, all of whom seemed genuinely awed by the new Guild boss.

At the end of that ritual they were ushered into a vast, glittering ballroom. Lydia thought she was prepared for the setting because she had seen it so many times at home on the rez-screen and in magazine photos.

But no film or picture could do justice to the true splendor of the hall. Massive chandeliers dominated the gilded and mirrored ceiling. Huge murals on the walls told the story of the violence of the Era of Discord and the triumph of the Last Battle of Old Cadence.

"I should have brought my camera," Lydia whispered to Emmett.

He was amused. "Don't worry, there will be plenty of pictures in the papers tomorrow."

There was no time to say anything else because people materialized immediately around Emmett. As Melanie had predicted, he was one of the most powerful men in the room and that meant that everyone wanted to be seen chatting with him.

She was wondering if anyone would notice if she slipped away to get a closer look at the scenes in the massive murals when someone put a glass of sparkling champagne in her hand.

"You look very lovely tonight, Lydia," Gannon Hepscott said.

She turned quickly, delighted to see a familiar face in the crowd. "Mr. Hepscott. I should have realized that you would be here."

He smiled, looking as exotic as ever in an all-white tuxedo. His heavy mane of silver-white hair was tied back with a strip of leather again tonight, just as it had been when she had met with him in his office.

"I was just thinking that this bash was going to be even more boring than usual when I saw you and your husband walk in," Gannon said.

"Do you attend every year?"

"Yes." He shrugged. "It's good business. Frankly, I'd rather be at home with a beer and a bowl of popcorn, watching the festivities on the rez-screen."

She laughed. "That's what I usually do." She waved a hand to include the brilliant scene. "I've got to tell you, this makes a pretty exciting change of pace."

He chuckled and glanced at Emmett, who was involved in a conversation with the mayor of Cadence. "Your new husband looks like he's going to be busy for a while. May I have this dance?"

"I'd be delighted."

She put her glass down on a passing tray. As if the tiny clink of sound had caught his ear, Emmett suddenly glanced in her direction. The corners of his eyes tightened almost imperceptibly. She wiggled her fingers and smiled very brightly to let him know that she was fine and that he didn't have to worry about her becoming a wallflower. Then she turned back to Gannon and allowed him to lead her out onto the floor.

The musicians were playing a sedate dance number. Gannon took her into his arms. She was amused to notice that he was careful to keep her at a polite, respectful distance. What man in his right mind would want to irritate the new Guild boss by dancing too closely with his wife?

"I have to tell you, the news of your marriage came as something of a shock, Lydia," Gannon said dryly. "I was aware that you were seeing London but I had no idea that the two of you were serious."

"Mmm." She couldn't think of anything more intelligent to say.

"I suppose the situation with Mercer Wyatt prompted you and London to move your plans forward?"

"Mmm."

"I realize that in your new role as the wife of one of the most powerful men in town you're going to be extremely busy. Does this mean that I should be looking for a new antiquities consultant?" Gannon asked.

Horrified, Lydia stumbled and would have fallen ignominiously on her rear right there in the middle of the dance floor if Gannon had not steadied her.

"No," she said, anxious to reassure him. "The marriage changes nothing. Really. I fully intend to continue to pursue my professional career, Mr. Hepscott."

"You're sure? A man in London's position probably makes a lot of social demands on his wife."

"Hardly any," she said airily. "Certainly none that will interfere with my professional activities. I've already made a lot of progress on your project. I've notified several of my best contacts on Ruin Row and I've made some appointments to look at some very interesting relics."

"I'm relieved to hear you say that. I'll admit that I've been looking forward to working with you. Don't laugh, but I have to tell you that if life had turned out a little differently for me, I might have gotten a degree in para-archaeology, myself."

"Is that so? What happened? Did you realize that you could make a lot more money in real estate?"

"No. Believe it or not, making money was never a big goal for me. It just came with the territory, so to speak. You know how it goes. You agree to work in the family firm for a few years after you graduate and then one morning you wake up and discover that you're running the business and that several hundred people are depending on you for a paycheck."

"I understand." She smiled to hide the wave of old sadness and lingering loss that still had the power to surprise her with its depths now and again at unexpected moments. "Well, sort of. I have to admit I never had to worry much about family pressure."

His hold tightened imperceptibly and his pale eyes softened. "But not for a good reason, I take it?"

"My folks were ruin explorers. They went on expeditions to find and map lost sites in remote locations. They were killed in a freakish storm that caused a massive landslide that wiped out their base camp."

"And now you're all alone in the world?" Gannon asked gently.

"No, she is not alone in the world," Emmett said in a stunningly dangerous voice. "She's got a husband."

Gannon brought Lydia to a halt, released her, and turned to face Emmett. "I don't believe we've been introduced."

Lydia could feel the tension sizzling in the air. It baffled her at first, and then, when she realized that Emmett was doing the intimidation thing with his eyes, she got annoyed.

"Mr. Hepscott, this is my husband, Emmett London," she said swiftly. "Emmett, this is Gannon Hepscott, my new client. I've men-

241

tioned him on several occasions. The Underground Experience Resort project?"

"Hepscott."

"London." Gannon's smile could only be described as taunting. "I'm looking forward to
working closely with your wife. I was just telling
her that I have always had a keen interest in
para-archaeology."

"Is that right?" Emmett said.

Gannon's smile held an unmistakable challenge. He was either supremely confident in his
own position and power or else he just wasn't
very bright, Lydia thought.

"Lydia and I are going to make a terrific
team," Gannon said, loading the words with nu-
ance.

Emmett's brows rose slightly. "Think so?"

"How can we miss?" Gannon chuckled. "I've
got the money and she's got the brains. Should
make for a perfect partnership."

Lydia went from annoyed to nervous. What
was going on here? She could have sworn that
Gannon was deliberately baiting Emmett.

"My wife is a very busy woman," Emmett
said.

"For now." Gannon shrugged. "But I hear the
two of you got an MC, not a Covenant Marriage. A year goes by very quickly, doesn't it?"

She had to do something and she had to do it
fast, Lydia decided. She stepped smartly between the two men.

"Do you know this is my first time inside the

242

Restoration Hall ballroom," she said lightly. "I'm so impressed with the murals. I've read about them and seen reproductions, of course, but I had no idea of the size and scale. Aren't they magnificent?"

Emmett and Gannon looked at her.

"The scope and the brilliance of the painting takes your breath away, doesn't it?" Lydia waved grandly at the closest mural, which depicted a battle between a band of intrepid ghost-hunters and Vincent Lee Vance's minions. "Of course, the subject matter is so inspiring. I mean, it was such a near thing, wasn't it? Vance came so close to establishing his crazed vision of a dictatorship. If it hadn't been for the Guilds who knows where we would all be today?"

"The hunters certainly earned their pay during the Era of Discord." Gannon glanced at Emmett with amused disdain. "And we've been paying them off ever since."

He inclined his head to Lydia, gave Emmett his shoulder, and walked away into the crowd.

Emmett watched him go. Lydia did not like the expression on his face.

"Don't even think about causing a scene, London," she warned out of the side of her mouth. "I will never, ever forgive you."

"Okay, but you know, I really hate it when a guy like that gets the good exit line."

She was so relieved she started to giggle. The heads of several people who had been listening discreetly to the exchange between the two men turned toward her in open curiosity. Horrified, she clapped a hand over her mouth but her shoulders were shaking with laughter and she could feel her eyes threatening to tear. Panicked at the thought of ruining her carefully applied makeup, she blinked rapidly.

Emmett swept her out onto the dance floor before she could make a complete fool of herself.

The moment of hysteria passed. She started to wonder if she was dreaming. She was in the arms of the man she loved and she was dancing at the Restoration Ball. Amberella, eat your heart out.

An hour later she found herself standing with a group of women that included the wives of two representatives to the City-State Federation, a famous actress, and a prominent socialite.

The conversation was not going well. The glamorous excitement of the evening was fading fast as reality set in. Oh, sure, the dancing was fun and she was taking mental notes on every celebrity she saw so that she could report back to Melanie. But the grim necessity of making small talk with a lot of boring, superficial people who seemed interested only in making sure that everyone else knew how much power and influence they wielded was becoming extremely tiresome.

It was just an upscale version of the old game

of one-upmanship, she thought. All in all, not much different from the dull sherry hours she'd been obliged to attend while on the faculty at the university. Except that the clothes here were a lot better.

"An interesting gown," the socialite said, giving Lydia's dress an appraising look. "I heard it was a Finella but it certainly doesn't have her classic signature look. A knockoff, from one of the other salons, perhaps?"

Translated, that meant that everyone now knew she wasn't wearing one of the designer's originals, Lydia thought. The actress and the two politicians' wives perked up immediately. Red meat at last.

Lydia smiled at the socialite. Did the blonde fool think she could be intimidated so easily? She'd dealt with arrogant, ambitious professors who could slice another scholar to ribbons with one scathing crack about the quality of the other person's research.

"Finella's designs are beautiful but a bit too, well, shall we say, *traditional* for my taste," Lydia said. "I prefer a more cutting-edge look. This gown was created by a new designer who works in Finella's salon. His name is Charles. Finella thinks he's a genius. I agree."

There was a short pause while they all absorbed that sally. If they did not go along with her they would find themselves in the position of disagreeing with the taste and judgment of the great Finella. On the other hand, if they showed approval they would be acknowledging that Lydia's gown was spectacular.

Unfortunately, before any of the women could untangle herself from the trap Lydia had set, Emmett materialized at her elbow. Instantly all attention switched to him. Lydia was sure she saw naked lust in the actress's eyes.

"Ladies." Emmett acknowledged the small group and took Lydia's arm. "Would you mind if I steal my wife away for another dance?"

"Newlyweds," the actress said, sarcasm dripping like poison. "They're so cute."

Lydia pretended that she had not heard the remark and made her farewells.

Emmett drew her quickly into the densest part of the crowd. Her first reaction was relief at the speedy escape from the unpleasant company.

"Am I glad to see you," she said. Then she noticed that they were on the opposite side of the ballroom, heading toward a side door, not the dance floor. "What's going on?"

"We're leaving, but I want to slip out without attracting any attention."

"Why?"

"I just got a message from Verwood. He's waiting out back with the Slider."

"What is it? Did Wyatt take a turn for the worse?"

"No. Verwood found his former mistress Sandra Thornton."

20

Lydia sat tensely in the front seat of the Slider. Emmett was at the wheel, easing the car through a maze of side streets in order to avoid the traffic and congestion on the main thoroughfares. Verwood loomed large in the rear seat.

The two had explained Sandra Thornton's role in the affair. A hasty plan of action had been hatched, but Lydia did not like it. She had decided to make her feelings on the subject known.

"I think you should take me with you when you go talk to this Sandra Thornton," she said.

"I told you, I want you to stay out of this." Emmett did not take his eyes off the dark streets.

"We've been through this before. You can't keep me out of it. We both know that."

Verwood had not said much after greeting her with a respectful nod but she knew that he was taking in every word of the argument. Given his position there in the backseat, it would have been impossible for him not to hear every word. Emmett was probably not real happy about having his security chief listening to what amounted to a domestic spat but she refused to back down. Her intuition told her that it was important that she go with him.

"Mr. Verwood says she's living alone," Lydia continued. "Just imagine how she's going to feel when she finds the two of you at her front door at this hour. She'll probably panic."

"That'd be the right thing to do," Verwood said, "if she shot the boss, that is."

"But what if she wasn't the one who shot him?" Lydia struggled to hang on to her patience. "And even if she did have something to do with the shooting, you need information from her, not hysterical panic. If she sees me, she'll be a lot less likely to rez-out on you."

"Huh." Verwood appeared to be somewhat struck by that observation. "Y'know, she's got a point, sir."

"Yeah." Emmett slowed the Slider to a crawl and drove along a narrow lane that led into the Old Quarter. "She does, doesn't she?"

Verwood folded his arms on the back of the seat. "Guys down at the Guild Hall are all talking about you, ma'am."

Lydia winced. "Is that anything like having the guys in the locker room talking about me?"

" 'Course not." Verwood was shocked by the analogy. "The guys are really impressed. Some of them worked with you while you were at the university. They said you're one hell of a tangler."

"Oh." She was taken aback by that news. She hadn't realized that the hunters gossiped about such things, she mused.

"Everyone down at the hall knows how you managed to find your way out of the tunnels after you'd been lost down there all on your own without any amber, for two whole days," Verwood added. "Pretty impressive."

"Mmm." She decided not to mention that the reason she had found herself in that predicament was because two members of the Guild had abandoned her.

"Most people who went through something like that, assuming they survived, would've ended up in a nice quiet para-psych ward." Verwood tapped his forefinger against his temple. "Probably never be able to work underground again. But we all know how you helped Mr. London, here, find his nephew after the boy got himself kidnapped. The guys say you went back into the catacombs just as cool as you please and never blinked."

"The reports of the effects of my underground disaster were greatly exaggerated," Lydia retorted.

"And this afternoon everyone was talking about how you took Jack Brodie and his girlfriend out to lunch at the fanciest place in town and made 'em give you a table even though the snooty head waiter tried to pretend they didn't have a reservation."

"It was a misunderstanding," Lydia mumbled.

"There were some who claimed that you weren't a real Guild wife on account of you weren't born into a Guild family and didn't know our traditions. But they sure changed their tune after they heard how you walked into that meeting of the Council today and told 'em how you were there to claim your Guild wife rights." Verwood whistled. "It was just like you'd been born and bred in the Guild."

"Yes, well —"

"You sure shut down Dorning's plans to issue a challenge," Verwood said happily. "Never did like that guy. Real ambitious and he doesn't care how he gets to the top. Fact is, the first thing I did after I heard about the boss getting shot was check out Dorning's alibi for that night."

"You did?" Lydia turned quickly in her seat to peer at him through the shadows. "I take it he was in the clear?"

"Yeah, but it doesn't mean he didn't hire someone to do his dirty work, right, Mr. London?"

"It's a possibility," Emmett conceded.

"So, there are some other suspects besides this Sandra Thornton," Lydia said softly.

"Oh, yeah." Verwood shrugged. "Guild bosses always have enemies. Part of the job description."

"Yes, I've heard that." Lydia shuddered and turned back to face the windshield. Please let this be over soon, she thought.

Emmett shot Verwood a warning glance in the rearview mirror. "I think you've said enough."

"Yes, sir." Belatedly realizing that he had annoyed his boss, Verwood tried to recover from his conversational faux pas. "Anyhow, down at the Guild Hall, everyone's talking about how they can sure see why you married this nice lady, Mr. London."

"What can I say?" Emmett muttered. "It seemed like a good idea at the time."

The apartment house where Sandra Thornton lived was located on one of the darker, meaner streets in the Old Quarter. Emmett got out of the Slider and studied the shabby-looking building. Most of the windows were dark. A couple were boarded up. You could almost smell the decay.

"Are you sure about the address, Verwood?" Emmett asked.

"Yes, sir." Verwood extricated himself from the back of the Slider and joined him on the cracked sidewalk. "I watched her come and go a couple of times this afternoon. She's got a key to the front door. Her car is that old Float parked near the curb. She lives here, all right."

Lydia walked around the front of the Slider, frowning at the heavily shadowed doorway across the street. In spite of the distractions presented by the business at hand, Emmett was intensely aware of her. Dressed in the sleek midnight-blue gown and sexy high heels, with little whispers of stray psi energy writhing around her, she made him want to head straight for the nearest bedroom. Or the backseat of the Slider, for that matter.

He got a flashback to the glittering ballroom they had just left and thought about his reaction to the sight of Lydia dancing with Hepscott. The thought of her working closely with the developer for the next few months was deeply disturbing.

"What's wrong, Emmett?" Lydia asked quietly.

He pulled himself back to the present. There would be ample time to brood over the problem of Gannon Hepscott in the future.

"I've got to tell you that I'm a little surprised that Sandra Thornton is living in a run-down place in a bad part of town." He shrugged. "Whatever else you can say about him, the fact is Wyatt has a reputation for being generous with his women. When he ends a relationship, he usually softens the blow with a few valuable parting gifts. Jewelry. Stock in Guild funds. That kind of thing."

"I see," Lydia said neutrally. "In other words if Sandra was Wyatt's mistress for any length of time, she should have been able to afford to live in a better neighborhood."

"Yeah."

"You said that Wyatt stopped seeing Sandra nearly two years ago. Maybe she ran through whatever money and jewelry he gave her."

"Hey, maybe that's why she called Mr. Wyatt the other day," Verwood volunteered. "To tell him she was broke. Probably knew she could get more cash out of him if she gave him a good sob story."

"If that was the case, I doubt she would have shot him in the back before identifying herself," Lydia said. "Hard to get cash out of a dead man."

"Huh." Verwood raised both hands. "She's got a point, Boss. Maybe we're off the mark a little here. Maybe Sandra Thornton didn't have anything to do with it."

"But there are other reasons besides money why a woman might want to kill a man," Lydia said quietly.

Emmett glanced sharply at her but he could not read her expression in the darkness.

"Well, we're not going to get any answers standing around out here," he said. He started toward the front door of the apartment house. "Let's go ask her."

He led the way across the narrow street, Verwood immediately behind him. Neither of them made any noise but Lydia's high heels rang faintly on the pavement.

Emmett went up the steps and tried the front door. It was locked.

"I'll take care of it, Boss." Verwood stepped in close to the door, took a pick out of his pocket, and applied it to the lock. Ten seconds later the door opened.

"That lock-pick gadget can't be legal." Lydia did not bother to conceal her disapproval. "Do all hunters carry one?"

"Uh —" Verwood broke off and looked quickly at Emmett, seeking guidance.

"What lock-pick gadget?" Emmett asked. "I didn't see any lock-pick gadget."

He moved through the doorway into a dimly lit hall. Lydia and Verwood followed.

Emmett examined the hand-lettered plaques on each door he passed. He stopped at the one that read *S. Thornton.*

"Let me knock," Lydia said. "It will be a lot less threatening."

She was right, Emmett thought. He stepped aside.

Lydia rapped her knuckles lightly against the panel and stood directly in front of the peephole.

There was no response.

She tried again, louder, sharper, more authoritative this time.

When there was no answer, Emmett took Lydia's place. He ignored her frown and knocked once.

"Ms. Thornton? This is Emmett London. I want to talk to you about Mercer Wyatt. This is a Guild matter."

"Oh, hey, that's real subtle," Lydia told him. "If I were her, I'd be climbing out the rear window about now."

No, you wouldn't, he thought. You'd fling open the front door and start chewing me out for having the nerve to wake you up at this hour.

"You want me to go downstairs and watch the alley in case she tries to sneak out that way, Boss?" Verwood asked.

"No." Emmett was about to order him to use

the pick again but he remembered to try the door first. It turned easily in his hand.

"Sheesh." Lydia shook her head. "I can't imagine leaving your front door unlocked in this neighborhood."

"Neither can I." This was not a good sign. He eased the door open. "Ms. Thornton?"

The unnatural stillness and the scent of burnt spice told its own tale.

Verwood wrinkled his nose in disgust. "She's into Chartreuse. Well, that explains how she went through whatever cash and goodies the boss gave her when they split."

"Something's wrong," Lydia whispered. "It's too quiet in there."

Emmett went through the doorway first with Verwood on his heels. He opened all his senses, listening for the slightest sound and feeling for any trace of psi energy, but he caught nothing. He glanced back at Lydia and Verwood. They both shook their heads.

The light from a single floor lamp slanted across a small living room that was nearly empty of furnishings.

Verwood surveyed the space with disdain. "She must have sold everything to buy the dope."

Emmett went down the short hall, glancing into the tiny bath before continuing on into the bedroom.

The smell of death mingled with the smoky scent of the Chartreuse.

Another weak lamp was lit in this room. It revealed a woman dressed in a scarlet nightgown. Her head was turned away from them, facing the window. Blond hair tumbled across the pillow.

A small Chartreuse burner sat on the table beside the bed.

They all looked at the body.

"Dear God, not again," Lydia whispered. She put her hand on her stomach.

Emmett went to the bed and touched the cold skin of the woman's throat. "She's been dead for several hours."

"Just like Professor Maltby." Lydia's gaze was riveted on the woman.

Emmett did not like the sound of that. "Do me a favor and don't get started on any new conspiracy theories, Lydia. Maltby and Thornton were both Chartreuse users."

"I know, but you've got to admit this is something more than a coincidence."

"I don't have to admit anything of the kind." He was about to tell Verwood to make the call to the cops when he saw the sheet of paper lying on the nightstand beside the drug apparatus.

There was a note written in an extremely shaky hand. He did not pick it up but he read it aloud to Lydia and Verwood.

My beloved Mercer:

Please forgive me. You always said that I was impulsive, didn't you? You told me that it was one of the things that you loved about me. I doubt that you expected that I might someday try to kill you on impulse, though, did you?

The papers say that you will probably live. Believe it or not, I'm glad to know that I did not succeed. But I can't go on any longer seeing you with her and knowing that I will never have you. I was good enough to be your mistress but not good enough to be your wife.

Farewell, my love.
Sandy

"I told you there were other reasons why a woman might try to kill a man," Lydia whispered. "Obsession and jealousy are right up there at the top of the list."

"It explains a lot of things," Emmett said, "like why Wyatt went out alone late at night to meet her and why he kept insisting that it was not Guild politics."

"Looks like we've got the shooter," Verwood said. He sounded relieved and satisfied.

Emmett nodded. "Better call Martinez."

21

It was after two in the morning before they got back to the town house. Martinez had had a lot of questions and she was, as Emmett had expected, not real happy with him. The detective had made several pointed remarks about how nice it must be to have the financial resources and the manpower of the Guild at one's disposal and how pleasant it would be to be able to conduct an investigation just once without worrying about budgetary constraints.

"You owe me for this, London," had been her parting remark. "I hear the Guild always repays its debts. I'll be waiting."

But despite the grumbling, he knew that Martinez had been deeply relieved to be able to close the high-profile case.

Emmett folded his arms behind his head and contemplated the night view of the Dead City through the floor-to-ceiling windows. The spires and towers that rose above the high walls were bathed in moonlight tonight. The effect was surreal, mysterious, and always compelling.

What was it about the magnificent ruins that called to people like Lydia and himself, people who resonated on the psychic plane with the psi energy that spilled from the ancient colony?

Beside him Lydia stirred, turned onto her side, and propped herself on one elbow. Fuzz, nestled between them at the foot of the bed, opened one of his four eyes and then promptly closed it.

Lydia put her palm on Emmett's bare chest. "Can't sleep?"

"I wonder where she was during the past two years," he said.

"Sandra Thornton?"

"Verwood says that it's as if she disappeared right after the relationship with Wyatt ended. Then, nearly two years later she reappears and tries to murder Wyatt. A couple of days later Verwood gets an anonymous tip that she's living in a run-down apartment in the Old Quarter. And a short time later she's dead from an overdose."

"Maybe she left Cadence for a while. She might have been living in Resonance or Frequency or one of the smaller towns."

He thought about that. "I'll have Verwood keep looking. I'd really like to know where Thornton spent the past couple of years."

There was a short silence during which Fuzz wriggled around a little and made himself more comfortable.

"I've got a few questions of my own." Lydia settled herself back on the pillows. "I can't get past the fact that Sandra Thornton checked out

the same way Professor Maltby did. An overdose of Chartreuse in both cases seems like too
much of a coincidence to me."

He thought about that. Okay, he had problems with her anti-Guild attitude and her tendency to blame ghost-hunters for anything and
everything that went wrong underground, but
he had learned the hard way to respect her intuition.

"What possible connection could there be between Maltby and Sandra Thornton?" he asked.

"There's one real big connection. Us. You and
me, Emmett."

He turned his head to look at her serious,
shadowed face. "What are you talking about?"

"Think about it," she said earnestly. "We were
on the scene both times the bodies were discovered. Doesn't that strike you as good grounds
for a conspiracy theory?"

"No," he said flatly.

"Okay, then how about this one? A lot of
people seem to have disappeared in both cases."

"I'll admit that Sandra Thornton apparently
dropped out of sight for a couple of years but
she eventually turned up again. Who have you
got on your list?"

"Everyone who was close to Troy Burgis fifteen years ago."

It was his turn to prop himself up on one
elbow. "You've got my attention. Now tell me
what the hell you're talking about?"

"I told you that I contacted Troy Burgis's

alumni association. Well, this morning I got a call from someone who knew Burgis in college, Karen Price. Turns out that within a few months after he vanished into the catacombs beneath Old Frequency, the other three members of his band, his girlfriend and two ghosthunter buddies, were supposedly killed in various accidents."

"Supposedly?"

"Get this: None of the bodies were ever found. What do you say to that?"

He wanted to tell her that she was letting her imagination run off with her common sense but for some reason he couldn't seem to summon up a logical counterargument.

"Huh," he said instead.

"Admit it, London. It's pretty darn weird that all four of them disappeared within a few months, isn't it?"

"Okay, it's weird, I'll give you that."

"While we're on the subject of a conspiracy theory," Lydia said, "there's something else that's been bothering me about Sandra Thornton."

"I'm listening."

Lydia's brows came together in a perplexed frown. "If she was so obsessed with Mercer Wyatt, why wait nearly two years to try to kill him? You'd think that the fires of passion would have cooled after so much time apart."

What was she talking about? he thought. Didn't she understand?

He leaned over her, trapping her beneath him, savoring the warmth and softness of her, losing himself in the hot rush of need.

"Don't know about Sandra and Wyatt," he said. "But I can guarantee you that two years apart from you wouldn't do a damn thing to cool this fire."

The huge vase filled with flowers was waiting for her the next morning when she walked into her office. It sat right in the middle of her desk. The glorious blooms and lush, artfully arranged greenery spilled out over the top in a massive waterfall of color that covered the entire surface.

Lydia's heart leaped. After-the-ball flowers from Emmett.

"Aren't they gorgeous?" Melanie called, hurrying toward her down the hall. "They arrived just before you got here. I took the liberty of reading the card. Couldn't resist. Guess who loves you and worships the very ground upon which you walk?"

Lydia smiled and walked to the desk to cup a dark pink orchid in one hand. "It was very sweet of him. He's so busy these days, I can't believe he found the time to order the flowers."

"Don't know how busy he was before you wore *Midnight* to the ball last night, but he's sure gonna be a whole lot busier from now on, thanks to you."

Lydia stopped smiling and picked up the card.

Midnight becomes you. I am your devoted slave forever.

> *Yours in gratitude,*
> *Charles*

"You should have seen yourself on the rez-screen last night. You were fabulous. It was so exciting to watch you and Emmett walk into Restoration Hall. Just take a look at these pictures in the papers." Melanie waved a handful of tabloids. "That dress was perfect and Charles is now the hottest designer in the city."

Lydia took the copy of the *Tattler* from her and examined the photo that covered the front page. It showed her walking along the red carpet on Emmett's arm, heading toward the doors of the ballroom. He looked great, she thought. Cool, confident, totally in control. Power formed an invisible aura around him. He could have stepped right out of one of the ballroom murals, a modern-day Jerrett Knox leading the forces of good against Vincent Lee Vance's evil legions.

She, on the other hand, had the glassy-eyed gaze of a deer caught in the headlights. Probably the fault of all those camera lights, she decided. But she had to admit that the dress looked good.

"Amazing what the right clothes will do for a woman," she said.

"I'll say." Melanie inhaled the fragrance of

one of the blooms. "All right, pal, let's have the whole story. Remember, you promised me every little detail."

"Don't worry, I took notes." Lydia started to toss the *Tattler* aside but paused when she noticed the second glaring headline.

Wyatt Shot by Ex-Lover. Woman Takes Own Life. New Guild Boss and Bride Find Body

"Oh, yeah," Melanie said, following her glance. "It says you and Emmett rounded off your big evening by discovering the body of the woman who shot Wyatt. You two really know how to have fun, don't you?"

"It was ghastly." Lydia shuddered. "She was wearing a scarlet nightgown that the cops think Wyatt gave her during the time of the affair."

"So, it was a lovers' triangle all along, huh? But it involved one of Wyatt's old flames, not Emmett and his ex-fiancée."

"That's the assumption. But I have to tell you that something about the whole thing feels off. Emmett agrees with me. We both wonder if —"

Lydia stopped talking in midsentence when the cadaverous figure of her employer loomed in the doorway of her office.

"What's going on in here?" Shrimpton peered at the flowers through his gold-rimmed spectacles. "Where did those come from?"

"Just a gift from a grateful patron of the museum, sir," Melanie said smoothly.

Shrimpton grunted. "Thought maybe London had sent them."

Lydia concentrated on rezzing the kettle. "Emmett is very busy these days."

"He's got his hands full, all right, what with running the Guild and finding dead bodies," Shrimpton agreed. "Word is, Wyatt's going to make it. Should be interesting to see if he can get control of his organization back from London when he gets out of the hospital."

"What?" Lydia spun around, cup in hand. "Are there rumors of some sort of power struggle between Emmett and Mercer Wyatt? That's ridiculous."

Shrimpton shrugged his bony shoulders. "Wyatt's not a young man anymore and the Guild Council has accepted London."

Melanie nodded. "Good point. It's a done deal. It certainly won't be easy for Wyatt to grab his job back if Emmett decides to hang on to it. And why would London give up power now that he's got it?"

"Because he doesn't want to run the Guild on a permanent basis," Lydia said, clutching the handle of the teapot very tightly. "Emmett told me that, himself. He's just doing the Cadence Guild a favor by holding things together until Wyatt is back on his feet."

"If that's really what he's doing, it's one heck of a favor." Melanie chuckled. "Everyone knows that, historically, whenever there's a temporary power vacuum at the top of the Guild because a boss gets seriously ill or injured, someone else takes over. When the old chief recovers he rarely gets his office back."

Shrimpton nodded. "Very true. If London does hold things together for Wyatt and then steps down when the old man comes back, one thing's for sure."

"What's that?" Lydia asked warily.

It was Melanie who answered. "Wyatt will owe London, big time. You know what they say, the Guild always repays its favors."

Shrimpton squinted at Lydia. "Let's get to what's important to us here at this museum. We've got to make the most of this opportunity. As long as you're married to the current Guild boss, Lydia, you're a hot attraction."

"That's for sure," Melanie chimed in. "After all the media coverage last night, you're now an even bigger draw than you were when you were just the Mystery Mistress. We're talking sex, murder, and a terrific dress."

Lydia groaned and flopped down into her desk chair. "I can't stand it."

Shrimpton ignored that. Clearing his throat portentously, he held up a page of handwritten notes. "This is an updated list of reservations for private group tours to be escorted personally by you, Lydia. The first one today is a Hunter-Scout group at ten-fifteen."

"Not another group of Hunter-Scouts." Alarmed, Lydia sat bolt upright. "I barely survived the last one. I lost all control. The little monsters crawled all over the artifacts in the Tomb Wing and tried to summon flickers. It's a wonder they didn't manage to set fire to the museum."

Melanie tsk-tsked. "Don't whine, Lydia. You know that every Hunter-Scout troop in the city wants a tour conducted personally by the boss's wife herself."

"More to the point, thanks to the Hunter-Scouts' interest in you, Lydia, we've quadrupled our income from student and youth groups in the last few days." Shrimpton rattled his notes. "Now, then, after the morning group tour you're free until five. Then you'll be escorting a VIP after-hours tour."

"Hold it right there, sir." Lydia sat forward and glanced at her calendar. She saw the note she made and smiled in anticipation of triumph. "I can't do the tour this afternoon. Melanie will have to handle it. I'm scheduled to oversee the transfer of the Mudd Sarcophagus, remember? The movers arrive at five."

"Oh, sorry, I forgot to tell you," Shrimpton said. "The sarcophagus isn't leaving today, after all. The collector's assistant called late yesterday to postpone the pickup until Monday. Something about not being able to coordinate the security arrangements and the moving company."

"All right, I give up." She shrugged. "With Emmett working so late every evening, I suppose it doesn't matter if I stay late here tonight." She checked the time on her watch and looked at Shrimpton. "But if I'm going to be stuck here until six-thirty, I assume that you won't have any objection to me taking a long lunch hour this afternoon?"

"No, no, of course not." Satisfied that she wasn't going to raise any more objections to the VIP tour arrangements, Shrimpton gave her a toothy smile and hastily backed out of the doorway.

Melanie looked sympathetic. "Don't worry, all these special group requests will dry up real quick if and when Emmett goes back to being a private consultant."

"When, not if," Lydia said forcefully. "He is going to step down, I tell you."

"Yeah, sure. So, why the request for the long lunch hour? Going to check out some galleries for the Hepscott project?"

"No, it's a personal matter."

"Hey, if you're going to shop for shoes and charge it to the Guild, the least you can do is invite your best friend to go along," Melanie pleaded. "I'm sure I can talk Shrimp into letting me have some extra time."

"I'll bet you could," Lydia said. "But I don't think you'll want to come with me on this errand. I'm not going to shop. I'm going to visit the home of a dead man."

Melanie grimaced. "See? That's your problem in life, Lyd. Your idea of how to have fun just isn't normal."

22

A few minutes after noon, Lydia knocked on the door across the hall from Professor Lawrence Maltby's apartment. Cornish opened it cautiously.

"You're back." He squinted at her with deep suspicion. "How come?"

"I want to take another quick look inside Professor Maltby's apartment. But the door is locked now."

"Owner came by and locked up yesterday."

"I see." She shot a speculative glance at the closed door on the other side of the corridor. "I wondered if, by any chance, Maltby might have given you a key?"

"Key?"

"Neighbors do that sometimes," she explained.

Cornish snorted. "Not in this part of town, they don't."

"Oh." Well, so much for the easy way. She thought about the window that opened onto the alley. The intruders had busted the lock the night she and Emmett had discovered them inside. Perhaps the owner of the building had not had time to get it replaced.

Cornish looked sly. "But Maltby was always lockin' himself out on the nights he went down into the tunnels. He took to hidin' a key under a loose floorboard on the back stairs. I saw him use it a couple of times. He never knew I knew about it. Expect it's still there."

"Will you show me where it is?"

"Depends." Cornish squinted. "Heard you and London got married. That makes this a Guild matter, right?"

She cleared her throat. "Sort of."

"So if I do you a favor, it's like doing one for the Guild."

She cleared her throat. "Sort of."

"A hundred will get you the key."

"If I pay you, it's not exactly a favor."

Cornish shrugged. "Up to you."

She sighed and reached into her purse. "Try twenty bucks."

"Get real. The other night London paid me a hundred just to tell him a couple of things about Maltby. That key's gotta be worth at least that much."

"A hundred bucks to show me where the key is hidden? That's outrageous."

"Take it or leave it."

"I don't have a hundred on me."

Cornish did not appear concerned. "If this is a Guild matter, London won't stiff me. He can send the cash tomorrow."

She did not have a lot of options here, Lydia reminded herself. "Okay, okay. A hundred bucks. Payable tomorrow. If the key works in that door."

"It'll work." Cornish darted out into the hall and scuttled down the dingy corridor toward the fire stairs. "Used it myself a few times to see if he'd left any Chartreuse behind when he went out."

"It's so nice to have neighbors you can trust."

Key in hand, she let herself into Maltby's apartment and closed the door. She stood quietly for a moment, taking in the stale, sad feel of the place. No one had cleaned yet. Maltby's books and papers still littered the floor. The overturned furniture, torn cushions, and crumpled rug appeared to be in the same positions in which the intruders had left them. It did not look as if they had returned to risk a second search. Perhaps they had concluded that whatever they were looking for was not here.

She put her purse down on the kitchen counter and began to wander slowly through the small space. The first time she had been here, there had been no opportunity to do a thorough search because there had been a dead man lying on the floor and Emmett and the cops had been pounding on the door.

When she and Emmett had come back it had been at night. They had had only the flashlights for illumination. The trapped milk carton had been a major discovery so they had not lingered to do a more in-depth search.

Today she was hoping that there might be something else of interest here. She did not know what she was looking for or what she hoped to discover, but there was simply no place else to go. All the leads from the Old Frequency College Alumni office had led to dead ends, literally.

She rezzed a light switch and discovered that the building's owner had turned off the power in the apartment. Luckily she had remembered to bring along a flashlight. More important, today she had the added benefit of natural light coming through the small windows in the front room and the study.

She opened the refrigerator to see if there was anything else of interest inside and immediately regretted the move. In the short time that the power had been cut off, the few items of food stored inside had gone very bad.

Holding her breath, she opened her psi senses, probing for illusion-trap energy. Nothing.

Hastily she closed the door and moved on to the kitchen cupboards. In the dull light of day, she saw several small things that had escaped her notice on the first two visits: a box of matches, some poison meant for various types of urban vermin, a foul-smelling sponge. But none of the odds and ends looked promising. None carried the taint of psi energy.

She moved back out into the living room and methodically went through every book and journal on the floor and the few that had been left on the shelves. She got down on her hands and knees and searched beneath the overturned sofa.

Nothing.

She did the grimy bathroom next, checking inside tissue boxes and investigating drawers.

Nothing.

She saved the small room that Maltby had used as a study for last on the assumption that, between the intruders and Emmett and herself, it had been thoroughly searched. Nevertheless, she took her time, painstakingly exploring every nook and cranny.

She was on her hands and knees beneath the desk, about to give up, when she saw the little amber bead.

It had rolled into the corner and lodged in a dusty cobweb. The filmy stuff coated the bead, dimming the natural glow of the amber. If not for the weak sunlight plus the beam of the flashlight, she doubted that she would have noticed it at all.

Leaning forward, she poked the hilt of the flashlight into the abandoned web, breathing a sigh of relief when no seriously annoyed spider made an appearance.

The bead rolled free, making a delicate clatter on the wood floor. She picked it up and scrambled out from under the desk.

Rising to her feet, she blew off the dust and debris and held the bead to the light.

The amber gem was about half an inch long, cut in an oval shape and pierced so that it could be threaded on a string. No doubt it had once been part of a necklace or a bracelet.

Don't get too excited, she thought. It had probably belonged to Maltby. He had been a tangler and, according to Cornish, he had spent a lot of time underground. That meant he would have worn amber.

But few men wore rez-amber in the form of beads or bracelets; besides, she had noticed Maltby's amber the day she found his body. It had been set in an inexpensive ring.

Had Maltby had a female visitor before he died?

She rolled the bead in the palm of her hand. A small, elegantly inscribed letter A had been cut into one side. The owner's initial?

A memory tingled at the back of her mind. Recently she had heard a woman's name that began with the letter A.

She concentrated for a few seconds and then it came to her. Burgis's girlfriend, the woman who had been Karen Price's roommate at Old Frequency College, had been named Andrea Preston.

Excitement flashed through Lydia. *Coincidence? I think not.*

Okay, so she was feeling smug. She had a right. The bead was a genuine clue.

She removed a tissue from her shoulder bag and carefully wrapped it around the bead. She could hardly wait to show the amber to Emmett tonight.

23

At five o'clock that afternoon, Melanie appeared in the doorway of Lydia's office. She wore a very short, red leather trench coat belted snugly around her waist. Her purse was tucked under one arm.

Lydia looked up warily. "What?"

"Nothing much," Melanie said a little too lightly. "I'm on my way home. Just stopped in to say good-bye. See you Monday."

"What's so funny?"

Melanie grinned. "Well, if you must know, I just saw your VIP tour group gathering in the lobby."

Lydia braced herself. "A Hunter-Scout troop?"

"Nope."

"Thank heavens for small favors. Garden club?"

"Nope. Try again."

"Charity organization?"

"Getting warmer."

"I give up."

"I'm not going to tell you," Melanie admitted. "Mostly because I want to see your face when you get a good look at this bunch of VIPs."

Resigned, Lydia got to her feet. "You know, the sooner Emmett steps down from his job at the Guild, the better. I'm tired of being a museum attraction."

Melanie stepped aside and swept out a hand to usher her through the door. Lydia heard her make some suspicious noises in the hall behind her.

"Stop snickering," Lydia ordered.

"I'm not snickering. I'm chortling."

"You're snickering."

Before Melanie could defend herself from that charge, Lydia turned the corner and saw the group that awaited her.

On the positive-rez side, it was a small crowd, only about half a dozen.

The negative-rez was that they all had shaved heads, long, green robes, and unnaturally serene expressions.

"Oh, boy," Lydia said under her breath. "Greenies."

"If I were you," Melanie whispered as she went past her toward the door, "I'd give them the same tour you give the Hunter-Scout troops. You know, concentrate on the Tomb Wing. Something tells me they'll want to see the really weird stuff."

At that moment the six Greenies noticed Lydia and bowed respectfully. By the time they raised their bald heads, she had her tour-guide smile firmly fixed in place.

One of them, the leader, apparently, stepped

forward. "I am Acolyte Clarence. It is very kind of you to make this time available to us. We are eager to learn."

The museum emptied out quickly at five, thanks to the new obsessive-compulsive night guard. Benny Fellows was young, but he took his duties seriously.

" 'Evening, Miss Smith." Benny touched his cap when she paused at the entrance to his small office with the Greenies in tow. "Everything is in order for the tour this evening. I've got the lights on in all the galleries."

"Thanks, Benny. We'll be finished in about an hour and a half."

"Yes, ma'am." Benny waved the group on into the main gallery.

Thirty minutes later, Lydia decided that she had been much too hasty in her assumptions concerning the Greenies' level of intellectual interest in antiquities. Their questions were thoughtful and showed that the group had done a fair amount of study.

Whatever else you could say about the cult, she thought, it was obvious that the Greenies did not starve their members. All six of the men in this group looked strong, solidly built, and quite fit. They varied in age but they all appeared to be somewhere between twenty and forty. Clarence was the oldest. He was also the one who asked the most questions.

The museum took on an eerie ambience after

closing time, she reflected as she led her group into the Tomb Wing. The long galleries were always on the dark side, of course, even during regular hours, because Shrimp liked the creepy effect. But this evening they seemed drenched in ominous mystery.

"In this gallery we house the various objects that the experts believe were associated with the alien burial rites," Lydia said, turning the corner and gesturing toward the dramatic entrance of the Tomb Wing.

The Greenies appeared suitably impressed by the over-the-top décor. Shrimpton had pulled out all the stops to induce a sense of spectral gloom in this wing. It was darker than the other galleries. The sarcophagi, urns, and other strange objects inside had been carefully arranged to create the most morbid effect. Each artifact was illuminated with a narrow beam of green light that left great pockets of shadows around the relics.

"Watch your step, please," Lydia said briskly. "It's quite dark in here."

A ripple of excitement went through the group. There were several murmured comments and exclamations.

She paused beside a green quartz urn that was dramatically accented with acid green light reminiscent of the interior glow of the catacombs. Nothing made by humans could precisely reproduce that unique radiance but Shrimpton's small staff had come close.

"This urn was discovered in a chamber that was heavily guarded with several very complex illusion traps," she said. "There were also a number of powerful energy ghosts in the vicinity. The assumption is that the original owner wanted to ensure that his tomb would not be disturbed."

Clarence surveyed the abstract designs on the urn. "Does anyone know what the decorations mean?"

"Unfortunately, the nature and purpose of the carvings found on so many of the artifacts remain unknown." She traced the elegantly curved decoration that circled the urn. "Many para-archaeologists, myself included, believe that these designs are examples of Harmonic writing."

"Real words? Oh, wow." One of the members of the group stepped forward to take a closer look. "But what does it say?"

"That's the problem," she said patiently. "We don't know. If these are meaningful symbols they are, in a sense, locked in code. Until para-archaeologists find a key to the code, the alien writing will remain nothing more than a series of attractive decorations, as far as we humans are concerned."

"Hey, look over there." Another Greenie pointed excitedly across the room. "A coffin."

The group hurried past the urn to examine the relic.

Lydia followed. "You are fortunate to be able

to view this object today. This is the last day it will be on display."

"Why is that?" someone asked.

She patted the edge of the uncovered coffin. "It was purchased from the museum by a private collector and it's due to be picked up on Monday. It's called the Mudd Sarcophagus after the P-A who discovered it. You will notice that the interior is large enough to hold a full-grown person but that the shape is not quite right for a human."

The six Greenies all leaned over to peer into the empty sarcophagus.

"Weird," one of them muttered. "The aliens must have had big chests and short legs."

She opened her mouth to respond to that observation but at that instant she heard the unmistakable clink of a string of beads.

Clarence was leaning over the open coffin. The long necklace that until now had been concealed by the folds of his green robes had fallen forward and dangled in midair. The thin spear of light from the ceiling fixture glinted on a series of oval-shaped amber gems.

Lydia stopped breathing. She was absolutely certain that if she could get her hands on Clarence's necklace and compare the beads on it to the single amber gem she had found in Maltby's apartment, she would discover that they were identical, probably right down to the little letter A carved on one side.

A for Amatheon, not Andrea.

Clarence straightened, absently tucking the beads back inside the folds of his gown. He smiled benignly at Lydia.

"You will forgive what no doubt appears to be our somewhat morbid interest in funerary artifacts, Miss Smith," he said. "Please understand that locating the tomb and the sarcophagus of the great philosopher, Amatheon, is of extreme importance to our Order. Naturally, that goal has given all of us a fixation with ancient tomb relics of every kind."

As he spoke, the other five Greenies drifted away from the sarcophagus. She had the unpleasant feeling that they were starting to circle her like so many sharks.

She was suddenly acutely aware of just how empty the museum was at this hour. The realization that she was alone with Greenies struck her with the force of a glacial wind. She was amazed that her teeth did not chatter.

Trying to appear casual, she edged toward the nearest alarmed display case. It contained an array of tomb mirrors. A small quartz box sat atop a pedestal a short distance away. She slipped between the case and the pedestal.

"No problem," she said coolly. "Almost everyone is interested in tomb relics. Human nature, I suppose. Death rituals and preparations for the afterlife hold a deep fascination for most people."

Was it her imagination or were the Greenies closing in around her? She tried to count the robed figures but it wasn't easy to keep track of all six in the deep shadows.

"Have you read the *Thirteen Steps to Bliss*, Miss Smith?" Clarence asked gently.

"No, actually, I haven't had a chance." She drew a breath and very casually put her hand on the top of the display case.

Immediately she felt a little safer and more sure of herself. If she so much as jiggled the lock the alarm bells would sound throughout the museum, summoning Benny.

"You really should read it," Clarence said.

"The thing is, I can't even keep up with my professional reading," she said lightly. "You wouldn't believe how many journal articles, conference papers, and books I have stacked up in my office, just waiting for me to get to them."

Clarence regarded her with an expression of grave reproof. "Some things are more important than a journal article."

"You know, you're right about that. I'll have to get a copy of the *Thirteen Steps* this afternoon and take a look." She could only count five Greenies now, including Clarence. Where was the sixth?

Then she sensed the rush of movement directly behind her. The sixth Greenie.

She started to spin toward him but she was too late. He clamped a hand around her mouth and placed a damp, medicinal-smelling cloth over her nose.

The odor was shockingly, horribly familiar. She had breathed this foul stuff once before.

One of the hidden memories of her Lost Weekend leaped forth from the dark depths of amnesia. The image snapped into crystal-clear focus.

The hunters who had abandoned her in the catacombs had used this stuff to subdue her.

She had no time to deal with the implications of the recollection. Another Greenie had grabbed her right arm. A third seized her ankles and hoisted her off the floor.

Struggling not to breathe, she swept out her free hand, groping for the little box on the pedestal. Her fingers closed around it. Twisting, she smashed the relic into the top of the display case. Glass cracked and shattered.

To her horror, no alarm sounded.

Her first, outraged thought was that Shrimpton had neglected to pay the security firm's bill.

"Hurry," Clarence ordered. "Benny told the van to pull up to the loading dock five minutes ago."

Benny, the new security guard, was in on this. No wonder the alarm hadn't gone off.

She could not hold her breath any longer. She had to inhale. The instant she sucked in air, the world around her wavered. Whatever had been used to soak the cloth over her nose was going to make her pass out quickly. She had very little time left in which to act.

She still had the little box in her hand. She

flailed wildly, slamming it against the chest of the nearest Greenie.

"Ghost-shit." The man released her involuntarily, bending over in pain.

"Don't let her go, you idiot," Clarence said.

"I think the witch cracked some ribs."

"I don't give a damn about your ribs."

Lydia twisted in her captors' grip. Her hand snagged on a string of beads. They all wore the amber necklaces under their robes, she realized.

She ripped at the beads and felt the string snap. Amber gems clinked and tinkled as they hit the floor, scattering and rolling in every direction.

"My beads," a Greenie hissed. "She broke my beads."

"Forget the amber," Clarence said grimly. "Benny will sweep up after we're gone. Move, you fools."

The fumes imbedded in the cloth were working swiftly. Lydia felt her consciousness leak away like water down a bathtub drain. No matter how hard she tried to twist and writhe, her muscles were going limp. Her eyes closed against her will.

She was vaguely aware that the Greenies were lowering her. At first she thought they intended to put her down on the floor. Maybe she was wrong about the amber bead connection. Perhaps what was happening was nothing more than a simple robbery.

It occurred to her as the world faded away

that she might have done her job too well here at Shrimpton's. Before she had joined the staff, the quality of the relics had been mediocre at best. No serious thief would have looked twice at any of the antiquities on display. But in the past few months she had obtained some rather nice acquisitions for the museum.

If these bastards were antiquities thieves, they would surely try to take the little dreamstone jar out of its special display case. It was far and away the most valuable relic in the place. They would have a surprise coming if they grabbed it. The alarm in that cabinet was not linked to the rest of the system. It was connected directly to the offices of Guild Security, Inc. The museum would soon be crawling with ghost-hunters.

But instead of the cold floor she felt the unmistakable touch of quartz against her back and legs. A fresh wave of panic flashed through her. They were putting her into the sarcophagus.

"Is she out yet?" Clarence asked urgently.

"Just about."

"Get the lid."

Lydia got her eyes open one last time and wished she hadn't bothered. The Greenies were lowering the cover of the sarcophagus onto the burial box.

She was profoundly grateful when the last of her conscious awareness winked out.

24

Emmett leaned back against the desk and quickly scanned the file Perkins had just handed him. "What do you mean, both men have disappeared? Benefits is still sending out monthly checks to each of them, right?"

Perkins twitched a few times, glanced uneasily at Verwood, who stood by the windows, and adjusted his spectacles with fingers that trembled ever so slightly. "Well, yes and no."

Emmett closed the file and dropped it on the desk behind him. "Explain."

"Yes, Benefits is still cutting the checks and putting them in the mail each month," Perkins said patiently. "But, ah, when I tried to verify the addresses to which the checks were sent I learned that both men had signed forms indicating that they wished their monthly retirement pay to be donated directly to a charity. That is exactly what Benefits has been doing for the past few months."

"These two guys decided to contribute the entire amount of their hunter benefits to charity?" Emmett shook his head once. "I'm not buying that."

"It is a little odd, I must admit," Perkins said. "But that appears to be the case."

"What's the name of this charity?"

"I made a note." Perkins pulled out a small notebook and opened it. "Here it is. The Order of the Acolytes of Amatheon."

"The Greenies?" Emmett straightened slowly, unable to believe what he had just heard. "Those two signed over their monthly retirement benefits to a cult?"

"Apparently that would be the case, sir," Perkins said.

"It may not be as strange as it sounds, Boss." Verwood rubbed the back of his neck. "I finally got a couple of leads on those two guys. They both disappeared into the cult a couple of months after that formal inquiry at the university."

"What does *disappeared* mean?" Emmett asked evenly.

"Well, seems like when you enter the Inner Circle of the Order you leave behind all the stuff that ties you to your old life." Verwood shrugged. "You ditch your friends, relatives, personal possessions, that kind of thing. You know how cults work."

Emmett set his back teeth. "And in this case, you sign over all of your assets to the organization."

"You got it." Verwood snorted in disgust. "Not a bad racket if you're the one running the cult. I did some checking. The Greenies opened up for business about three years ago. They've been growing steadily in numbers ever since.

Got a couple of thousand members here in Cadence. Same in the other cities."

"Who the hell is running the cult?" Emmett asked.

"Guy named Herbert J. Slattery. Leastways that used to be his name. Now calls himself Master Herbert. Claims to channel some old alien philosopher named Amatheon."

"Got an address for Slattery?"

"Just the cult's office downtown. But Perkins, here, could get Slattery's personal address pretty damn quick if you want it. He's good at that."

"Thank you, Mr. Verwood," Perkins said, pleased by the praise.

A lot of things were suddenly starting to resonate in what might prove to be a pattern, Emmett thought. He glanced at his watch. It was almost 6:30. Lydia was probably still at Shrimpton's. She had left a message earlier today telling him that she had a special after-hours tour scheduled for that afternoon. With luck she would be finishing up right about now. He leaned over his desk and grabbed the phone.

"Sir?" Verwood's broad features tightened in a frown of bewilderment. "I don't get it. What do those screwball Greenies have to do with this?"

"Maybe everything."

He punched out Lydia's number. There was no answer. He cut the connection and called her on the little phone she carried in her purse.

When he got no response, he tried the town house. Then he dialed her apartment number. *Too damn many phones these days.*

Out of options, he pulled out the short list of phone numbers he carried in his wallet and dialed Melanie's home number. She answered on the first ring.

"I left the museum just as she was getting ready to conduct the special tour," Melanie said. "She should have finished by now. Why? Something wrong?"

"I can't get hold of her at any of the usual numbers."

"She's probably in a place where the signal won't resonate. Give her a few minutes and try again." Melanie chuckled. "Don't worry, I doubt that she ran off to join the Greenies."

He went cold. "What made you say that, Mel?"

"Hey, it's just a joke. Sorry."

"I'm serious. Why the joke about Greenies?"

"I guess it popped into my head because that special tour she escorted after hours today was for half a dozen Greenies. I told her they'd probably be interested in the Tomb Wing, just like the Hunter-Scout troops."

"Sonofa . . . Mel, listen to me, I need the number of the guard's office there at Shrimpton's. Do you have it?"

"Hang on, I'll get it for you." Melanie was starting to sound worried. "What's wrong?"

"Just get me the number."

"Here it is." She rattled off a string of numbers. "The new guy's name is Benny Fellows."

"Thanks."

"Emmett, you're starting to scare me. What is this all about?"

"Later."

He severed the connection and tried the guard's number. When he got no answer he tossed down the phone and headed for the door.

"Let's go, Verwood."

Emmett drove, piloting the car through the busy streets with an intensity of purpose that other drivers noticed. Vehicles melted out of the Slider's path.

Night had fallen, the darkness complicated by a gathering fog. The streetlights created small circles of glare but not much in the way of useful illumination.

He parked in front of the entrance to Shrimpton's a short time later. Pounding on the front door brought no response. There was no sign of the guard.

Emmett led Verwood around the side of the building, found the window he wanted, and smashed it open with the heel of his boot. Glass fractured, shattered, and then rained down in tiny shards.

Verwood glanced nervously over his shoulder. "Uh, Boss, that's bound to set off an alarm. Cops will be here any minute."

"You hear any alarm?" Emmett reached through the busted window and unlocked it.

"Uh, no." Verwood's brows rose. "Now that you mention it, I don't hear any alarm. Seems kinda strange for a museum."

"Yes, it does." The lack of clanging bells and sirens was a real bad sign, Emmett thought.

"You'd think a place like this would have a security system."

"It does." Emmett went through the window.

Verwood scrambled after him. "I gotta tell you, Boss, it might not look too good in the papers if you get arrested breaking into a museum. Know what I mean?"

"Relax. The owner owes the Guild a couple of favors," Emmett said, thinking of the dreamstone arrangements.

Verwood brightened. "Oh, well, in that case." He wedged his large frame through the open window.

Emmett did a quick survey of the surroundings. The shelves full of journals, books, and gallery catalogs looked familiar. This was Lydia's office, all right. In the gloom he could see a massive object on top of her desk.

"What the hell?" He crossed the room, flipped on the light, and scowled at the sight of the huge bouquet. "Some bastard sent my wife flowers."

"Uh, Boss, maybe you could worry about the flowers later?"

"I'll bet it was Hepscott." Emmett spotted the card lying on top of the desk and picked it up.

"If it was, I'm going to have his head on a platter." He ripped the card out of the envelope. "*Your devoted slave.* Charles." Emmett tossed the card on the desk. "Charles. *Charles.* Rings a bell but I can't place it. You know anyone named Charles, Verwood?"

"Know a coupla guys named Chuck," Verwood said. "And one who goes by the name of Chase. Don't think I know anyone who calls himself Charles, though."

"When this is over, I want you to find this Charles."

"No problem, Boss."

Emmett went through the desk drawers quickly. "Her purse is gone."

"Probably means she left for the day and everything's okay."

"Optimism is not a desirable quality in a security expert, Verwood."

Verwood exhaled heavily. "Yeah, Mr. Wyatt told me that once or twice, too."

They went down the hall, past the other offices, and then turned into the corridor that led to the museum lobby. A single fluo-rez tube burned in the empty office used by the museum's tiny security staff.

"Evening-shift guy is probably making his rounds," Verwood offered. "Maybe he doesn't know the alarm system isn't working."

Emmett went back out into the hall. "Or maybe he had something to do with the malfunction."

"You know, you and Mr. Wyatt sure do think alike when it comes to figuring out what folks might be getting up to," Verwood said admiringly. "It's like you both zero right in on the worst-case scenario. Guess that's why you both made Guild boss, huh?"

Emmett decided to ignore that. The observation struck a little too close to home. It was, after all, Mercer Wyatt who had taught him how to analyze the motives and ambitions of others.

"Melanie said the Greenies would be interested in the Tomb Wing relics." Emmett turned in that direction. "We'll start there."

Halfway along the hall, he realized that there was something different about the Tomb Wing. Instead of being darkened entirely for the night or dimly lit with the creepy green lighting used for daytime display, all of the overhead fluo-rez tubes were ablaze.

He halted at the entrance. The guard was inside the gallery, his back to Emmett and Verwood. He was busily sweeping up a lot of broken glass. The headphones he wore explained why he had not heard anyone approach.

"Hell of a way to stand guard," Verwood growled. "We could empty out the place before he even realized there was anyone else around."

"Wonder how he knew that glass display case was broken," Emmett said.

"Maybe he accidentally broke it himself."

Emmett went down the long gallery and tapped the guard on the shoulder.

The man started violently. "What? What?"

He dropped the industrial-sized broom and grabbed at the headphones, yanking them off his ears. Simultaneously he twisted around and tried to back away.

The awkward movement brought him up against a low, wide green quartz bowl that looked as if it had been designed as a wading pool. Emmett had seen it on an earlier tour of the gallery and knew that Shrimpton billed it as an alien embalming tub.

The guard tripped, cried out, flailing, and then toppled backward into the shallow pool. He landed on his back in an awkward sprawl.

Emmett braced one foot on the edge of the quartz pool. "Benny, I presume?"

"Yeah, I'm Benny. What's going on here?" Benny levered himself up to a sitting position and glanced nervously at Verwood. Then he switched his attention back to Emmett. "Who are you? What are you doing here? Wait, I recognize you. Emmett London, right? The new Guild boss? I saw your picture in the papers."

"Then we can skip the formalities. I'm looking for my wife."

Benny's jaw sagged. For a few seconds he seemed truly bereft of speech. Then he swallowed visibly.

"Your . . . your wife? Miss Smith?"

"She's Mrs. London now, Benny."

Benny froze. "Yes, sir. But what makes you think I know where she is?"

"She had a tour at five o'clock. A bunch of Greenies."

"Sure. Right. The special tour. I remember."

"When did she leave?"

"I'm not exactly sure," Benny spoke quickly. "I was busy supervising the loading of the sarcophagus, you see. That's why the alarm system is shut down. Had to turn it off so that I could open the loading-dock doors."

"My wife left a message at my office telling me that the sarcophagus wasn't going to be moved until Monday and that she had the Greenie tour instead."

"There was some sort of mix-up," Benny said, talking a little more steadily now as if he was on more certain ground. "Miss Smith, I mean, Mrs. London was busy with the tour group when the moving van arrived. So I handled the transfer. I figured Mr. Shrimpton would appreciate me showing initiative."

"Is that what you call it?"

Benny looked offended. "All the paperwork was in order. I've got it in my office. See for yourself."

Emmett looked at the broken glass on the floor. "What happened in here, Benny?"

Benny followed his gaze with a jerky movement of his head. "The movers are responsible, sir. When they picked up the coffin and its lid, they accidentally banged one corner into that display case. Nothing's missing, though. I checked."

Emmett took his foot down off the rim of the pool and crossed to the broken display case. Several tomb mirrors were clustered inside.

"I told you, nothing was stolen." Benny grabbed the edge of the pool and hauled himself to his feet. He started to put one foot over the side but stopped when Verwood moved toward him. "The sarcophagus was an authorized transfer. The museum got a lot of money for it."

Emmett glanced down at the pile of glittering glass shards that Benny had succeeded in assembling with his broom. Here and there in the sparkling slivers he caught the unmistakable gleam of polished amber.

He took one of the tomb mirrors out of the display case and used the handle to stir the chunks of glass. Two oval-shaped beads appeared. He picked them up and examined them in the light.

"They were made for a necklace," he said to Verwood.

"Whoever busted the case must have broken a string of beads at the same time." Verwood pointed toward the foot of a nearby pedestal. "There's another one. And I see a couple more over there by that table."

"That's one possible explanation." Emmett rose to his feet and turned toward Benny. "The other is that the necklace was broken in the course of a struggle."

Benny blanched. "No," he whispered. "Nothing like that happened, I swear it."

Verwood picked up the headphones that the guard had ripped off a few minutes earlier. A long cord connected them to an audio player. He held the right phone up to his ear.

Emmett watched him. "Music?"

"Nope." Verwood lowered the headphones, his expression grim. "Don't think you're gonna like this, Boss. It sounds like one of those Thirteen Steps to Bliss lectures. Lot of stuff about that Amatheon guy."

"No." Benny gave a choked cry and leaped out of the quartz pool.

He dashed toward the entrance of the gallery.

Emmett stuck out a foot and grabbed his arm as he went flying past. Benny stumbled and went down heavily. Verwood moved in to anchor him to the floor.

Benny thrashed violently. Verwood was obliged to use some force. In the course of the struggle, the buttons of the guard's uniform gave way.

A string of amber beads gleamed on Benny's hairy chest.

Emmett walked forward and stood looking down at him. "Let's try this again from the top, Benny. I'll run through it. You tell me if I get anything wrong. Those Greenies kidnapped Lydia this evening, didn't they? Took her out of here in that damn sarcophagus."

Benny's eyes darted from side to side. He twitched a few times but he held his silence.

"You were the inside man, weren't you,

Benny?" Emmett continued gently. "You turned off the alarms. The paperwork that authorized the transfer of the coffin was supposed to let you off the hook if anyone got suspicious, wasn't it? Your alibi was going to be that you were busy supervising the loading of the relic when Lydia disappeared."

"It wasn't . . . it wasn't like that," Benny squeaked.

"But something went wrong. Lydia wouldn't have gone without a fight. In the process, the case got broken and somebody lost his amber necklace."

Benny just stared at Emmett, mouth open, bottom lip trembling.

Verwood was staring, too. "Well, damn," he declared. "If that don't beat all. Only other hunter I've seen pull a ghost this far outside the Wall is Mr. Wyatt."

Emmett became aware of the tiny wisps of psi energy snapping and cracking in the air around him. A small ghost had coalesced. It promptly disintegrated only to reform and fall apart over and over again. He was standing in the center of a light shower of green fireworks.

Benny finally pulled himself together. "It's a trick."

Emmett glanced at the small ghost hovering off to his left, exerted enough concentration to keep it together for a moment, and sent it floating toward Benny.

"No, please." Benny tried to scuttle backward

but Verwood pinned him. Sweat bathed his forehead. "Stop it. Stop it. Don't let it touch me."

Emmett tightened the grip on the urgency and rage that was fueling his para-rez abilities. There was no point terrorizing Benny. The guard was barely out of his teens, a young man who somewhere along the line had been emotionally or physically damaged to such an extent that he had become easy prey for a cult.

It was unlikely that Benny knew anything helpful, anyway. He was obviously a low-ranking member of the organization. No one would have entrusted him with hard information.

Annoyed with himself, Emmett de-rezzed the ghost.

Verwood tilted his head slightly, angling his gaze up at Emmett. "Guess we go talk to that guy who runs the Greenies, right, Boss?"

"That's one approach," Emmett said, thinking about other possibilities.

Benny shook his head. "You can't just go barging in on Master Herbert. He spends most of his time meditating and communicating with the spirit of Amatheon. It requires a tremendous amount of his time and an enormous degree of psychic energy. He needs rest between his sessions with the Philosopher. Nobody gets to see Master Herbert without an appointment."

Emmett closed his fist around the amber beads. "Don't worry, Benny. Got a hunch Master Herbert will see me this evening."

25

Lydia opened her eyes to the familiar green light of the catacombs. Relief swept through her. A moment ago, when awareness had begun to creep back, she had been terrified that she was coming awake inside a closed coffin. In those first few seconds all she could think about was how long it would take her to go mad.

She had a feeling that the image of the lid of the sarcophagus descending downward, blotting out the light and sealing her into the quartz burial box, would provide her with an ample supply of nightmares for the rest of her life.

As if she didn't have enough weird dreams already.

She sat up cautiously. Her stomach swam and her head spun. Whatever they had used to put her out had some unpleasant side effects. *Just like last time.*

After a moment she decided that she was not going to throw up. Her head cleared a little. She started to shift positions again and discovered that she was on a pallet, not the hard quartz floor of the small chamber.

The space in which they had confined her was about the size of her office at Shrimpton's. But given that it was a lot bigger than the sarcophagus she decided that she would not complain too loudly about the accommodations. At least not yet.

There was a comforting familiarity about the chamber. She had spent a lot of her professional life underground in these catacombs. The walls, ceiling, and floor were oddly proportioned to the human eye but they were not uncomfortable. Every surface in the space glowed with a soft green radiance just like all of the other passages and chambers and hallways that the aliens had built below ground. As with the proportions, the light took some getting used to but after a while it felt natural, like sunlight or moonlight.

The experts had never been able to figure out the source of the luminous glow. It seemed to be a property of the particular type of green quartz that had been used to construct the catacombs. So far as anyone knew, the illumination had never so much as flickered or dimmed anywhere in the endless miles of underground corridors that had been explored thus far. Nevertheless, para-archaeologists, hunters, ruin rats, and everyone else who went down into the tunnels always carried spare flashlights, just as they carried spare amber and spare water.

The eerie light and the design of the room weren't the only things she found comforting, she thought, pushing herself to her feet. Psi energy pulsed heavily everywhere down here in the catacombs. It was invigorating.

Her stomach settled and her mind cleared. She looked toward the entrance of the chamber and saw a row of human-engineered steel bars and a lock. The aliens had not used doors or gates to seal their rooms. They had relied on various types of illusion traps to ensure privacy and security. But someone had obviously decided to go low-tech here to make sure that she did not escape. A smart move, given that she had never met a trap she couldn't untangle.

That thought made her glance at her wrist. She was relieved to see that her kidnappers had left her with her bracelet.

There was a tiny room off the main chamber, its entrance closed by a curtain. She pulled the drape aside and found that someone had thoughtfully installed a portable rest room, complete with commode, shower and basin. It was the same make and model as those that were standard equipment on most professionally run excavation sites.

She made use of the facilities and felt even steadier after she washed her face.

When she was finished, she went to stand at the bars of her cell and looked out into the corridor. A short distance away down the hall three people with shaved heads and green robes were seated at a long folding table. There was a stack of sandwiches and several cans of Curtain Cola in the middle of the table.

One of the Greenies, a woman, noticed her and quickly pushed back her chair.

"She's awake," the woman announced excitedly. "Acolyte Martin, go and tell the assistants. They said that Master Herbert wanted to see her as soon as she was alert."

"I'm on it." Martin took off, sandwich in hand, and disappeared around a bend in the corridor.

The third Greenie, another woman, peered at Lydia. "How do you feel?"

"Like I could dance until dawn." Lydia leaned heavily on the bars and tried to look as wan as possible. "Too bad I didn't bring my new dress."

"Hey, don't get smart mouthed with us," the first woman snapped. "We're just doing our job."

"Are you going to tell me why you went to all this trouble to grab me?"

"We don't know why the Master wants you here," the second woman said.

Lydia nodded. "Well, that's a real conversation stopper, isn't it?"

The first woman hesitated. "My name is Acolyte Frances. You want something to eat?"

Lydia did a quick status check on her stomach. Things appeared to be under control in that department. Maybe it would be a good idea to take some nourishment. She might need energy later.

"Got any rez-tea?" she asked.

"Sure."

"I'll take a large cup and one of those sandwiches, please."

By the time Acolyte Martin returned to inform everyone that she was to be escorted into the "Master's Chamber" Lydia felt almost normal, assuming she ignored the fact that she was both very mad and very scared.

Frances told Lydia to stick her hands out between two of the cell bars. The Greenie bound her wrists with some tape and then unlocked the door.

Lydia concentrated on orienting herself silently, using the amber in her bracelet to draw a mental map of the route to the Master's Chamber. She'd had a great deal of experience navigating underground and a professional's feel for alien architecture.

Her three escorts guided her through a short series of halls and intersections. They passed a number of chambers that had been converted into offices, complete with desks and files. There were no phones, of course. For some reason, a property of the illuminated quartz no doubt, most communications systems did not work underground.

One passage caught her attention. It was blocked with a gate of illusion shadow. Two burly-looking Greenies were stationed on either side of the darkened entrance.

"What's in there?" she asked her escorts.

"That's classified," Acolyte Martin intoned. "Only those with a need to know go in there."

"Need to know, huh?" Lydia glanced back over her shoulder as she was led past.

There was a small sign propped on one side of the passage. It read AREA 51.

The next hallway contained a row of small chambers that had been outfitted as offices. Each was staffed with a Greenie or two. If it hadn't been for their bizarre robes and shaved heads, they would have looked like normal clerks.

"What are all these people doing?" Lydia asked.

"They handle the financial and business affairs of the Order," Frances explained. "The contributions and donations we receive amount to a great deal of money. The funds have to be invested and managed wisely according to the instructions Master Herbert receives from Amatheon if we are to prosper and grow."

"You guys make a lot of money off those *Thirteen Steps to Bliss* books?"

"The books are one of our sources of income," Frances said. "There are others."

"Such as?"

"Save your questions for Master Herbert," Martin said.

They halted at a doorway that was cloaked in illusion shadow. Another pair of Greenies with broad shoulders and tough-looking features greeted Lydia's escorts.

"The Master is ready to see her," one of them said. "You are instructed to take her to the Philosopher's Chamber."

Lydia watched intently to see which of the

two guards de-rezzed the trap that shuttered the entrance. It was the one on the right. The other was probably a hunter, she decided.

She felt psi energy shiver in the air for a few seconds and a moment later the illusion shadow evaporated. She and her escorts walked into a large, imposing green hall. Behind them, the shadow reappeared. The guard had reset the trap.

She surveyed the grand hall and almost laughed, in spite of the fear that was snaking through her. Hysteria, she thought. Get a grip.

But that was easier said than done. The room was really quite amazing. Human furnishings invariably seemed very much out of place when they were moved into the ruins and the catacombs. The clash of perspectives and proportions was simply too great to allow for any harmonious blending of styles. When people did bring furniture into the catacombs, as was sometimes necessary, they generally stuck to simple, utilitarian pieces.

But whoever had done this space had clearly felt compelled to go for drama. The walls were hung with great swaths of red and gold velvet draperies. Intricately patterned carpets were spread out on the floors. The furnishings were large, heavy pieces in the style that had been popular at the time of the Era of Discord. The sofas, chairs, and tables were hand carved and gilded to a fare-thee-well.

In addition to looking distinctly odd in the

ancient, nonhuman setting, the thick carpets and heavy wall hangings cut down the natural light that emanated from the quartz. The result was an over-furnished, dimly lit room that was probably supposed to appear aristocratic and imposing.

Lydia looked at Frances and raised her brows. "Who was your decorator? It looks like a stage set for a low-budget horror movie."

Frances and the other two were obviously stunned by her lack of good taste but before they could lecture her on issues of artistic design, a short, plump figure in a green robe bustled forth from another shadowed room. Amber beads clinked.

"I am Acolyte Rich," he announced.

"Okay, that settles it," Lydia said. "You're of the masculine persuasion. I wasn't sure. Those unisex robes complicate things, you know."

"My Master considers you an honored guest," Rich stated. He sounded offended by her failure to immediately recognize his sex.

"Yeah?" Lydia held up her bound wrists. "If this is the way you treat your guests, I'd sure hate to see how you handle folks you don't like very much."

Rich looked at Frances and the other two.

Frances shrugged. "She's been real chatty ever since she woke up. Probably a side effect of the drug they used to bring her in."

"Chatty?" Lydia frowned. "You call this chatty? You haven't seen anything yet. Five will get you ten that I can talk any of you right into the ground. Come on, let's see your money."

Rich's eyes glinted angrily beneath the hood but when he spoke he kept his voice calm and polite. "Please come with me, Miss Smith. The Master is expecting you."

"Gee, I sure hope he isn't expecting too much." Lydia walked forward. "I'm not. Let's go talk to the murdering bastard."

There was a horrified silence from the Greenies.

"What are you saying?" Frances whispered. "That's a lie."

"Master Herbert would never hurt anyone," Rich growled. "He is the First Acolyte of Amatheon. The Philosopher teaches that Bliss can only be achieved through peaceful means."

"How dare you accuse the Master of murder?" Martin took an ominous step toward her. "You owe him an apology."

The velvet curtains shifted again and another figure appeared. Like the others he wore green robes but his gown was trimmed at the sleeves and hem with lots of intricately worked letter As stitched in gold thread.

The cowl was thrown back to reveal a tall man in his mid-thirties. In other garb he could have passed for a successful CEO or an academic on the fast track to department head. He was striking in appearance with a high, aristocratic forehead and prominent cheekbones. But it wasn't his looks that drew the eye. It was the way he commanded the space around him. He had a stage actor's charisma, Lydia thought.

"Enough, Acolytes," he said in a deep, mellifluous voice that rolled like dark honey through the entire room. "Miss Smith has had an unpleasant experience and is upset. There is no need to make the situation worse. I'm sorry to say that she has good reason to feel negative toward all of us at the moment." He turned toward Lydia and bowed slightly. "I am hoping to change her opinion."

"You must be Herbie," she said.

The acolytes threw her annoyed looks but the newcomer merely smiled tolerantly.

"Allow me to introduce myself," he said. "I am, as you guessed, Master Herbert. I know you have questions." He paused a beat. "I have answers."

"Well, Herb, I don't know why you went to all the trouble to kidnap me, but I can tell you one thing: My husband is going to be really pissed about this."

26

"I don't get it, Boss." Verwood, seated on the passenger side of the Slider, frowned at Fuzz, who was perched on the back of the seat. "Why did we have to stop by your place to pick up this little varmint before we go nail the guy who's running the Greenie cult?"

"Fuzz is a dust-bunny, not a varmint." Emmett eased the Slider through a narrow Old Quarter lane. "And he's a lot smarter than he looks."

"That probably wouldn't take much. I mean, how smart would the little critter have to be to have more brains than a wad of dryer lint?"

Fuzz paid no attention. He was braced on the seat back, straining forward as if eager to leap straight through the windshield. All four of his eyes were open.

"Watch yourself, Verwood," Emmett said. "Remember what they say about dust-bunnies."

"Yeah, yeah, I know. By the time you see the teeth, it's too late." Verwood took a pretzel out of the sack on his lap and offered it to Fuzz who accepted it in one paw. "He's kind of cute in his own way. You know, I've seen a few dust-bunnies living in alleys in the Old Quarter and out in the country near some of the smaller ruins but I never met anybody who kept one as a pet."

"Lydia says he adopted her, not the other way around." Emmett sent the Slider creeping through another fogbound street. "I think the two of them have formed some sort of psychic connection, although Lydia says she isn't aware of it on her end. But Fuzz found her once before when she was lost underground and I can't think of any other way he could have done that unless there's some psi-link. I'm praying he can work his magic act again tonight."

Verwood's face was grim in the light from the dashboard. "You really think they took her underground?"

"There's only one explanation I can come up with to rationalize why someone would grab her."

"Ransom? Everyone knows you're rich in your own right and you've got the deep pockets of the Guild to back you up if you need more cash. But, shit, the risk. I mean, what kind of idiot would kidnap the wife of a Guild boss? The guy's gotta know he's signing his own death warrant."

"This isn't about money. According to the information you and Perkins turned up, the Greenies have rivers of income flowing in from a variety of safe, perfectly legal sources. Everyone knows that a well-run cult is a money machine."

Verwood screwed up his face in a quizzical expression. "You think maybe they need Mrs. London's opinion on some antiquities?"

"She's a terrific para-archaeologist but there are a fair number of those around." Emmett slowed the Slider and brought it to a halt at the end of a short lane. "The one thing that makes her different from any other P-A is that she survived forty-eight hours underground without amber and came out with her para-rez faculties intact."

Verwood whistled softly. "You think this is connected to what happened back when she disappeared for two days?"

"Yes." Emmett de-rezzed the engine and cracked the door. "I also think that Lydia was right all along. She *was* the victim of a conspiracy. But one that was orchestrated by the Greenies, not the Guild. Come on, Fuzz."

He reached into the Slider for the dust-bunny. Fuzz, clutching the unfinished pretzel in one of his six paws, hopped onto his arm and scurried up to his shoulder.

Verwood got out of the Slider and walked around the front to join Emmett. "What are we doing here? Thought we were headed for the Greenie headquarters."

"With any luck at all, that's what the Greenies will assume, too. Probably figure they can stall us indefinitely there."

"So, where are we?"

"This is the former address of Dr. Lawrence Maltby."

"Thought he was dead."

"He is."

Emmett led the way across the empty, mist-shrouded street and went up the steps to the darkened front door of the aging apartment building.

The lock had not been repaired. They went inside and down the dingy hall. Emmett halted at the door across from Maltby's, made a fist, pounded three times.

"This is London. Guild business. Open the door or we'll break it down."

There was a frozen silence from inside the apartment. Then Emmett heard a series of quick steps. The peephole went dark.

A few seconds later the door opened about two inches. Cornish peered out nervously. He did not unhook the chain.

"What do you want, London?"

Emmett flattened his hand on the wall beside the door frame. "I want you to tell me the location of Maltby's secret rat hole, the one he used when he went down into the catacombs."

Cornish's eyes widened in exaggerated innocence. "How would I know that?"

"Something tells me you're an opportunist, Cornish." Emmett smiled slowly, showing a few teeth. "Got to be to support a serious Chartreuse habit."

Cornish flinched. "Now, see here, I don't know where you're going with this, but it's got nothing to do with me."

"I think you probably followed Maltby a few times when he went out at night. How could you resist? Maybe you figured you could steal a couple of relics or even some dreamstone from his hoard."

"I didn't do anything wrong."

Emmett gritted his teeth against the irritating whine in the little man's voice. "I'm not here to get you in trouble. I just want to know where Maltby went when he spent a night in the catacombs. It's worth a thousand to me."

Cornish's face went slack. "A thousand?"

"That'll buy a lot of Chartreuse, won't it?"

"Hang on," Cornish said. "I'll get a coat."

"I regret the inconvenience and the fear that you went through this evening, Lydia." Herbert sat down on a velvet-covered chair that bore a strong resemblance to a throne. "May I call you Lydia?"

"No," Lydia said.

"Please forgive me, but I felt that I had no choice but to arrange for you to be brought here in a somewhat unconventional manner. I was afraid that you would never agree to assist us of your own free will. There is a great deal of prejudice against the Order in the outside world. It is not easy to overcome."

"What makes you think I'll help you now, Herb?" Lydia asked.

Some progress had been made, she thought. Herbert had ordered Frances to remove the

314

tape that had bound her wrists and she was no longer in a barred cell. Instead, she was comfortably seated on a red velvet sofa, drinking rez-tea from a beautiful little cup and snacking on cookies.

This was probably Herb's idea of shrewd para-psychology, she thought, a sort of good Greenie–bad Greenie routine. He wanted her to think that he was the good Greenie, the one she could trust.

"Believe it or not, I'm sure that once I have explained the situation, you will feel a strong professional interest in assisting us, Miss Smith."

"That's Mrs. London to you, Herb."

Herbert's handsome jaw tensed but his warm smile did not slip by so much as a fraction. His compelling eyes were gentle with understanding.

"Why don't I start by answering some questions for you," he said persuasively.

"Okay, my first question is, when are you going to let me out of here?"

"All in good time, my dear." Herbert took a swallow of tea and deliberately lowered the cup. "I was referring to questions you no doubt have concerning the unfortunate incident you suffered in the catacombs a few months ago."

Lydia froze in the act of reaching for another cookie. "Your Greenies were involved in that? And here I've been blaming those two hunters who abandoned me —" Enlightenment struck. "Well, jeez, now I get it. Those bastards were working for you, weren't they? They were closet Greenies."

Herbert sighed. "We prefer to use the proper name of our organization, Mrs. London. We are the Order of the Acolytes of Amatheon."

"Yeah, sure." She took a big bite out of the cookie and munched. "Just tell me what you and your cult had to do with what happened to me."

"We rescued you, Mrs. London."

She swallowed twice to get rid of the last of the cookie and then shook her head. "That's a lie. When I regained consciousness I was alone in the tunnels. There was no one else around." Except for Fuzz, of course, but there was no reason to mention him to Herb. She had never told anyone except Emmett and her closest friends about Fuzz's role in her adventure.

Herbert's mouth curved in a sad, weary smile. "It's the truth, although I admit there's no way I can prove it now. You were found unconscious by one of our excavation crews."

"You operate your own teams?" She hesitated as something else became clear. "Yes, of course you do. That's how you created this little underground empire, isn't it? You have your own equipment and a private staff of tanglers and hunters."

"Many fine dissonance-energy and ephemeral-energy para-rezes have become members of the Order. We also have a number of other professionals with various skills. Accountants, bookkeepers, administrators, clerks. We even have our own medical clinic. In short, we have created a complete community down here, Mrs. London."

"Do you have a license to excavate?"

"Of course. We obtained it in the name of one of our many business enterprises. This entire sector was turned over to us. It was unexplored when we acquired it. Our people cleared the traps and ghosts and mapped the passages."

"You know the Antiquities Act states that no individual or organization can lay exclusive claim to any of the ruins. You can own artifacts and relics, but you can't just claim as private property whole sections of the catacombs."

"Ah, yes, but there is a lovely little loophole, isn't there?" Herbert looked amused. "A business or institution can, with the appropriate certification, stake a claim for a period of several years for purposes of excavation, exploration, and research. During that time the organization has complete control over the entire sector in which it is licensed to operate."

He was right. There was no point arguing the finer points of the Antiquities Act with Herbert. He obviously knew it backward and forward.

She helped herself to another cookie. "You were saying something about having rescued me." Might as well keep him talking, she thought. Time was critical. The longer she stalled, the better the chances that Emmett would find her.

"Yes." Herbert rose from his over-gilded chair

and began to pace the carpet. His strides were slow, thoughtful, imbued with an aura of grave importance. "One of our crews discovered you in a chamber in this sector. You were still unconscious. You were taken to the infirmary where you were diagnosed as showing all the symptoms of a bad ghost burn."

"What did your medics do to me?" she asked, not bothering to conceal her deep suspicion.

"You were given the customary psi-calming drugs that are usually administered in such situations. As I'm sure you are aware, people who have been singed are generally very agitated and confused when they awaken."

"In other words, you drugged me."

"I assure you, the medics followed standard emergency procedures. The drugs allowed you to fall into a normal sleep. We were then faced with a dilemma."

"What to do with me?"

"I regret to say that was precisely the problem. You see, the Philosopher has made it clear that we are to keep our work here in the catacombs secret until we have achieved our objective."

"Which is?"

Herbert came to a halt in front of a floor-to-ceiling wall hanging that featured a scene of the towering gates that guarded the Dead City above ground. He managed to position himself so that he was framed by the two great pillars. Lydia was sure that wasn't an accident. You had to hand it to Herb. He had flair.

"We are searching for the tomb of the great Amatheon," Herbert said. Awe and reverence reverberated in his words. "We have reason to believe that it is in this sector. We are very close to our objective, Mrs. London. But secrecy is vital at this stage."

"Why? You said yourself you control this entire sector. You can do whatever you want down here."

"Please, Mrs. London, don't act naïve. You know as well as I do what it is like here in the catacombs. No sector can ever be completely mapped, charted, or secured. No matter how thoroughly the survey crews do their job, they cannot possibly locate and clear, let alone protect, every single chamber or corridor."

"Mmm," she said, going for noncommittal. She could not argue with him. He was right.

"Worse yet, once the word gets out that valuable antiquities have been discovered in a sector, the ruin rats descend like the human vermin they are. Somehow, they always manage to find their own entrances."

"In other words, you didn't want the outside world to find out what you were doing down here. You knew that if you called the authorities and told them to come pick me up from your infirmary, your secret would be out."

"Yes." Herbert shook his head. "I apologize, but in our defense, I must tell you that we only did what we felt was both reasonable and right at the time. While you were sleeping under the influence of the medication, we took you to one of the sectors that is administered by the university and left you at a regularly used entrance. We knew that you would be found very quickly and that was exactly what happened."

Liar. Her fingers tightened around the handle of the cup. She had walked for miles underground before locating an exit. Herbert was relying on her well-documented amnesia to cover up the cracks in his version of the truth.

"I see." She crossed her legs and tried to project an expression of reluctant interest. "Well, that does explain a few things. I suppose you know that I have no memories of those forty-eight hours."

Herbert nodded in sympathy. "It's common knowledge that amnesia is normal following a bad burn. Often the effects are even worse. Most people who go through what you went through are not quite, shall we say, normal, afterward."

"A lot of people still don't think I'm normal. I was fired from my job at the university because the para-psychologists didn't think I'd ever be able to work underground again."

"You can hardly blame them for their opinion, Mrs. London. Very few para-rezes are ever able to go back into the catacombs after experiencing serious dissonance trauma." Herbert gave her a blinding smile. "But you are obviously an exception to the rule."

"Mmm."

"I'd like to think that the reason you survived

with your psi faculties intact was because we found you so soon after your encounter with the ghost and were able to treat you immediately with the latest medications."

He really was a great actor, she thought. Herbert was able to mix the truth and lies together in a seamless tale. If she hadn't regained some whispers of her memory, she might have bought the whole story.

But Herb had made a serious mistake. He obviously did not know about Fuzz's role in her rescue.

She knew exactly how she had escaped. Her memory of awakening in an empty corridor to find Fuzz crouched beside her, licking her face with his raspy little tongue, would be with her forever.

"Let's cut to the chase here, Herb. As long as I appeared to be just another burned-out pararez with a case of amnesia, you didn't care what I did aboveground. But when you realized that I had recovered fully and was able to work again, you decided to grab me."

"To be blunt, yes."

"I went back into the catacombs for the first time last month." She swung her ankle, thinking quickly. "The news was in the papers because of the dreamstone find. Was that when you found out that I was resonating on all frequencies again?"

"Yes. I am delighted to say that you surprised all of us, Mrs. London."

"What do you want from me?"

Herbert clasped his hands behind his back and regarded her with somber determination. "We need you, Mrs. London. In fact, we are quite desperate for your assistance. You are our last hope."

She eyed him skeptically. "Yeah?"

Herbert unclasped his hands and started toward her. "Come with me. I want to show you something that will astonish you."

27

Emmett felt the psi energy leaking out of the hidden rat hole long before Cornish and Verwood had finished pushing the empty shipping casks out of the way. His senses weren't picking up the usual fleeting wisps of power that were common in the Old Quarter, rather the strong, steady pulses that indicated an entrance into the catacombs. He was aware that Fuzz, still perched on his shoulder, was tensed as if he was about to spring.

"I followed Maltby here a couple of nights." Cornish stepped back to dust off his hands. "He never saw me. He went inside and stayed gone for hours. Figured this was where he had his hole. I came back one evening when I knew he was passed out from doing Chartreuse. I poked around a bit." He waved a hand at the floorboards. "There's a trapdoor there."

Verwood aimed the flashlight at the boards and glanced at Emmett. "Want me to open it, Boss?"

"Go ahead."

The dilapidated building in which they were standing was in the old warehouse district near the South Wall. All of the buildings along this section of the riverfront had been abandoned and boarded up years ago. Eventually it would probably be redeveloped but not for a long time. There were other, more fashionable sections of the Quarter that would get the gentrification treatment before this one did.

Verwood reached down to pry up the hinged section of flooring. The door into the catacombs opened with a squeak and a groan.

They all looked down into impenetrable darkness.

Cornish grinned. "Illusion trap. Maltby installed it to protect his little hole."

Emmett looked at him. "You didn't mention that it was trapped."

Cornish jerked as if Emmett had touched him with the point of a blade. "Hey, hey, it's okay." He stepped back hastily. "I'm a pretty fair tangler. Used to work the ruins on a regular basis. I can de-rez this for you. I did it the night I found it and then reset it so Maltby would never know."

"Do it," Emmett said evenly. "Destroy it so that it can't be reset."

"Sure, right, no problem." Cornish skittered closer to the opening.

Emmett and Verwood exchanged glances and then both moved back several paces. The first rule of working in the catacombs was not to stand too close to a tangler who was de-rezzing illusion shadow, no matter how small. That went double if you had never seen him work before and didn't know how competent he was. One small mistake on the tangler's part and everyone in the vicinity got caught in the explosion of nightmares that swept out on paranormal frequencies.

Cornish worked the shadow quickly and then held up both hands with a magician's flourish. "There you go, one trap de-rezzed. Maltby kept a little base station down there. Fixed it up real nice. When I went in I found one of those small, one-man mag-sleds, bottled water, food, even a portable lav."

Emmett moved back to the opening in the floor and looked down. A flight of rickety, human-made steps disappeared into deep darkness. But the flashlight beam cut through it with no trouble. Not illusion shadow, just an absence of light.

"I'll check it out," Emmett said to Verwood. "You stay with Cornish."

"Hey, I'm outta here," Cornish howled. "You promised I could go if I showed you the rat hole. I even de-rezzed it for you."

Emmett ignored the protest. "Watch him, Verwood. He doesn't leave until I verify that there are no more traps."

"Got it, Boss."

Cornish subsided, grumbling.

Emmett and Fuzz descended the shaky steps. The flashlight picked out the damp walls of a tunnel that had been dug with human tools. The atmosphere was dank and humid. The close confines triggered a latent claustrophobia Emmett hadn't known he possessed.

But the pulse of psi energy was stronger now and he knew that Fuzz was feeling it, too. The dust-bunny's little claws were squeezing and contracting on his shoulder and the small beast was leaning forward so far he was in danger of falling off his perch.

The steps spiraled downward and turned a corner. The tunnel walls were so tight now that Emmett had to force himself to breathe normally.

Then he saw the reassuring crack of green light up ahead. The fact that there were no suspicious dark patches and no suspicious tingles of energy meant that it was untrapped. He paused at the entrance and called back up to Verwood.

"I'm going in."

"Right, Boss." Verwood's voice was muffled and far away.

Emmett turned sideways to slide through the opening in the catacomb wall. The very existence of such cracks in the green stone had puzzled the experts for years. After all, the quartz seemed virtually indestructible, so how was it possible that slits and holes and crannies had occurred?

A number of theories had been advanced, including the possibility that at some time in the past massive earthquakes had proved more powerful than the alien-engineered quartz.

Others had concluded that the damage had

been done in the construction process and had gone unnoticed. A third school held that the rat holes had been created by the thieves, renegades, and outlaws among the ancient Harmonics who had had access to the tools and machines that had been used to build the underground maze.

Whatever the cause, the rat holes were scattered around all of the ancient cities. As long as they existed there was no way to completely limit access to the catacombs. There would always be ruin rats, illegal antiquities hunters, thrill seekers, and criminals who would be willing to take their chances underground.

Once through the crack, Emmett found himself confronted by a standard-looking passageway. There were several intersections ahead, each with a number of branching corridors that would, in turn, lead to more intersections and branching passages and so on for miles. Without amber he would become disoriented and lost as soon as he turned the first corner.

He sent a small pulse of psi power through his watch face, orienting his para-rez senses. The tuned amber functioned as a compass. Now, no matter where he went down here, he would be able to find his way back to this spot. He could use someone else's amber to navigate if necessary.

Near the entrance were the supplies and equipment that Maltby had accumulated during his years of ruin hunting. Emmett stepped up into the mag-sled, pulsed the key, and glanced at the amber-rez directional locator situated on the dash. It was functional. Now he had a backup compass.

The little vehicle hummed to life.

Fuzz growled, sounding agitated and impatient. Emmett reached up and took him down from his shoulder. He held the dust-bunny up so that he could look the creature straight in all four of his eyes.

"This is it, pal. You're on. We're playing the Find Lydia game for real. You did it once before. Let's see if you can do it again."

Fuzz blinked. His hunting eyes gleamed. His sleek, sinewy little body quivered beneath the ratty fur.

Emmett put him down on top of the sled's hood directly in front of the wheel, facing the corridors.

"Find Lydia."

He set the sled into motion, moving at a slow speed, praying that Fuzz would send some kind of signal with his body language at the first intersection.

Fuzz leaned forward as if sniffing the scent on some invisible wind. If he was right, Emmett thought, the dust-bunny was actually sending out some sort of psychic probe.

At the first branching in the corridors, they confronted the entrance to five different passages. Emmett looked at Fuzz who was staring fixedly at the second tunnel on the right.

Experimentally, Emmett started to veer to the left.

Fuzz stiffened, bounced a few times, and uttered a series of sharp little growls. His distress was plain.

Emmett obediently turned toward the tunnel that had caught Fuzz's attention.

The dust-bunny settled down, satisfied, and went back to staring straight ahead.

"Fuzz, old buddy, you make one hell of a hood ornament."

28

The endless cascades of illusion shadow plunged in seething waves from ceiling to floor. The thick, churning darkness formed an ominous curtain of energy across one entire wall of the vast chamber.

Lydia stared at it, awed and seriously thrilled in spite of the fact that she had other priorities at the moment. Priorities such as figuring out how to escape the clutches of the Greenies.

"You were right, Herb," she said, trying not to let her excitement show. "It's incredible. Absolutely huge."

"About two hundred feet across and nearly forty feet high," Herbert said. "None of the tanglers on our crews can even come close to figuring out how to de-rez it."

She found herself succumbing to her professional curiosity. "Did you check the records?"

"I assure you, I've spent hours searching excavation reports all the way back to the founding of the colonies and there is no record of anyone ever encountering anything like this. As far as we can tell it is unique."

Lydia did not point out that *unique* was a high-risk word in para-archaeology. Just because an unusual illusion trap or a particular type of relic appeared to be one of a kind did not mean that there weren't a thousand more of them somewhere down here in the unmapped sectors awaiting discovery. She was not, however, in the mood to discuss archaeological theory and practice with Herb.

"You really think you're going to find the tomb of this Amatheon character behind that illusion trap?" she asked. She had not yet been able to figure out if Herbert had bought into his own cult beliefs or not.

"Amatheon has guided us to this place," Herbert intoned. "This incredible wall of trap shadow was obviously set to protect some great secret. It can only be the Philosopher's tomb."

"No offense, Herb, but if you really believe that you're channeling Amatheon, you should probably make an appointment with a good para-shrink first thing in the morning."

Herbert did not take offense. He merely inclined his head politely. "I know you do not follow the teachings. That is your choice. But if it makes you feel any better, I will tell you that in addition to Amatheon's guidance, I had the help of a map."

"Good grief, you found a genuine Harmonic map and you didn't turn it over to the authorities? Do you have any idea of how valuable such a discovery is? In two hundred years we haven't found any written records, at least none that we've been able to decipher. A map of even a portion of the catacombs would be an incredible thing."

"Calm yourself, Mrs. London." Herbert raised his brows. "I didn't say that the map was drawn by the Harmonics."

"Oh." Lydia took a deep breath and got herself back under control. "So, who did create it?"

"I believe that the chart was hand drawn by Vincent Lee Vance."

"You're joking, right? Are you telling me that the revolutionary leader found this place a hundred years ago and drew a map?"

"That is exactly what I am telling you. I suspect that Vance established his second headquarters on the other side of that curtain of energy in the tomb of Amatheon."

Several pieces of the jumbled puzzle settled into place.

"Where did you find this map?" Lydia asked cautiously.

"In Vance's first headquarters, in the catacombs beneath Old Frequency."

Lydia sucked in her breath. "You're Troy Burgis, aren't you?"

Real surprise flashed briefly in his eyes. He concealed it quickly. "Troy Burgis disappeared fifteen years ago, Mrs. London. He never reappeared."

"Okay, have it your way. Tell me, what makes you think that I can de-rez this monster?"

"I don't *think* you can do it, Mrs. London, I know you can."

"What do you mean?"

"You did it once before, the last time you were here."

Lydia spun back to face him. "What are you saying?"

"This is the chamber where we found you unconscious. There are only two ways to get into this room. We know for certain that you did not arrive here via the corridor that you and I just used because it is guarded at all times. There is only one other way you could have entered this place."

"You're saying that I came through that illusion trap?"

Herbert inclined his head. "As far as we know, you are the only person who has ever seen the inside of Amatheon's tomb and Vance's secret headquarters here in Cadence."

"You kidnapped me so that I could show you how I de-rezzed that massive trap?"

"As I said, we are desperate. In exchange for showing us the path into the tomb we are prepared to let you have full excavation rights. You, Mrs. London, will have the honor, not to mention the enormous prestige, of being the lead para-archaeologist on the team that documents and records whatever lies behind that barrier. You've been looking for a way to regain your reputation. This project will make you a legend in the world of para-archaeology."

"There's just one problem," Lydia said. "I don't remember how I did it the first time."

★ ★ ★

The Greenie robe smelled unpleasantly of someone else's body odor but at least it fit reasonably well. Fuzz had the worst of it because he was inside, tucked under Emmett's arm.

The dust-bunny had guided him to a sector that was listed as *Unmapped* on the sled's built-in locator. There was a note that a privately held corporation named Ama-Green had taken out a license to excavate for purposes of research and exploration.

At the first evidence of human occupation — discarded newspapers and trash in the tunnels — Emmett had abandoned the sled, taking Fuzz with him.

They had encountered the first guard station a few minutes later. Emmett had managed to slip into an empty passageway just in time to avoid discovery.

Using Fuzz as a directional indicator, Emmett had worked his way deeper into the Greenie compound, bypassing two more guard stations. But as they had worked their way through the sector it had become increasingly difficult to find corridors that were not teeming with guys in green robes. Camouflage had become a necessity.

Emmett had been obliged to let the first three prospects for a robe donation go by because they had all been too short.

When the fourth Greenie, a young man of twenty or twenty-one, had entered a chamber that had been converted into a laundry room, Emmett had decided the length of the robe was about right.

He had stepped out from behind the huge stack of folded towels and summoned a small ghost. The terrified Greenie had given up his robe without protest.

Emmett had left the robe donor securely bound and gagged in a closet, tucked away behind a large, industrial-size washing machine.

The corridor outside the laundry room was empty. Emmett paused at the first intersection and allowed Fuzz to poke his nose out through the opening in the robes.

"Well, buddy?"

Fuzz swiveled his head to the right and leaned heavily in that direction.

"Got it."

Lydia saw the newcomer arrive in the hallway outside her cell and immediately stopped her restless pacing. The man wore a green robe like the others. He had the cowl pulled up over his head and his back was to her as he went toward the three acolytes who were guarding her.

She felt a tingle of awareness. All of her senses had been functioning at high-rez for hours now and were no doubt over-sensitized. Nevertheless, there was something about the way this green-robed figure moved that was very familiar.

"Open the door," Emmett said in a cool, calm

335

voice that rang with authority. "I've been ordered to move her to a different location."

Martin and Frances looked baffled. The third young guard frowned.

"Gee, I don't know," she said. "Maybe we better check with someone."

"Yeah." Martin started to get to his feet. "I'll get hold of the sector chief and just make sure —"

Ghost light flared violently in the passage. The three young people leaped to their feet and flattened themselves against the wall. They stared in shock at the wildly pulsing UDEM.

"Shit," Martin yelled.

Frances opened her mouth to scream.

"Nobody moves," Emmett said quietly. "And nobody gets singed. Give me the key to the cell."

Fuzz appeared from under Emmett's robes. He tumbled excitedly across the floor and slipped through the bars of Lydia's cell.

She scooped him up and kissed the top of his tatty little head. "About time you guys got here. What took you so long?"

Martin fumbled briefly under his robes and produced a rez-key. Emmett manipulated the ghost a little to one side and held up his hand.

"Toss it to me," he ordered.

Martin obeyed.

"You," Emmett said, looking at Frances. "Take off the robes."

Shaking visibly, Frances unfastened the garment, revealing the jeans and T-shirt she wore underneath. She wadded up the robe and hurled it at Emmett.

"You'll never make it out of here without getting caught," she snapped, voice quivering.

Emmett nodded. "You might want to keep in mind that this type of ghost is agitated by loud noises. One good scream, for example, will probably cause it to go wild."

Leaving the UDEM to keep the three pinned to the wall, he unlocked the cell door.

Clutching Fuzz, Lydia rushed out.

"Put this on." Emmett tossed the robe to her.

She swung the green gown around her shoulders and pulled up the hood.

"Let's go." Emmett turned and went swiftly away down the corridor. "The ghost will hold them until someone comes along to de-rez it."

She hurried after him, Fuzz tucked in one arm under the robe.

There was a small utility truck around the next bend.

"Right where I left it," Emmett said, leaping into the open cab and rezzing the engine. "Things are looking up."

Lydia scrambled up beside him. Fuzz poked his nose out from under the robes.

"Is that true what you told those three?" she asked. "About the ghost getting agitated by loud noises?"

"No, but with luck, they'll believe it long enough to give us a head start."

"How did you get hold of a truck?"

"I stole it off a bunch of Greenies who were having lunch."

"Nice going," she said.

Emmett checked the gages and dials on the dash and whipped the vehicle around a corner. "Fuzz got me in here but now we can use the locator to head for the nearest exit."

They passed another truck driven by a man in a green robe. The driver started to lift a hand in greeting and then did a double take and frowned.

"This place is crawling with security," Lydia warned.

"I got that impression." Emmett glanced at the locator and made another turn. "What the hell is going on down here?"

"The archaeological discovery of the century. Maybe of two centuries. The leader calls himself Master Herbert."

"That would be Herbert Slattery, Greenie boss, right?"

"Actually, I think he's really Troy Burgis."

"Yeah?"

"Listen to this. He claims he found an old map that was drawn by Vincent Lee Vance. He thinks it shows the location of Vance's second headquarters. He says that what Vance actually found was the tomb of this Amatheon character. Problem is, there's a huge wall of illusion shadow at the entrance."

"He really believes his own spiel about Amatheon?"

"I got that impression, but I have to tell you the guy is a good actor. I honestly can't say if he was putting me on or not. But he definitely wants to get into the chamber that Vance marked on the map."

"Did they grab you because Herb or Burgis or whatever his name is thinks you can de-rez the big trap?"

"It's a long story." Lydia clamped a hand around the side of the cab to hang on as Emmett sent the truck humming down another corridor. "But the punch line is that I did it once before during my Lost Weekend. That's why they wanted to get me back. Apparently I'm the only tangler who has been able to get into the chamber."

"And you've got amnesia about that whole forty-eight hour period," he concluded softly.

She smiled humorlessly. "Talk about your ironic twist, huh? I saw what no human has seen since the days of Vincent Lee Vance and I have no recollection of it. Just think, if things had gone a little differently seven months ago I'd probably be heading up the entire Department of Para-archaeology at the university today instead of working at Shrimp's."

"I take it you didn't offer to untangle this monster for Herb?"

"Nah. He promised me the sun, moon, and stars if I'd get him into that chamber but I told him I couldn't remember how I'd done it the first time. Then I explained that the knockout drug they used on me had given me a headache. I said I needed some rest before I made an attempt."

"That's why you were in the cell when I came looking? You were supposed to be resting up for the big event?"

"Actually, I was trying to buy some time. I had a hunch you would probably show up sooner or later."

He turned another corner and braked to a sharp halt. "Damn. Looks like the word is out that you're gone."

Lydia sucked in her breath at the sight of the big double ghost that blocked their path. Through the chaotic, pulsing green glare of psi energy, she saw two figures moving on the other side of the UDEM. Hunters, she thought, working in tandem to increase their power.

As she watched a third man appeared, adding his energy to the flaring, whirling firestorm.

"Forget that." Emmett threw the truck into reverse, braced one hand on the back of the seat, and turned slightly in the seat to check the corridor behind the vehicle. He stomped hard on the accelerator. "The first two are simple rez-patterns. I could handle them without any trouble. But the third guy is good. I'd have to burn amber to get rid of his ghost plus the other two and we can't risk that yet."

She understood. Once Emmett used the kind

of power that would melt amber the countdown would begin to the inevitable aftereffects. A bad case of lust would be the least of his problems. She knew that he could control that. But there was nothing he could do to hold off the desperate need for sleep that would soon overtake him. He could not afford such a severe expenditure of psi energy until they were in a location where it would be safe for him to crash.

At the next intersection, Emmett glanced at the locator, spun the wheel, and turned sharply to the right.

Alarmed shouts rang in the corridor. Greenies appeared. Two small ghosts flared. Emmett derezzed them, but instead of forcing the truck past the gathering crowd, he checked the gauges and made a left turn that took them down still another corridor.

They didn't get far. A fresh team was waiting in the next passage. Emmett slammed to a halt, reversed course again, and turned to the right.

This glowing corridor was empty but psi power surged in waves down the hall, flowing around them like the currents of an invisible river.

"Bad news," Lydia whispered. "This looks familiar."

"Yeah?"

"Herb brought me here." She turned her head, searching for reference points. "This is the corridor that leads to the chamber where that wall of illusion shadow is located. Once we're in there, we'll be trapped in more ways than one."

Emmett checked the rearview mirror. "Guess that explains a few things."

"Such as?"

"Why they left three kids to guard you instead of a couple of trained hunters. Hell, they're not trying to catch us. They're herding us in the direction they want you to go. Doubt if they were expecting me. I'm probably a complication they could have done without, but they wanted you to make an escape attempt."

She frowned. "Why would they do that?"

"So that they could block all the routes out of here except one," Emmett said.

Another memory shimmered and coalesced with startling clarity in her mind. "Just like last time."

"What?"

"Little creep."

"Who?"

"Herb." Fresh outrage flashed through her as more memories of her Lost Weekend came together. "I knew he was lying, I just wasn't sure which of the details he gave me were true and which were false. But now I recall that I didn't arrive in this sector by crashing through from Amatheon's tomb. I *escaped* that way."

"What the hell?"

"It's all coming back to me now. Never mind, I'll explain later. Keep going."

Someone yelled behind them.

Emmett checked the rearview mirror again. "Maybe it's time I gave those guys something else to think about."

He reached inside his robe and withdrew a dark, lethal-looking object.

She stared at the weapon in his hand. "That's a mag-rez gun. Where did you get it?"

"Supply cabinet."

"Oh, yeah? And just what supply cabinet contains illegal weapons like that?"

"The one Wyatt keeps in his office. Also known as his private wall safe."

"Guild bosses," she muttered. "What can you do with 'em?"

Emmett checked his mirror again. She saw his hand tighten on the gun. A new jolt of alarm went through her.

"Emmett, you can't use that thing in here. You know how dangerous it is to use any kind of firearms inside the catacombs. The bullets ricochet all over the place. What's more, the psi energy you use to rez the trigger is unpredictable inside the walls. It could easily summon a lot of wild ghost energy."

"All of which will cause some major distractions," he said coldly. "Which may be just what we need."

She heard a small rumble of protest and looked down to see that Fuzz was wriggling gently in her hands, trying to free himself. She realized that she was holding him very snugly.

"Sorry, Fuzz. Guess I'm a little tense." She relaxed her grip.

Fuzz scrambled off her lap and perched on her shoulder. He was all sleeked out now, four eyes glittering with the ice and fire of a born predator. The same chilling heat burned in Emmett's eyes, she noticed.

By the time you see the teeth, it's too late.

She drew a deep breath. "Don't worry, we're going out of here the same way I did the last time. I'll untangle the trap that guards Vance's secret chamber."

"I thought you told Herb you couldn't remember how to de-rez that wall of shadow."

"He lied to me so I lied to him."

29

Emmett drove through the doorway of the ante-chamber and braked hard. With a few deft movements, he succeeded in parking the big vehicle so that it blocked the entrance.

Ghost light flared wildly in the entrance they had just driven through. The pulsing energy was so close that Lydia flinched. Emmett had summoned a large UDEM.

"What are you doing?" she asked.

"Setting up a roadblock. It won't hold them for long but it will buy us some time." He motioned her to get out of the cab. "End of the line, let's get moving."

Lydia scrambled out of the vehicle, Fuzz on her shoulder. Emmett followed swiftly.

She heard shouts and yells in the long hall behind them. The ghost Emmett had set effectively blocked the entrance. It would take time and skill to de-rez it.

They ran toward the great, crashing waves of psi energy that spilled and roiled along the far wall. Lydia thought she was prepared for the monster trap this time but the sight of that endlessly shifting darkness nevertheless made her mouth go dry.

Emmett surveyed the scene and whistled softly. "Okay, I'm impressed."

Fuzz growled softly.

"Herb said there was no record of any other trap like it in the official excavation records and on that point, I'm inclined to believe him," Lydia said. "It would have been worth an entire graduate seminar course in P-A school."

Emmett reached out to pluck Fuzz from her shoulder. "I'll take care of my buddy here while you do what you have to do." He glanced toward the entrance. "But whatever it is, please do it fast."

"Don't worry, now that we're in here, the Greenies will keep their distance until I do something with this thing." She moved slowly toward the cascading night.

"Guess the thought of being caught in this monster's backlash is what you might call a major deterrent."

"Yes." She shivered and turned quickly toward him. "Emmett, if I'm wrong about this, if I can't untangle it again, I honestly don't think anyone standing this close will survive. It would be best if you moved into one of those alcoves along a side wall. The quartz will block some of the energy."

"Forget it; Fuzz and I know you can handle this. But it would be nice if you hurried things up a bit."

"Right."

She turned back to face the trap and concentrated on the silent waterfall of dark energy in front of her. She probed gently, feeling for the patterns within the patterns of pulsing, seething psi-power. There was no way a single tangler working alone could possibly summon enough energy to de-rez the entire trap at once. Herb had told her that the Greenies had attempted to use two tanglers in tandem in one desperate experiment but the results had been disastrous. The effort had provoked dangerous, unpredictable changes in the complex rez patterns.

The answer was obvious, once you saw it, she thought. If you could not tear down a wall or go around it, you had to tunnel through it.

She was vaguely aware that the shouts and cries at the entrance of the chamber had ceased. A great hush had fallen. She sensed the intensity of the observers. No doubt Master Herb was there somewhere among the watchers.

"A couple of them have guns," Emmett said quietly. "I think the idea is to wait until you de-rez this thing, then they'll take down my ghost and try to kill us both before you can reset the big trap."

"Sounds like a plan." If the Greenies managed to murder them both before she could reset the giant snare, they would achieve their goal of getting into the secret chamber.

"Lydia, listen to me, once the trap comes down, take Fuzz and run, as fast as you can. Don't stop, no matter what happens, understand?"

She knew then that he intended to use the mag-rez gun to buy her some time. Once the bullets started ricocheting off the walls of the antechamber and wild, chaotic ghost energy started flying around, a lot of people, including Emmett, were going to get hurt, burned, or killed.

"The trap's not coming down, Emmett. Get ready to follow me."

He flashed her a quick, questioning look but he said nothing.

She chose the section of the energy wall that was directly in front of her and then set about coring through the dark rush of power.

She caught the pulse of the resonating energy pattern in one small spot and gently dampened it. Not the simplest work she had ever done, she thought, but in an odd sort of way, it wasn't the most complicated, either. The trick was to not think about the great mass of nightmarish energy that could be so easily triggered with one misstep.

A section of night opened, slowly at first and then widening more quickly. She caught a glimpse of familiar green light coming from the mysterious chamber on the other side of the barrier.

She worked carefully until she had a tunnel wide enough to accommodate the three of them. Then she cleared the section of flooring so that they could walk through the churning passage.

"Let's go," she said.

Emmett, who had been watching the crowd at the entrance, turned. "It's still there —" he started to say and then broke off, grinning with appreciation, when he saw the opening. "Well, damn, lady, that is one really good trick. I never knew an illusion trap could be handled that way."

"There's never been any reason to try such a technique until this monster came along. Ready?"

"Go," Emmett ordered.

She moved into the tunnel and was immediately enveloped in a strange, rushing silence. Dark energy crashed and rolled overhead and on every side except for the strip she had cleared along the floor. It was as if she were caught inside the hollow curl of a tremendous ocean wave. A great sense of exhilaration swept through her, making her almost giddy.

She glanced back and saw that Emmett had followed her into the passage. He was moving quickly but she could not hear his boots ring on the floor. His mouth opened and she knew that he was speaking to her but even though she was only a yard from him she could not hear a word. When he realized that the psi energy was cloaking all sound, he grimaced, shook his head, and closed his mouth.

Fuzz crouched on Emmett's shoulder, his fur standing out all over his body in a halo of gray fluff. All she could see were his four gleaming eyes. The giddy sensation grew stronger. She started to laugh at the little furball and then she noticed the wild red-gold snakes dancing and writhing in front of her face. Her own hair was also responding to the enormous amount of ambient psi energy in the air. So was Emmett's. All three of them looked like they'd just touched a live wire carrying enough power to light up a small town.

The wall of energy was unusually thick. The tunnel she had created was at least twenty feet long.

Emmett paused midway and turned to look back over his shoulder. Lydia followed his gaze. Through the opening in the other end she glimpsed figures dashing around in the antechamber. The Greenies had managed to de-rez Emmett's ghost. Any second now one of them would brave her tunnel to give pursuit.

"I'll close it," Lydia shouted and then realized Emmett couldn't hear a word she was saying.

She sent a psi probe back to de-rez the entrance of the tunnel. It closed quickly. Swirling night sealed the opening and cut off the green glow from that end.

She did not doubt that soon Herb or one of his strong ephemeral-energy para-resonators would take the risk of trying to repeat her success. But even knowing now that it could be done, they would use extreme caution around this extraordinarily powerful trap. She and Emmett and Fuzz had a little time, she thought.

She was about to congratulate herself when she noticed that the tunnel seemed to be narrowing slightly. Only then did she realize that she was tiring. The effort to hold the passage open against the pressing weight of an untold amount of psi energy was drawing down her reserves.

She beckoned quickly.

"Run!" she screamed although she knew Emmett could not hear her.

Nevertheless, he seemed to understand what was happening. With one hand around Fuzz to secure him to his shoulder, Emmett broke into a run.

Lydia whirled and raced toward the far end of the energy tunnel.

The tunnel continued to narrow. It seemed to her that she could feel the pressure of the energy bearing down on her, no longer exhilarating, but oppressively heavy. She fought back with a burst of psi power. The whirling waves drew back slightly but not for long.

The opening at the far end was closer. Just a few more paces.

Almost there.

Lydia plunged out of the collapsing tunnel with Emmett right on her heels. Her foot caught on an object on the floor. She tripped and went down hard. Emmett stumbled over the same obstacle but managed to stay on his feet. He reached down, grabbed Lydia by the collar of her shirt, and hauled her away from the entrance of the collapsing tunnel.

There was no need to reset the trap, she thought. The passage she had opened was rapidly closing itself, *just as it had the last time.* Emmett stopped a safe distance away from the cascade of endless nightmares. Together they watched in amazement as restless, seething energy refilled the void Lydia had created.

A wall of illusion shadow once again separated the two chambers.

"You okay?" Emmett shoved the mag-rez gun into his belt.

"Yes, I think so." She started to get to her feet, struggling to recover her breath. "Sorry about that. My memory seems to be coming back in bits and pieces. I remember now that the wall resealed itself when I escaped. I didn't have to try to reset it."

In fact, she had barely made it through.

Fuzz scurried over to her. She picked him up and examined him closely. He appeared to be fine.

"Looks like you aren't the only person to have come this way." Emmett motioned toward the object that she had tripped over on the way out of the tunnel.

She followed his gaze and saw a grinning skull and a bundle of pale bones. The skeleton was still partially covered in the tattered remains of a red-and-gold uniform that she recognized from pictures in history books and the scenes painted on the walls of Restoration Hall. The burnished glow of the famous amber-and-gold signet that had once been pinned to the chest of the jacket was undimmed after a hundred years.

Nearby lay a second skeleton garbed in a similar style. An amber pendant necklace had fallen through the rib cage.

"I remember them," Lydia said softly. The chill that went through her was disturbingly familiar. "They were here last time. Meet the remains of Vincent Lee Vance and Helen Chandler."

30

"So this is where they came to die after the Last Battle of Cadence." Emmett studied the skeletons. "According to the old legends they had made a suicide pact and vowed to carry it out if they were defeated. But I've got a hunch that they were a little more practical than that. Probably intended to hide from the Guild hunters until the heat died down."

"I'll bet something went wrong when she tried to de-rez a tunnel in the trap," Lydia whispered. She thought about how close to disaster they had all come a moment ago when the opening she had made through the wall of shadow had begun to narrow without warning. "It wouldn't have taken much. One tiny miscalculation and they would have been caught in the backlash when the trap shut."

Emmett nodded. "They would both have been exhausted from the battle and the desperate retreat through the catacombs. Some of the firsthand accounts claim that Vance had been singed. One thing is for sure, by the time they reached this place neither of them would have been in any shape to tackle this monster trap."

Lydia rubbed her arms against the prickly chill that had raised goosebumps on her skin. "They got caught. The effects of a trap as massive as this one would probably be enough to kill a human outright. At the very least it would have plunged them both into deep comas. Without medical help, they would have eventually died right where they fell without ever awakening."

"The historians are going to be rewriting a few chapters in the textbooks after this place gets taken apart by the pros."

"What a truly dreadful way to go." Lydia shivered again and reached up to touch Fuzz. "Trapped in an alien nightmare."

"Hell with 'em, they deserved it." Emmett leaned down and picked up Vance's infamous amber signet. "These two nearly destroyed the colonies trying to conquer them. The punishment fit the crime."

She smiled ruefully. "Okay, that's definitely a point of view."

"What the hell is this place?" Vance's amber in his hand, Emmett turned on his heel, surveying the great circular chamber. "I've never seen anything like it in the excavation reports. I'm damn sure it isn't a tomb, though."

Lydia followed his gaze. The vaulted ceiling was high, much higher than in the antechamber. A number of wide, curving balconies had been cut into the quartz walls. They rose in tiers almost to the top. There were a number of niches and openings Some of them appeared to connect to other, smaller chambers.

Many of the relics in the chamber were familiar in style and design. She had seen similar pedestals, urns, and abstract sculptures at excavation sites and in museums and galleries. But the long rows of shallow quartz boxes topped with ornately carved lids were new to her.

"You ever seen anything like these before?" Emmett crossed to one of the long boxes and ran a finger along the elaborate designs that decorated it.

"No, I haven't." Lydia went to stand beside him. "We can't be sure that this isn't some kind of very elaborate tomb built for a great leader. Maybe Herb was right. Maybe this is the burial site of Amatheon."

"Don't think so."

She frowned. "What makes you so certain? No offense, but you're a hunter, not a trained P-A."

Emmett shrugged. "The place doesn't feel like a tomb."

"You can't go by feel. The truth is, we know almost nothing about how the Harmonics used any of the rooms and chambers we've excavated in the past two hundred years."

"True."

Cautiously she raised the lids of several of the long boxes. There was nothing inside. "I wonder what they kept in these trays?"

He glanced back at the seething wall. "We

don't have time to do an archaeological report. We've got to get out of here."

"I just want to take a quick peek in a couple more of these trays."

"Damn it, Lydia —"

She had the lid of another box partially open. There was an object inside. Her first thought was that it was a smaller version of the outer container. It was intricately decorated with the familiar, flowing abstract designs that appeared on so many of the relics.

"Look, it's hinged on one side just like the cover of a . . . oh, jeez, Emmett." She hardly dared to breathe. "*Emmett*, look."

"Save it for later." Emmett grasped her arm to haul her away. He glanced impatiently at the object that held her riveted to the spot. He went very still. "I don't believe it."

They both stared at the first of several extraordinarily thin sheets of quartz. Each was covered with still more abstract designs.

"A book." Lydia swallowed and gently turned a page. "I think it's a real *book*, Emmett. The first one that has ever been found in the ruins."

The thrill of the discovery threatened to overwhelm her. Very carefully she turned another page.

Something shimmered on one of the green quartz sheets. A section of the page wavered before her eyes. She yelped in surprise, yanked her hand away, and took a quick step back. Fuzz grumbled about the sudden movement and dug his small claws into her shirt to maintain his balance.

Emmett leaned over the book and cautiously examined the shimmering section. "I think it's a picture of some kind. But it's out of focus. The reader probably had to activate some mechanism to make it clear."

"Psi powered?" She studied the wavering page. "I can feel a trickle of energy."

"So can I."

"It doesn't feel dangerous."

"Famous last words from a P-A." Emmett tightened his grip on her arm. "We're sure as hell not going to run any experiments here. For all we know the energy ghosts and illusion traps may have been the least lethal of the psi-tech gadgets the aliens left behind."

"I won't argue, but you know what this place feels like, Emmett? It feels like a library."

"You P-As are always warning everyone not to draw parallels between humans and the Harmonics, remember? You say we're not supposed to make assumptions about the aliens' culture based on our own."

"I know, but for now I'm going with my intuition. I think this was a library or something similar. At some point they packed it up, perhaps when they abandoned their colonies. But they left one book behind. Maybe it wasn't very important to them. Or maybe it just got overlooked. But it is our first Harmonic text. They're going to go wild at the university."

"And you'll go down in the records as the one who found it."

She closed the cover and gently lifted the book out of the long storage box. It was lighter than it looked. "I'm taking this with me."

"Lydia —"

"I'll be careful, I promise. I won't open it again until I've got it in a research lab. Emmett, please, I can't leave it. Last time amnesia wiped out my memories of this chamber and the people who knew the truth lied about everything. I just can't take the chance of losing it all again."

His face hardened and for a moment she thought he would refuse, but in the end, he just nodded once, very curtly.

"All right," he said. "How do we get out of here?"

Relieved, she clutched the book in both hands and angled her chin toward an opening flanked by two elegant columns. "I remember that passage, I think."

"Is there another illusion gate that way?"

She frowned, trying to summon up the memories. "Yes, but it's a much smaller one."

Emmett scooped Fuzz off her shoulder and put him down on the floor. "We'll let you go first, buddy. You've got better senses than either of us. Home, pal."

Fuzz promptly scuttled off, leading the way through the twin columns.

Lydia and Emmett followed. Fuzz tumbled

and bounced through another chamber, past more mysterious objects, and then he turned into a short hall and stopped abruptly. His fur flattened against his sinewy little body.

Illusion shadow blocked the path.

"No problem," Lydia said.

She de-rezzed the barrier quickly.

And nearly blundered into the massive ghost waiting on the other side.

It was huge. Green fire ebbed and flared in a terrible, unpredictable rhythm. There was a narrow space between the leading edges of the ghost light and the wall.

Emmett caught hold of her and yanked her back out of range.

"Now I remember that thing." Lydia watched the ghost pulse and glow and swirl. The last of her missing memories flooded back.

"Is this the one that singed you?" Emmett asked, studying it intently.

"Yes." She shuddered, clutching the book close. "There was no other way out. I couldn't go back. So I waited until the pulses seemed to ebb somewhat and then I tried to slide past, hugging the wall. But it flared suddenly and scorched me. I was running on pure adrenaline at that point and I managed to keep going a few more yards. I got as far as the next intersection, turned into another passage, found a chamber, and collapsed. The next thing I remember is Fuzz licking my face."

Emmett bent down and picked up an object

lying on the floor. He held it between thumb and forefinger.

"My bracelet," she breathed. "This is where I lost it. I broke the catch when I escaped from the guards so I clutched it in my hand. It got me this far, but when that ghost brushed me I must have dropped it."

Emmett eyed the huge ghost. "If that chamber we just left really is a library, I guess this would be the circulation desk."

"Staffed by the librarian from hell."

Emmett tossed Vincent Lee Vance's amber signet into the air and caught it in his hand.

"Lucky for us I've got my library card," he said.

31

Monday morning Lydia lounged in her office chair, sipped hot rez-tea, and surveyed her small, attentive audience. Melanie was propped on the edge of the desk, skirt riding high. Shrimpton hovered in the doorway.

"That's pretty much the end of the story," Lydia concluded. "After Emmett used Vance's signet to de-rez that big ghost blocking our path, we made our way to the nearest exit. Emmett immediately got in touch with Verwood and Detective Martinez and briefed them on the situation down in Greenie Land. Martinez went in with a contingent of cops and hunters and mopped up. It was a huge coup for her, of course."

"Too bad Herbert Slattery or Troy Burgis or whatever his name is got away," Shrimpton said dourly.

"They'll find him," Lydia said.

Melanie nodded. "Meanwhile, finding that cache of illegal weapons in that corridor the Greenies called Area 51 will pretty much guarantee that Martinez gets a huge promotion."

"By the time Martinez receives her new promotion, Emmett will be an *ex*–Guild boss,"

Lydia said firmly. "Wyatt's recovering nicely, thank goodness. He's going home from the hospital today."

Shrimpton scowled thoughtfully. "Have they figured out what this Herbert-Burgis character was planning to do with all those guns?"

"Burgis is the only one who can answer that question for certain but I wouldn't be surprised to find out that he had plans to follow in Vance's footsteps."

"Conquer the city-states?" Melanie was appalled. "Impossible. There's no way he could have done that."

"I think he dreamed of finding some alien technology in that so-called tomb of Amatheon," Lydia said slowly. "By all accounts he's been obsessed with Vance for years. Got a hunch he figured that Vance had discovered some great secret in that chamber."

"And Burgis thought that if he got his hands on that secret, he could accomplish what Vance failed to do, is that it?" Melanie asked.

"That's the current theory," Lydia said. "Like I said, we'll know more when they get Burgis."

"Shouldn't take long to find him," Shrimpton said. "Something tells me that if Martinez doesn't catch him right quick, the Guild will hunt him down very soon."

"That's for sure." Melanie chuckled. "Jack says every hunter in every city in the Federation is looking for Burgis. He can run for a while but he won't be able to hide for long."

Shrimpton heaved a mournful sigh. "So much for the great deal on the Mudd Sarcophagus. There never was a real private collector waiting to pay twice what it was worth. It was all a ruse to make the kidnapping possible."

Melanie's brows zipped together. "I don't get that part. Burgis must have known that if you disappeared in the middle of a Greenie tour someone would have suspected the Order of the Acolytes of Amatheon."

Lydia shook her head. "He didn't care if a few of the Greenies got picked up off the street and questioned. None of them knew anything. The ones who were involved in the kidnapping were all safely back underground. It never occurred to Herb that anyone could find his hidden empire."

"But he was wrong," Shrimpton said. "Professor Lawrence Maltby discovered it first and he tried to warn you, didn't he?"

"Yes." Lydia put down her empty cup. "Poor Maltby. He wandered for years down there in the tunnels. At some point he must have stumbled onto Burgis's operation. He obviously recognized Burgis and figured out that the Greenies were responsible for my Lost Weekend. He tried to warn me but by the time I got to his apartment, someone else had gotten to him first."

"Burgis or one of his Greenies," Melanie said. "Everyone in Maltby's neighborhood knew he used drugs. It wouldn't have been difficult to spike a batch of Chartreuse with something lethal."

"Yes," Lydia said. "I think the killer probably went in to make certain that the drugs had worked. Maltby must have still been alive. He'd been using Chartreuse for years and had no doubt built up some tolerance. It probably took him longer to die than the killer expected. There must have been a struggle."

"That's when the killer's necklace got broken," Melanie said. "Afterward, he picked up as many of the beads as he could find, but it was dark in the apartment and he was in a hurry."

"He missed the bead that I found," Lydia concluded. "He also missed the note that the professor had started to write, the one about the Amber Hills Dairy milk carton. Even if the killer noticed it, he probably assumed that it wasn't important. Just the start of a grocery list."

"I take it Burgis sent some more Greenies to search Maltby's place later that night just to make sure that nothing had been left behind that might give the cops a clue?" Melanie asked. "Those were the two guys you and Emmett surprised?"

Lydia nodded. "They didn't find the milk carton, either."

Melanie frowned. "What happened to Burgis's three pals? The ones who were with him in that pulse-rock band and later disappeared?"

"The cops haven't been able to identify them yet," Lydia said. "The assumption is that they are all living under other names and are part of the Greenie hierarchy. But it's going to take a while to get to the bottom of that organization."

There was a short silence while they all absorbed that fact.

"It's not fair, I tell you," Shrimpton said darkly. "The governor appointed the university to oversee the excavation of that library chamber and all of the big museums are going toe-to-toe to get a piece of the action. They're lobbying like mad and calling in old favors. But this institution is out in the cold. It's not right."

Melanie cleared her throat. "We don't exactly have the facilities to handle a major excavation like that one, sir."

"Nevertheless, we should have been allowed to be part of the team that will open up the library." Shrimpton slapped a hand against the doorjamb, his indignation rising. "But no. We don't get zip-squat. Not *zip-squat*, I tell you."

"It's okay, Boss," Melanie said soothingly. "Take it easy. Remember your blood pressure."

"The devil with my blood pressure. It was a Shrimpton employee who discovered the way into that chamber. If there was any justice this institution should have been granted the lead license to excavate."

Lydia exchanged a glance with Melanie. Referring to Shrimpton's House of Ancient Horrors as an *institution* and making it sound as though it belonged in the same category as the Department of Para-archaeology at the university or the renowned Cadence Archaeological Museum was pushing it. But neither of them had the heart to point that out to Shrimp.

"I know just how you feel, sir," Lydia replied. "No one from my old department at the university even bothered to invite me to join their crew as an outside consultant."

"It's your own fault, if you ask me," Melanie said. "You should never have given your ex-colleagues in the department the secret to getting through that illusion wall."

"I know, I know." Lydia spread her hands. "The thing is, it was clear that they were going to attempt to de-rez it on their own. If someone had screwed up, there would have been a terrible accident. I didn't want that responsibility on my shoulders."

Shrimpton snorted. "The bottom line here is that we've got nothing, absolutely nothing, to show for our contributions to this momentous discovery. In fact, we actually lost something: a perfectly good sarcophagus. Those things don't grow on trees, you know."

"I have it on good authority that the Guild will see to it that the sarcophagus is returned," Lydia assured him. "Emmett says it's the least the hunters can do under the circumstances."

Shrimpton huffed. "Well, that's something to

be thankful for, I suppose. But who's going to compensate us for losing you, Lydia?"

"You've still got me, sir," she said quickly.

"Yes, yes, of course we have you as a member of the staff," he continued, "but let's face it, the moment London steps down from his position as the boss of the Cadence Guild, you'll no longer be the big draw you've been lately."

Melanie chuckled. "Sad to say it, Lyd, but he's right. When you are no longer Mrs. Guild Boss, I doubt if we'll be able to convince folks to pay extra for a private tour of the museum conducted by you."

"Like I said, we get zip-squat," Shrimpton concluded mournfully. "Be lucky if this institution even gets mentioned in a footnote in one of the countless articles and books that will be written about that alien library."

Lydia had been waiting for this very moment. "I regret that I will no longer be a major attraction here at Shrimpton's House of Ancient Horrors, sir, but I think I can guarantee that this museum will get a bit more than a footnote out of this affair."

He blinked a couple of times. "How's that?"

"Mr. Shrimpton," she said very earnestly, "you gave me a job when no one else in the city would even consider of hiring me because they thought I'd been burned out. In addition, you have been very generous about allowing me to develop a private consulting business outside my duties here. And then there was all that time off you gave me to prepare for the Restoration Ball. I owe you a great deal."

"Nonsense." Shrimpton turned an odd shade of red and flapped a hand. "You've been an excellent addition to the staff. Happy to have you with us."

Lydia sniffed a couple of times and managed a watery smile. "The point I'm trying to make is that, regardless of my outside activities, I consider myself first and foremost a member of this, uh, institution's staff. My professional loyalties lie here at Shrimpton's, not up at the university."

Shrimpton dug a handkerchief out of his pocket and dabbed at his cheeks. "Very touching, my dear. Very touching, indeed."

Melanie sighed. "If you two are going to burst into tears, I'll have to leave."

Lydia wiped her nose and quickly got to her feet. "Because of my allegiance and affection for this museum, I wouldn't dream of allowing it to come out of this business with nothing but zip-squat."

"Yeah?" Melanie began to look interested.

Shrimpton put his handkerchief back in his pocket. "What do you mean?"

Lydia reached down, opened her bottom desk drawer, and took out the large cardboard box she had placed there when she had arrived at the office that morning. Setting the box on the desk, she removed the lid with a flourish.

Shrimpton shuffled forward to take a closer

look. Melanie leaned over the desk. They both stared at the book that Lydia had brought out of the alien library.

"Oh, my goodness," Shrimpton whispered. "Is that for us?"

"For a while," Lydia said wryly. "Sooner or later we'll have to let the university experts examine it. But they're going to be very busy for quite some time inside that library. I figure we can put this book on display as soon as we get the Guild to arrange security, say, this week. We should be able to exhibit it for at least a month or longer before the crowd up at the university realizes what's going on and starts screaming bloody murder."

"Well, well, well." Melanie grinned. "I do believe Shrimpton's House of Ancient Horrors has got its next big attraction."

Shrimpton was dazzled. "People will be lined up all the way to the river to see this book."

"They sure will," Lydia said. "Especially when they find out it has pictures."

"*Pictures!*" Melanie exclaimed. "Are you serious?"

"Oh, my," Shrimpton said, aghast at the prospects. "Oh, my goodness gracious. Pictures?"

"There is a tiny bit of psi-energy coming from it," Lydia explained. "I wanted to be sure it was safe. Yesterday I took it to a private lab to get it checked out. The techs did some fiddling and testing. They figured out that anyone who can rez a lightbulb or a door key can operate this thing."

Very carefully she opened the quartz covers and turned to the place she had marked.

Melanie and Shrimpton looked at the small section at the bottom of the page where the quartz paper seemed to shimmer and waver.

"It's easy enough to do once you get the hang of it," Lydia explained. "Watch this."

She sent out a small pulse of psi energy. The shimmering section snapped into focus. A clear holographic picture formed in midair above the page.

"Isn't he adorable?" she said. "He looks just like Fuzz."

They all gazed in wonder at the life-sized picture of a dust-bunny. There were two versions; one showed the creature with just its baby blues open. The other showed it with all four wide open.

"We rezzed each of the photos in the book at the lab," Lydia explained. "Every single one is a picture of an animal commonly found here on Harmony. The lettering seems large for the size of the page."

Melanie's face lit up with sudden comprehension and delight. "Oh, my goodness. A children's picture book of animals."

Lydia touched the page reverently. "So unimportant and insignificant that it was overlooked and left behind when the aliens packed up the contents of that chamber and left town.

But the clear connection between the pictures and the lettering will give the experts a crack at decoding Harmonic writing at last."

Shrimpton beamed. "Our very own Rosetta Stone," he whispered.

Lydia and Melanie both looked at him.

"What's a Rosetta Stone?" Melanie demanded.

"I don't understand, sir," Lydia said. "It's not a stone, it's a book."

"Bah, that's the trouble with the modern educational system," Shrimpton declared. "They don't teach the history of Old Earth archaeology in school the way they did when I was a lad." He grinned with benign satisfaction. "Never mind. The important thing is that Lydia is right. This is going to be an even bigger draw than having the Guild boss's wife on the staff."

32

Emmett delivered the news when he walked through the door of the town house that evening.

"They found Herbert's body this afternoon," he told Lydia while he peeled off his jacket. "Or maybe I should say Troy Burgis's body."

"Dead?"

"Suicide. He used a mag-rez gun. Messy."

Fuzz hopped from Lydia's shoulder to Emmett's and settled down to finish a pretzel that he had been munching.

"I'm not surprised, if you want to know the truth." Lydia handed Emmett a glass of wine. "The destruction of his underground operation meant the end of his driving obsession with Vincent Lee Vance."

"He probably would have been real disappointed to find out that there was no tomb after all, just a library with only one book." Emmett took a swallow of wine and followed Lydia into the living room. "I can't say that I'm sorry the son of a bitch is dead, but it would have been nice to get some more answers out of him first."

"The answers will come eventually. It's going to take the authorities a while to sort it all out."

Emmett unfastened the collar of his shirt and

dropped onto the heavily cushioned sofa. He took off his shoes and stacked his heels on the coffee table. Fuzz scampered down to his knee and perched there contentedly, nibbling on his pretzel.

It was good to be home, Emmett thought, raising the glass to his mouth. Good to smell dinner rezzing on the stove. Good to think about the night ahead.

Good to be married to Lydia.

He watched her walk toward him carrying a small plate of crackers and cheese and wondered how she felt about being married to him.

She put the plate down on the table and dropped lightly onto the sofa beside him. "Any news about Burgis's three pals?"

"Not yet. Martinez thinks they probably all had emergency escape plans in place and used them to disappear. They'll show up eventually in one of the other cities."

She curled one leg under herself. "It's hard to believe that those four really thought that they could establish their own private army of fanatics down in the catacombs."

"Burgis was obviously mentally unstable and dangerously obsessed right from the start. His friends were very likely equally unbalanced. But after fifteen years underground searching for Vance's lost chamber, all four of them must have become raving lunatics. They had probably lost all touch with reality."

"How's Mercer Wyatt doing?"

"Recovering nicely. He's as tough as old quartz. He's going to start coming back into the office part time next week. He should be back full time at the end of the month."

She watched him with deep, serious eyes. "What about you, Emmett?"

"Me?" He helped himself to a cracker and some cheese. "I go back into private consulting next week."

"So soon? You don't have to wait until Mercer returns to work full time?"

"Nope. Mercer plans to employ another consultant to help him run the Guild for a while."

"For heaven's sake, who?"

"Tamara."

Lydia's jaw dropped in surprise. "Oh, my."

"Mercer has finally given up trying to convince me to be his handpicked successor. He told me that he has a scheme to get Tamara onto the Council. An advisory position at first, naturally. But I've got a hunch he intends to find a way to make her the next president of the Cadence Guild."

"Oh, my," Lydia said again. She shook her head in wonder. "A female Guild boss. Talk about taking the organization into the modern age in a hurry."

"If anyone can pull it off, it's Wyatt."

"Whew. It's finally over."

A long time later, he opened the door of the steamy bathroom. Lydia stood in front of the mirror, a large, fluffy towel secured around her breasts. Her hair was pinned up in a careless knot on top of her head. She had just finished showering and brushing her teeth.

She turned off the water in the sink and met his gaze in the mirror. She frowned. "Emmett? Is something wrong?"

He moved to stand behind her and put his hands on her shoulders. She was warm and damp from the shower. Little tendrils of red-gold hair had escaped the pins.

"Earlier this evening, you said something about it being over. It's not."

She went very still beneath his hands. "What's not over?"

"Our marriage."

She tensed. "It's only for a year."

"I'm well aware of that."

"I told you, I'm sorry I got you into this mess." She waved her hands. "I just couldn't think of anything better at the time."

"I can," he said.

She watched him warily. "You can what?"

"Think of something better."

She swallowed. "Oh."

"I love you, Lydia."

"Oh."

He raised his brows. "Is that all you can say?"

"No." Her smile was radiant in the foggy mirror. She turned to face him. "No, it isn't all I can say. I love you, too."

"Enough to consider a Covenant Marriage

to a hunter who is about to become an ex–Guild boss?"

"Oh, yes, *yes*." She put her arms around his neck. "I do love you so."

Happiness and certainty whirled through him. He kissed her forehead. "Let's make it as soon as possible."

She raised her head quickly, frowning a little as she concentrated. "If we skip all the expensive stuff like the big church wedding and reception, we can probably arrange it within a couple of months. There's still a lot of paperwork, of course."

"But we're not going to skip the expensive stuff," he said firmly.

"Really, Emmett, there's no need to spend a fortune on a fancy wedding."

"I'll take care of everything."

"You will?"

He started to remove the pins in her hair. "I'm not trusting you to arrange another marriage for us. The last time you handled things we ended up with a tacky, five-minute Marriage of Convenience at the registrar's office. No fancy clothes, no great food, no dancing, no presents. I learned my lesson. This time things are going to be different."

She blinked. "They are?"

Her hair tumbled down to her shoulders. Satisfied, he unknotted the towel. It fell to the floor. He surveyed her from head to toe, taking his time. She turned very pink under his gaze.

"Yes," he said eventually. "Things are going to be very different this time."

She started to giggle. He kissed her until she stopped laughing and started making the sweet little murmurs of pleasure and anticipation that set fire to his blood.

After a while, he picked her up and carried her into the bedroom and put her down on the turned-back bed. She watched him from the shadows as he got out of his clothes.

He lowered himself beside her and pulled her into his arms. The curve of her bare thigh was perfect under his palm. He slid one leg between hers and bent his head to kiss her breast.

He took his time making love to her. When she shivered in his arms and whispered his name, he entered her, sinking deep and savoring the connection on every plane from the physical to the paranormal.

In the end he surrendered to the pounding satisfaction, embracing the release in a way that he had never been able to do with any other woman.

He covered Lydia's mouth with his own in a kiss that was as hot as ghost fire.

33

It was pouring rain. Lydia fumbled with the umbrella getting out of the cab. The driver watched her drag her purse and large portfolio case out of the vehicle.

"You sure this is the right address, lady?" he asked, doubtful.

Okay, so she didn't look like the kind of person who hung around with the upscale crowd here on Ruin View Hill. There was no need for the cabbie to point it out.

"Yes, it's the right place." Irritated, she paid him and stuffed her wallet back into her purse.

"Want me to wait?"

"No, thanks. I'll call another cab when I'm ready to leave," she said icily.

"Suit yourself, I was just trying to help." The driver's eyes widened. "Hey, wait a second, I know you. Saw your picture in the papers. Didn't recognize you because of those big dark glasses and that scarf. You're the new Guild boss's wife, aren't you? The tangler who was with London when he found the skeleton of Vincent Lee Vance."

So much for her pitiful disguise, Lydia thought. It was Melanie who had suggested the

379

large scarf and the oversized dark glasses so that she could walk the streets without being asked for an autograph every five steps. It had worked, up to a point, but clearly it wasn't enough to fool the cab driver.

Lydia had been desperate enough to try any tactic to evade reporters and autograph seekers. The glowing accounts of the Guild's heroic role in the discovery of Vance's remains and the destruction of the Greenie empire were still making headlines daily. While most of the attention had been directed at Emmet, who coolly referred all inquiries to the Guild's public relations department, she had been accosted on the street every time she left Shrimpton's.

Today, in addition to the scarf and glasses, she had taken the extra precaution of slipping out of the museum through the loading-dock entrance before she had hailed the cab on a side street.

"Mr. London is going to be the ex–Guild boss very soon," she said crisply. "You won't be seeing my picture in the papers much in the future." Thank heavens, she added silently.

"You sure you don't want me to wait? Don't mind doin' London's wife a favor." The cabbie winked. "Never hurts to be on the right side of the Guild."

"Not necessary, thanks." She made to turn toward the high gates that barred the drive of the huge estate.

"Could I have your autograph for my wife?"

the cabbie asked. He thrust a blank receipt and a pen out the window. "Here, I'll hold your umbrella for you. If you could just sign this for me, she would be really thrilled."

Lydia hesitated and then surrendered the umbrella. "I've got a better idea," she said, digging into her purse to pull out one of her business cards. She scrawled her name and a short note on the back and handed it to him. "Take your wife to Shrimpton's House of Ancient Horrors to see the Harmonic book. This will get you in through the VIP entrance so you won't have to stand in line."

"The VIP line? Oh, man, wait'll I tell Betty." He bobbed his head. "Thank you, ma'am. This is gonna make my Betty's day."

"May I please have my umbrella back?"

"Oh, sure. Sorry. You're sure you don't need me to wait?"

"I'm sure."

"Okay." He rezzed the engine. "You have a good day now, Mrs. London."

"Thank you."

She waited until the cab was gone before she tromped through the rain to the high gates and pressed the buzzer.

"May I help you?" a graveled voice asked politely.

"Lydia Smith . . . London to see Mr. Hepscott. I have an appointment."

"Yes, of course, Mrs. London. I see you are on foot. There's a sheltered area just inside the gates. Please wait there after you come through the gates. I'll pick you up in a moment."

"Thanks."

The massive gates swung open. Lydia walked through them and along the drive to a small stone gazebo. A moment later a tall, distinguished-looking, gray-haired man dressed in formal butler attire arrived in a cart.

She was whisked to the grand entrance of the mansion and ushered into a vast reception hall. Her dripping raincoat and umbrella were taken from her and she was shown into a handsomely appointed library.

"Mr. Hepscott will be with you in a moment," the butler assured her before retreating from the room.

As soon as she was alone, Lydia set her purse and portfolio case down near a low table and went to stand at the wall of windows. The views from the big estates along Ruin View Hill were generally acknowledged by real estate agents to be the finest in the city. The claims were true, she thought. But as spectacular as the sight of the Dead City was from up here on the ridge, she much preferred to live in the Old Quarter where she could pick up the wispy traces of psi power.

Speaking of stray bits of psi energy.

She could feel some right here in this room. Curious, she opened her senses more fully. Small currents of power definitely hummed in the atmosphere. It was rare to pick up traces this far from the Old Quarter.

She searched the room, looking for the source. Then she saw it: a wide, gleaming glass case filled with a large number of alien artifacts. Even a cursory glance from across the room assured her that it was an excellent collection. The remnants of psi energy clinging to so many ancient relics massed together was enough to stir her senses.

She started toward the glass case and stopped when the door opened.

"Good afternoon, Lydia."

Gannon Hepscott walked into the room. He was dressed in a white shirt and a pair of white slacks. White shoes, a white belt, and a white silk scarf at his throat finished the outfit. His silver white hair was tied back at his nape, as usual.

"It's nice to see you again," she said warmly, meaning every word. It was a great relief to return to her normal work schedule.

Gannon shook her hand and motioned her to the sofa. He looked concerned.

"I understand you've been rather busy since we last met." He frowned. "I trust you were not injured during your adventures down there in the catacombs?"

"I'm fine, thanks. It's been a little hectic lately but things are quieting down. I'm delighted to be able to resume work on your project. I know we lost a little time but I think we can make it up fairly easily."

"I'm not worried about it." Gannon walked to

a leather-and-polished-wood cabinet. "Can I offer you wine or rez-tea?"

"Tea sounds great." Lydia opened her portfolio to take out her notes and sketches. "It's a little damp outside."

"I noticed." Gannon picked up a pot and poured tea into two delicate cups decorated with charming garden scenes. He brought the cups and saucers to the low table and set them down.

Lydia opened her notebook. "You'll be happy to know that this morning I received a call from a private collector who is rumored to own three remarkable quartz wall panels," she said briskly. "Seems that she is in rather dire straits financially and would like to find a buyer for the panels."

"Excellent." Gannon lowered himself into one of the gray leather chairs. "You were able to keep my name out of it?"

"Yes. As far as she's concerned she's dealing with a knowledgeable, moderately wealthy collector who appreciates the value of the panels. But I made it clear that we'll walk away if she tries to drive the price out of sight. She's willing to negotiate."

"Given your recent experiences with private collectors, I'm amazed that you're still willing to do business with unknown parties over the phone."

She grimaced. "The tabloids certainly made a big deal out of how I was kidnapped and carried off in an alien sarcophagus."

"It made for great newspaper sales but it must have been terrible for you."

"It would have been a lot worse if I hadn't been unconscious while I was inside that coffin."

"I can imagine. It was extremely fortunate that your husband stumbled onto the scheme shortly after you disappeared and was able to follow your kidnappers."

"Mmm." She concentrated on organizing some photos of a quartz urn.

Emmett had decreed that some details about the rescue operation were to be kept quiet. One of those concerned Fuzz's role in the affair. *"If scientists find out that dust-bunnies might be able to form psychic links with humans, there will be a rush to start experimenting on the little furballs in every lab in the Federation."* The thought of innocent dust-bunnies being turned into research subjects had been too terrible to contemplate.

The other detail that Emmett had ordered kept top secret was Cornish's involvement in the rescue. *"The Guild owes him a favor for showing me Maltby's hidden entrance to the catacombs,"* Emmett had said. *"Cornish may eventually come to grief because of his drug habit and his dealings in illegal antiquities, but it won't be because the hunters gave his name to the cops."*

The Guild always repaid favors, Lydia thought.

Gannon studied the photos of the urn. "Do you mind if I ask how London was able to find you down there in the catacombs? The media said the Greenie operation had gone undetected for several years. Yet your husband managed to locate you almost immediately. It was an amazing feat."

"Everyone knows that the Guild has its ways," she said lightly.

Gannon nodded. "Someone must have seen the sarcophagus being loaded into the van, got suspicious, and followed it."

"Probably. Emmett wasn't clear on that point. The Guild likes to keep its secrets."

He chuckled. "You mean even Guild boss wives are kept in the dark about some things?"

She moved one hand slightly. "I'm afraid so. I'll be happy when Emmett steps down, to tell you the truth. Being a Guild boss wife is not all it's cracked up to be."

"I can understand why you would feel that way." Gannon leaned forward to pick up one of the photos. "This is a very nice piece."

"The price is even nicer. The dealer hinted that the owner is desperate to raise cash."

Gannon tossed the photo down with a decisive air. "Let's get it."

She made a note. "I'll make the call later this afternoon. We don't want to look too eager."

Gannon settled back in his chair and studied her with a considering expression. "I don't suppose, given your connections with both the Guild and the university, that there's any chance of acquiring a couple of items from that library chamber for my project?"

"Are you kidding? The university has put up

386

so many guards and barricades around the entrances and exits of that chamber that the place looks like a crime scene. Only authorized personnel can go in now and I'm not on the list."

"I might be able to pull a few strings and get you appointed to a consulting position."

"It wouldn't do you any good. If I got on as a consultant, I'd no longer be able to work for you. It would be a conflict of interest."

"Ah, well, it was just a thought." There was a discreet knock. Gannon frowned slightly and glanced toward the door. "Come in, George."

The door opened. The butler loomed. "I'm sorry to disturb you, sir, but Mr. Anderson is on the phone."

"Thank you, George, I'll take it in my office." Gannon got to his feet. "Will you excuse me for a moment, Lydia?"

"Of course."

Gannon left, closing the door behind him. Lydia waited a moment and then rose and crossed the room to the antiquities cabinet.

The closer she got, the stronger the pulse of psi energy. She did not understand why it would be this thick. Granted, so many relics grouped together could create a trickle of power but not as much as she was picking up.

And then she caught it, the unmistakable aura of illusion trap energy. It was coming from the bottom bookshelf on the right-hand side of the cabinet.

She crouched down and saw a row of books. Behind the volumes there were dark shadows. A *lot* of dark shadows. Illusion trap energy crackled gently.

She took out a couple of books and saw the chunk of green quartz that was anchoring the shadow. The trap was small, but extremely complex. Nevertheless, she was able to de-rez it in seconds.

When the unnatural shadow evaporated she saw a clear box containing a half dozen recordings. Not the new amber audio discs that had appeared on the market a couple of years ago, but the older synch wave tapes that had been used for twenty years before that.

Each tape was sheathed in a plain, unmarked cover.

Ice-cold perspiration trickled down her ribs.

She listened intently but heard no footsteps in the hall outside the library.

Very carefully she opened the lid of the storage box and took out one of the tapes. The envelope that protected the recording was not marked with any of the familiar commercial music studio brand names. Instead, someone had used an ink pen to write simply *Number 5*.

She quickly replaced the recording and took another one out of its envelope. *Number 6*.

What was it Karen Price had said when she had called to talk about her old roommate? *"Burgis was obsessed with only two things. One of them was pulse-rock music. He went so far as to rent a studio so that his band could record a half dozen tapes. . . ."*

It was getting hard to breathe. Lydia was intensely aware of the enormous silence of the big house.

She had to get out of here, she thought. Right now.

She shoved the second recording back into the storage container and closed the lid.

She was about to reset the trap when intuition made her hesitate. She had no way to protect herself on the way out of this big house. What if the butler tried to stop her?

The little trap might come in handy.

Gingerly she picked up the chunk of quartz that anchored the ephemeral psi energy. It looked harmless now but she could feel the core of the illusion trap pattern resonating around it. Unless she deliberately destroyed it, the snare would continue to pulse, ready to be reset and re-triggered.

Quartz in hand, she leaped to her feet and ran to the table where she had spread out the photos and her notes. She put the still-resonating stone into her purse and gently reset the trap. She shoved her paperwork back into the portfolio, grabbed it and the purse, and rushed toward the door.

It opened before she was halfway across the room.

"I'm sorry, Lydia, but I really can't let you leave," Gannon said with polite regret.

Heart thudding in her chest, she stared at the mag-rez gun in his hand.

"There seem to be a lot of those around these days," she said hoarsely. "Part of your underground cache, I assume?"

Gannon shook his head. "I've been so damned careful for so long. I'd really like to know what it was that gave me away."

34

Emmett crouched beside the twisted and broken body. The remains of Foster Dorning were sprawled in the alley behind the City Center Parking Garage. A large trash container partially obscured the dead man. The rain that had been falling steadily all morning had soaked Dorning's clothing and sluiced off much of the blood. His personal phone lay in the muck nearby.

"Who reported it?" Emmett asked.

Verwood juggled the oversized umbrella he was using to cover Emmett and the body. "A delivery truck driver found him a few minutes ago. He notified the garage attendant who sent for me. Figured you'd want to know."

"Someone call the cops?"

"I told the attendant to take care of it. They'll be here any minute." Verwood looked at the body. "His assigned parking space is on the top floor of the garage. You think maybe he got out of his car, got disoriented in the rain, and fell over the edge?"

"No." Emmett rose slowly. "I think it's a lot more likely he was pushed. What the hell was he doing here at headquarters in the middle of the night?"

Verwood shrugged. "Who knows? Looks like the Guild is going to be in the news again this week. Never a dull moment, huh?"

Sirens hummed in the distance.

Emmett leaned down and picked up Dorning's personal phone and dropped it into his pocket just as the first police car turned into the alley, lights flashing.

The car doors opened. A familiar figure got out.

"Detective Martinez," Emmett said. "What a surprise."

"Personally I'm trying to look on the bright side," Martinez said. "At least your wife isn't involved this time."

Fifteen minutes later Emmett managed to escape Martinez's clutches.

Upstairs he walked into the reception lobby and dropped the phone on the desk in front of Perkins.

"The last number he called is blocked," Emmett said. "I assume you can get around that little obstacle?"

"Of course, sir. I'll have an address for you in a few minutes."

"Thanks." Emmett went toward the door of his office. "I'm going to call Wyatt. Let me know as soon as you track down that number."

Inside his office he reached across the desk, grabbed the phone, and dialed Wyatt's private number. Mercer answered on the first ring.

"Tell me everything you can about Sandra Thornton," Emmett said.

Mercer was silent for a moment. "Something else happen?"

"Dorning is dead. Apparently he fell from the top of the garage here at headquarters."

"Seems a little unlikely," Mercer said dryly.

"Struck me that way, too. I think someone is getting rid of loose ends. Talk to me about Sandra."

"You think maybe she was a loose end?"

"Yes. Lydia is right. The coincidences are getting a little too thick on the ground. What did you know about her? Where did she come from? Where did she go to school? Any family?"

"I slept with the woman for a time, Emmett, I didn't make her my best friend."

"She must have said something about her past during that time."

"Let me think for a moment."

The line went silent. Emmett leaned back against the desk and waited. A sense of urgency was building in him.

"She was stunningly beautiful," Mercer said after a while. "But not in a glamorous way, if you know what I mean. There was a sort of sweet, pure innocence about her. Hard to describe. She seemed fragile in some ways and in others she was sophisticated beyond her years."

Sophisticated in bed, for instance, Emmett thought. All he said was, "Go on."

"I remember one night when I arrived at her

apartment, she seemed sad," Mercer said slowly. "It was unusual for her to be down. One of the reasons I enjoyed her company, aside from the fact that she was lovely, was because she was always in a cheerful, upbeat mood. Not one of those whiney, demanding, clingy types."

"I need hard information, not your personal impressions about her personality."

"That night, I could tell she had been crying and drinking. Her face was all red and puffy. There was some obnoxious music playing on the stereo."

"What kind of music?"

"Some of that screaming-loud, high-rez stuff that no one my age can take for more than five minutes without going crazy."

A tiny alarm bell went off somewhere. "She say anything about the music?"

"She mentioned that the songs she was listening to went back to her college days. I got the impression she had once been involved with some young man who had had his own band."

Emmett stilled. "She say anything else about this guy?"

"I don't think so. She turned the music off right away. We had a couple of drinks together and that was all there was to it."

"She ever mention where she went to college?"

"Not that time. But a month or two later we happened to catch a late-night sports report on the rez-screen. The announcer was giving the

394

results of an upset game between two college teams. Old Frequency College had pulled out a last-minute save. Sandra got excited and said something like 'Go, Freaks.' "

"Did she attend Old Frequency?"

"I asked her that. Instead of answering directly, she brushed the question aside. I got the impression that she didn't want to talk about it. I figured maybe she had dropped out or flunked out and didn't want to admit it."

"And now she's dead, along with Master Herbert and Dorning," Emmett said softly. "That makes three. Someone is definitely mopping up."

"What the hell are you talking about, Emmett?"

The door opened. Perkins walked in, notepad in hand. He was clearly troubled.

"Hang on, Mercer." Emmett looked at Perkins.

"I have that address for you, sir," Perkins said. "It was somewhat complicated to track because it was unlisted and the first address that came up is evidently an error. I had to do some rather involved cross-checking."

"Just give it to me, Perkins."

"Number Twenty-seven Ruin View Drive." Perkins looked up, more anxious than ever. "It doesn't make any sense, sir. That's Gannon Hepscott's address. You know, the big developer?"

"Hell, I should have put it together sooner."

"What's going on there?" Mercer demanded. "I heard Perkins say something about Gannon Hepscott."

"Hold on," Emmett said. Leaving Mercer hanging on one line, he dialed Lydia's office.

"Shrimpton's House of Ancient Horrors," Melanie said cheerfully. "Be sure to see our latest attraction, the Harmonic children's picture book of —"

"This is Emmett, Mel. Where is she?"

"Who, Lydia? She had an appointment with her big-time client this morning. Left here about forty minutes ago. I had to help her sneak out the back way because the reporters are still loitering around in front."

"She went to Hepscott's office?"

"Not today. He asked her to come to his home up on Ruin View Drive. Just imagine; our Lydia is drinking tea in one of those big fancy mansions up there even as we speak."

"Shit." Emmett cut the connection and went back to Mercer. "Lydia's in trouble. She's in your neighborhood. I need some help."

"You're Troy Burgis," Lydia whispered.

She had dropped the portfolio but she clutched her purse very tightly and forced herself to look away from the gun. She had to watch Gannon's eyes, she thought. Like all technology from car keys to heavy construction equipment, the mag-rez gun required a small pulse of human psi energy to activate it. If she paid attention she might catch the telltale signs of increased concentration that meant he was sending power through amber to enable the trigger.

Gannon looked annoyed. "So Maltby did put it all together. I was afraid of that. I had him taken care of immediately after he was seen leaving the sector that night. He managed to break into some private files down there. But how the hell did he get the information to you?"

"Let's just say he put your face in a milk carton. But you've changed a lot since college, haven't you? I wouldn't have recognized you if it hadn't been —" She broke off quickly.

"Yes, Lydia? If it hadn't been for what? I need to know how you figured out that I used to be Troy Burgis. I make it a point to not repeat my mistakes."

She shrugged. "There were a lot of little clues along the way," she lied. "But the one that I finally picked up on today was the music. I found your old recordings."

"How did you know about my band?" he asked sharply.

She was not about to drag Karen Price's name into this, she thought. She would keep it vague. "According to your college yearbook you formed a band." She angled her chin toward the collection of unmarked recordings. "That's your music on those old tapes, isn't it? You rented a studio to make them but you couldn't afford to have fancy dust jackets created for them."

Gannon looked startled. "You got that information out of a yearbook?"

She didn't answer that question. "The clipping about your death mentioned that you were obsessed with Vincent Lee Vance. What was that about? The man was a wanna-be dictator, for heaven's sake. Not exactly a great role model."

"Vance was a brilliant, powerful man who came within a hairsbreadth of ruling all of the city-states."

"And you really thought you could finish the job? Sheesh, talk about delusions of grandeur. What gave you the idea? Finding his secret headquarters under Old Frequency?"

"Yes." Gannon hesitated and then shrugged. "He had left behind some of his early journals and a few battle maps. One of those maps appeared to show the location of the underground chamber that he intended to use as his headquarters when his forces took Cadence."

"The library."

Gannon's mouth twisted. "Vance did not know what was inside at that point. The note in his journal says that the chamber was unusually well guarded by a very difficult trap. He said he hoped that Helen Chandler would be able to de-rez it. He was convinced that the Harmonics had used the trap to protect some great secret inside that room."

"A secret that would be his when and if he got into the chamber."

Gannon nodded. "I assumed he and Chandler had died somewhere in the catacombs, but I decided to try to find the chamber he mentioned in the journals."

"You talked your three band buddies into disappearing with you so that you could all search for the tomb together."

Gannon shook his head ruefully. "We had such dreams in those early days. We were sure that whatever we found in that chamber would make us all rich and powerful. But nothing went right."

"What do you mean?"

"The maps were badly flawed. I suspect that Vance made the mistakes deliberately as a sort of code so that no one else could find the chamber. The result was that the four of us blundered around for over two years underground trying to find the chamber before we realized the enormity of the task."

"How did you survive during that time?"

"We used to slip out of the catacombs at night to steal food and supplies. It was a miserable existence, I assure you." Gannon grimaced. "Eventually I faced the fact that it would take a great deal of time and money to conduct a proper search."

"So you came out from underground and started investing in real estate."

"Yes." Gannon was amused. "Imagine my surprise when I discovered I had a knack for it. The beauty of real estate was that it allowed me to buy up huge plots of land directly above the sector of the catacombs that the four of us were exploring. Owning that property enabled us to maintain a measure of control over the rat holes and hidden entrances."

"Which meant you could keep out most of the ruin rats and treasure hunters."

"Yes. It didn't provide perfect security but it worked fairly well. But we soon realized that to clear an entire sector we needed a loyal workforce and we required security. Herbert, who used to be Norman Fairbanks, came up with the concept of the Order of the Acolytes of Amatheon. He established the various legal entities and took out the license to excavate. After we established the cult the money started to pour in so fast we could hardly count it."

"That's when your dreams really went over the top, isn't it? You saw all that money and all those loyal servants and it occurred to you that you had the makings of your own personal army. All you needed were some high-tech weapons. So you started stockpiling guns."

The intercom on the large desk chimed gently. The interruption rattled Gannon. He flinched and then punched the button.

"I thought I made it clear that I did not want to be disturbed, George."

"I'm sorry, sir, but there are visitors at the gates."

"Send them away."

George cleared his throat. "The visitors are Mr. and Mrs. Mercer Wyatt, sir."

"The Wyatts?" Gannon's jaw jerked. "What the hell are they doing here?"

"They probably just stopped by to borrow a cup of sugar," Lydia said sarcastically.

"Sir, Mr. Wyatt said that he and his wife were out for a drive and noticed a large plume of smoke coming from this house." George sounded agitated. "They said they've summoned the fire department. But none of our sensors show a problem."

Sirens blared outside on the street.

"What is going on here?" Gannon whispered hoarsely.

An interior alarm system screeched.

"Shit," Gannon said. "That's the perimeter security system. Someone is inside the gates."

"Sir, the fire department is demanding entry," George said urgently. "They insist that the house be evacuated immediately. They're sending men and equipment over the walls."

"Wyatt. That son of a bitch." Gannon cut the intercom connection and crossed to the curio cabinet. "A pity I didn't finish him off that night."

Lydia sucked in her breath. "You're the one who shot Mercer Wyatt."

"Who would have thought a man his age would survive two shots from a mag-rez?"

Gannon raised a lamp shade to reveal a small lever. He turned it swiftly. The large cabinet moved away from the wall on hidden rollers. An opening in the wall appeared. Lydia saw the top of a long flight of steep stairs leading downward into darkness.

The winds of psi power wafted out of the tunnel.

"Although I anticipated success all these years," Gannon said, "I made provisions for failure. When I discovered that this house had a rat hole that had gone undiscovered for nearly half a century, I bought it immediately."

"You're going to disappear again."

"I have another identity ready and waiting as well as a healthy supply of cash. I would have liked to have invited you to run away with me, Lydia. As I told London, I do believe you and I would have made a good team under other circumstances. But I can see that you are committed to your hunter."

"You got that right." She gripped the purse very tightly.

Gannon raised the barrel of the gun. "The least I can do to repay you for all the trouble you have caused me is to kill you."

This was it, Lydia thought. Her only chance. She prepared to hurl the purse toward Gannon, trying to brace herself for the mind-numbing horror of the nightmares that would envelop them both when she triggered the tiny trap anchored to the chunk of quartz.

The door slammed open an instant before she sent the pulse of energy to spring the trap.

Emmett exploded into the room, moving quickly.

Gannon jerked around to confront the new threat. The mag-rez gun roared just as Emmett dropped to the floor.

At the same time ghost light flashed and

flared in the tunnel entrance directly behind Gannon. Lydia knew that Emmett was summoning an enormous amount of raw dissonance energy from the catacombs below.

Gannon convulsed and writhed wildly in the chaotic green fire that swept over him. The gun fell from his hand and clattered on the floor.

A few seconds later, he crumpled. Lydia knew that he had to be dead. No human mind could have withstood such a direct encounter from such a massive ghost.

The dissonance energy snapped and sizzled and then winked out almost as swiftly as it had appeared.

Emmett levered himself to a sitting position and looked at her. "Are you all right?" he asked, raising his voice to be heard above the screaming alarms that reverberated throughout the house.

"Yes. But I'd better get rid of this thing before there's an accident." She reached carefully into the purse, picked up the quartz, and carefully de-rezzed it completely, destroying the vicious little snare.

He settled back against the nearest wall, watching her. "You were going to trigger an illusion trap?"

"Only if nothing better came along. Luckily you got here first." She set the quartz down and turned toward him. "How did you —" Then she saw the blood. "*Emmett.* Oh, my God."

She ran to his side and clamped a hand over

the bloody, ragged crease that the mag-rez bullet had opened on his upper arm.

"It's okay." Emmett looked down at the blood leaking through her fingers and grimaced. "I think."

"We need an ambulance." She kept her hand tight over the wound and tried to reach the phone on Gannon's desk.

Mercer Wyatt appeared in the doorway, leaning heavily on a cane. He fumbled with a small phone. "I'll make the call."

Tamara walked into the room followed by a number of firefighters and hunters. She took one look at Gannon and then, with quick, efficient moves, she unknotted the figured silk scarf at her throat and handed it to Lydia.

"Here, use this," she said as Mercer barked orders into the phone.

Lydia took the scarf and secured it snugly around the wound. To her relief the flow of blood had diminished considerably.

Mercer ended his call. "Medics will be here in a couple of minutes." He scowled at the crowd gathering in the room. "Someone turn off those damned alarms. Verwood, take a couple of men and detain that butler."

"Yes, sir," Verwood said. He motioned to several hunters.

A short time later the clanging bells and whistles went silent.

The firefighters checked the charred flooring and wall panels around Gannon's body but were soon satisfied that the ghost had not started a blaze. They left just as the medics pulled into the drive.

For a moment or two, Lydia, Emmett, Mercer, and Tamara were the only ones left in the room.

Emmett looked at Mercer, his mouth curving very slightly at one corner. "Thanks, Dad."

Mercer blinked. Then his specter-cat eyes, eyes that were mirror images of Emmett's, blazed with satisfaction. A slow, uncharacteristically warm smile transformed his face.

"Anytime, son."

35

"Martinez got the rest of the story from Gannon's faithful butler, George." Emmett settled deeper into the big chair, his heels propped on the ottoman, and absently scratched Fuzz, who sat on his lap.

He had enjoyed the role of invalid for the first day and a half, he decided. Having Lydia hover attentively was a pleasant novelty. But now he was getting a little bored. Lydia was not merely fussing, she was giving orders — a lot of them. The instructions covered everything from the amount of sleep he needed to what he should eat and how often the bandage on his arm had to be changed.

Luckily the mag-rez gun had not done any permanent damage. The wound was healing quickly. He was profoundly grateful that he had arrived on the scene before Lydia had been forced to use the trapped quartz in a last-ditch bid to save herself. After the ghost burn she had endured during her Lost Weekend, the last thing she had needed now was the para-psych trauma that would have accompanied an immersion in a sea of alien nightmares.

This morning Mercer and Tamara had arrived to help piece together the entire tale. Lydia had prepared a large pot of tea and set out a plate of cookies.

It was only tea and cookies, he thought, watching her pour, but it was the first time they had had company over. This was the kind of thing that married couples did.

"After years of searching that sector and securing the property rights aboveground as well as exploration rights below," Emmett said, "Hepscott and his followers finally found that massive wall of illusion shadow. They knew it had to be the gateway to Vance's lost headquarters but they couldn't get through it."

"Hepscott was a good tangler but he didn't want to take the risk of trying to de-rez such a vast, complex trap," Lydia said. Her jaw hardened. "So he ran several experiments using some of Herb's Greenies. Two of the Greenies died when they combined forces to untangle the trap. Later, two more Greenie tanglers wound up in para-psych wards. They never recovered."

"Must have been a little tough on morale among the Greenies," Tamara observed.

"It was," Emmett said. "Hepscott knew he couldn't afford to risk too many more followers. That's when he decided to kidnap a first-rate ephemeral-energy para-rez, someone who would be expendable. After doing his research, he chose Lydia."

"The two hunters I accused of abandoning me in the catacombs actually nabbed me. They used a knockout drug and stashed me in a hiding place. Then they pretended to search for me. Later, when the search was called off, they came and got me, intending to take me to Master Herb. I pretended to still be unconscious." Lydia shrugged. "They got careless."

"She escaped and fled into the antechamber," Emmett said. "Once there she understood intuitively that the only hope was to carve out a small hole in the trap. She made it into what we now call the library and out through another passageway."

"Which is where I ran into a huge ghost, got singed, and developed a case of amnesia that probably saved my life," Lydia concluded.

Tamara's elegant brows tightened quizzically. "Saved your life? Oh, I see what you mean. When Hepscott realized that you had no memory of what you had seen underground he decided not to take the risk of murdering you to ensure your silence."

"He had another reason for not getting rid of her seven months ago," Emmett said, adjusting the pillow Lydia had put under his injured arm. "She was, after all, the only person he knew who had ever made it through the illusion wall. If she had done it once, she might be able to do it again. So he decided to watch and wait to see if she recovered enough from the para-psych trauma to go back underground."

"I did recover," Lydia said. "But I didn't get a chance to prove that I could handle working in the catacombs until Emmett showed up at Shrimpton's looking for a P-A consultant a few weeks ago."

Mercer nodded slowly. "The next thing Hepscott knew, you and Emmett were seeing a lot of each other. He was aware of Emmett's Guild connections and he probably realized it would be extremely dangerous to grab you again. This time he'd have the entire Cadence Guild on his trail."

"Hepscott was aware of the risks involved," Emmett said. "But he was also growing desperate. Getting through that illusion wall was vitally important to him. He was convinced the secrets on the other side were worth any risk. But he had another problem, namely the Cadence Guild. He knew that it was the one organization that could stand in his way when he began to organize his forces into an underground army."

Mercer snorted. "So he made plans to take control of the Guild."

"What a manipulative bastard Hepscott was." Tamara was quietly furious. "First he sent Sandra Thornton to seduce Mercer, hoping to learn as much as possible about the inside workings of the Guild. Not that he got anything, of course," she added proudly. "Mercer wouldn't be so stupid as to give away his secrets during pillow talk."

Mercer's eyes glinted with rueful amusement. He patted her hand. "I appreciate your confidence in me, my love."

To Emmett's surprise, Tamara seemed to relax a little at Mercer's touch. The two of them exchanged a glance in one of those moments of silent, personal communication that could only take place between a couple that had formed a genuine bond.

Emmett looked at Lydia and saw that she, too, had picked up on the small flash of intimacy between Mercer and Tamara. She raised one shoulder in a tiny "who knew" shrug.

Hell, he thought, maybe that marriage was going to work, after all.

Lydia shuddered. "Hepscott used poor Sandra Thornton to lure you to that rendezvous site that night, Mr. Wyatt. He was the one who shot you. Later, when he wanted the investigation halted, he killed Sandra and wrote the suicide note himself. Can you believe it? After all those years together, he calmly set his lover up and killed her without a second thought just to further his plans."

"Meanwhile Hepscott had been using his money and influence to help Dorning move up quickly through the ranks of the Guild," Tamara said. "Dorning was a powerful hunter and thanks to Hepscott, he had the cash to grant a lot of favors. He made it all the way to the Council Chamber. From there it was only a step into the offices of the Guild boss."

"But no one had counted on Emmett taking charge of the Guild immediately after you were shot, Mr. Wyatt," Lydia said. "The transition in leadership went so smoothly that there was barely a ripple in the organization. Suddenly there was no power vacuum and Hepscott's plans for Dorning were in a muddle."

Mercer straightened his legs, wincing a little as he changed position in the chair. He looked at Emmett thoughtfully. "Dorning, I assume, was the one who sent that ghost to attack you on your wedding night?"

Emmett munched a cookie. "It was a test to see if he could take me. An old-fashioned formal challenge was the last option he had for grabbing control of the Guild in a legal way. Evidently Hepscott was reluctant to murder two Guild bosses in a row. Probably worried that the cops would notice a pattern."

Tamara frowned. "You de-rezzed his ghost that night when he tried to get a feel for your psi abilities, but he was obviously ready to go ahead with the challenge anyway."

Emmett shrugged. "Dorning was good but he knew he probably couldn't take me so he and Hepscott came up with Plan B. The scheme was to proceed with the formal challenge and then slip me a small dose of knockout drugs just before the match. The idea was to slow me down, not put me to sleep. I would have felt a little off, but I probably wouldn't be aware that I'd been drugged. Even if I did figure it out, it would have been difficult to stop the match just because I didn't feel in great shape."

Tamara picked up her cup. "In the end, when

411

he realized that his entire scheme had unraveled, Hepscott tried to get rid of all the loose ends before he pulled another disappearing act. Sandra Thornton was already out of the way so he killed Dorning and Master Herbert."

"Hepscott blamed me for all his problems," Lydia said. "So he summoned me to his mansion. He wanted to know where he'd made his mistakes. After he had his answers, he intended to kill me and dump my body into the catacombs where it would never have been found. Then he planned to disappear."

Emmett put his hand over hers. "He was right about one thing: You were, indeed, to blame for his problems. Because of you, everything went wrong for Gannon Hepscott."

Mercer contemplated Lydia for a long, thoughtful moment.

"It would seem that the Guild owes you some very large favors, my dear," he said.

Lydia choked on a bite of cookie. Gasping for air, she yanked her fingers out from under Emmett's palm and flung up both hands.

"Whoa. Stop. Halt," she wheezed. "Don't go there. Forget the Guild favor thing, okay?"

They all looked at her as if she had just suggested that the sun would not rise.

"The Guild never forgets a favor," Mercer assured her.

36

Three months later . . .

"Sheesh." Lydia stared at her reflection in the mirror. "This is almost as scary as going through that wall of illusion shadow."

The wedding gown that Charles had created for her bore the designer's signature in every detail. It was a mysterious and intriguing combination of ethereal feminine grace and sophisticated elegance. Layers of nearly weightless white silk curved deeply at the neckline, clung snugly around her breasts and waist and then spilled into a sea of skirts and a flowing train.

She could hardly believe that in another five minutes she would be walking down the aisle of the historic Old Quarter Church. Emmett would be waiting for her at the altar.

"Well, a Covenant Marriage is a very serious matter," Melanie said, uncharacteristically serious herself as she arranged the gossamer veil. "But you don't really have any doubts about a permanent marriage with Emmett, do you?"

"It's not Emmett I'm worrying about. It's that church full of people out there."

"Relax, you look gorgeous." Melanie stepped

back to survey her handiwork and nodded once, very briskly. "Absolutely gorgeous. Ready?"

"As ready as I'll ever be." Lydia picked up the bouquet of amber orchids and took a deep breath.

Melanie, wearing an amber-colored bridesmaid dress that had also been designed by Charles, collected her own flowers and prepared to lead the way.

Shrimpton, looking very fine and not nearly as dour as usual in a formal tuxedo, stepped forward to take Lydia's arm. He patted her gloved fingers with a paternal air.

"Don't be nervous," he whispered in a kindly manner. "You look very beautiful."

She was genuinely touched. "Thank you, sir."

The church was filled. The groom's side was packed. Mercer and Tamara Wyatt shared the family pew with Emmett's mother and her husband and Emmett's half brother, Daniel, the CEO of the Resonance Guild. Who said dysfunctional families couldn't get along? Lydia thought.

A host of eminent guests from Resonance City occupied five more rows. The rest of the section was filled with hunters from all ranks of the Cadence Guild.

The bride's side was full, too. In addition to Zane and his aunt, Olinda, the entire staff of Shrimpton's House of Ancient Horrors had turned out for the wedding. The remaining seats were occupied by a motley collection of gallery shop owners, ruin rats, and former colleagues from the university's Department of Para-archaeology.

Charles was in the last pew, looking extremely pleased at the sight of Lydia in his magnificent creation.

At the altar Emmett stood with his best man, Verwood. Fuzz was there, too, perched on Verwood's shoulder. The dust-bunny wore an amber satin bow that Melanie had tied somewhere in the vicinity of the top of his head.

Emmett turned to watch Lydia walk toward him. She saw the love and the complete certainty in his eyes and her brief attack of bridal jitters evaporated. She forgot about the hundreds of staring people around her.

The man she loved was waiting for her. She went to him with joy in her heart.

Several hours later Emmett unknotted the old-fashioned formal tie, opened the collar of his pleated shirt, and picked up the bottle of champagne. He grabbed a couple of flutes and walked out onto the night-darkened terrace.

Been here, done this, he thought. But he was going to make sure this wedding night went according to plan.

Lydia was stretched out in one of the loungers. The soft lights of the town house spilled through the windows and gleamed on the pale, delicate skirts of her wedding gown.

Fuzz sat on the table next to Lydia, munching

a pretzel. He was still wearing the satin ribbon Melanie had tied in his fur. Emmett had tried to remove the silly bow earlier but Fuzz had resisted. Evidently he had discovered a heretofore unsuspected sense of style.

Emmett sat down on the other lounger, poured two glasses of champagne, and handed one to Lydia.

He smiled at her and raised his glass. "To us, Mrs. London. I love you."

She smiled in the shadows. "To us, Mr. London. I love you."

They sat together, drinking in the night as well as the champagne and watched moonlight gleam on the spires and towers of the mysterious ancient city.

"Gosh," Lydia said after a while. "There aren't any ghosts around and no one seems to be trying to kill us. Do you really think we'll get to have a nice, quiet wedding night at last?"

"Not if I can help it." He put down his glass, got to his feet, and scooped her up off the lounger. The skirts of her wedding gown cascaded over his arms. "Nice and quiet was not at all what I had in mind this evening. I wouldn't want you to get bored on your second wedding night, my love."

She laughed. The sound danced in the darkness, mingling with the whispers of power that drifted out of the Dead City.

Love, stronger than any psi energy, enveloped them both.

Emmett carried her inside and down the hall to the welcoming shadows of the bedroom.

Out on the terrace the night continued to whisper its secrets. Fuzz moved closer to the bowl of pretzels and helped himself to another snack. He settled down to munch, waiting patiently.

After a few minutes she appeared, hopping down from the roof overhang to crouch on the terrace railing. She was the most beautiful dust-bunny in the world, a lovely ball of shapeless, colorless fluff.

Fuzz held out a pretzel in one paw. She blinked her charming blue eyes and tumbled off the railing to join him on the small table.

Accepting the pretzel with one of her six paws, she moved a little closer and began to nibble daintily.

There was a bowl of pretzels and a full moon over the ancient city. Who could ask for more?

Nights on Harmony were made for love.

About the Author

Jayne Castle, the author of *After Dark* and *Harmony*, is a pseudonym for **Jayne Ann Krentz**, the *New York Times* bestselling author of *Light in Shadow, Smoke in Mirrors, Lost and Found, Summer in Eclipse Bay, Dawn in Eclipse Bay, Eclipse Bay*, and other novels. She has been featured in such publications as *People* and *Enterainment Weekly*, and is also known for her books written under the name Amanda Quick. A former librarian with a degree in history, she is also the editor of an award-winning essay collection, *Dangerous Men and Adventurous Women: Romance Writers on the Appeal of the Romance*. You can find her online at www.jayneannkrentz.com.